AGENT MOOSE

WITH ART BY

Mo O'Hara   Jess Bradley

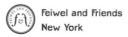

Feiwel and Friends
New York

With love to my mom—
my biggest supporter and my friend.
—M. O.

For my wonderful boys, John-Paul and Jacob.
Love you silly guys.
—J. B.

A FEIWEL AND FRIENDS BOOK
An imprint of Macmillan Publishing Group, LLC
120 Broadway, New York, NY 10271

AGENT MOOSE. Text copyright © 2020 by Mo O'Hara. Illustrations
copyright © 2020 by Jess Bradley. All rights reserved. Printed in China by
RR Donnelley Asia Printing Solutions Ltd., Dongguan City, Guangdong Province.

Our books may be purchased in bulk for promotional, educational, or business use. Please
contact your local bookseller or the Macmillan Corporate and Premium Sales Department
at (800) 221-7945 ext. 5442 or by email at MacmillanSpecialMarkets@macmillan.com.
Library of Congress Control Number: 2019948805
ISBN 978-1-250-22221-3 (hardcover)

Book design by Liz Dresner • Color by John-Paul Bove • Lettering by Micah Meyer
Feiwel and Friends logo designed by Filomena Tuosto
First edition, 2020

1 3 5 7 9 10 8 6 4 2
mackids.com

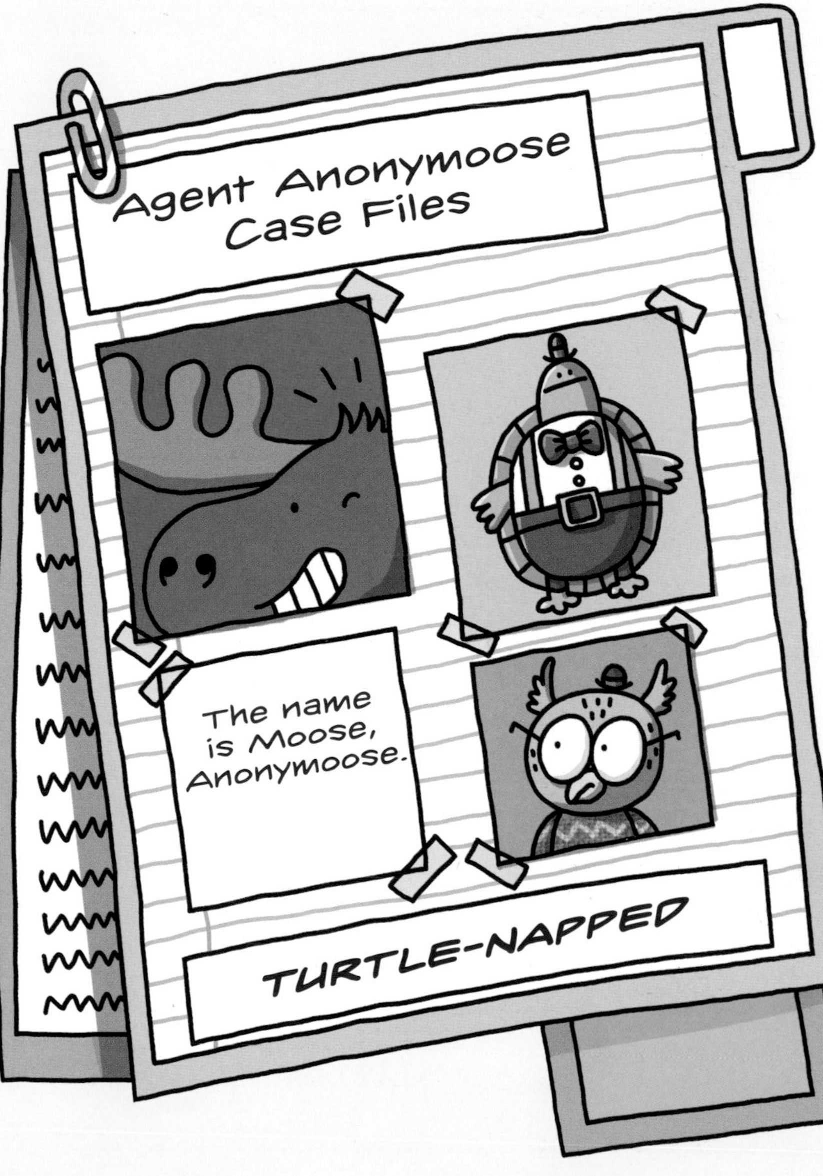
Agent Anonymoose
Case Files
The name is Moose, Anonymoose.
TURTLE-NAPPED

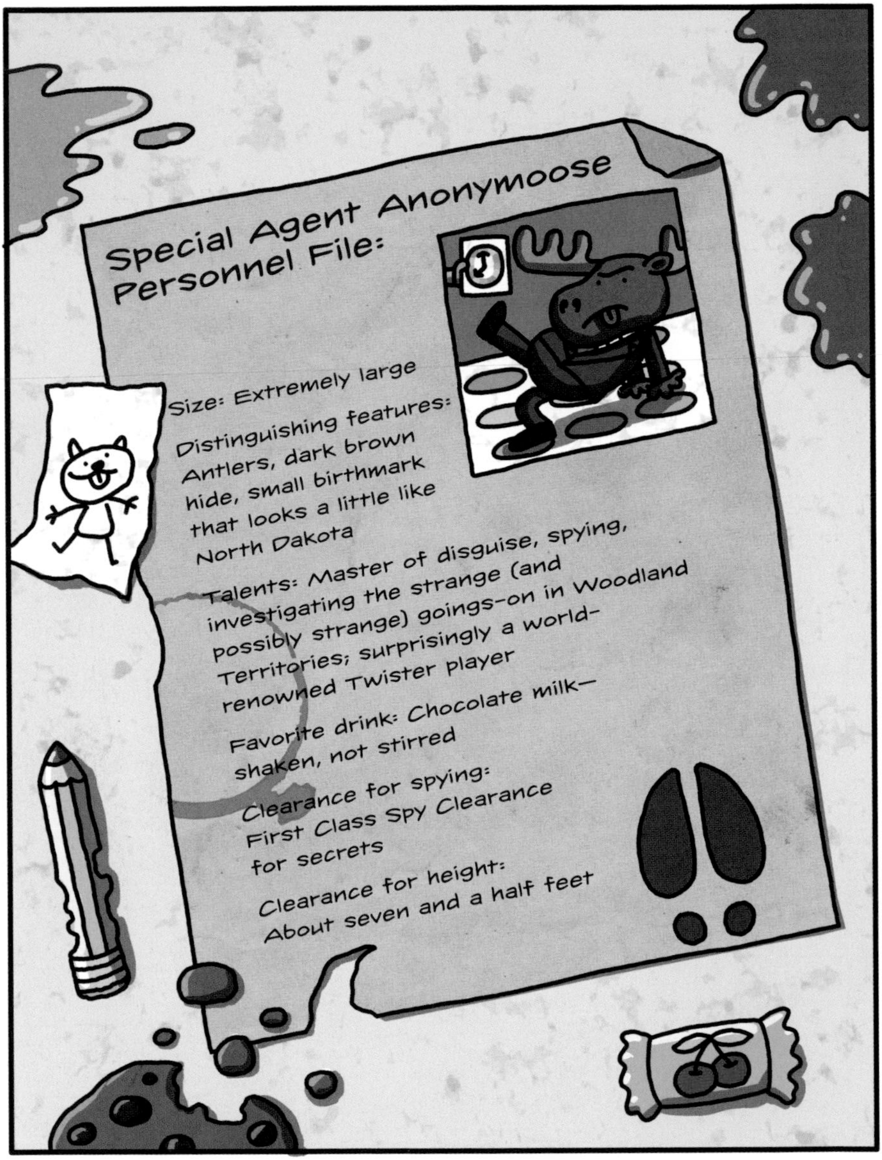
Special Agent Anonymoose
Personnel File:
Size: Extremely large
Distinguishing features: Antlers, dark brown hide, small birthmark that looks a little like North Dakota
Talents: Master of disguise, spying, investigating the strange (and possibly strange) goings-on in Woodland Territories; surprisingly a world-renowned Twister player
Favorite drink: Chocolate milk—shaken, not stirred
Clearance for spying: First Class Spy Clearance for secrets
Clearance for height: About seven and a half feet

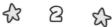

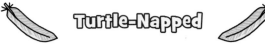

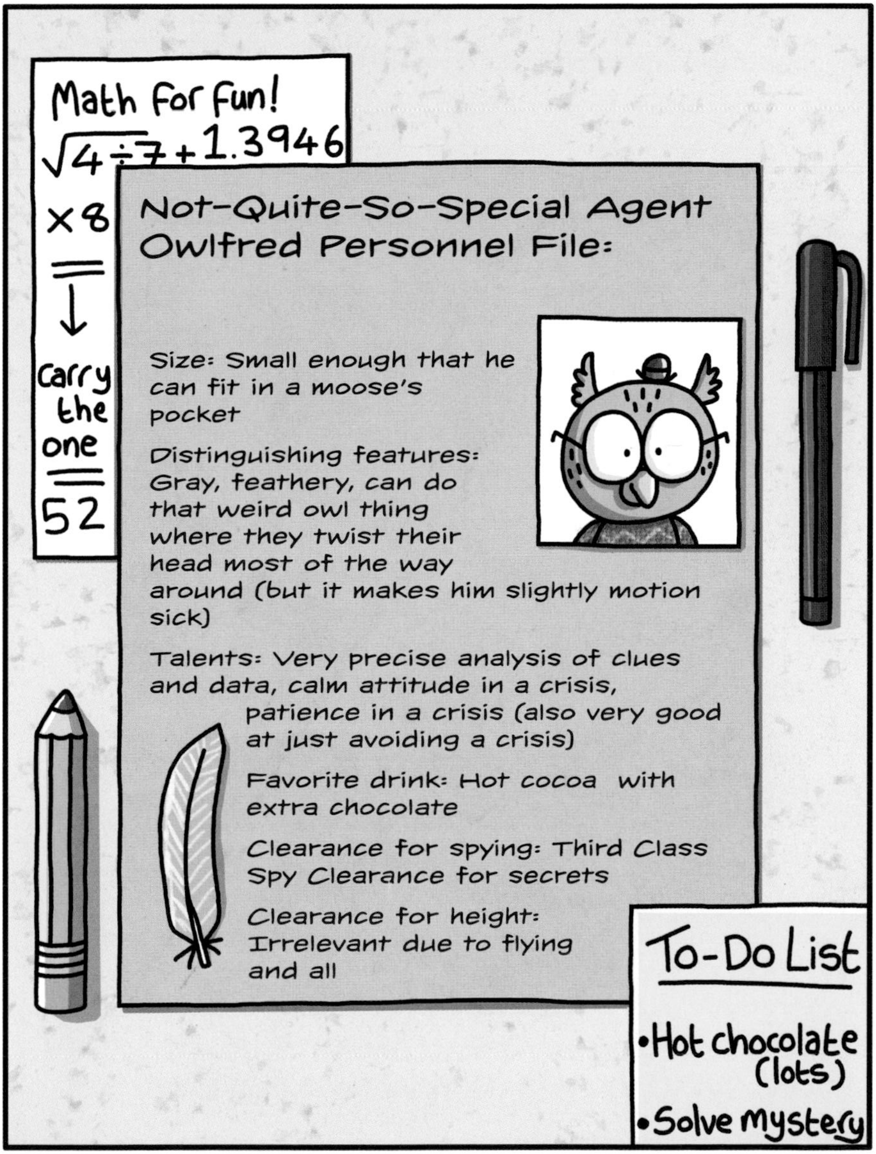
Math for fun!
√4÷7+1.3946
×8
=
↓
carry the one
=
52
Not-Quite-So-Special Agent Owlfred Personnel File:
Size: Small enough that he can fit in a moose's pocket
Distinguishing features: Gray, feathery, can do that weird owl thing where they twist their head most of the way around (but it makes him slightly motion sick)
Talents: Very precise analysis of clues and data, calm attitude in a crisis, patience in a crisis (also very good at just avoiding a crisis)
Favorite drink: Hot cocoa with extra chocolate
Clearance for spying: Third Class Spy Clearance for secrets
Clearance for height: Irrelevant due to flying and all
To-Do List
•Hot chocolate (lots)
•Solve mystery

Chapter 1

★ NEWS OF THE WILD ★

MOOSE MISJUDGES MANIC MOON MAYHEM

"No COMMENT," SAID MOOSE.

OCTOPUS WINS PRIZE

SHAKEN AND STIRRED

Shaken and Stirred

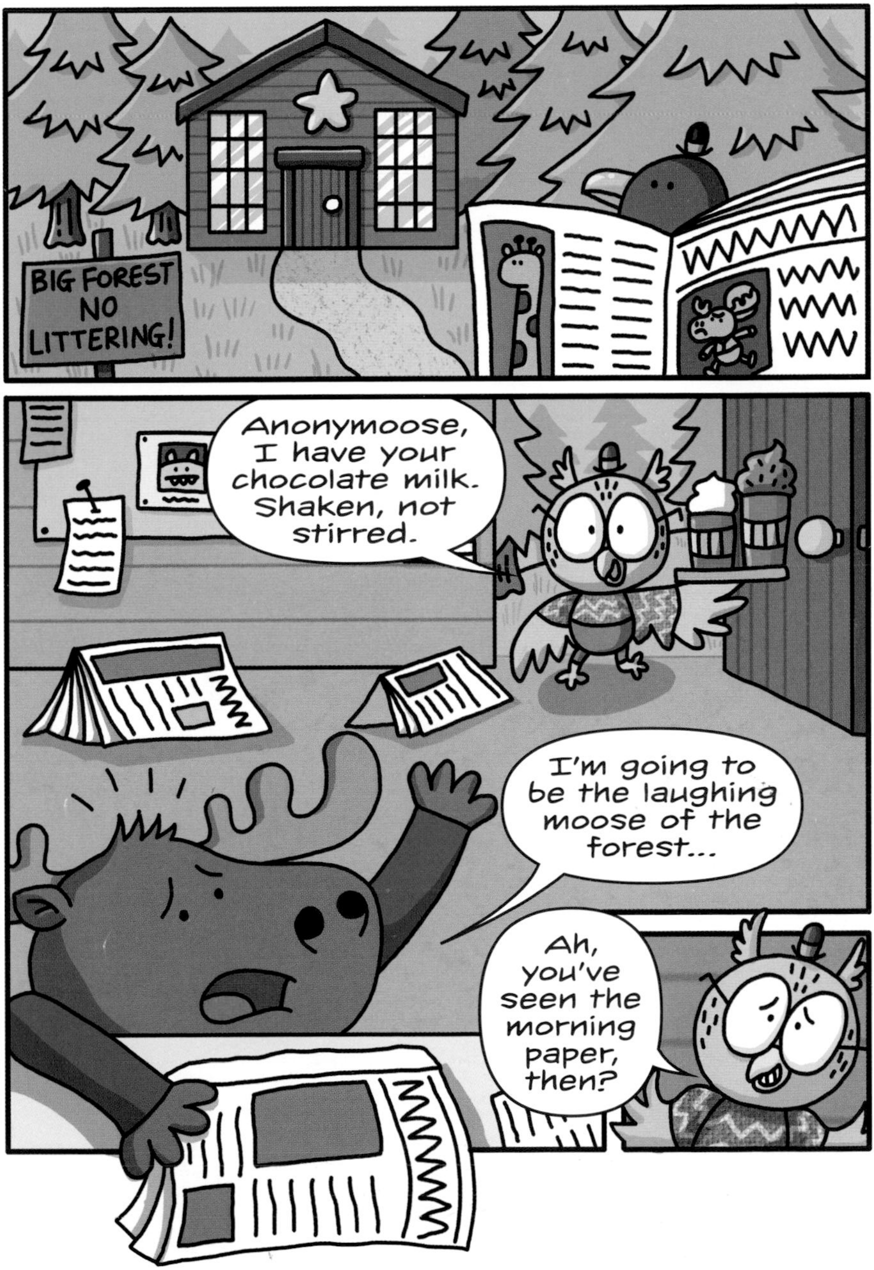
BIG FOREST
NO
LITTERING!
Anonymoose, I have your chocolate milk. Shaken, not stirred.
I'm going to be the laughing moose of the forest...
Ah, you've seen the morning paper, then?

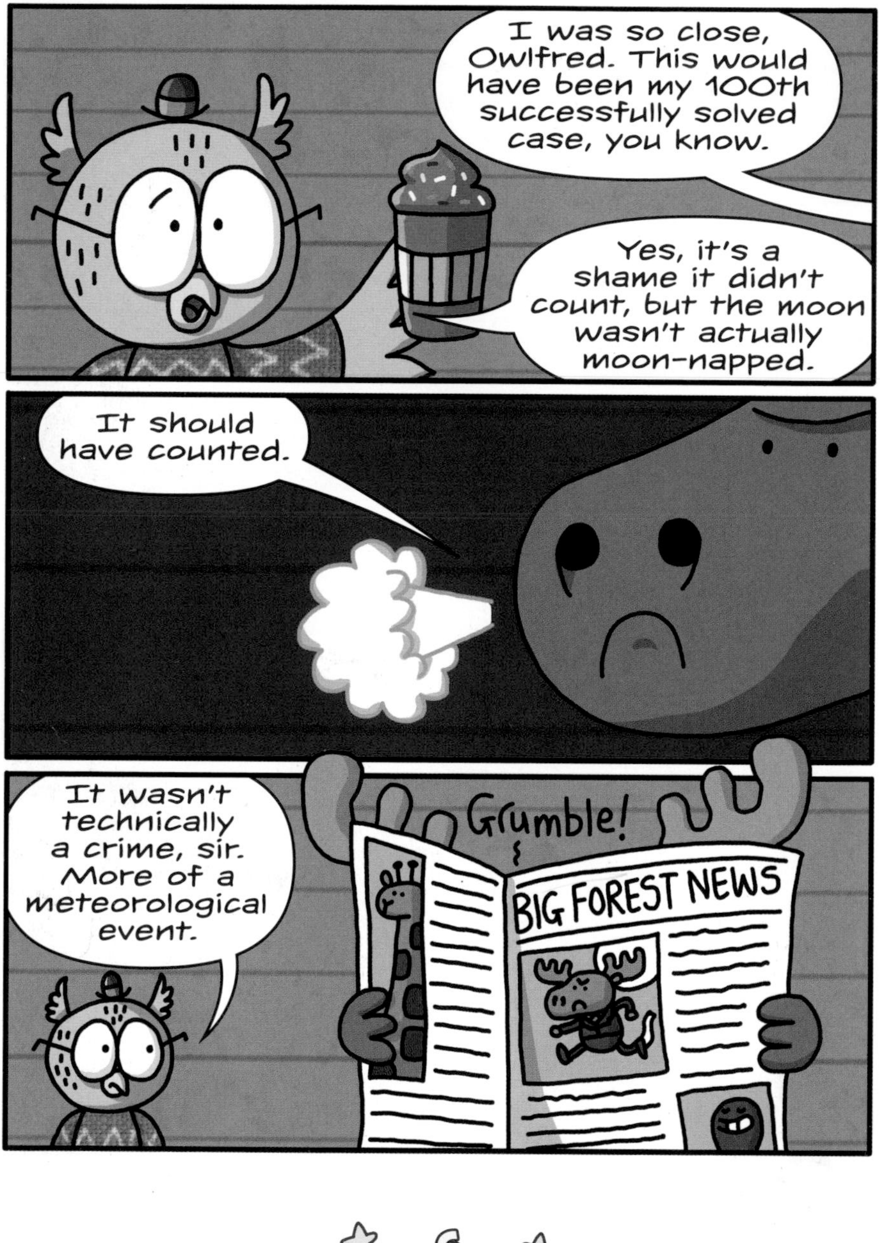
I was so close, Owlfred. This would have been my 100th successfully solved case, you know.
Yes, it's a shame it didn't count, but the moon wasn't actually moon-napped.
It should have counted.
It wasn't technically a crime, sir. More of a meteorological event.
Grumble!
BIG FOREST NEWS

Shaken and Stirred

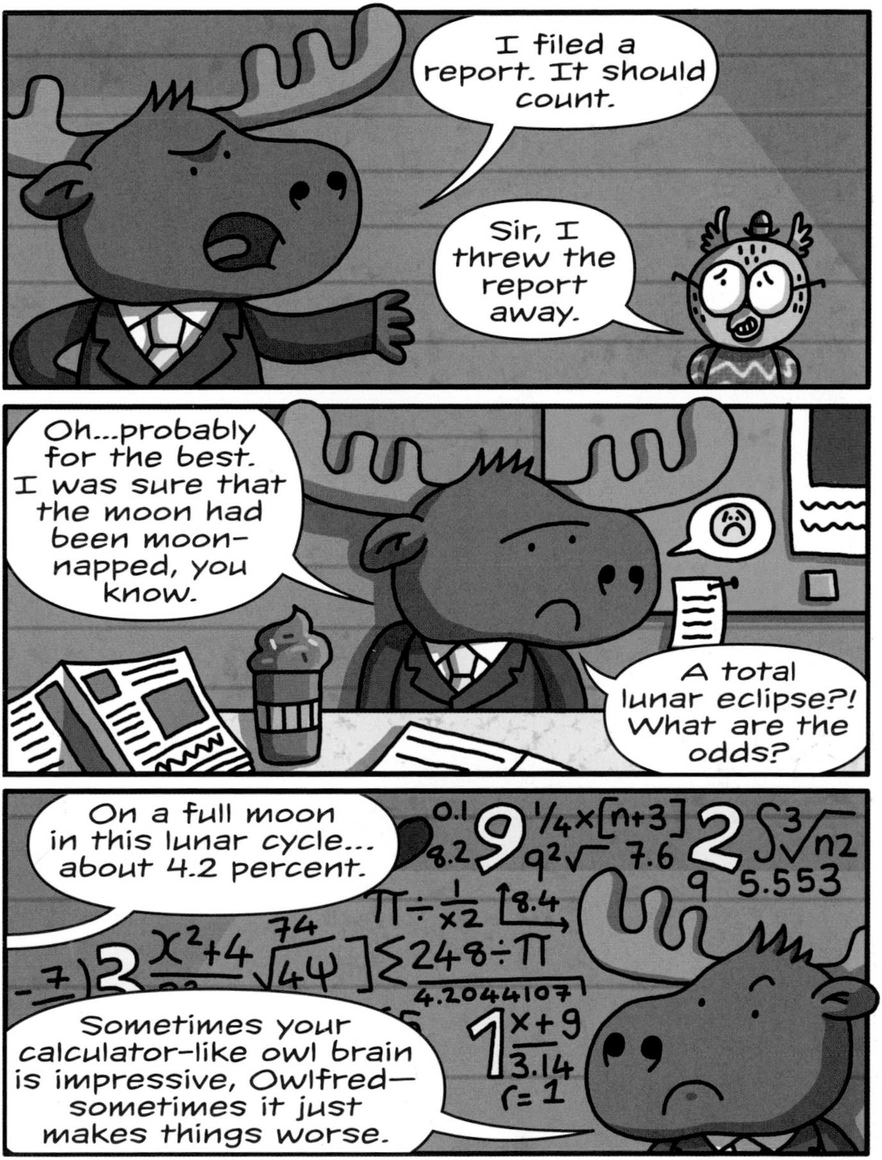

I filed a report. It should count.
Sir, I threw the report away.
Oh...probably for the best. I was sure that the moon had been moon-napped, you know.
A total lunar eclipse?! What are the odds?
On a full moon in this lunar cycle... about 4.2 percent.
Sometimes your calculator-like owl brain is impressive, Owlfred—sometimes it just makes things worse.

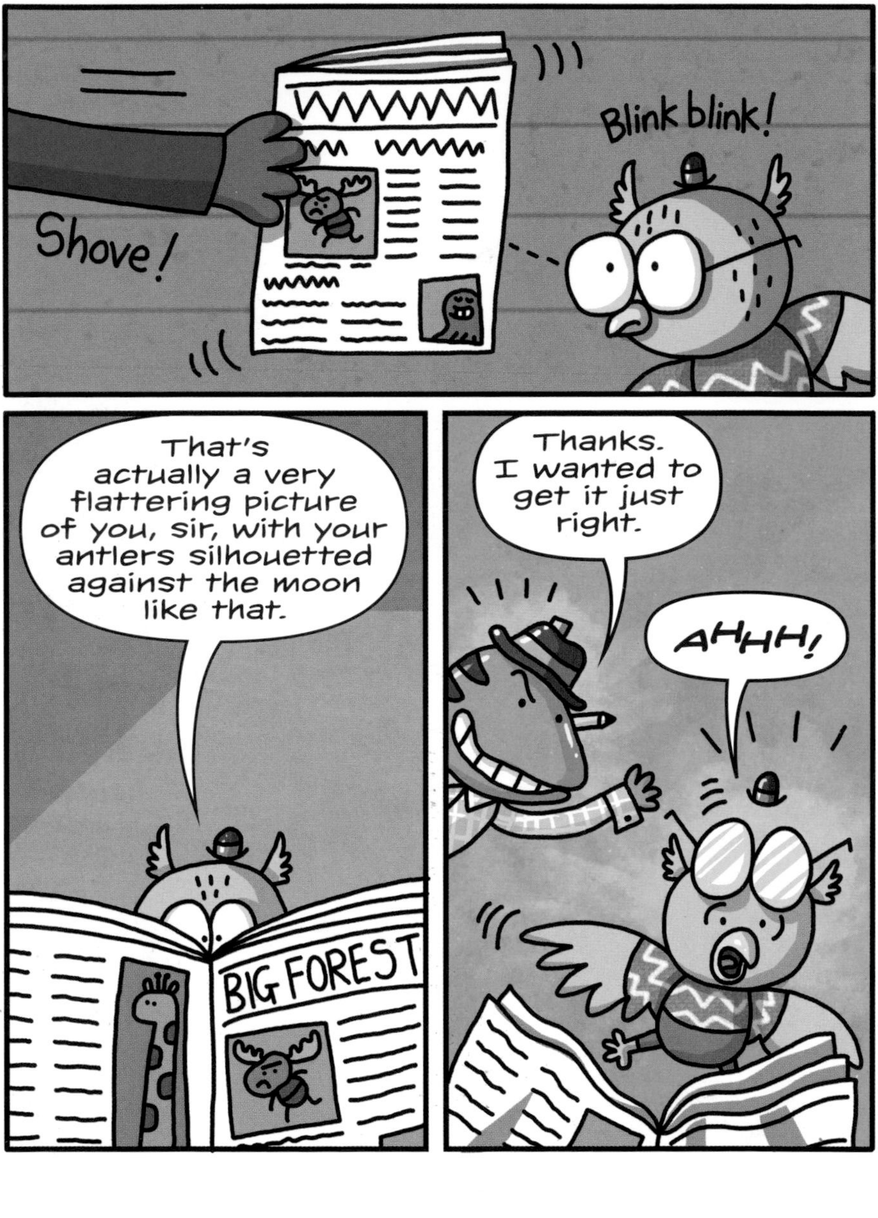
Shove!
Blink blink!
BIG FOREST
That's actually a very flattering picture of you, sir, with your antlers silhouetted against the moon like that.
Thanks. I wanted to get it just right.
AHHH!

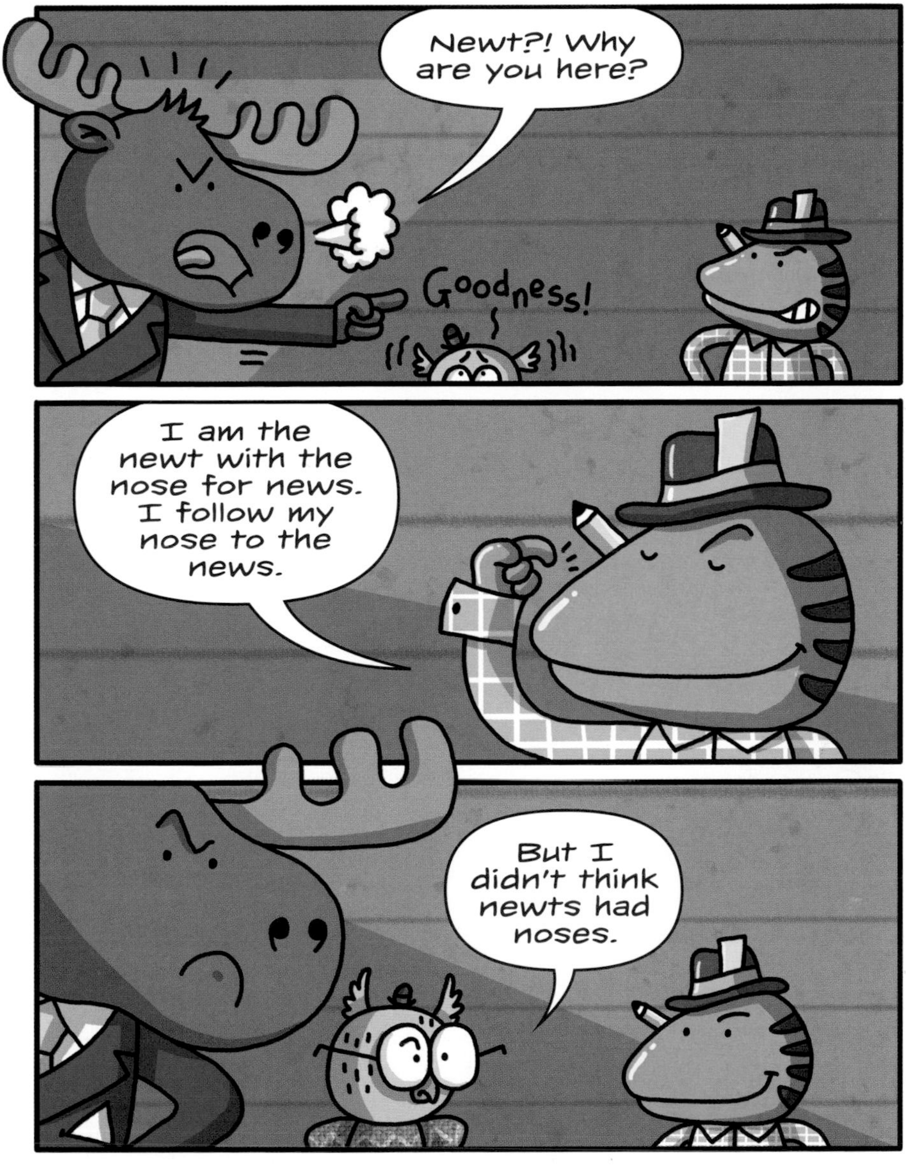
Newt?! Why are you here?
Goodness!
I am the newt with the nose for news. I follow my nose to the news.
But I didn't think newts had noses.

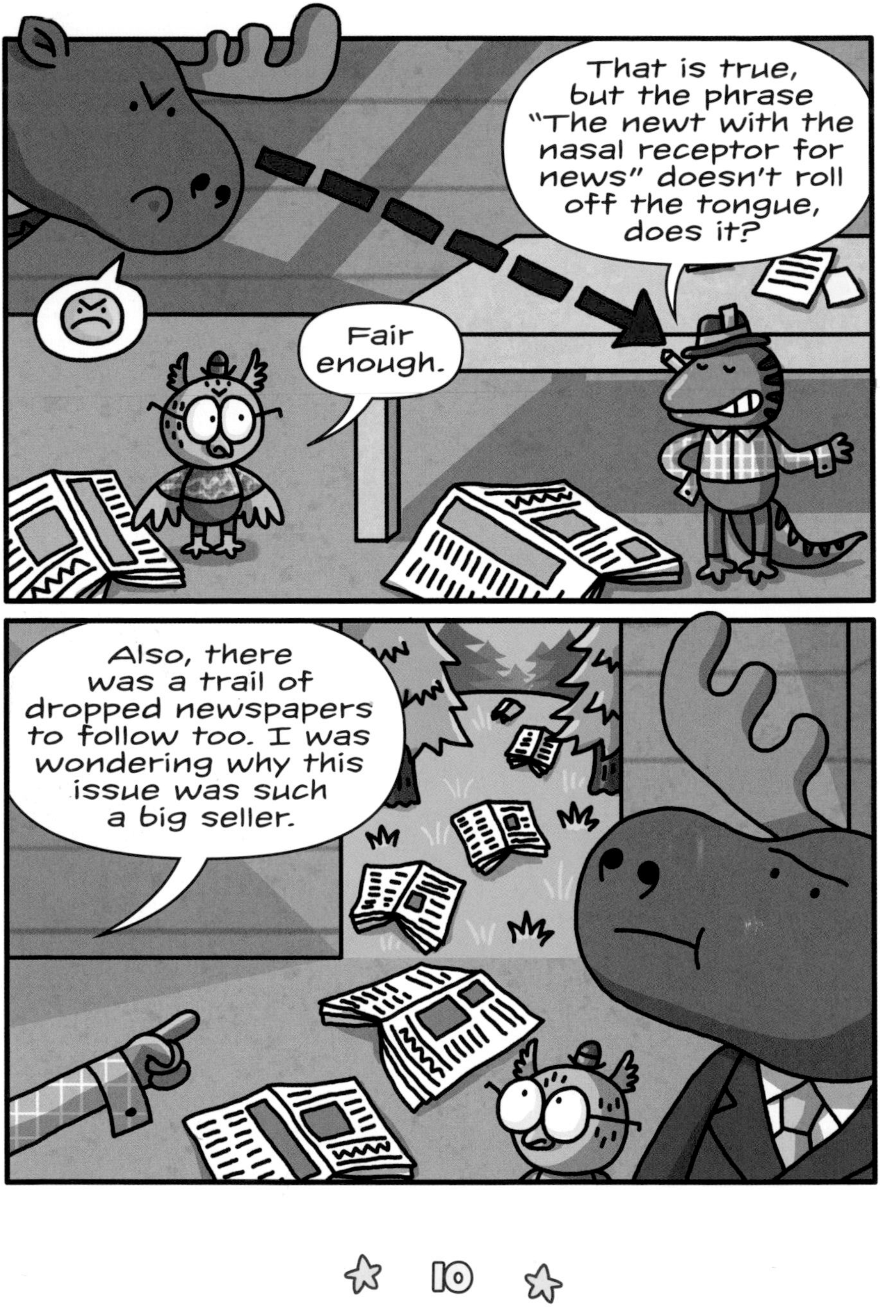
That is true, but the phrase "The newt with the nasal receptor for news" doesn't roll off the tongue, does it?
Fair enough.
Also, there was a trail of dropped newspapers to follow too. I was wondering why this issue was such a big seller.

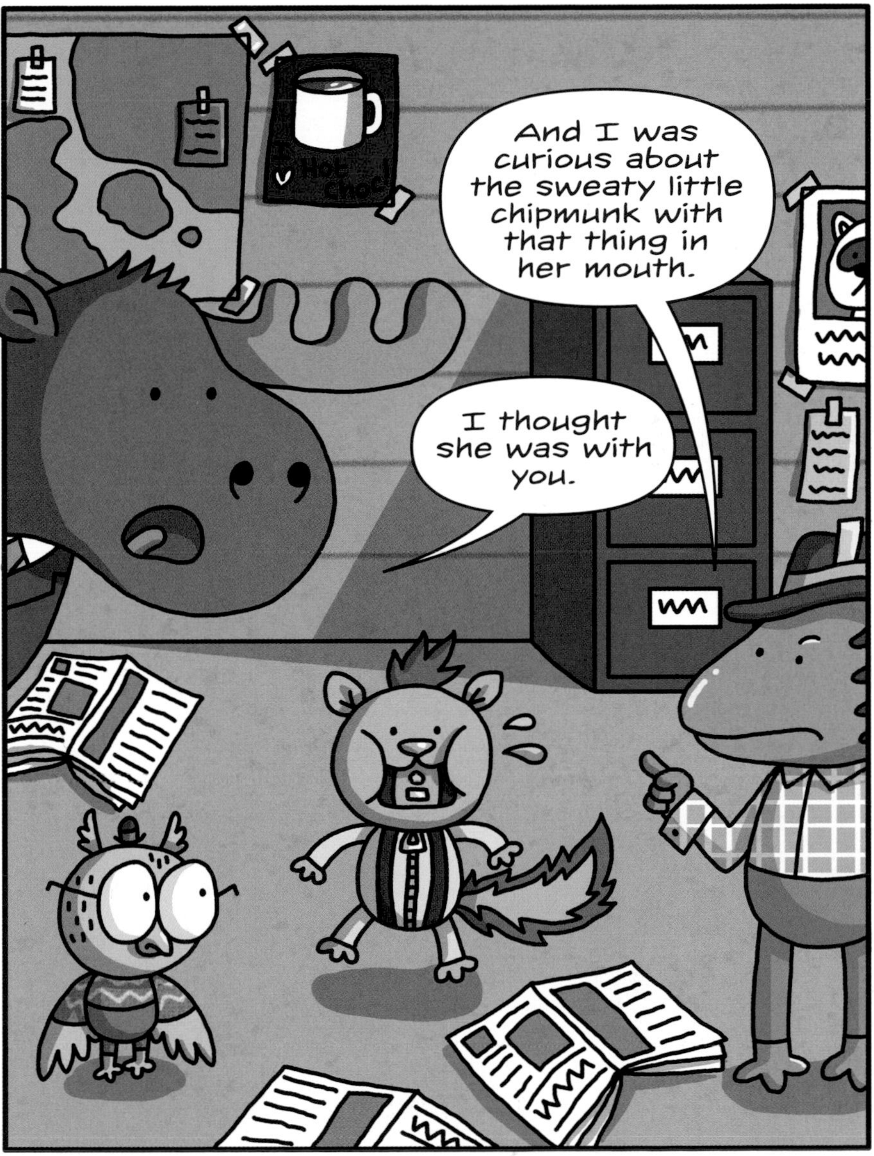
And I was curious about the sweaty little chipmunk with that thing in her mouth.
I thought she was with you.

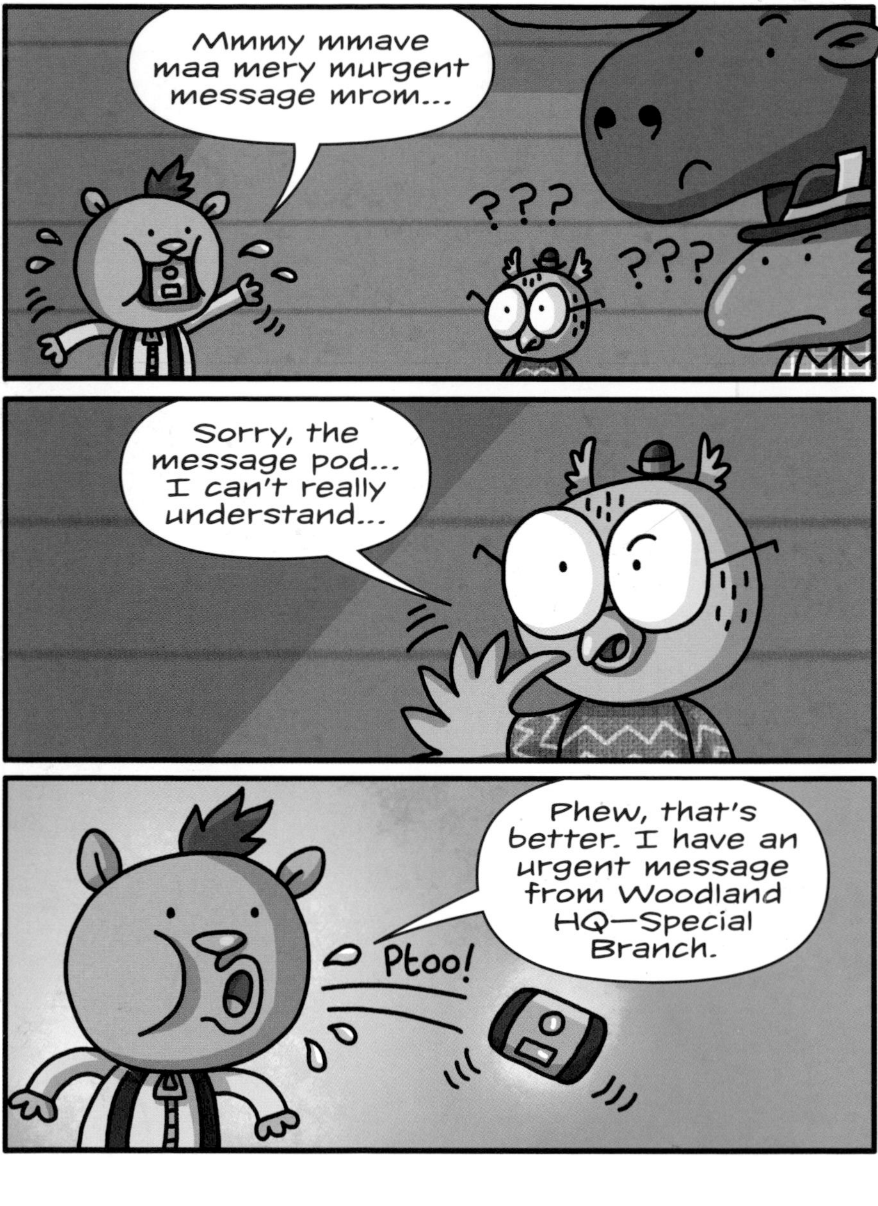
Mmmy mmave maa mery murgent message mrom...
???
???
Sorry, the message pod... I can't really understand...
Phew, that's better. I have an urgent message from Woodland HQ—Special Branch.
Ptoo!

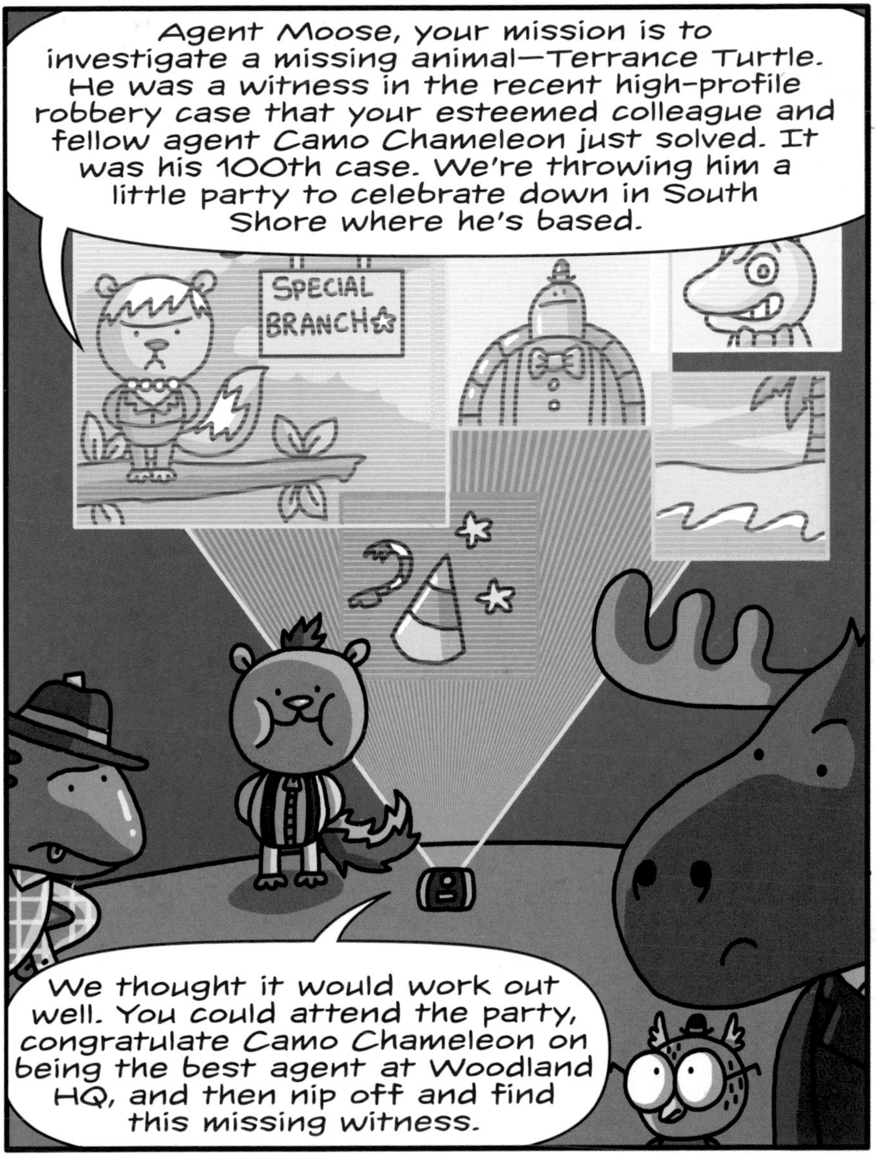
Agent Moose, your mission is to investigate a missing animal—Terrance Turtle. He was a witness in the recent high-profile robbery case that your esteemed colleague and fellow agent Camo Chameleon just solved. It was his 100th case. We're throwing him a little party to celebrate down in South Shore where he's based.
SPECIAL BRANCH
We thought it would work out well. You could attend the party, congratulate Camo Chameleon on being the best agent at Woodland HQ, and then nip off and find this missing witness.

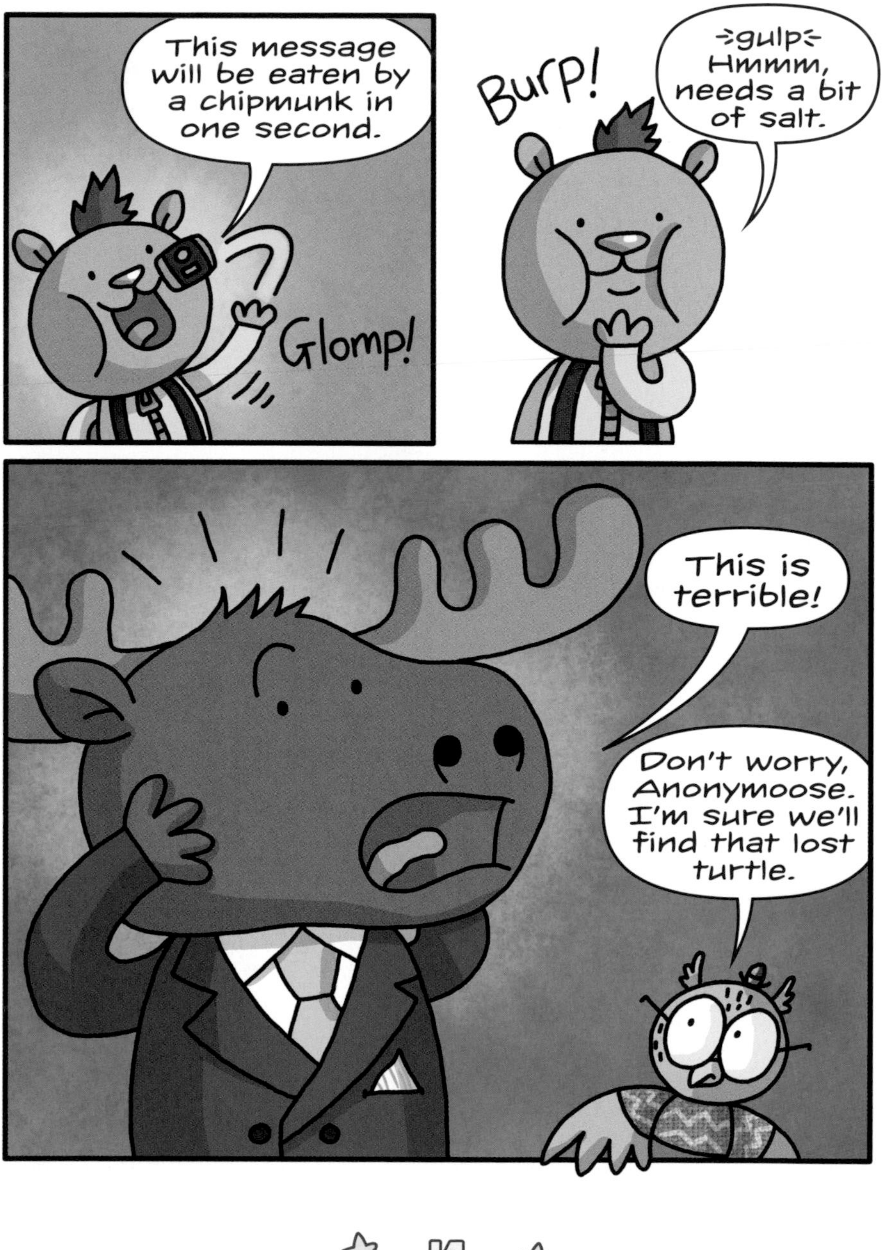
This message will be eaten by a chipmunk in one second.
Glomp!
Burp!
gulp
Hmmm, needs a bit of salt.
This is terrible!
Don't worry, Anonymoose. I'm sure we'll find that lost turtle.

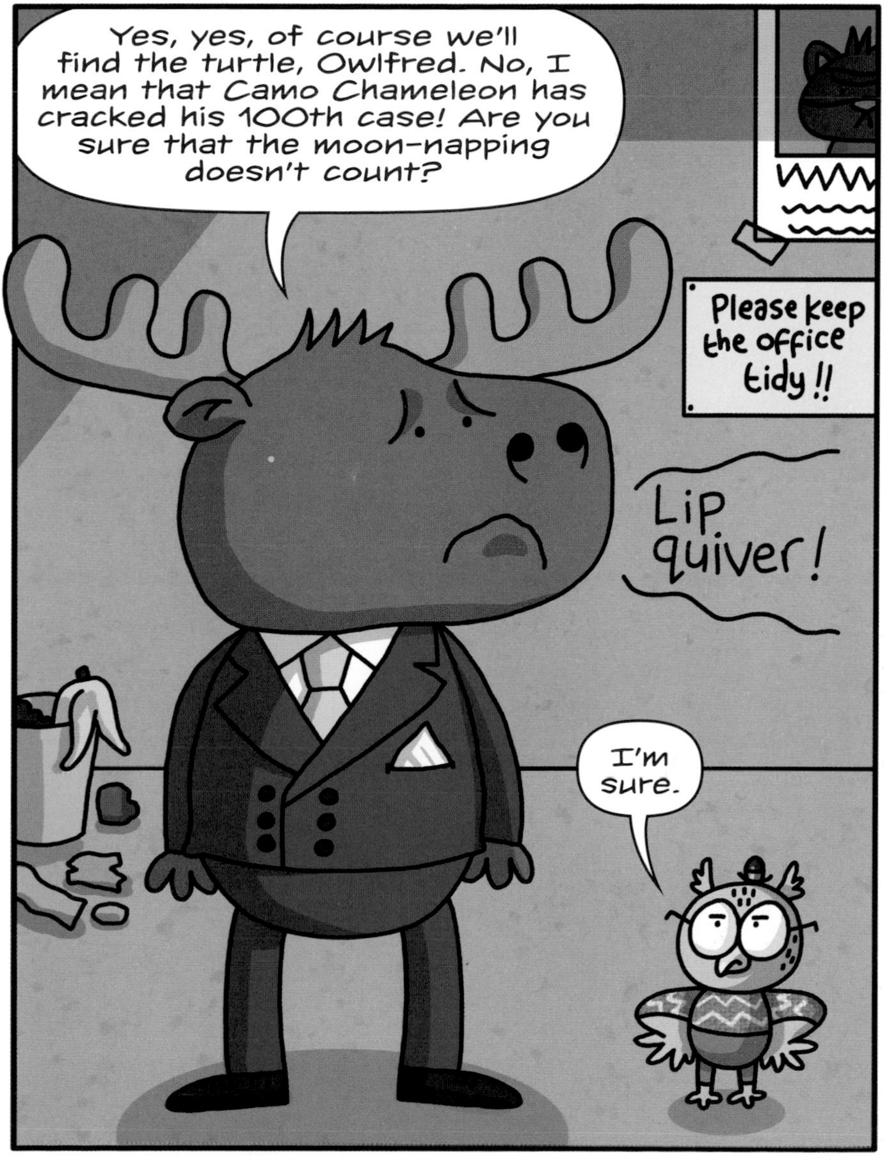
Yes, yes, of course we'll find the turtle, Owlfred. No, I mean that Camo Chameleon has cracked his 100th case! Are you sure that the moon-napping doesn't count?
Please keep the office tidy !!
Lip quiver!
I'm sure.

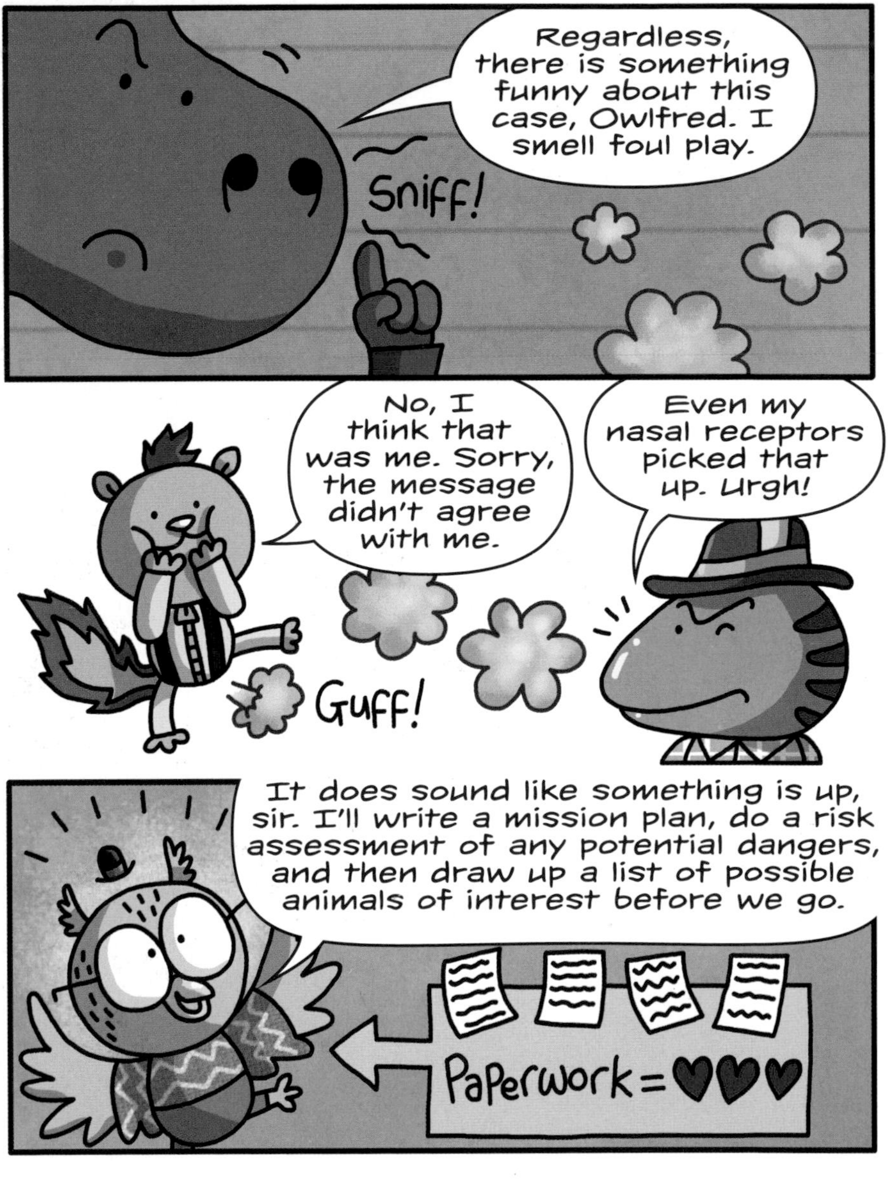
Regardless, there is something funny about this case, Owlfred. I smell foul play.
Sniff!
No, I think that was me. Sorry, the message didn't agree with me.
Guff!
Even my nasal receptors picked that up. Urgh!
It does sound like something is up, sir. I'll write a mission plan, do a risk assessment of any potential dangers, and then draw up a list of possible animals of interest before we go.
Paperwork=♥♥♥

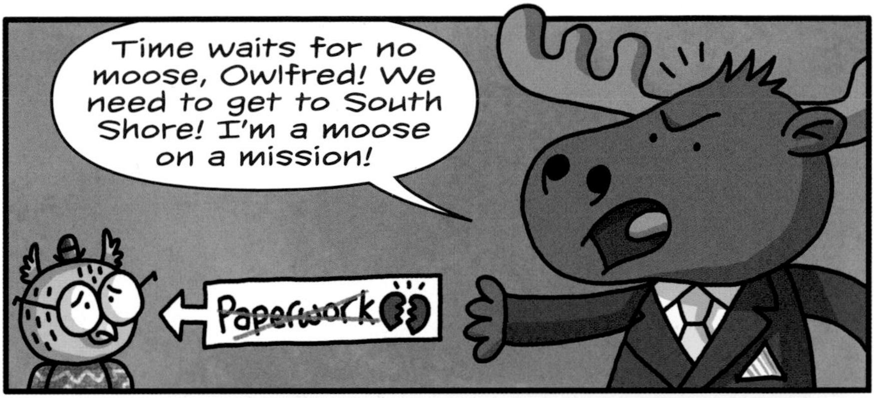
Time waits for no moose, Owlfred! We need to get to South Shore! I'm a moose on a mission!
Paperwork

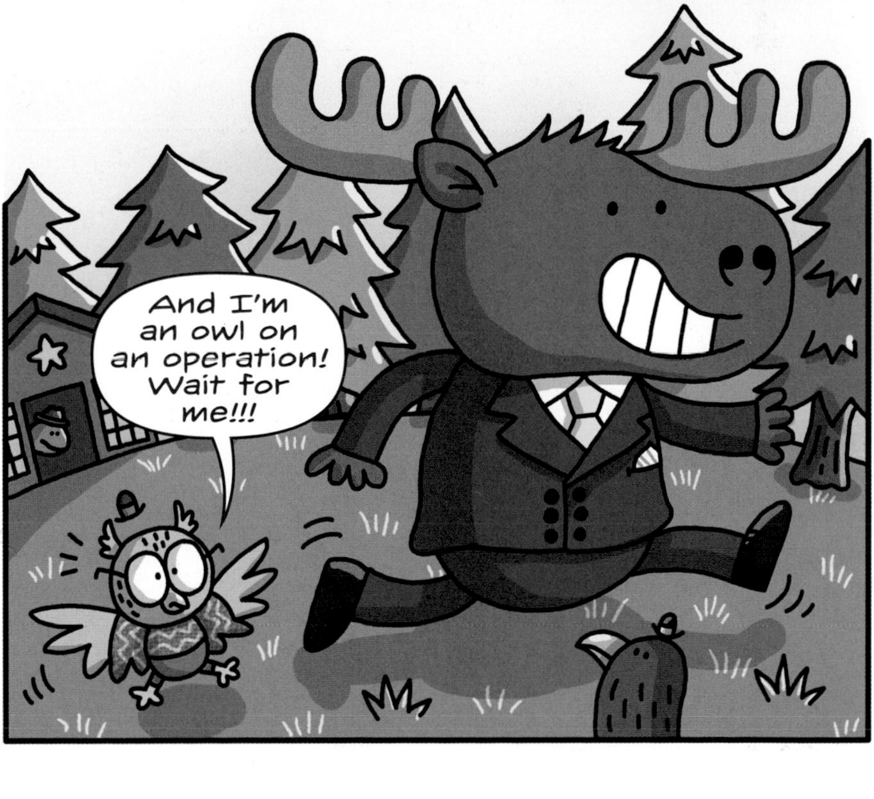
And I'm an owl on an operation! Wait for me!!!

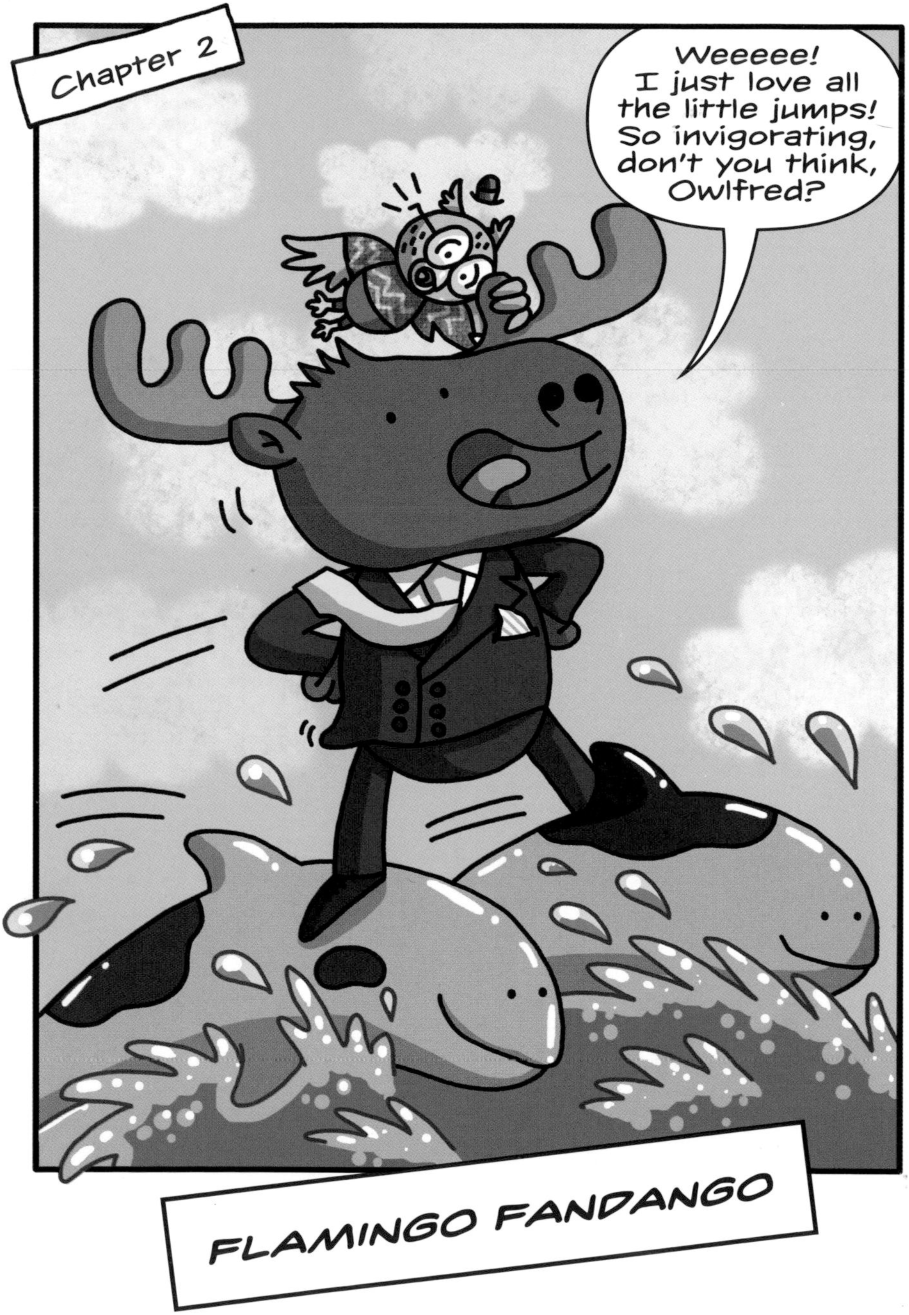
Chapter 2
Weeeeee! I just love all the little jumps! So invigorating, don't you think, Owlfred?

FLAMINGO FANDANGO

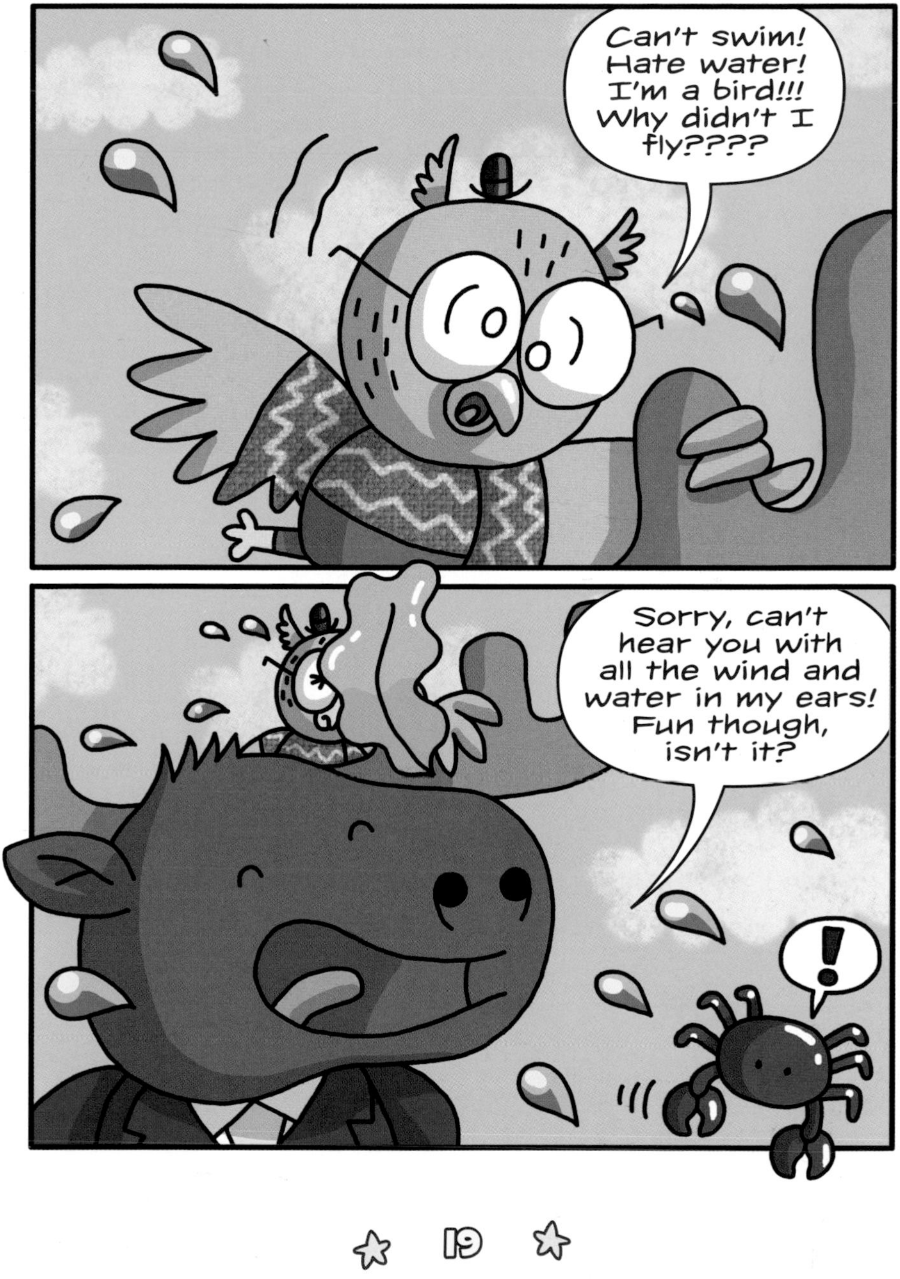
Can't swim! Hate water! I'm a bird!!! Why didn't I fly????
Sorry, can't hear you with all the wind and water in my ears! Fun though, isn't it?
!

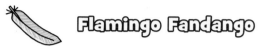

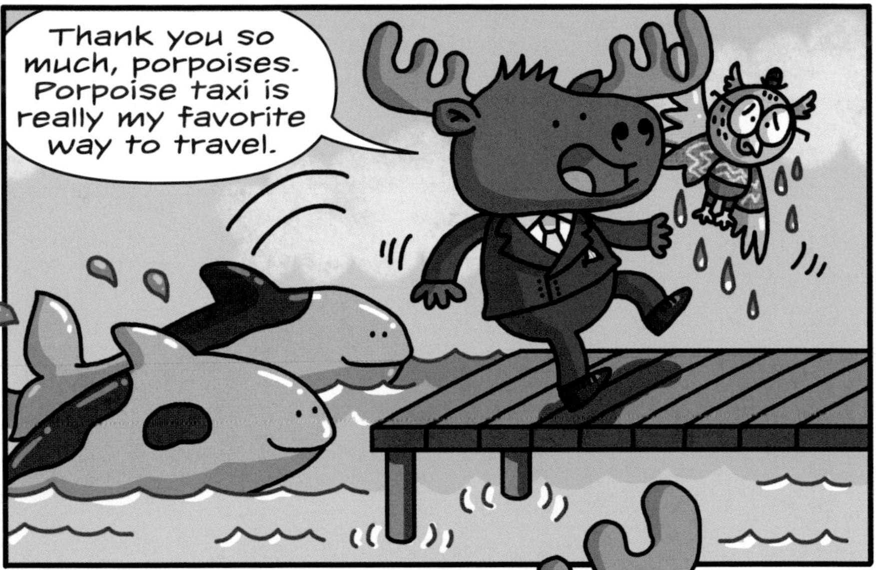
Thank you so much, porpoises. Porpoise taxi is really my favorite way to travel.

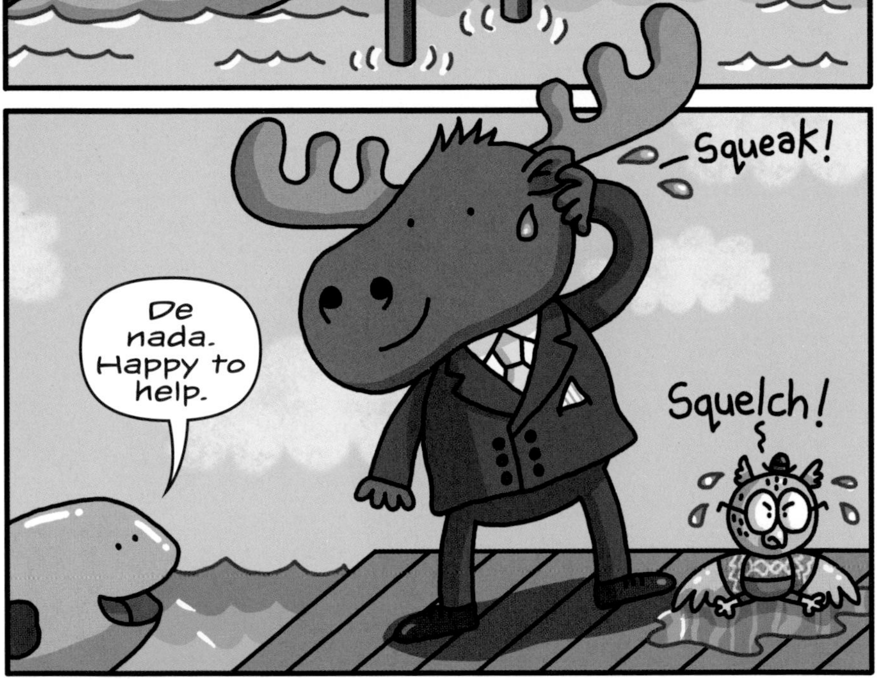
Squeak!
De nada. Happy to help.
Squelch!

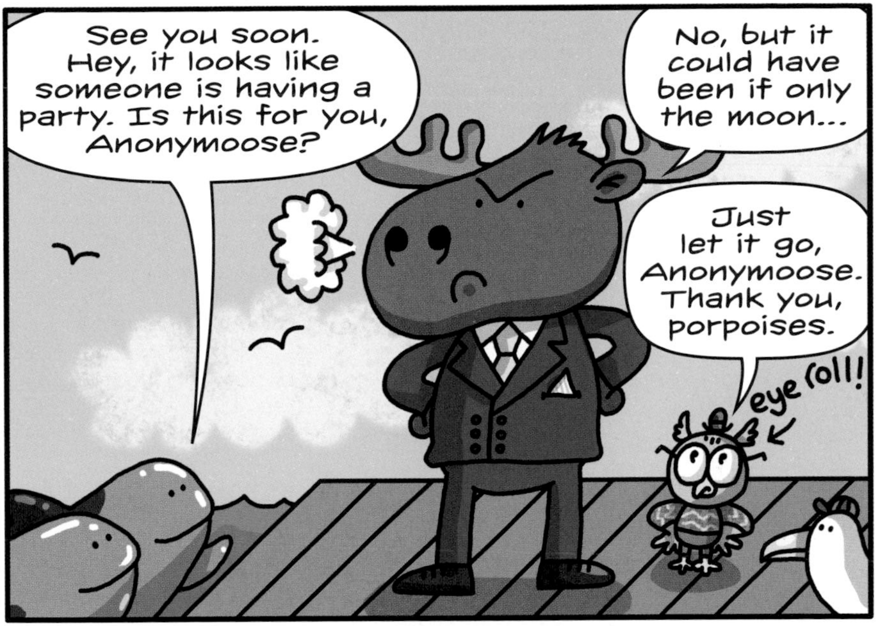
See you soon. Hey, it looks like someone is having a party. Is this for you, Anonymoose?
No, but it could have been if only the moon...
Just let it go, Anonymoose. Thank you, porpoises.
eye roll!

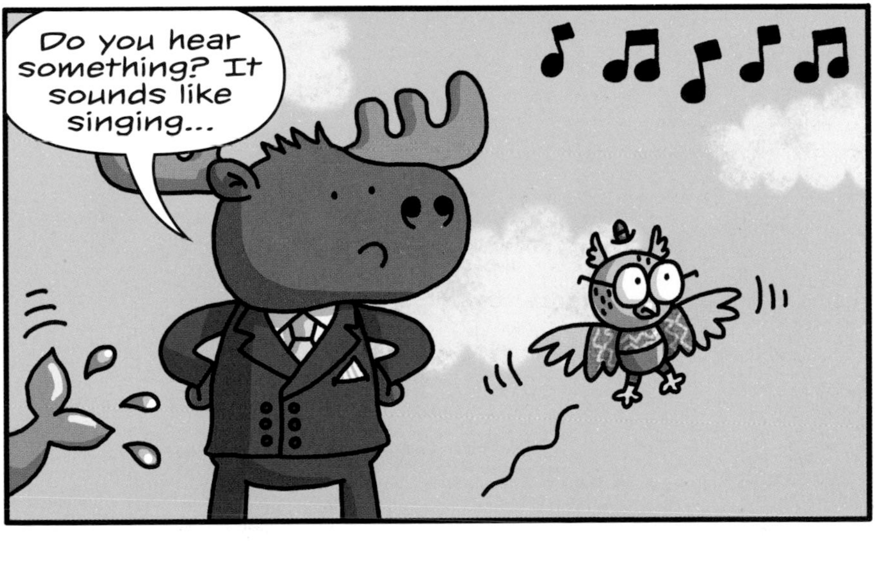
Do you hear something? It sounds like singing...

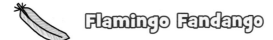

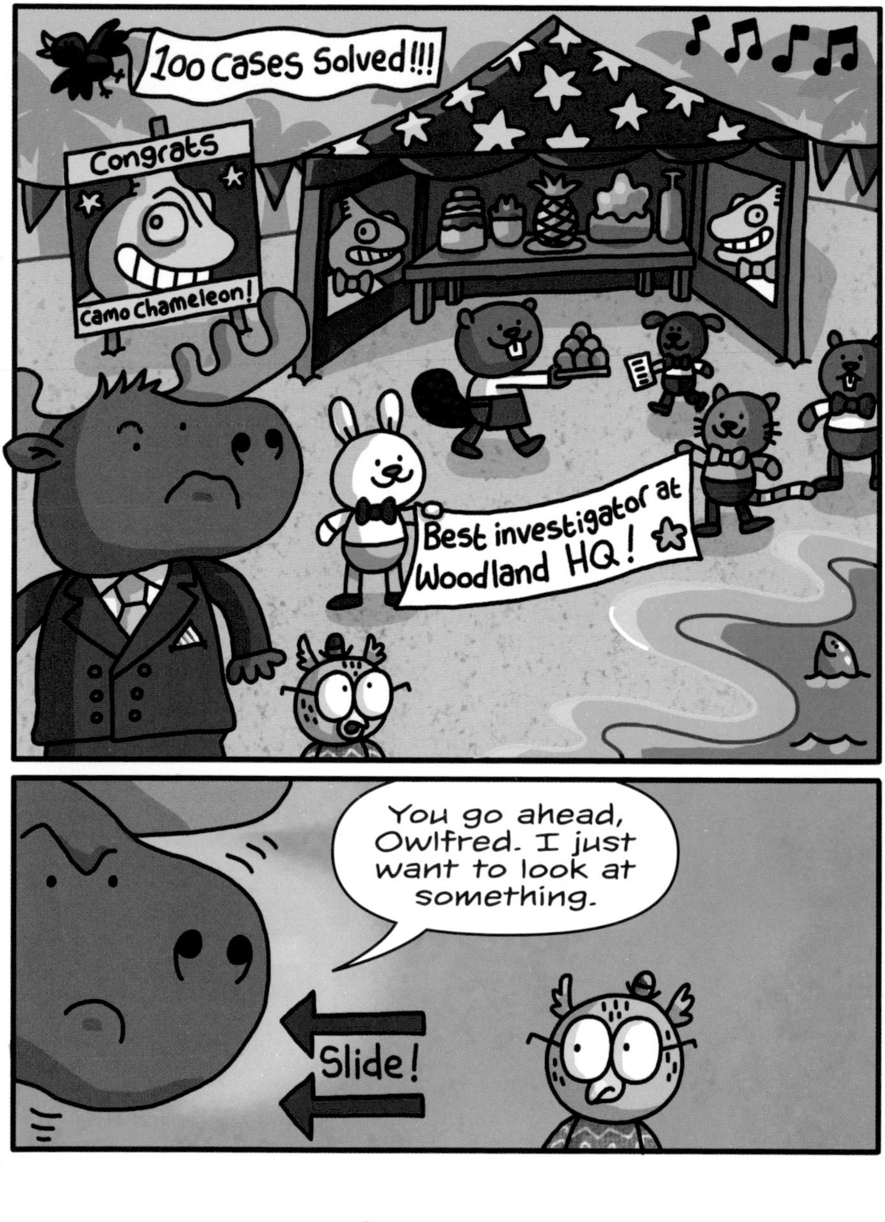
100 Cases Solved!!!
Congrats
Camo Chameleon!
Best investigator at Woodland HQ!
You go ahead, Owlfred. I just want to look at something.
Slide!

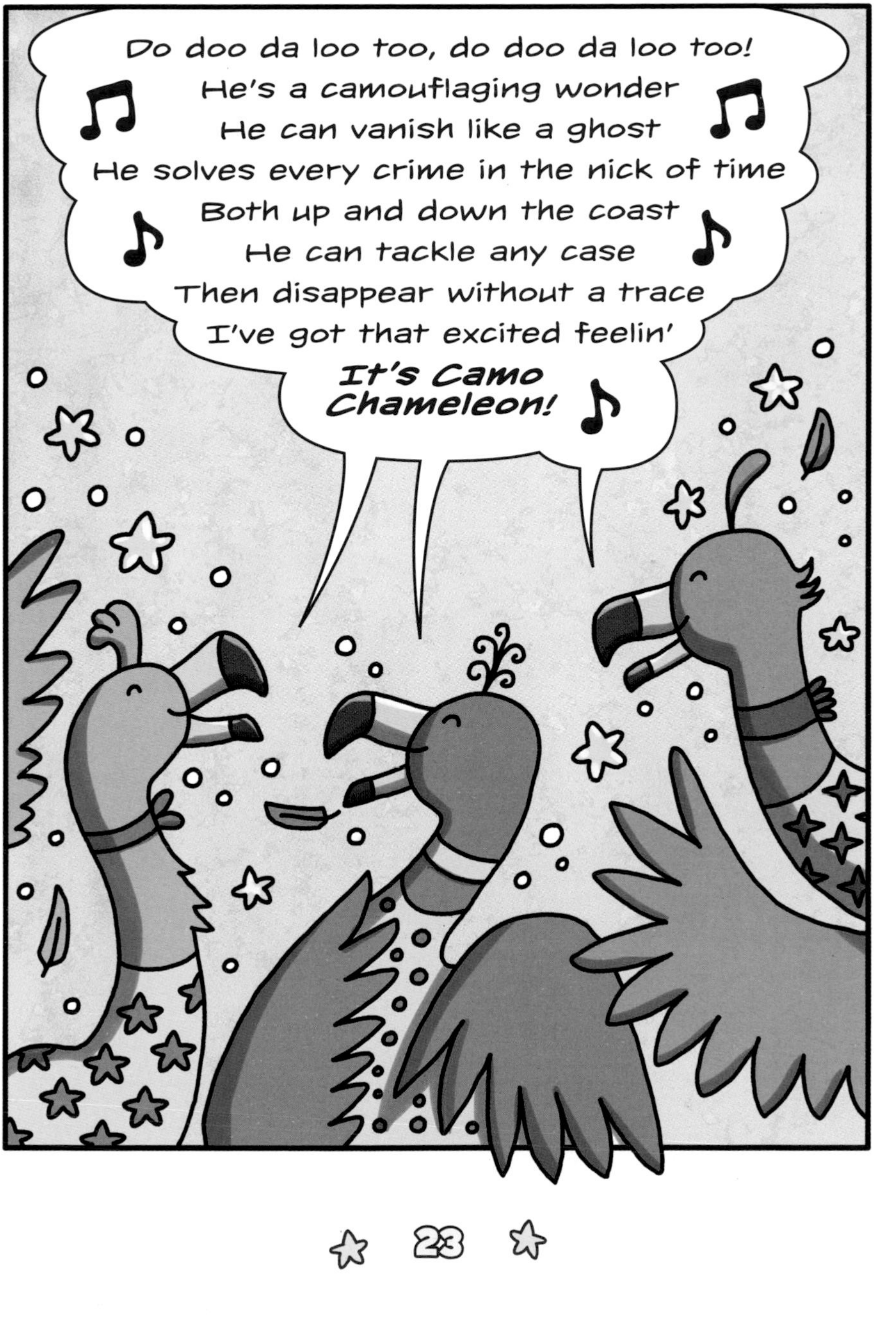
Do doo da loo too, do doo da loo too!
He's a camouflaging wonder
He can vanish like a ghost
He solves every crime in the nick of time
Both up and down the coast
He can tackle any case
Then disappear without a trace
I've got that excited feelin'
It's Camo Chameleon!

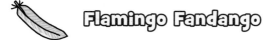

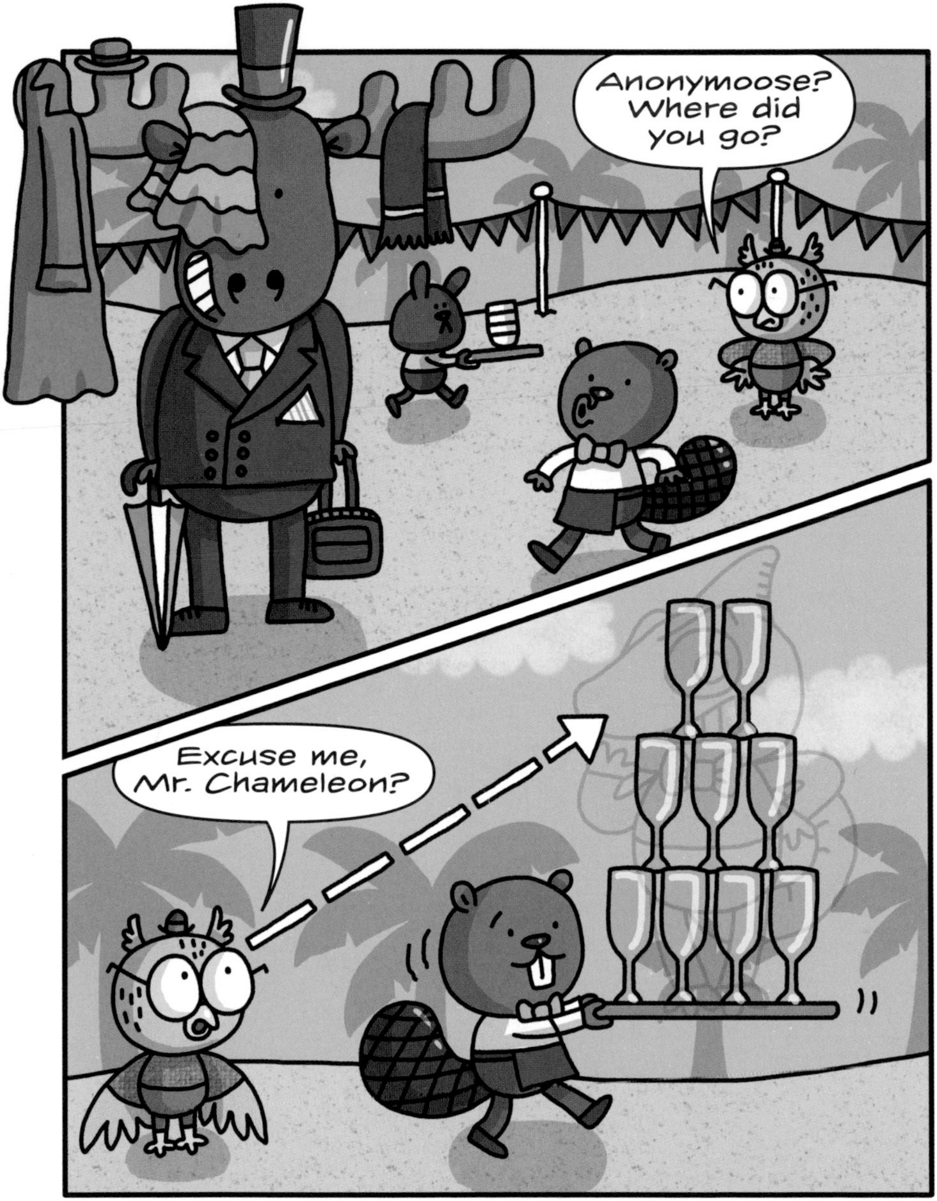
Anonymoose? Where did you go?
Excuse me, Mr. Chameleon?

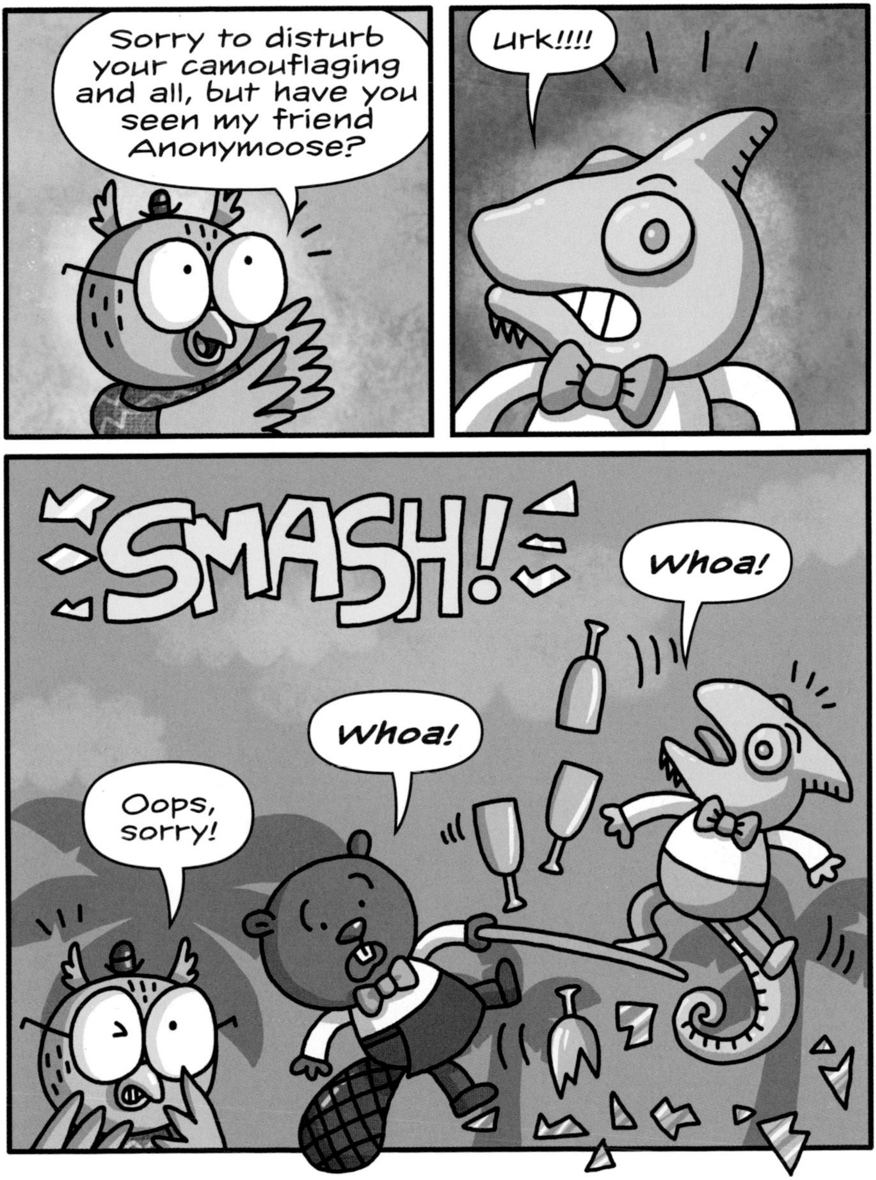
Sorry to disturb your camouflaging and all, but have you seen my friend Anonymoose?
Urk!!!!
SMASH!
Whoa!
Whoa!
Oops, sorry!

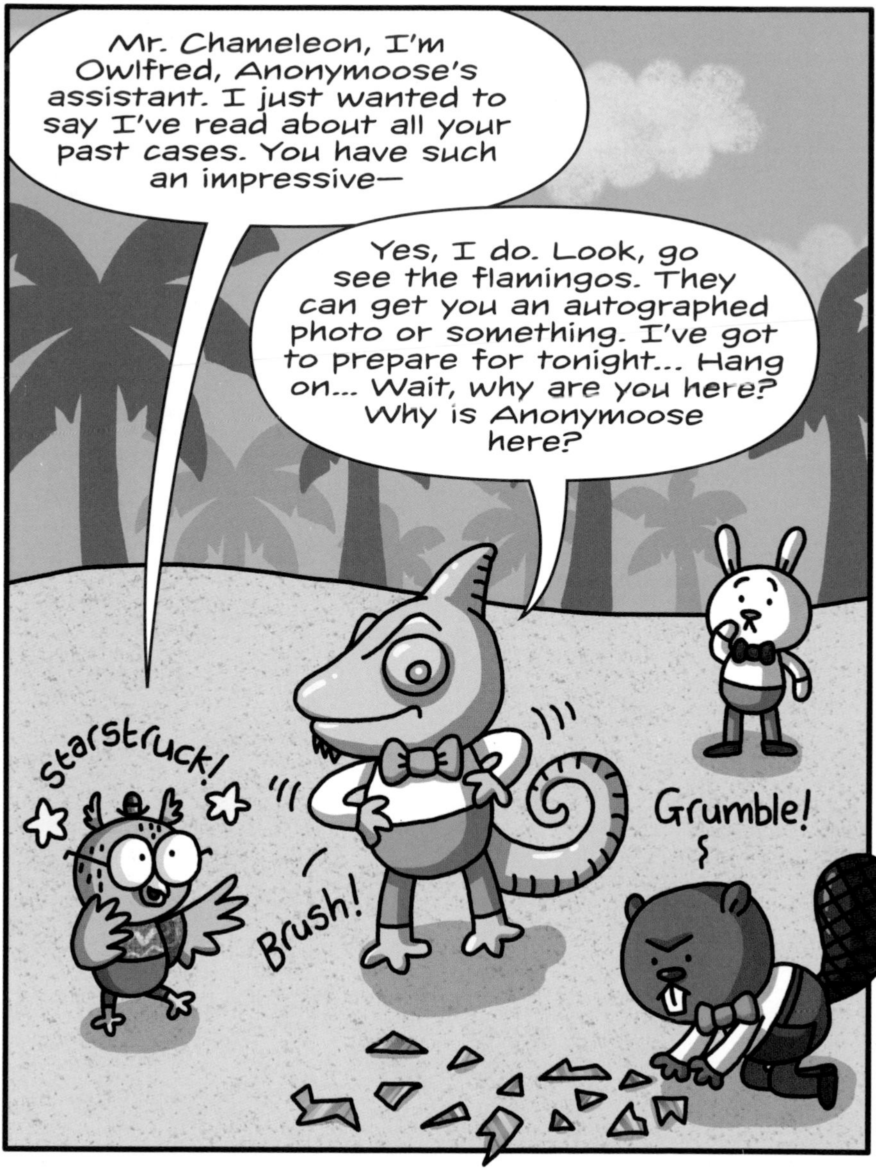
Mr. Chameleon, I'm Owlfred, Anonymoose's assistant. I just wanted to say I've read about all your past cases. You have such an impressive—
Yes, I do. Look, go see the flamingos. They can get you an autographed photo or something. I've got to prepare for tonight... Hang on... Wait, why are you here? Why is Anonymoose here?
Starstruck!
Brush!
Grumble!

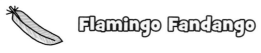

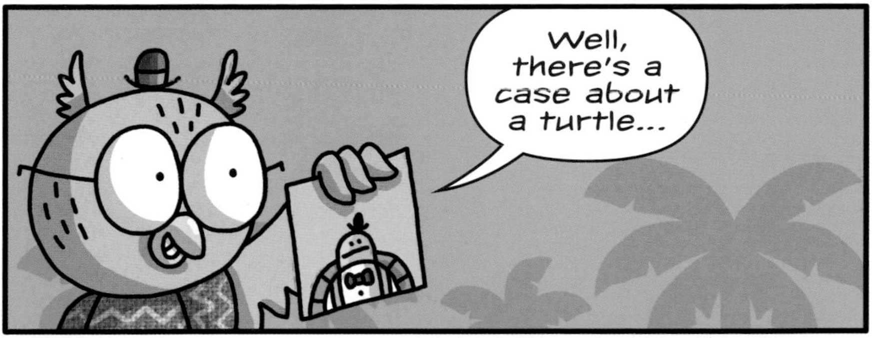
Well, there's a case about a turtle...

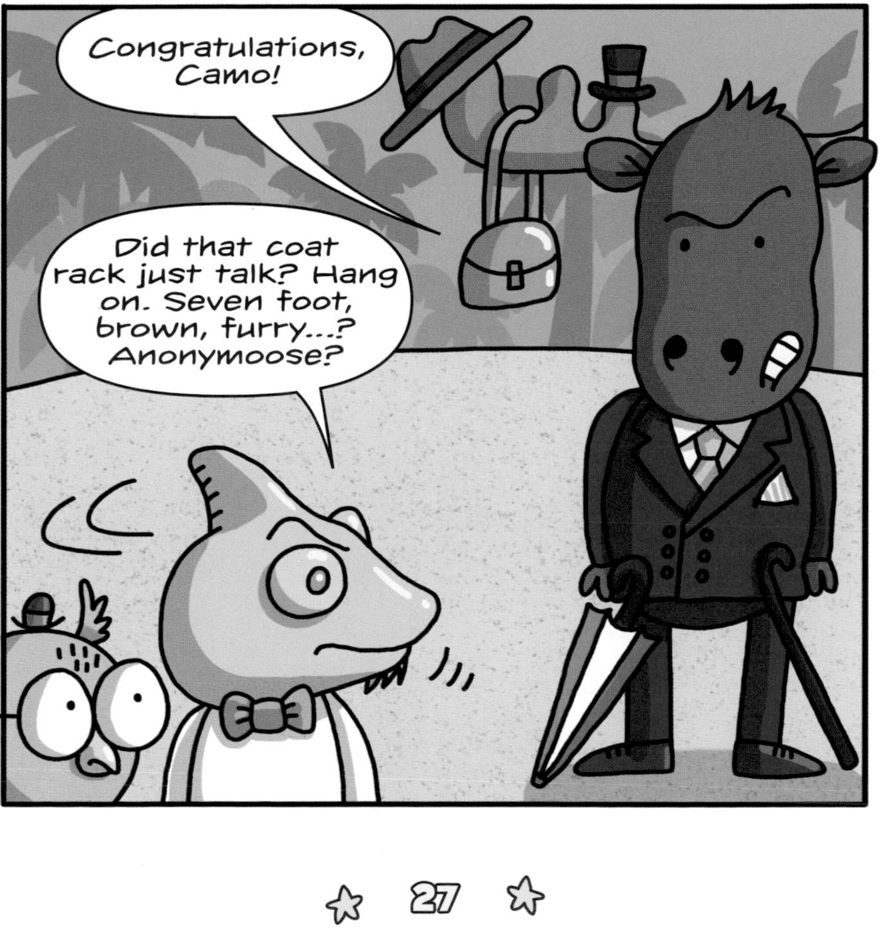
Congratulations, Camo!
Did that coat rack just talk? Hang on. Seven foot, brown, furry...? Anonymoose?

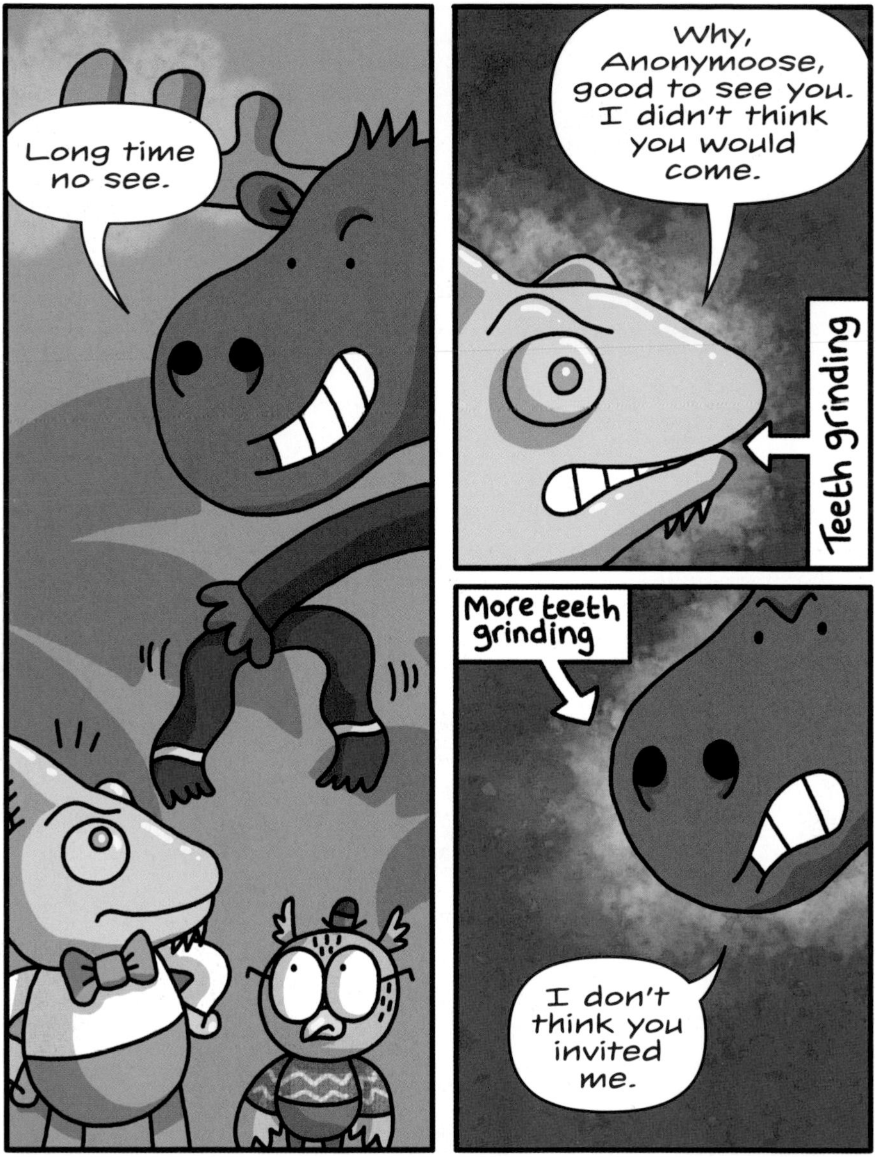
Long time no see.
Why, Anonymoose, good to see you. I didn't think you would come.
Teeth grinding
More teeth grinding
I don't think you invited me.

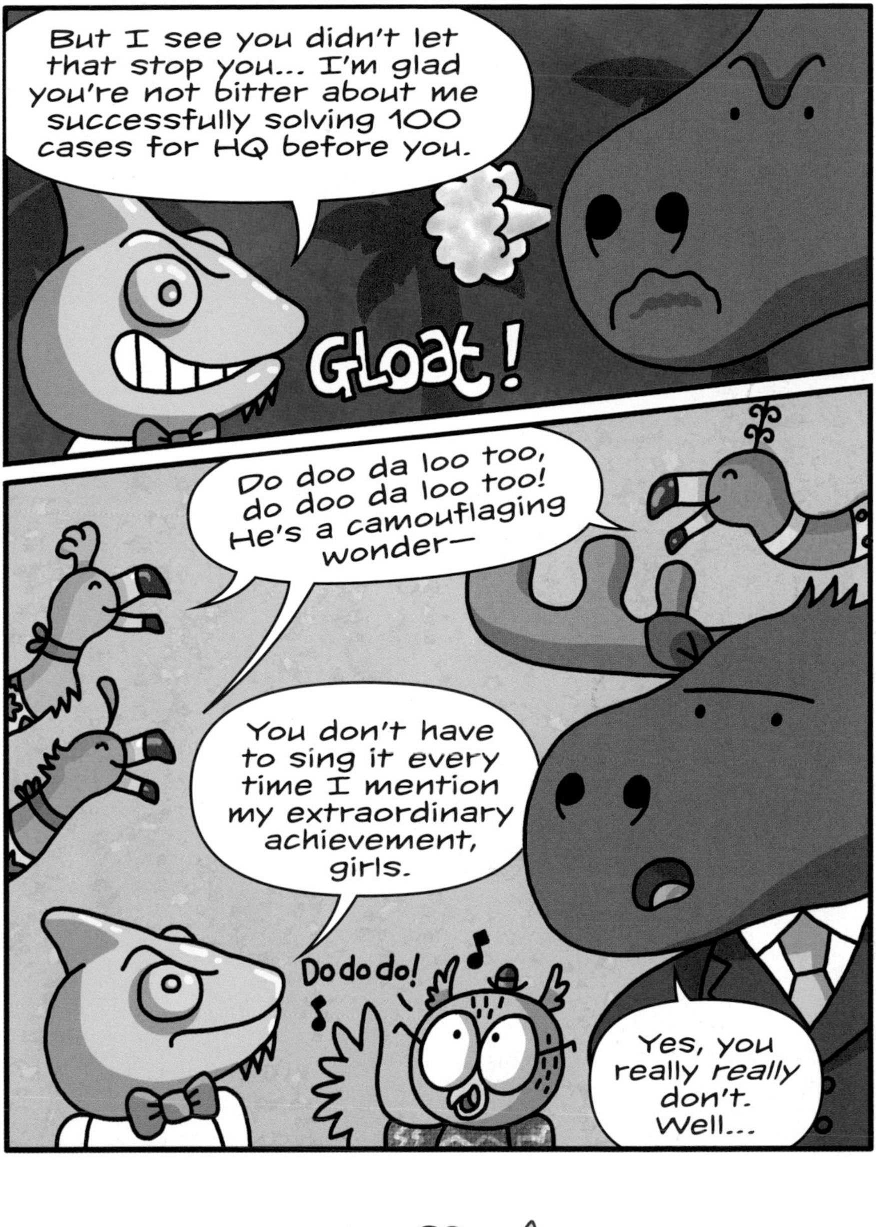
But I see you didn't let that stop you... I'm glad you're not bitter about me successfully solving 100 cases for HQ before you.
GLOAT!
Do doo da loo too, do doo da loo too! He's a camouflaging wonder—
You don't have to sing it every time I mention my extraordinary achievement, girls.
Dododo!
Yes, you really *really* don't. Well...

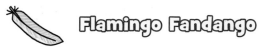

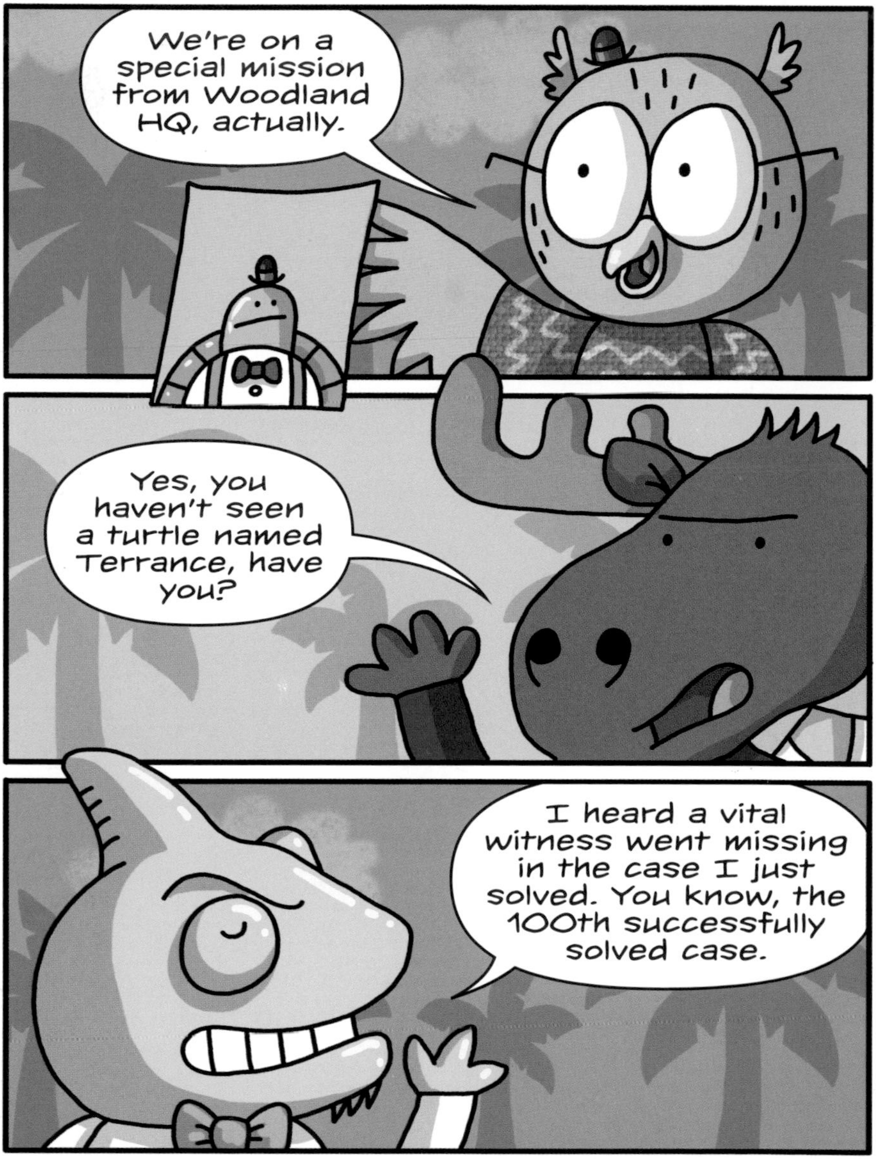
We're on a special mission from Woodland HQ, actually.
Yes, you haven't seen a turtle named Terrance, have you?
I heard a vital witness went missing in the case I just solved. You know, the 100th successfully solved case.

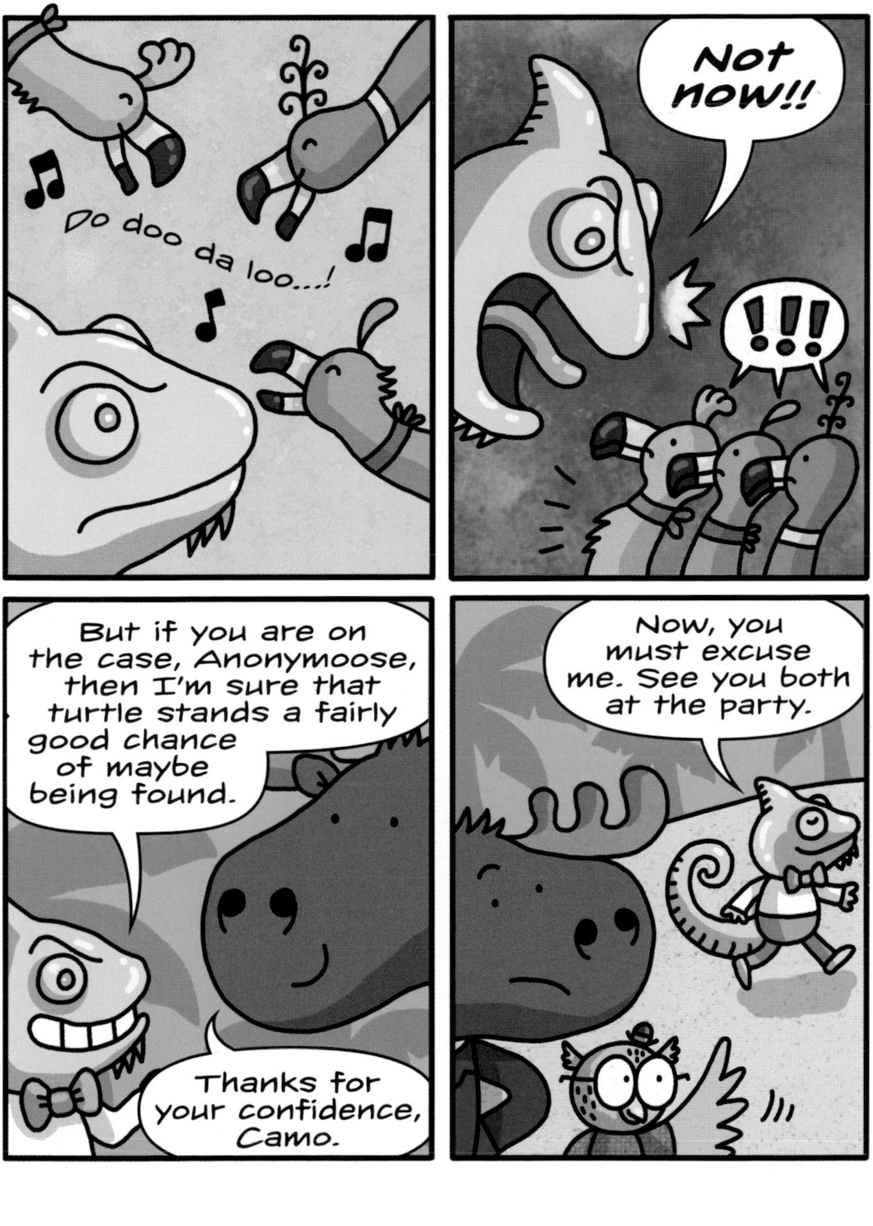
Do doo da loo...!
Not now!!
!!!
But if you are on the case, Anonymoose, then I'm sure that turtle stands a fairly good chance of maybe being found.
Thanks for your confidence, Camo.
Now, you must excuse me. See you both at the party.

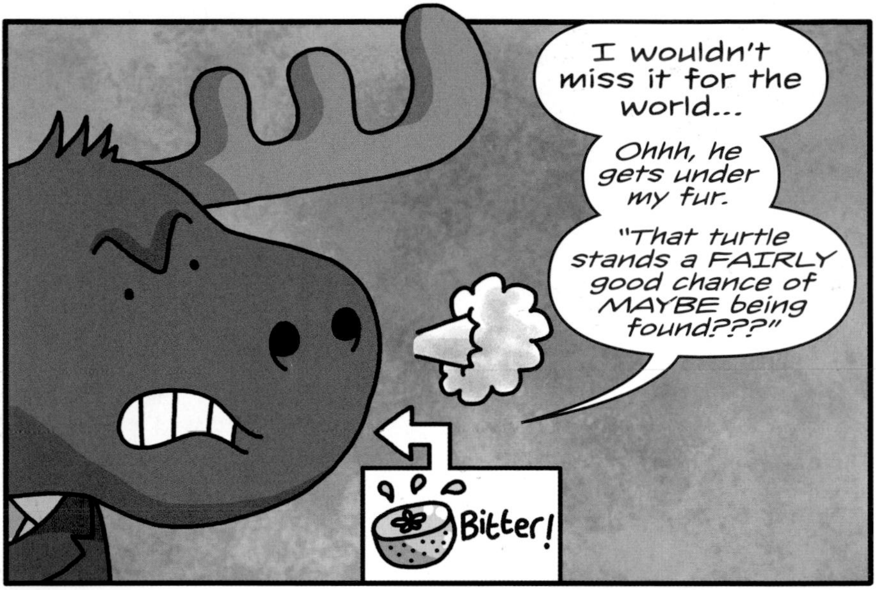
I wouldn't miss it for the world...
Ohhh, he gets under my fur.
"That turtle stands a FAIRLY good chance of MAYBE being found???"
Bitter!

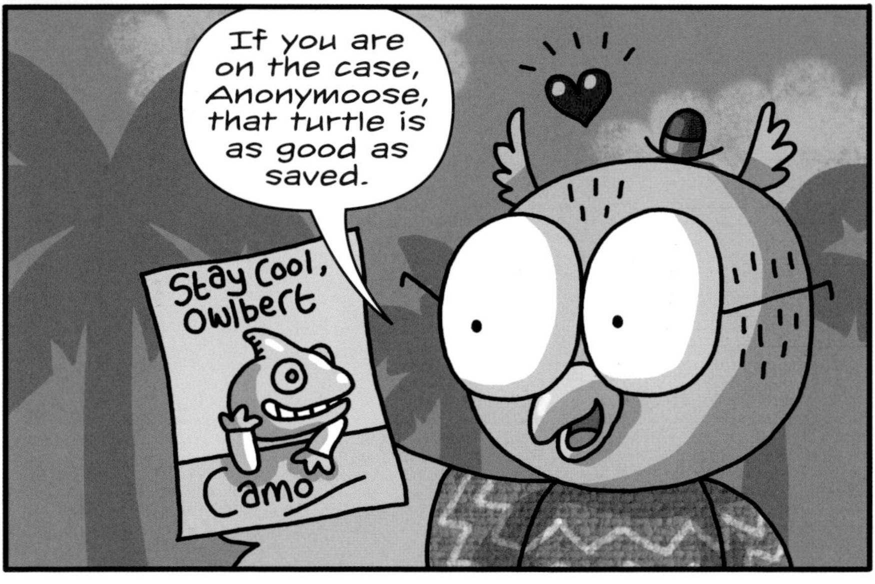
If you are on the case, Anonymoose, that turtle is as good as saved.
Stay Cool, Owlbert
Camo

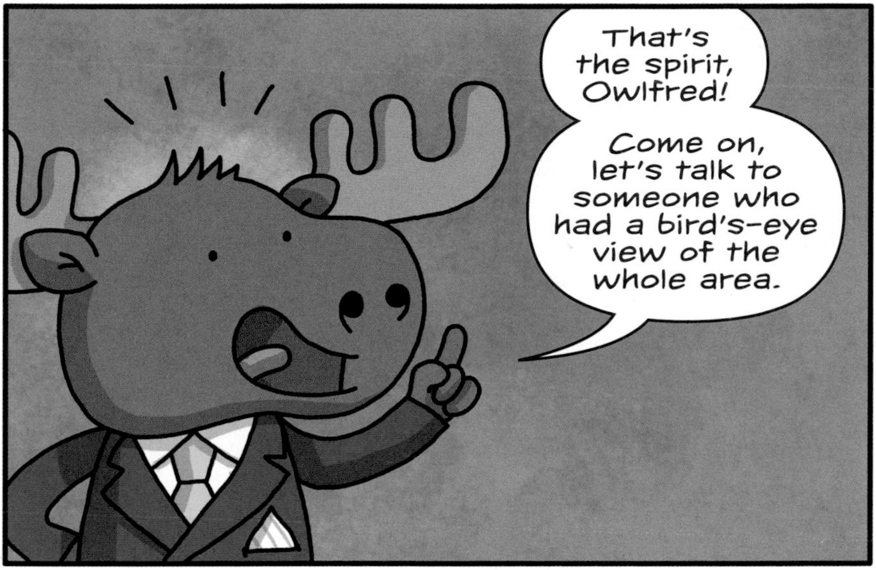
That's the spirit, Owlfred!
Come on, let's talk to someone who had a bird's-eye view of the whole area.

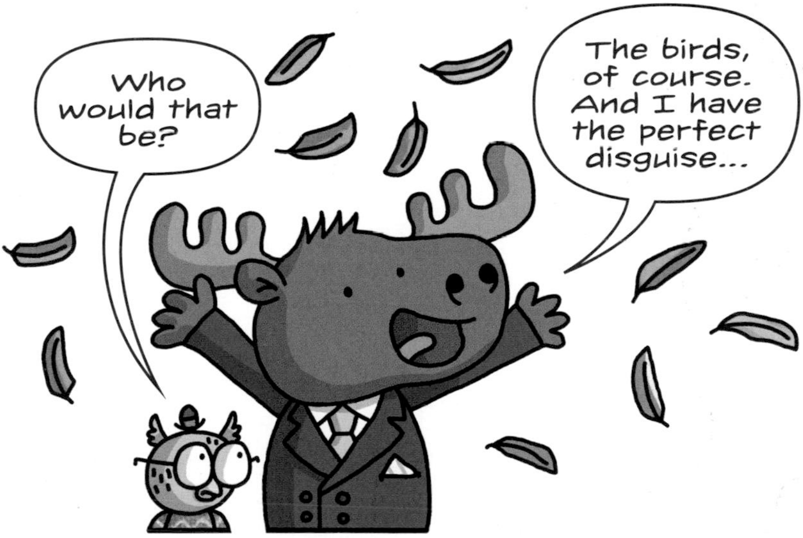
Who would that be?
The birds, of course. And I have the perfect disguise...

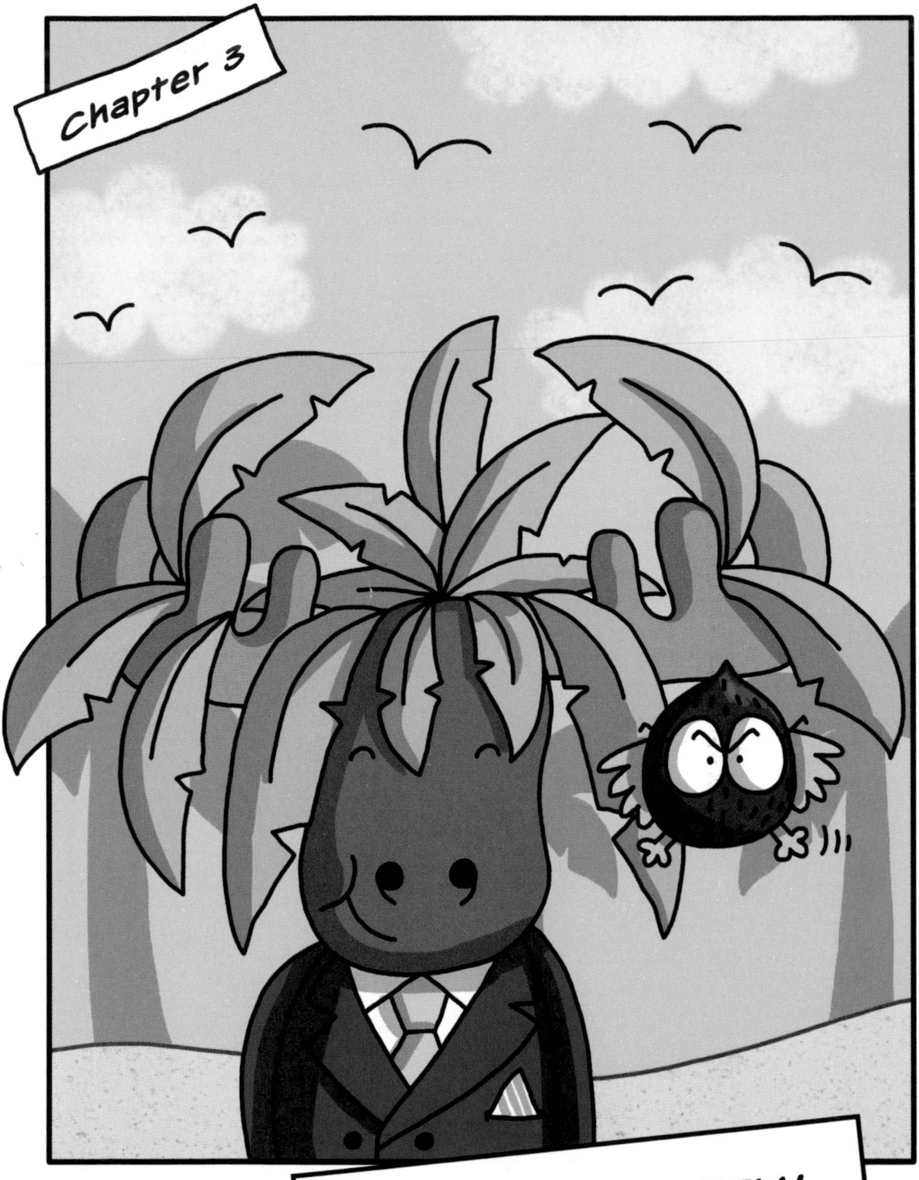
Chapter 3
BIRD'S-EYE VIEW

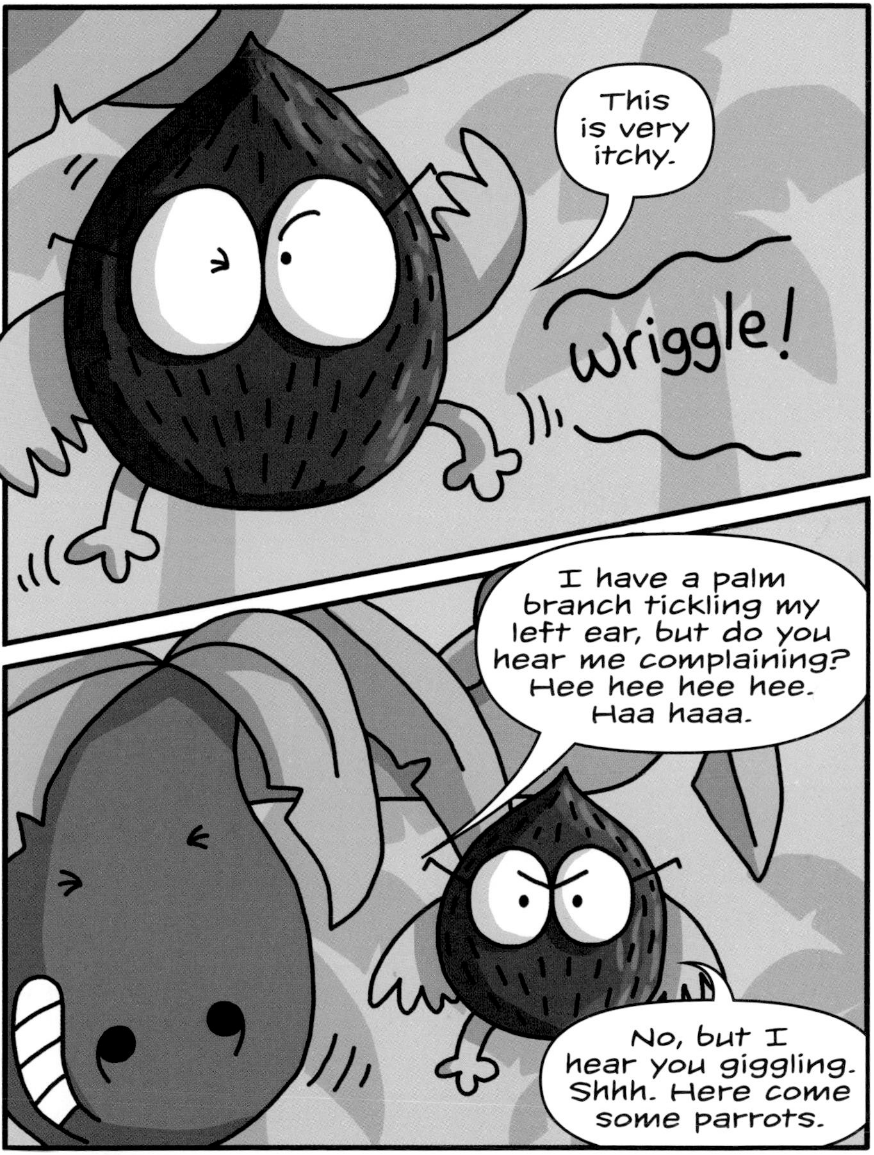
This is very itchy.
wriggle!
I have a palm branch tickling my left ear, but do you hear me complaining? Hee hee hee hee. Haa haaa.
No, but I hear you giggling. Shhh. Here come some parrots.

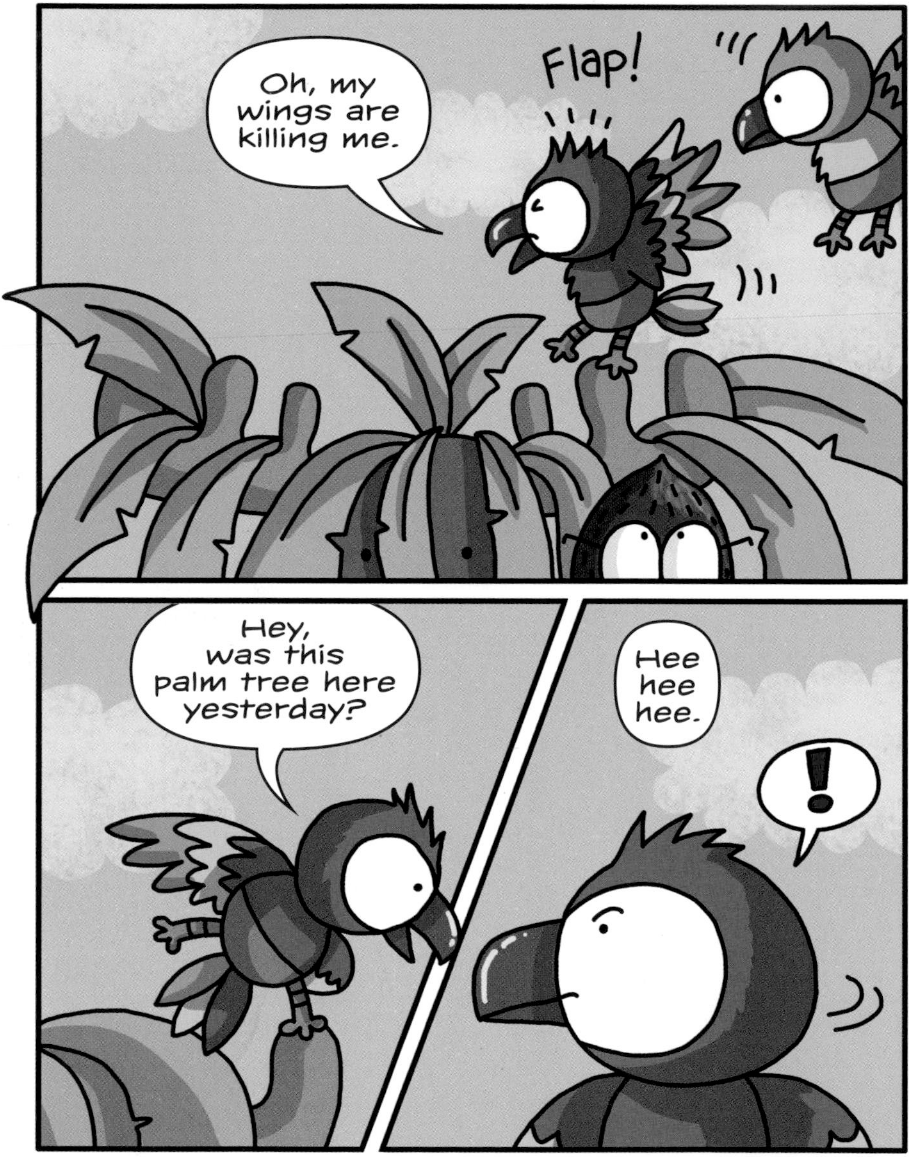
Oh, my wings are killing me.
Flap!
Hey, was this palm tree here yesterday?
Hee hee hee.
!

Bird's-Eye View

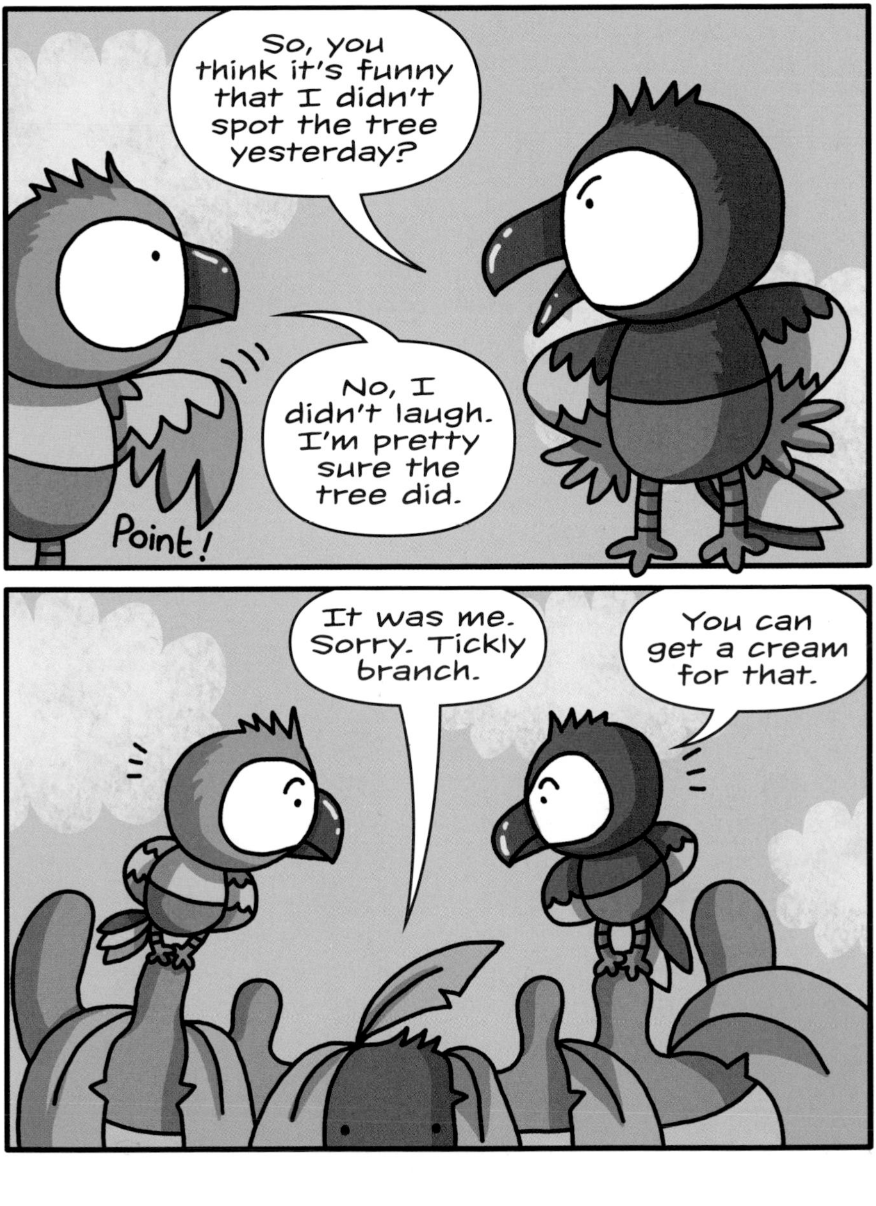
So, you think it's funny that I didn't spot the tree yesterday?
No, I didn't laugh. I'm pretty sure the tree did.
Point!
It was me. Sorry. Tickly branch.
You can get a cream for that.

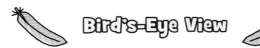

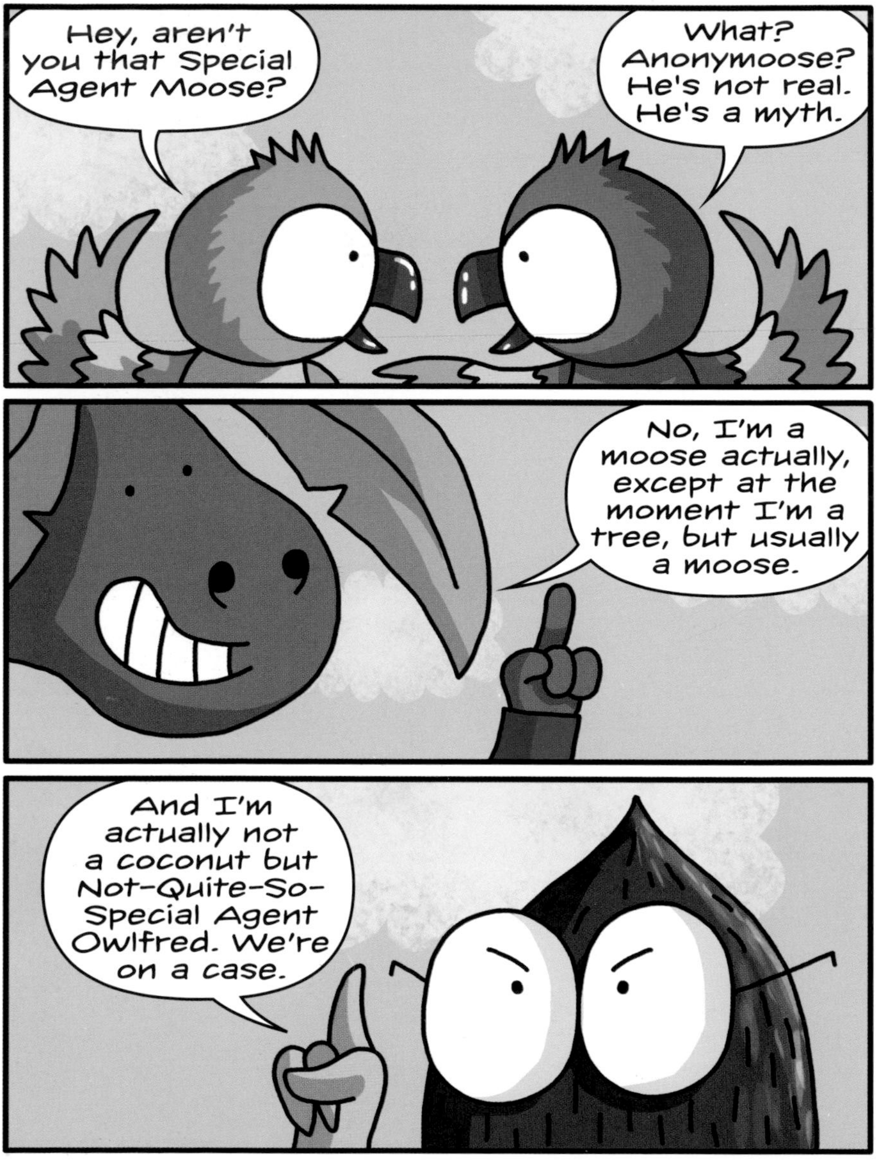
Hey, aren't you that Special Agent Moose?
What? Anonymoose? He's not real. He's a myth.
No, I'm a moose actually, except at the moment I'm a tree, but usually a moose.
And I'm actually not a coconut but Not-Quite-So-Special Agent Owlfred. We're on a case.

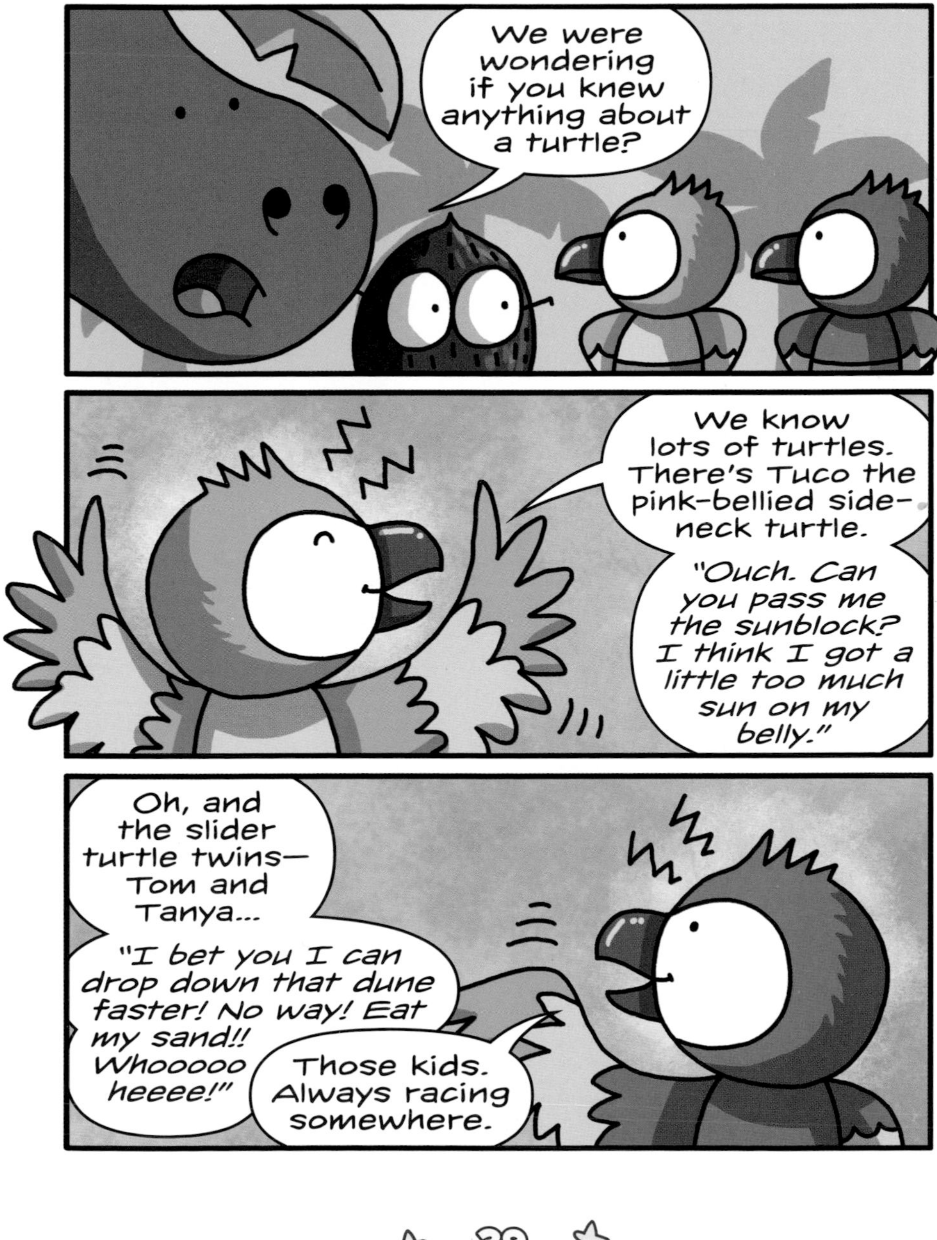
We were wondering if you knew anything about a turtle?
We know lots of turtles. There's Tuco the pink-bellied side-neck turtle.
"Ouch. Can you pass me the sunblock? I think I got a little too much sun on my belly."
Oh, and the slider turtle twins—Tom and Tanya...
"I bet you I can drop down that dune faster! No way! Eat my sand!! Whooooo heeee!"
Those kids. Always racing somewhere.

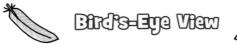

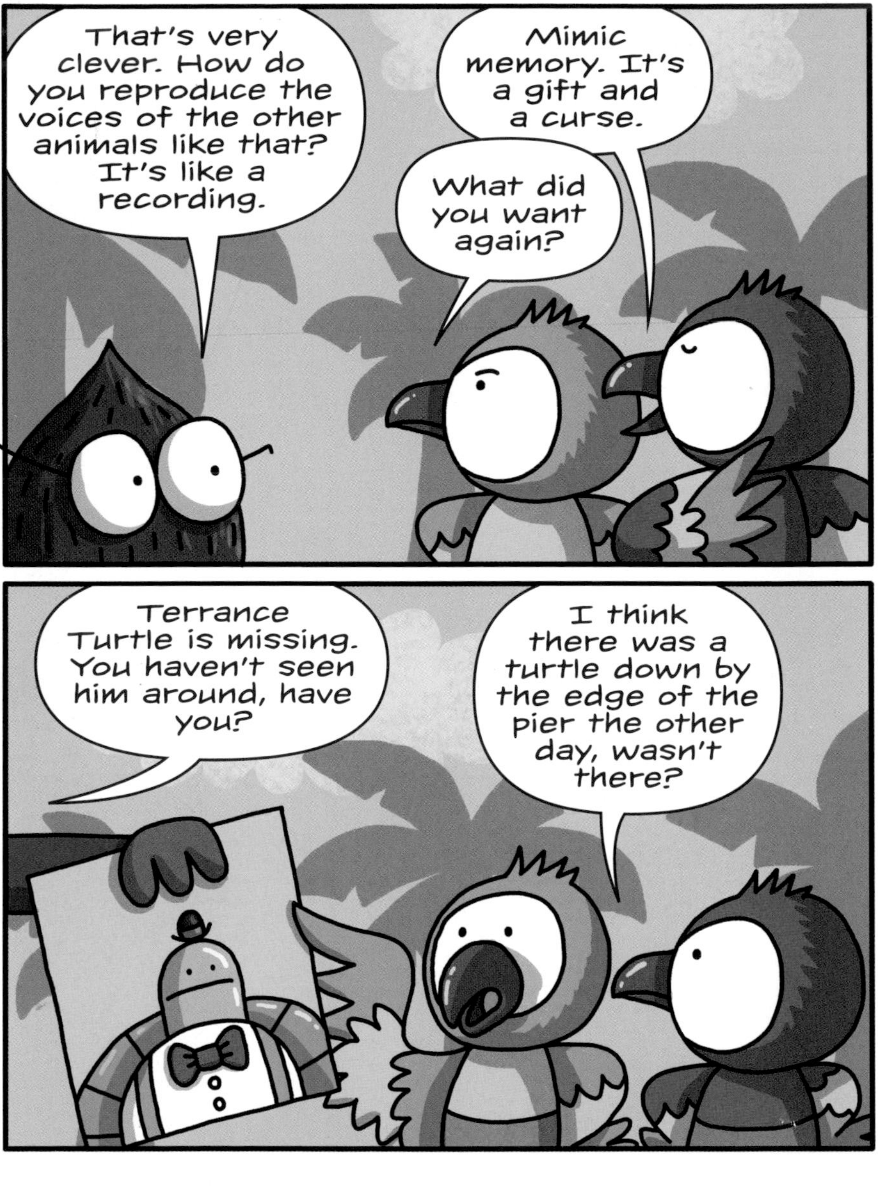
That's very clever. How do you reproduce the voices of the other animals like that? It's like a recording.
Mimic memory. It's a gift and a curse.
What did you want again?
Terrance Turtle is missing. You haven't seen him around, have you?
I think there was a turtle down by the edge of the pier the other day, wasn't there?

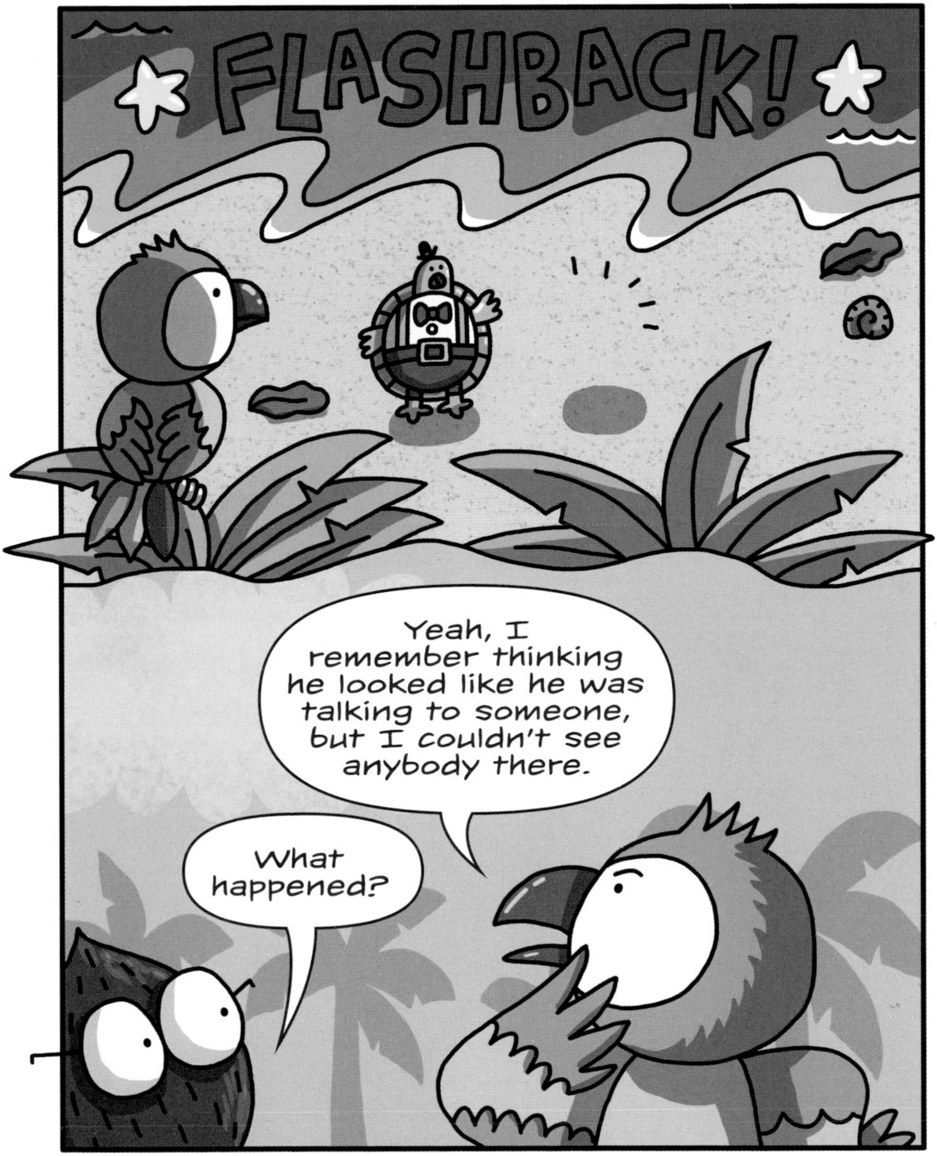
FLASHBACK!
Yeah, I remember thinking he looked like he was talking to someone, but I couldn't see anybody there.
What happened?

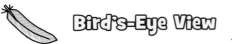

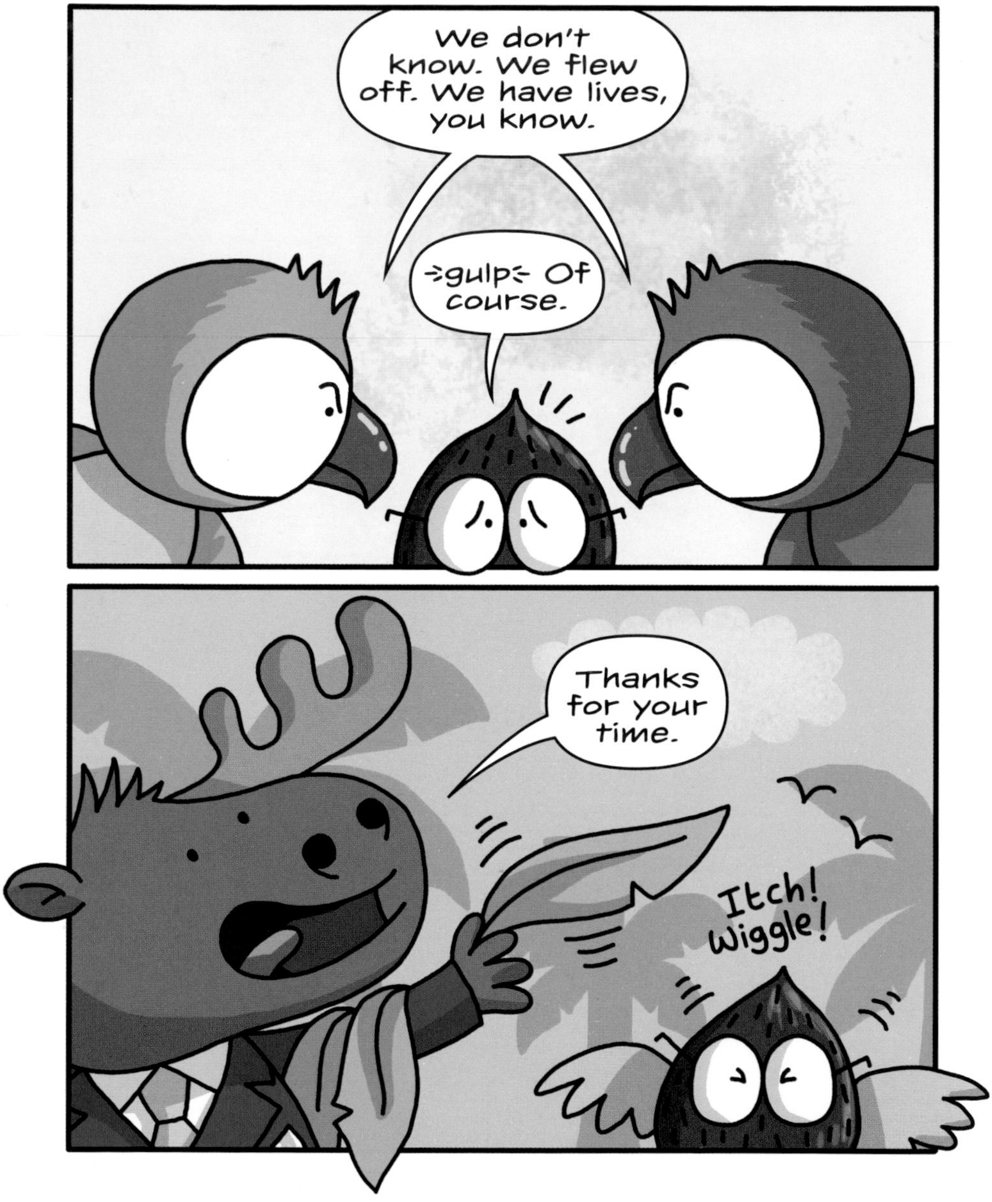
We don't know. We flew off. We have lives, you know.
=gulp= Of course.
Thanks for your time.
Itch! Wiggle!

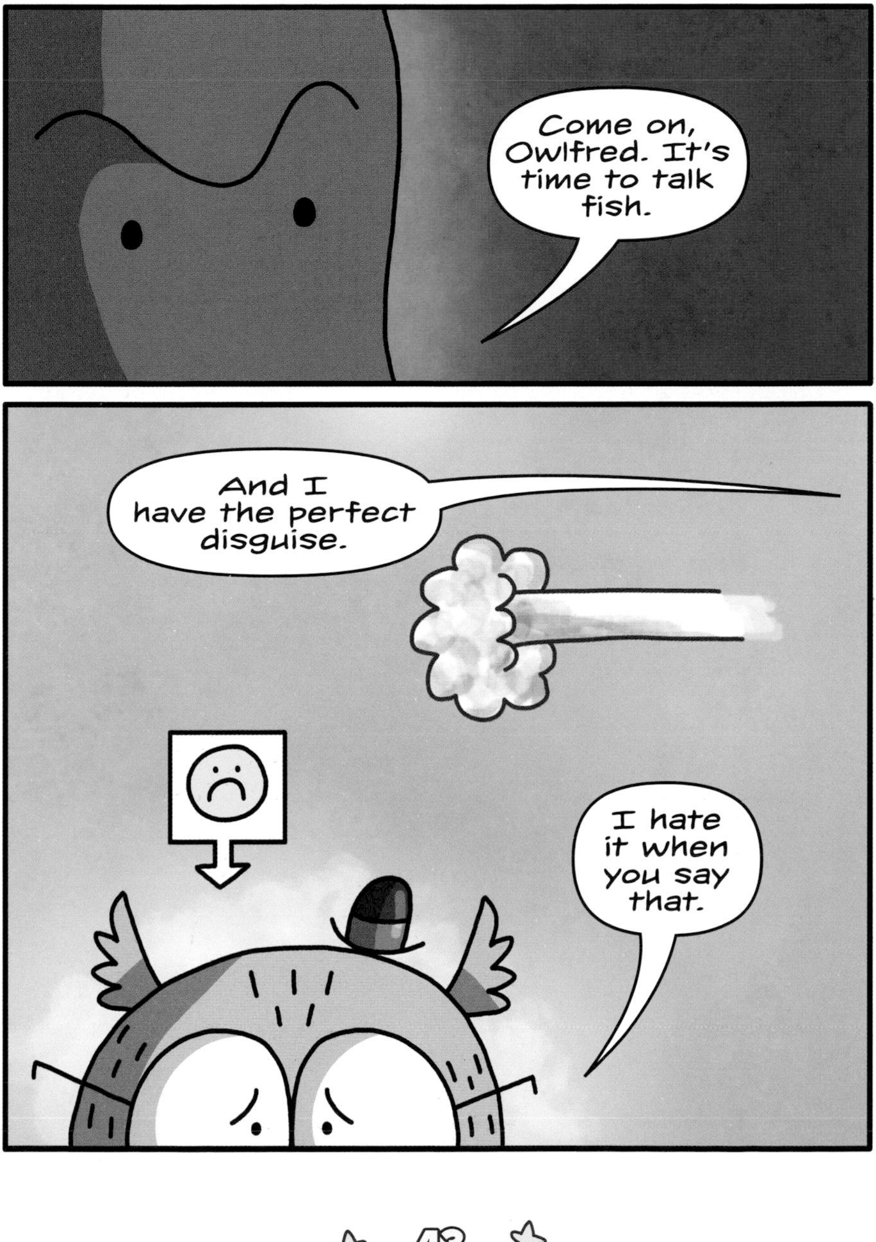
Come on, Owlfred. It's time to talk fish.
And I have the perfect disguise.
I hate it when you say that.

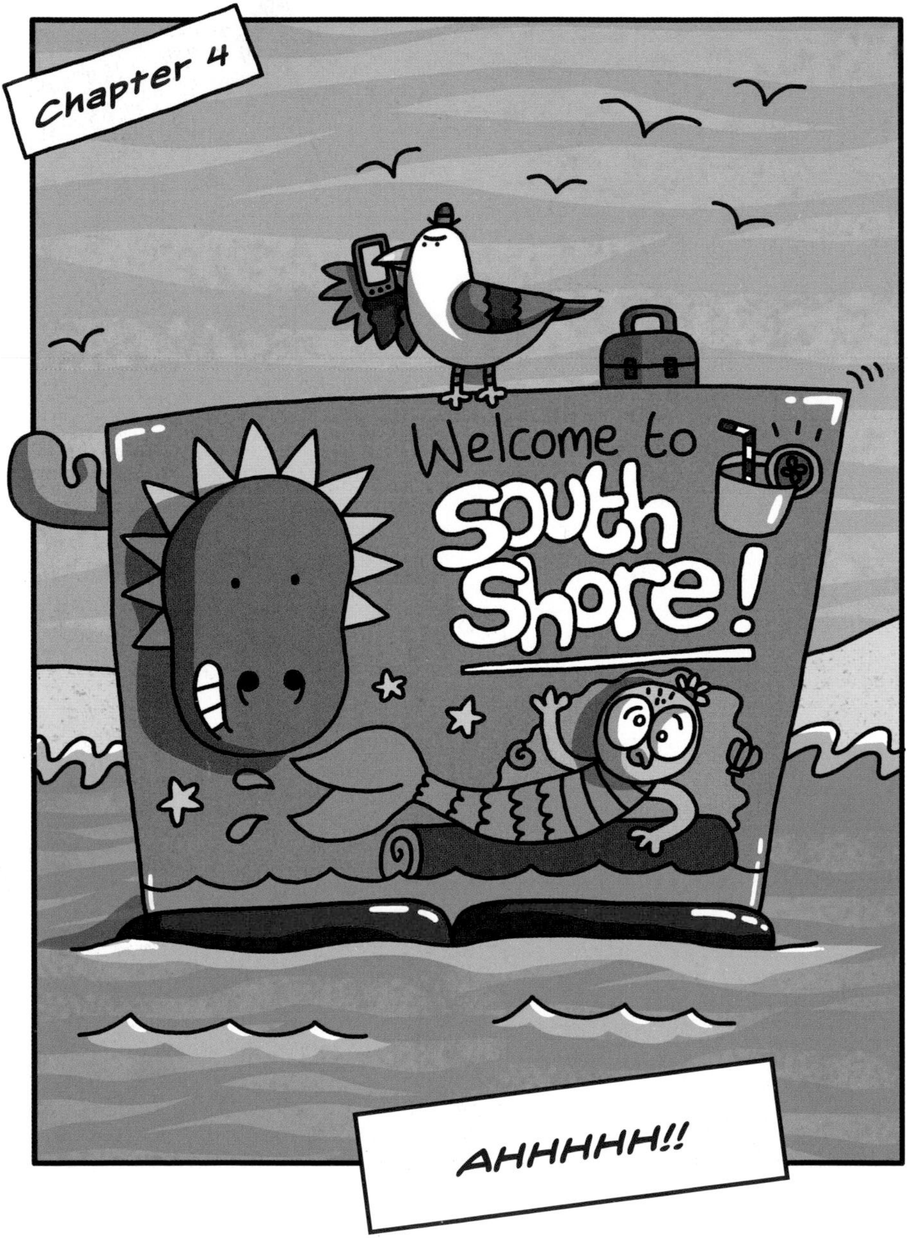
Chapter 4
Welcome to South Shore!
AHHHHH!!

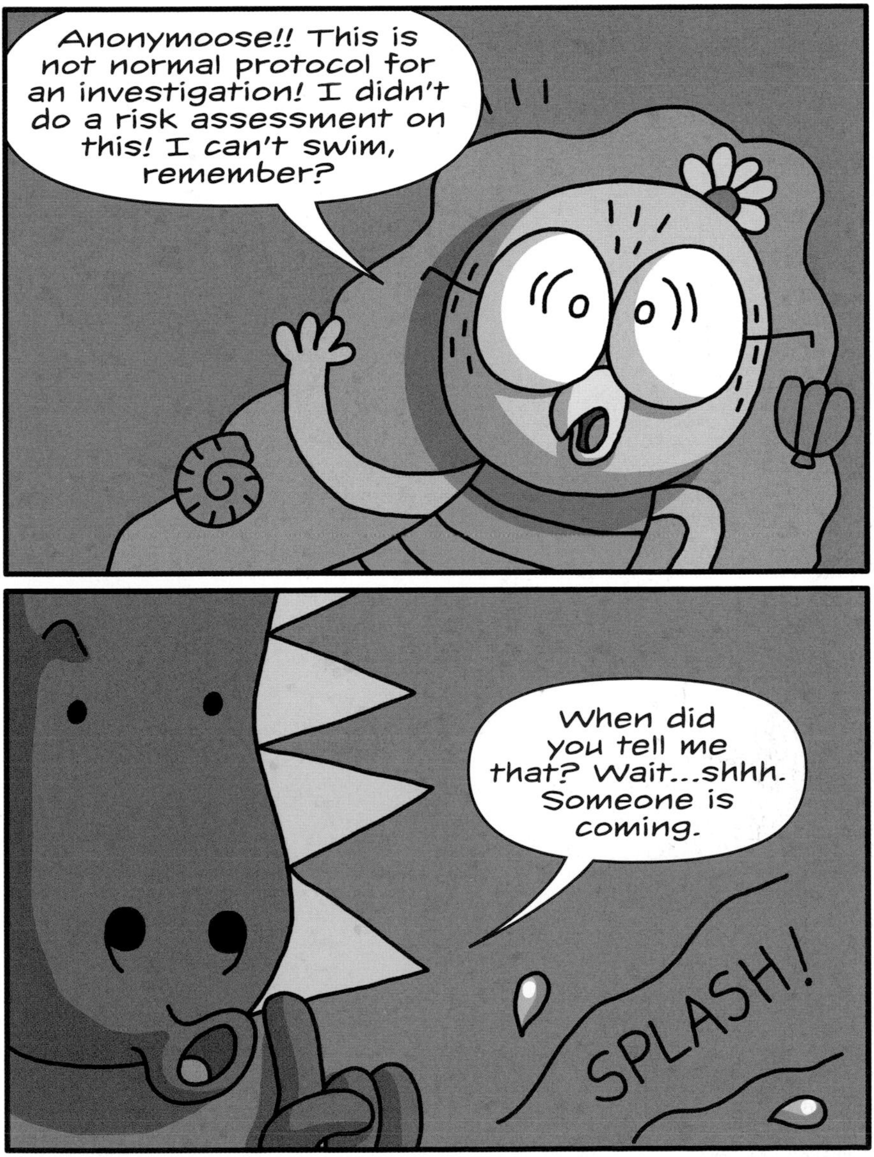
Anonymoose!! This is not normal protocol for an investigation! I didn't do a risk assessment on this! I can't swim, remember?
When did you tell me that? Wait...shhh. Someone is coming.
SPLASH!

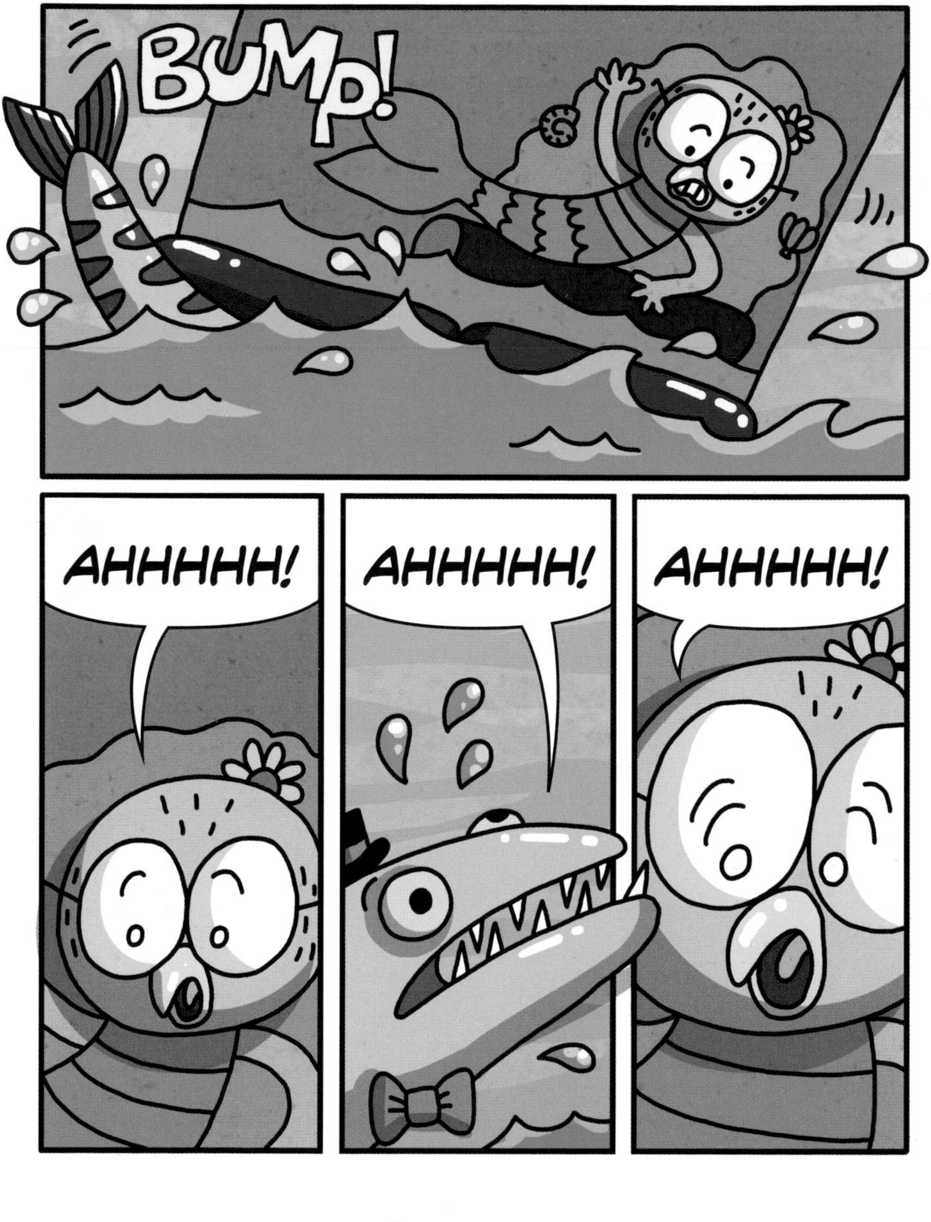
BUMP!
AHHHHH!
AHHHHH!
AHHHHH!

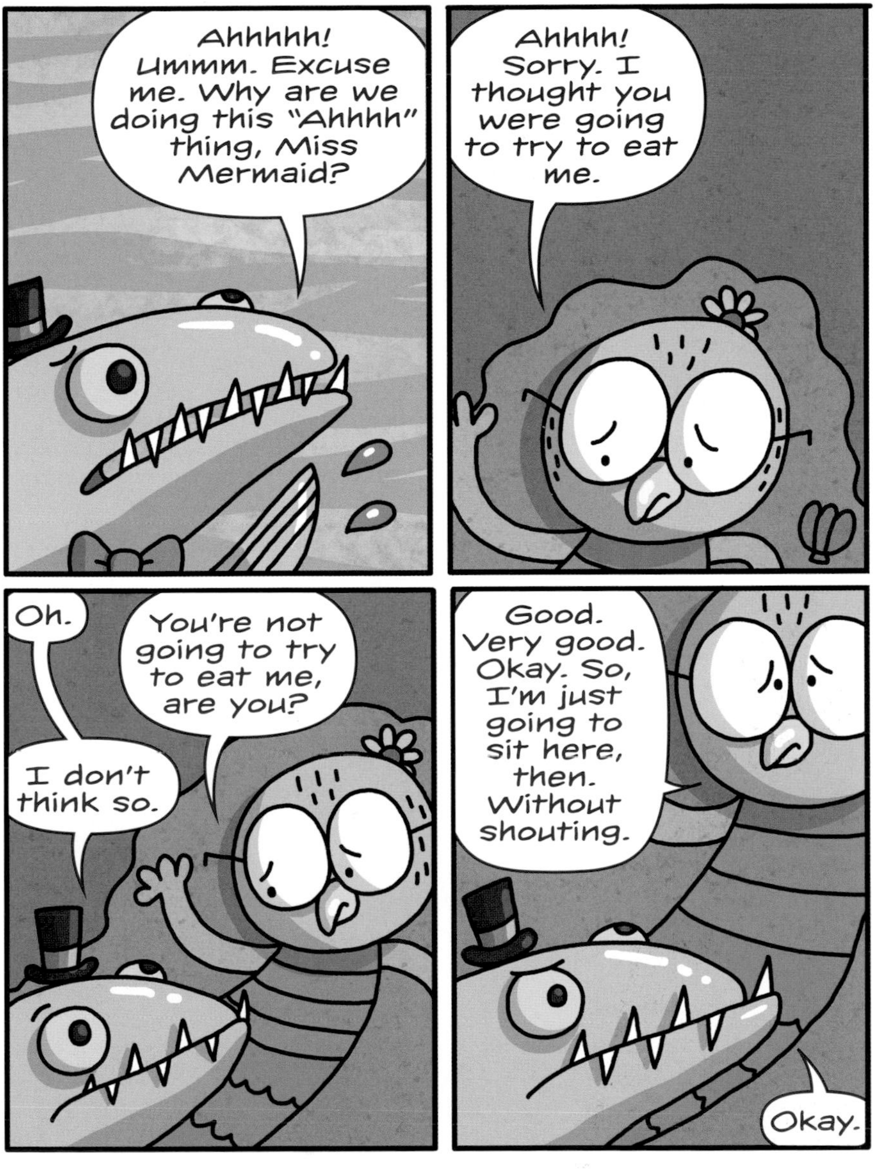
Ahhhhh!
Ummm. Excuse me. Why are we doing this "Ahhhh" thing, Miss Mermaid?
Ahhhh! Sorry. I thought you were going to try to eat me.
Oh.
You're not going to try to eat me, are you?
I don't think so.
Good. Very good. Okay. So, I'm just going to sit here, then. Without shouting.
Okay.

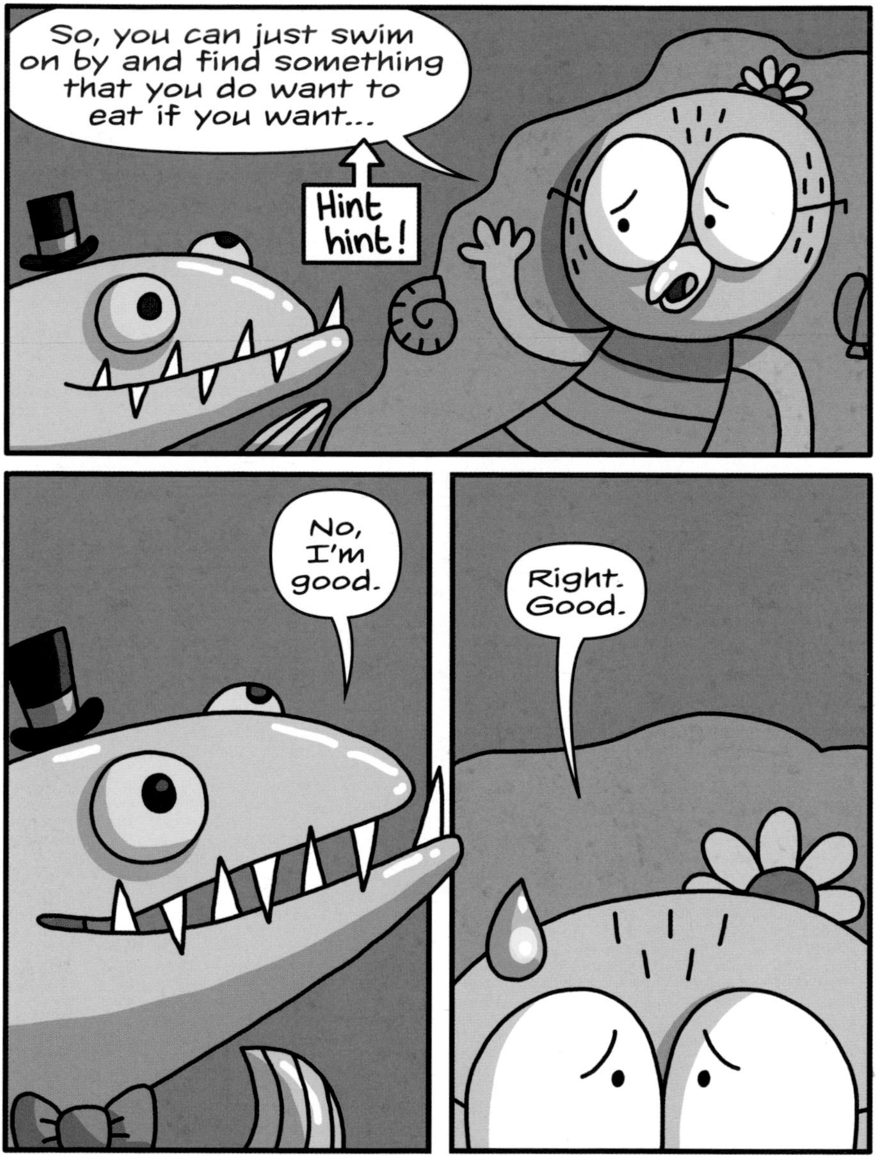
So, you can just swim on by and find something that you do want to eat if you want...
Hint hint!
No, I'm good.
Right. Good.

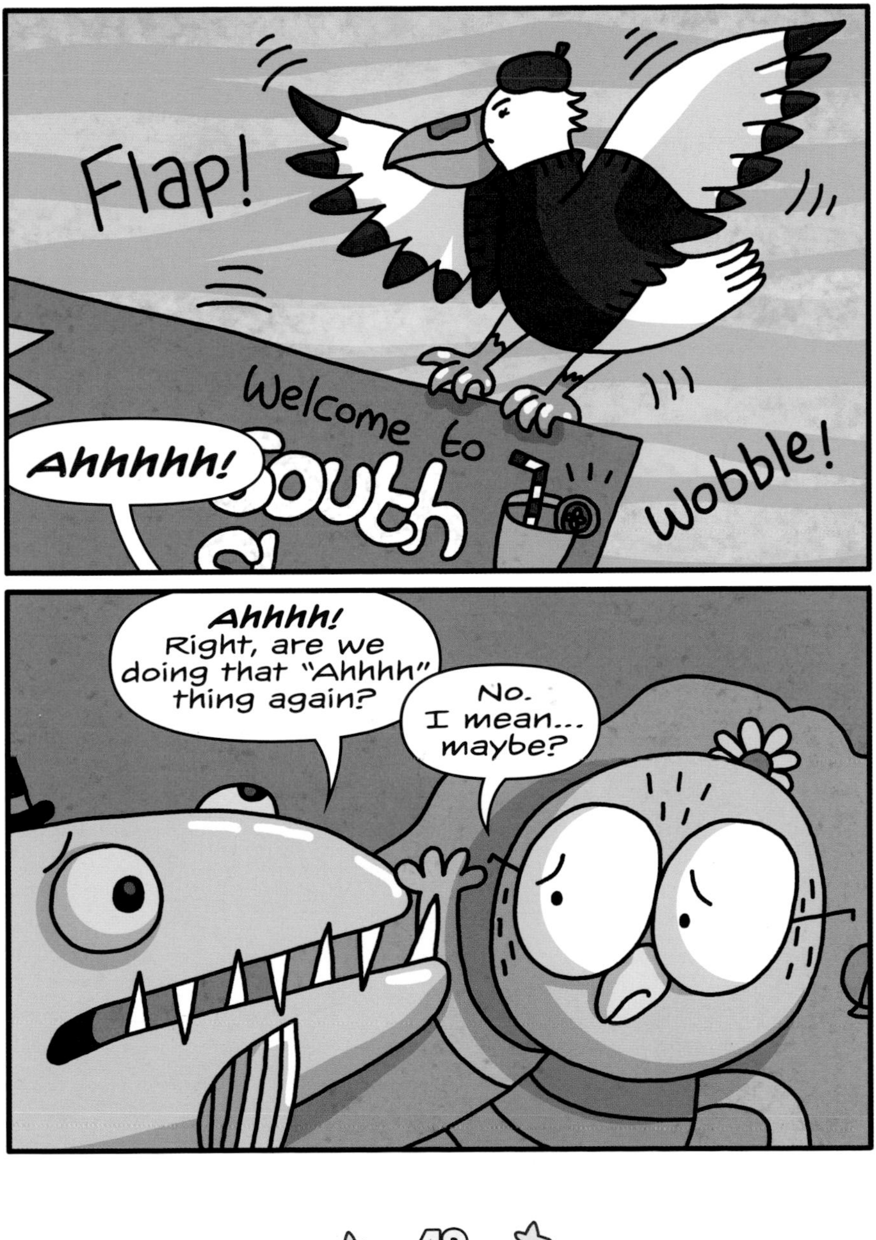
Flap!
Welcome to
South
Ahhhhh!
wobble!
Ahhhh!
Right, are we doing that "Ahhhh" thing again?
No.
I mean...
maybe?

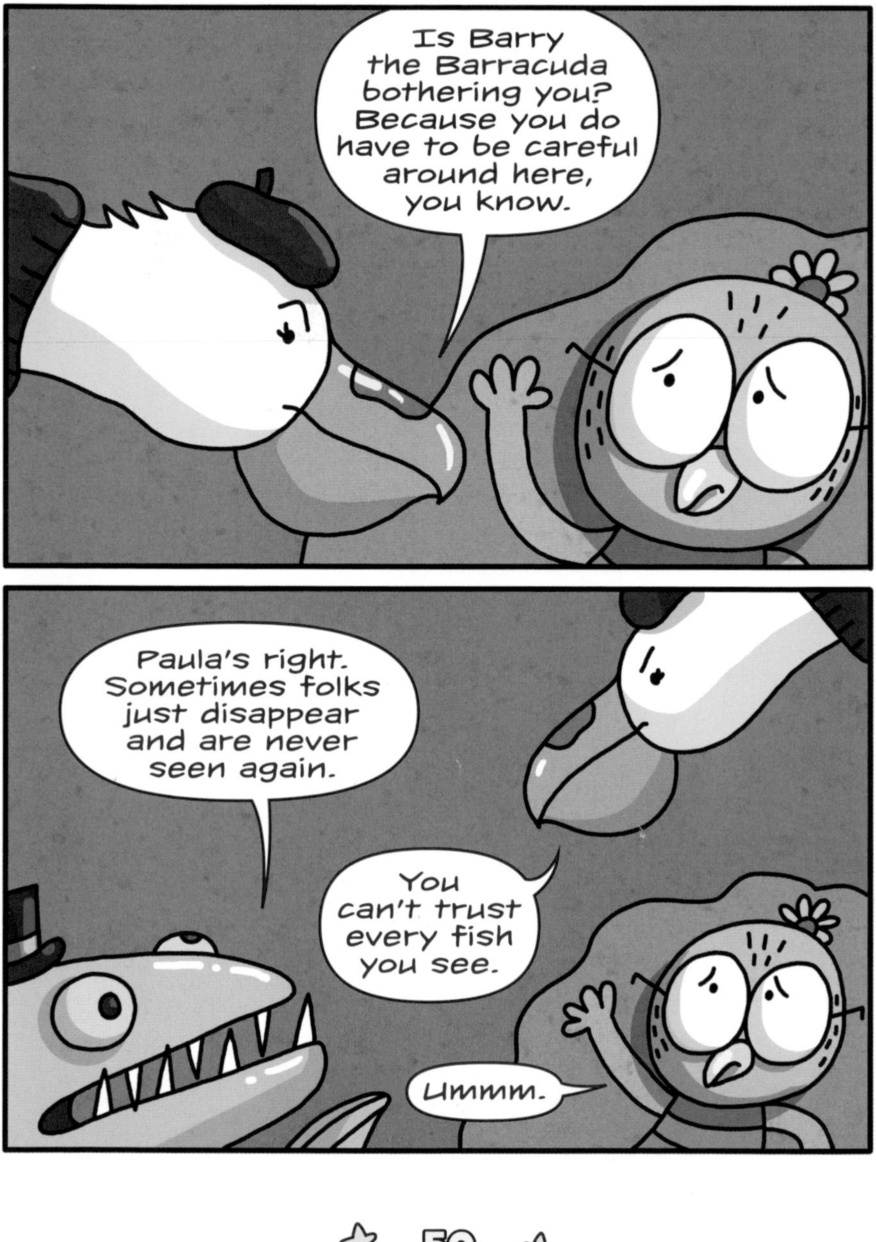
Is Barry the Barracuda bothering you? Because you do have to be careful around here, you know.
Paula's right. Sometimes folks just disappear and are never seen again.
You can't trust every fish you see.
Ummm.

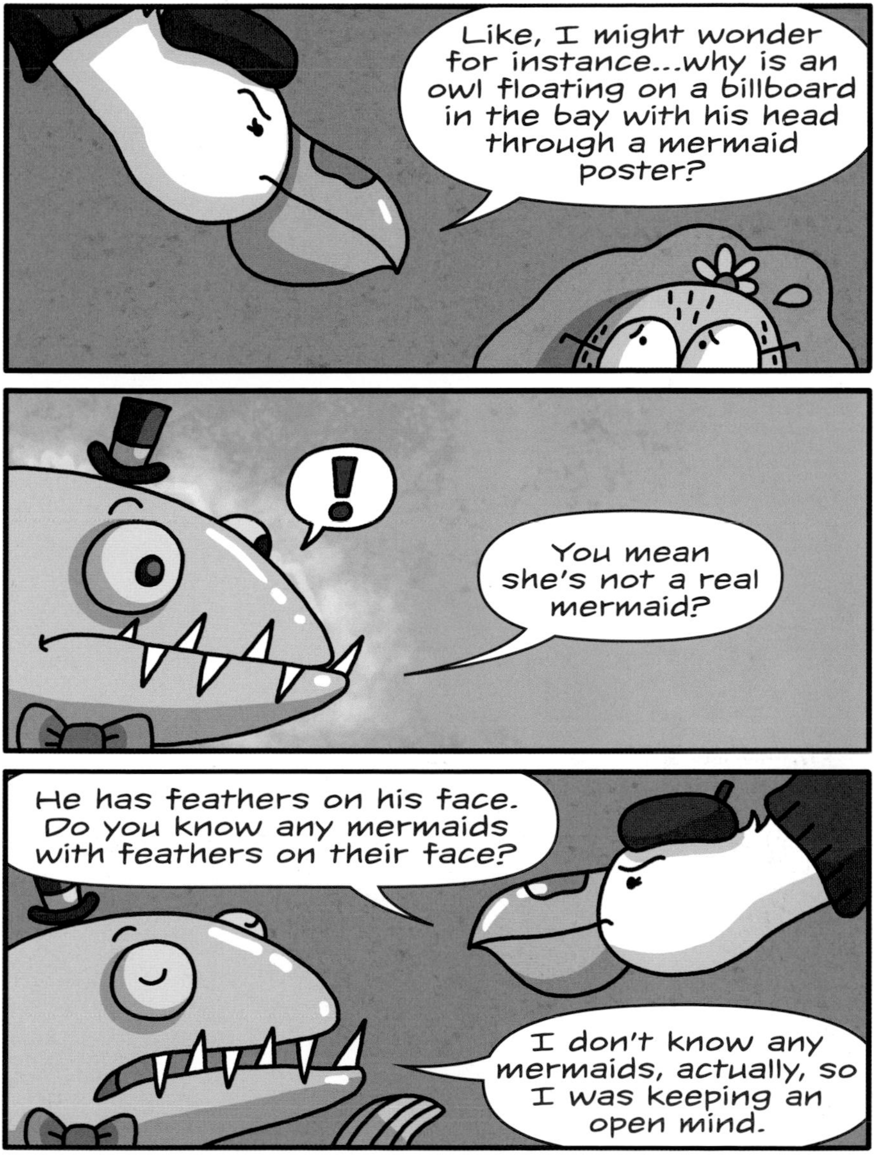
Like, I might wonder for instance...why is an owl floating on a billboard in the bay with his head through a mermaid poster?
!
You mean she's not a real mermaid?
He has feathers on his face. Do you know any mermaids with feathers on their face?
I don't know any mermaids, actually, so I was keeping an open mind.

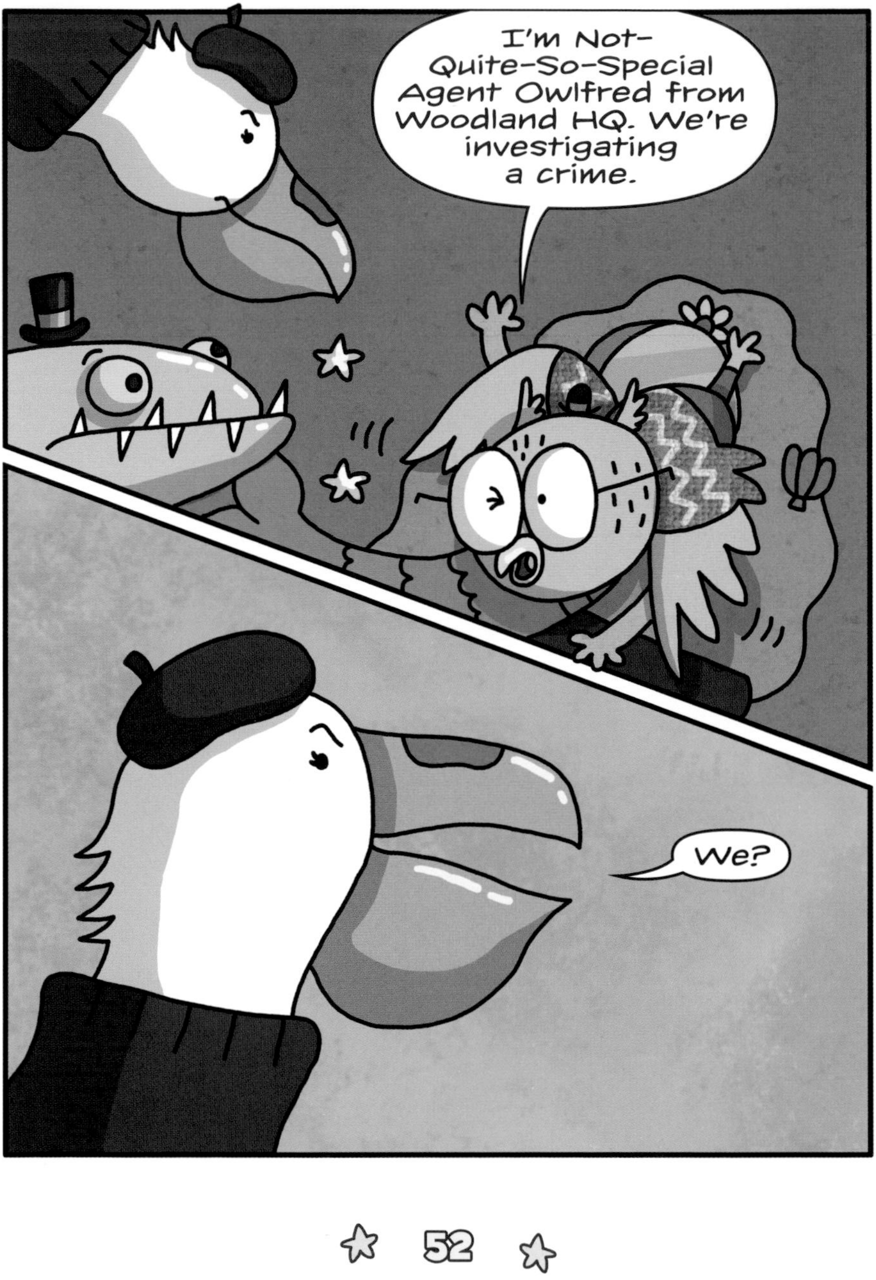
I'm Not-Quite-So-Special Agent Owlfred from Woodland HQ. We're investigating a crime.
We?

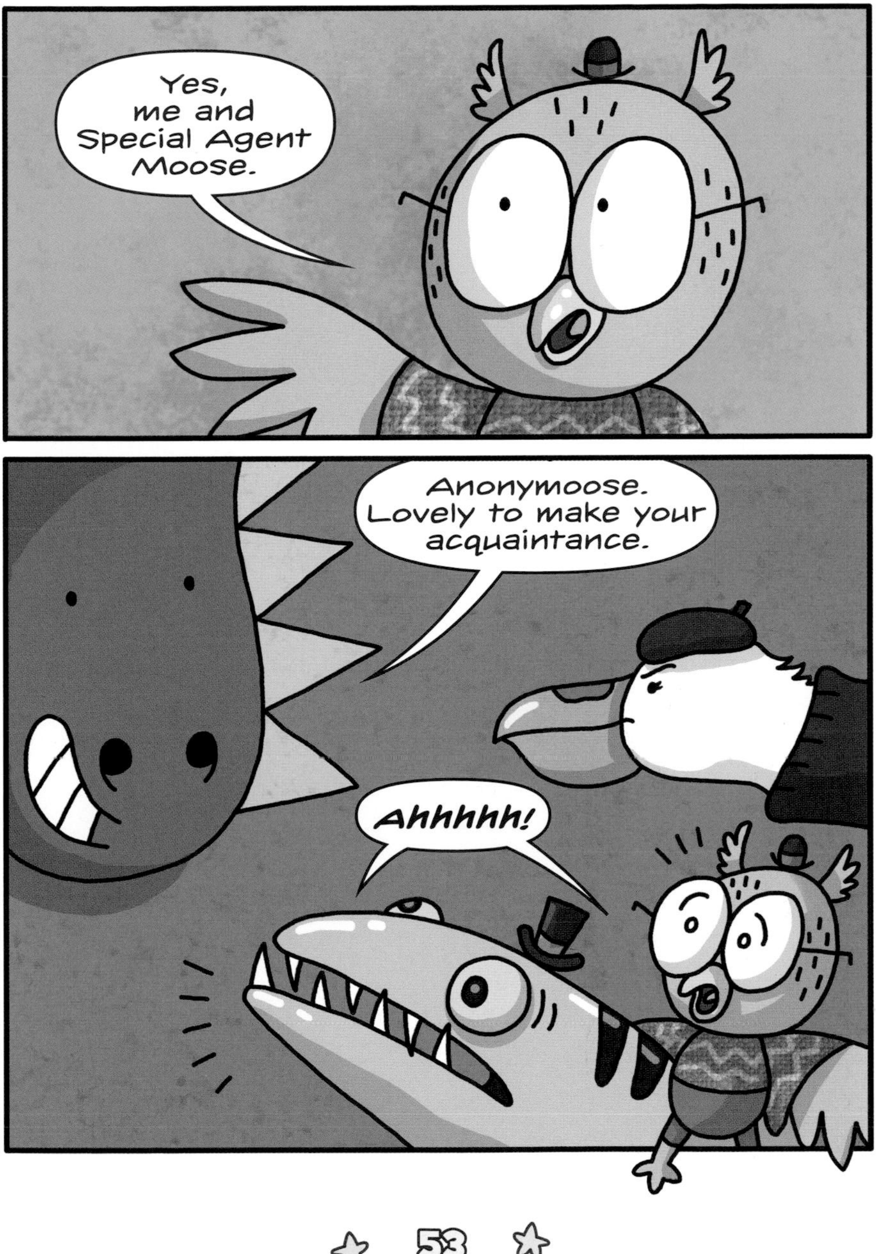
Yes, me and Special Agent Moose.
Anonymoose. Lovely to make your acquaintance.
Ahhhhh!

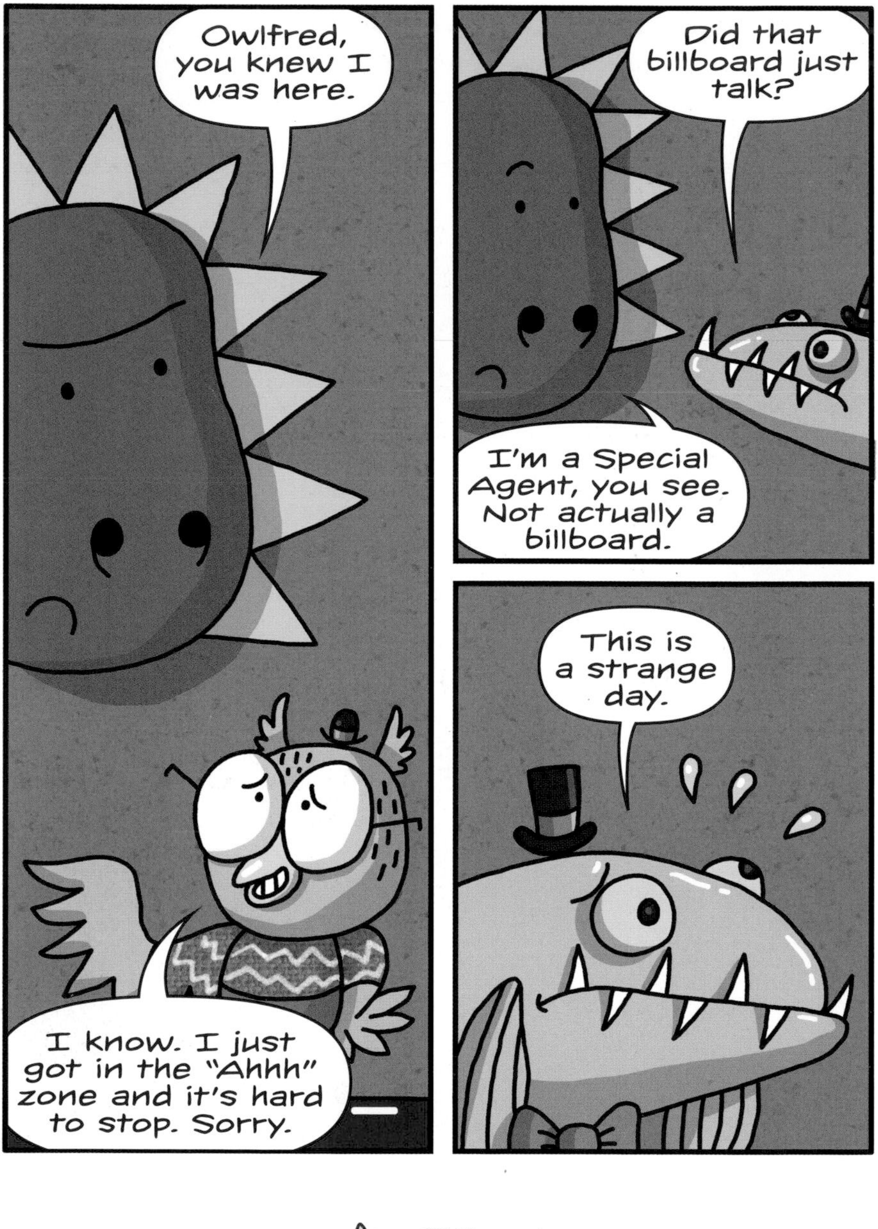
Owlfred, you knew I was here.
I know. I just got in the "Ahhh" zone and it's hard to stop. Sorry.
Did that billboard just talk?
I'm a Special Agent, you see. Not actually a billboard.
This is a strange day.

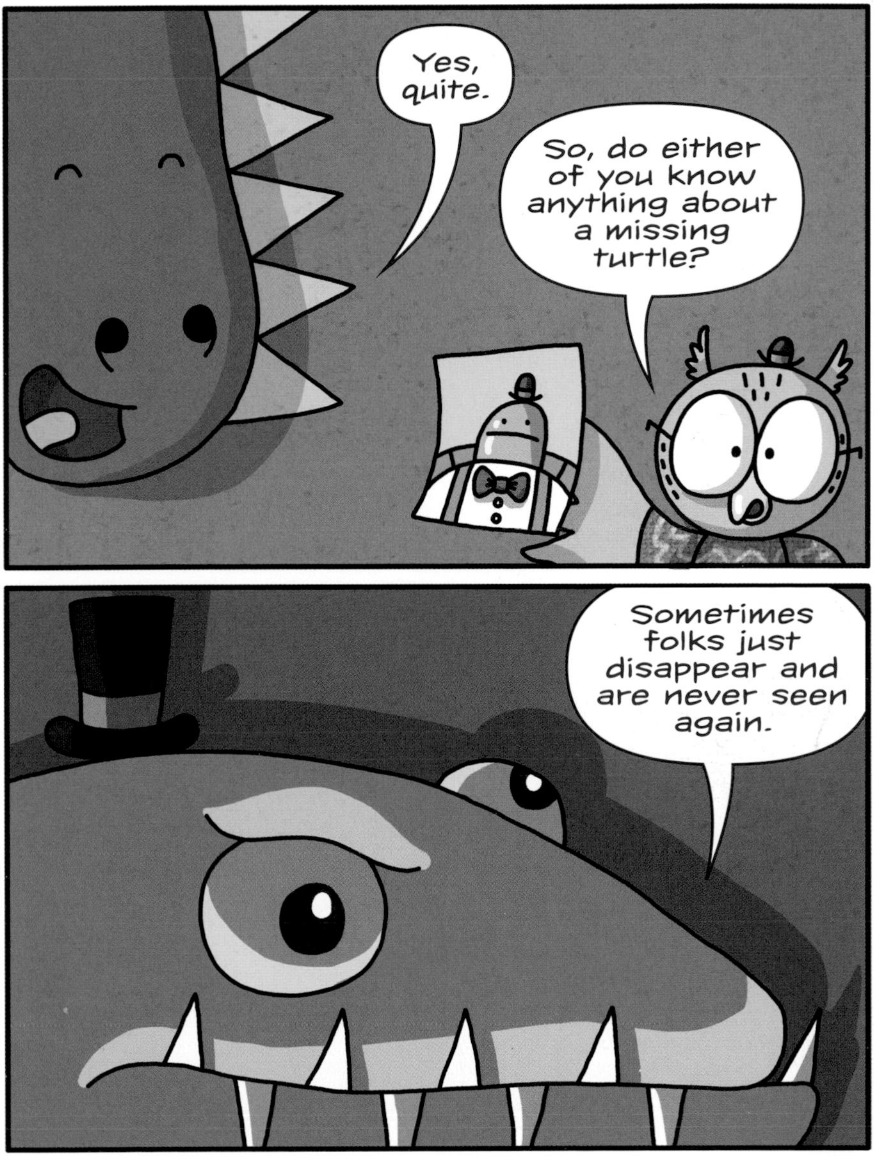
Yes, quite.
So, do either of you know anything about a missing turtle?
Sometimes folks just disappear and are never seen again.

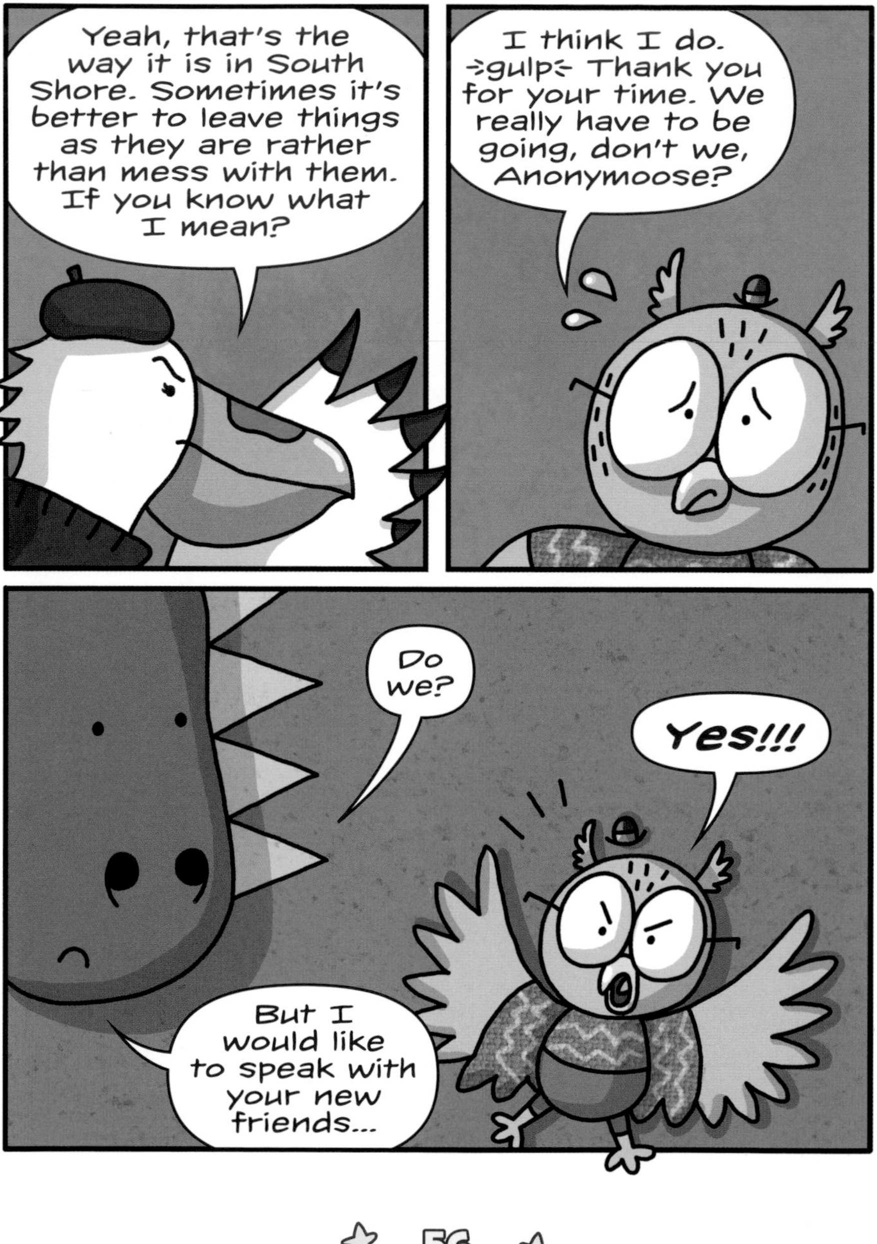
Yeah, that's the way it is in South Shore. Sometimes it's better to leave things as they are rather than mess with them. If you know what I mean?
I think I do. ⇒gulp⇐ Thank you for your time. We really have to be going, don't we, Anonymoose?
Do we?
Yes!!!
But I would like to speak with your new friends...

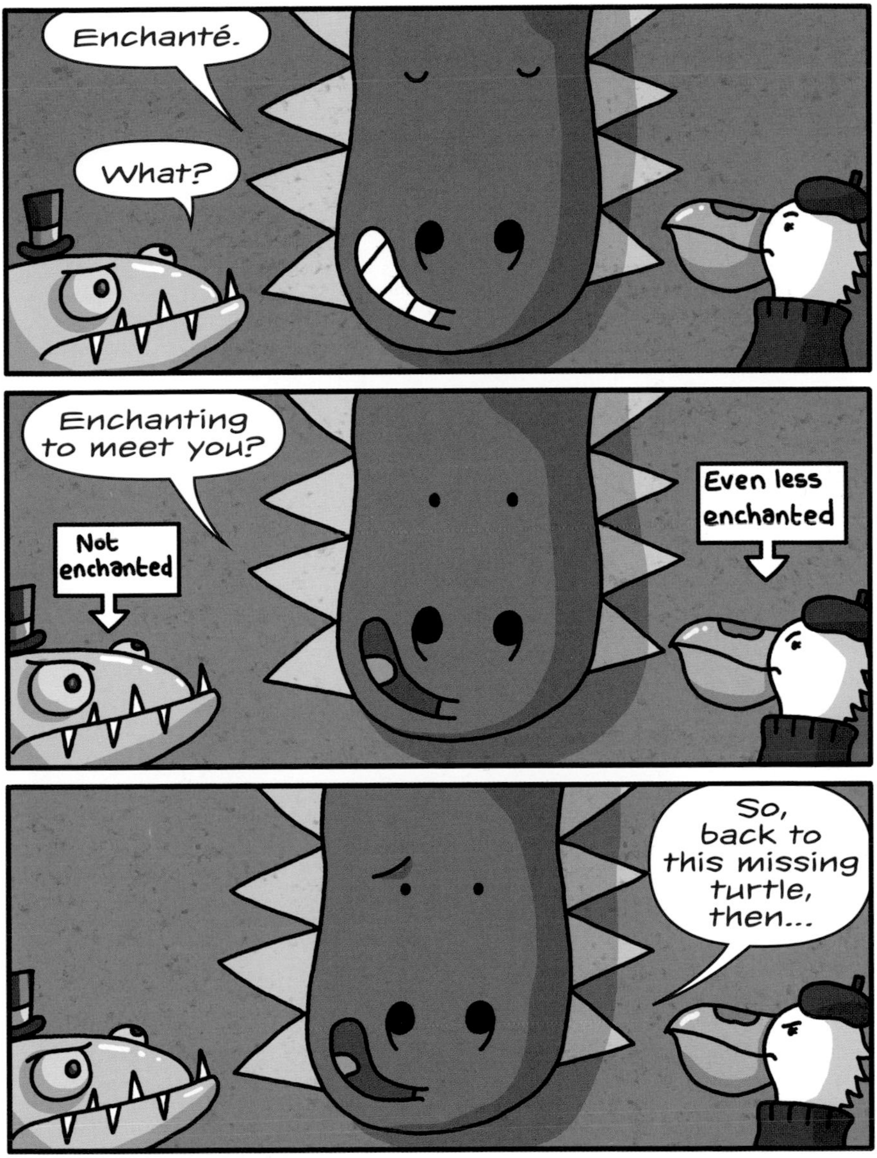
Enchanté.
What?
Enchanting to meet you?
Not enchanted
Even less enchanted
So, back to this missing turtle, then...

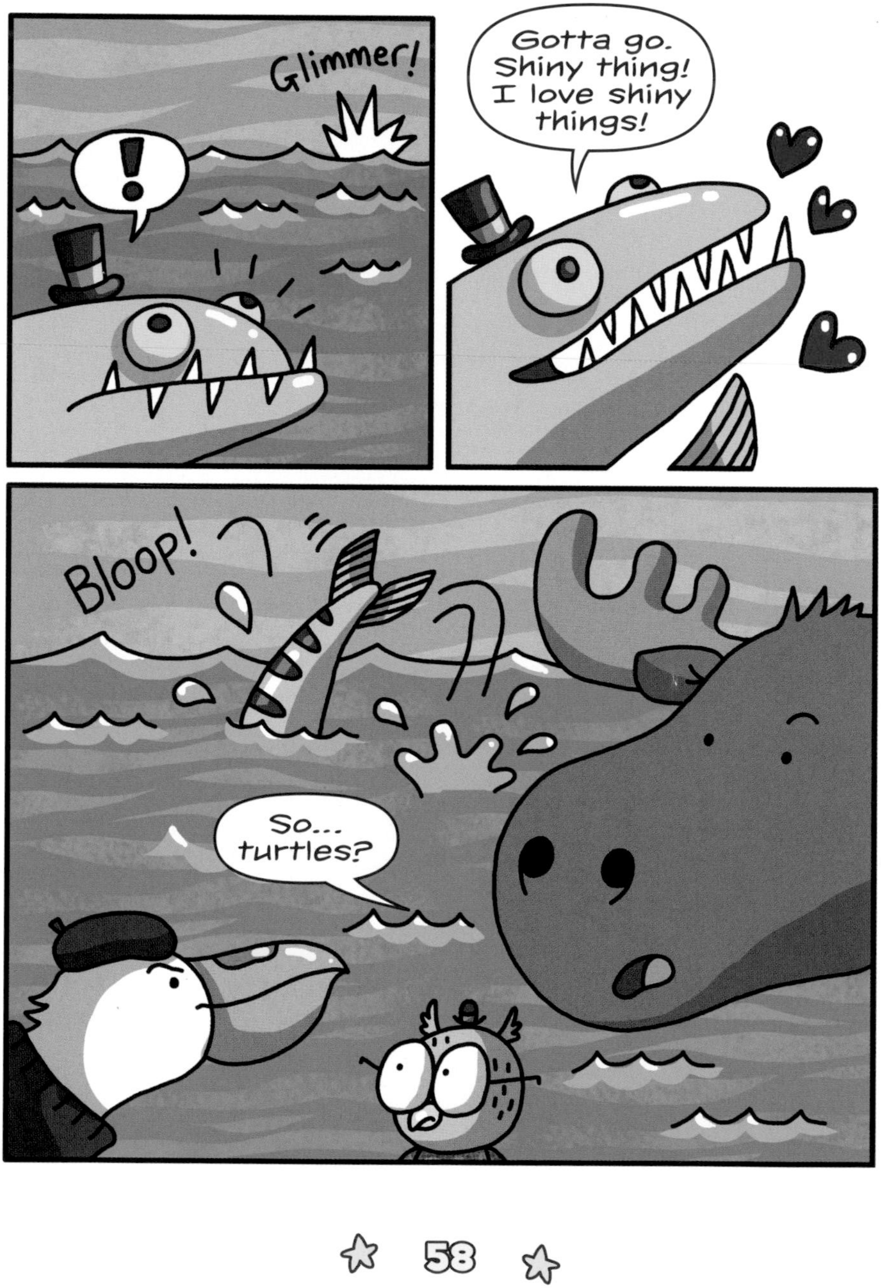
Glimmer!
!
Gotta go. Shiny thing! I love shiny things!
Bloop!
So... turtles?

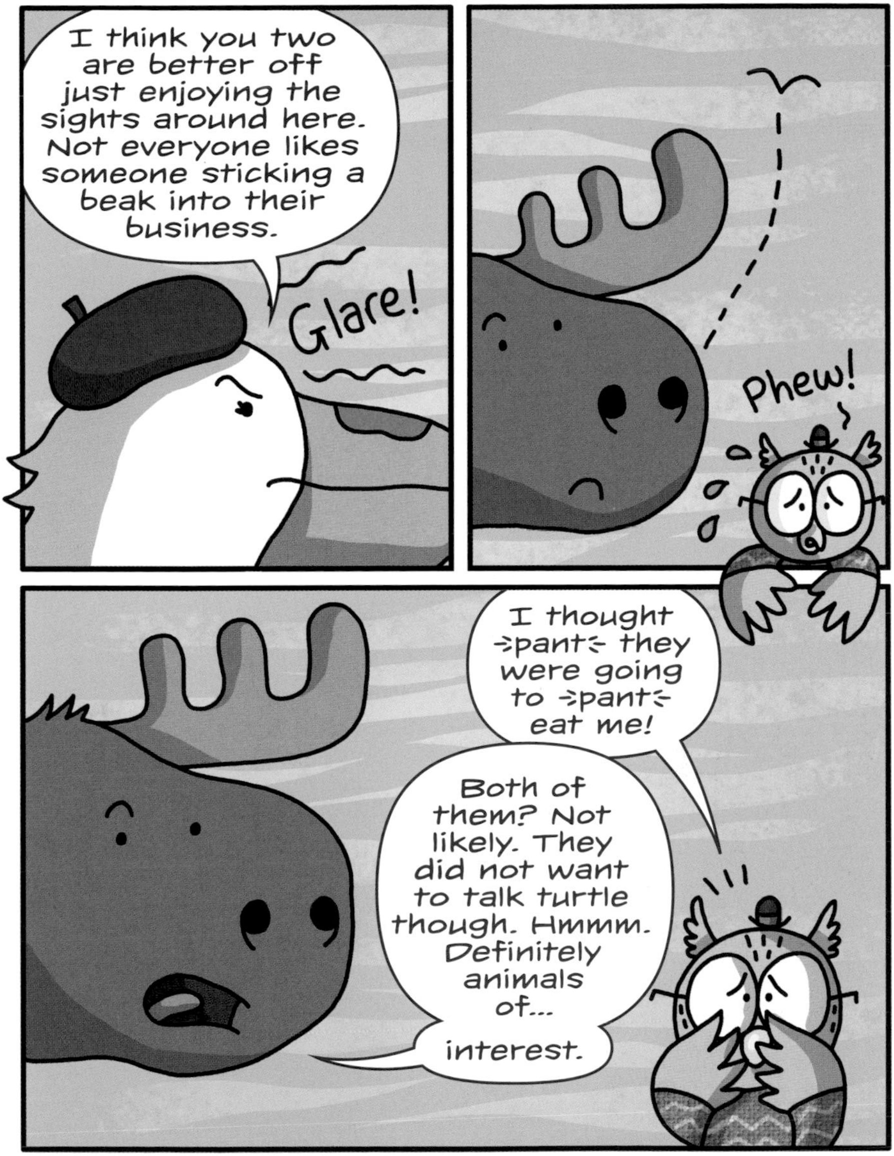
I think you two are better off just enjoying the sights around here. Not everyone likes someone sticking a beak into their business.
Glare!
Phew!
I thought ⇉pant⇇ they were going to ⇉pant⇇ eat me!
Both of them? Not likely. They did not want to talk turtle though. Hmmm. Definitely animals of...
interest.

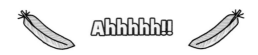

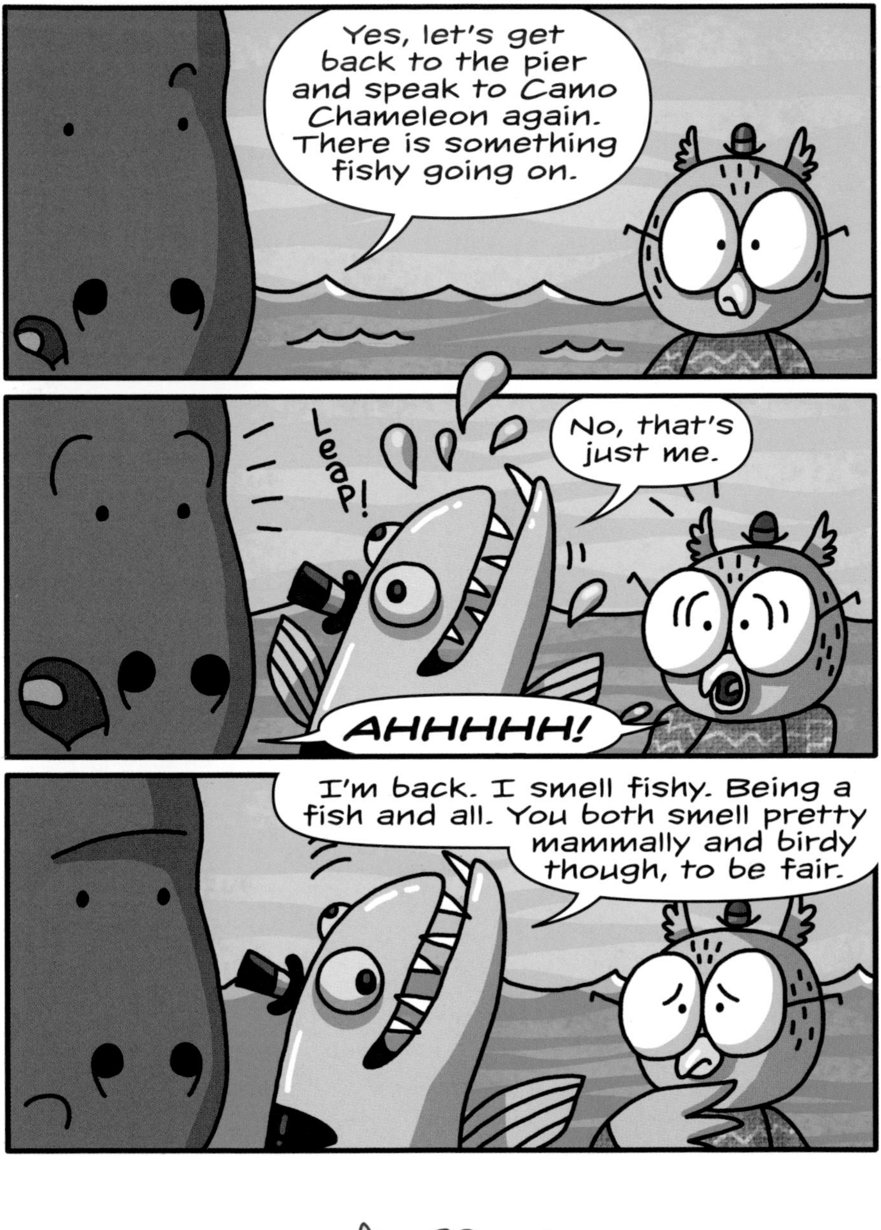
Yes, let's get back to the pier and speak to Camo Chameleon again. There is something fishy going on.
Leap!
No, that's just me.
AHHHHH!
I'm back. I smell fishy. Being a fish and all. You both smell pretty mammally and birdy though, to be fair.

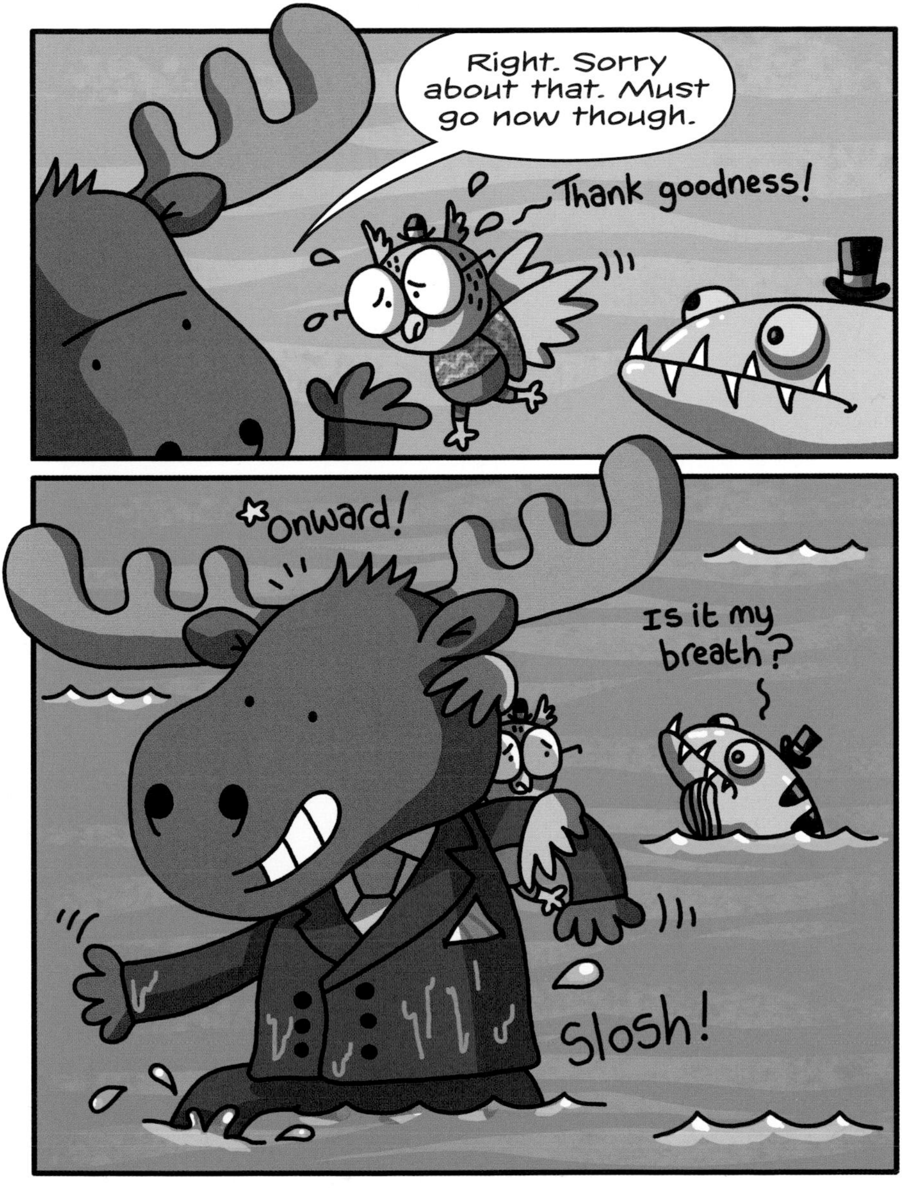
Right. Sorry about that. Must go now though.
Thank goodness!
Onward!
Is it my breath?
Slosh!

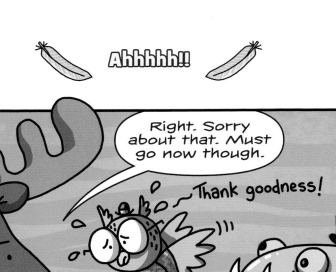

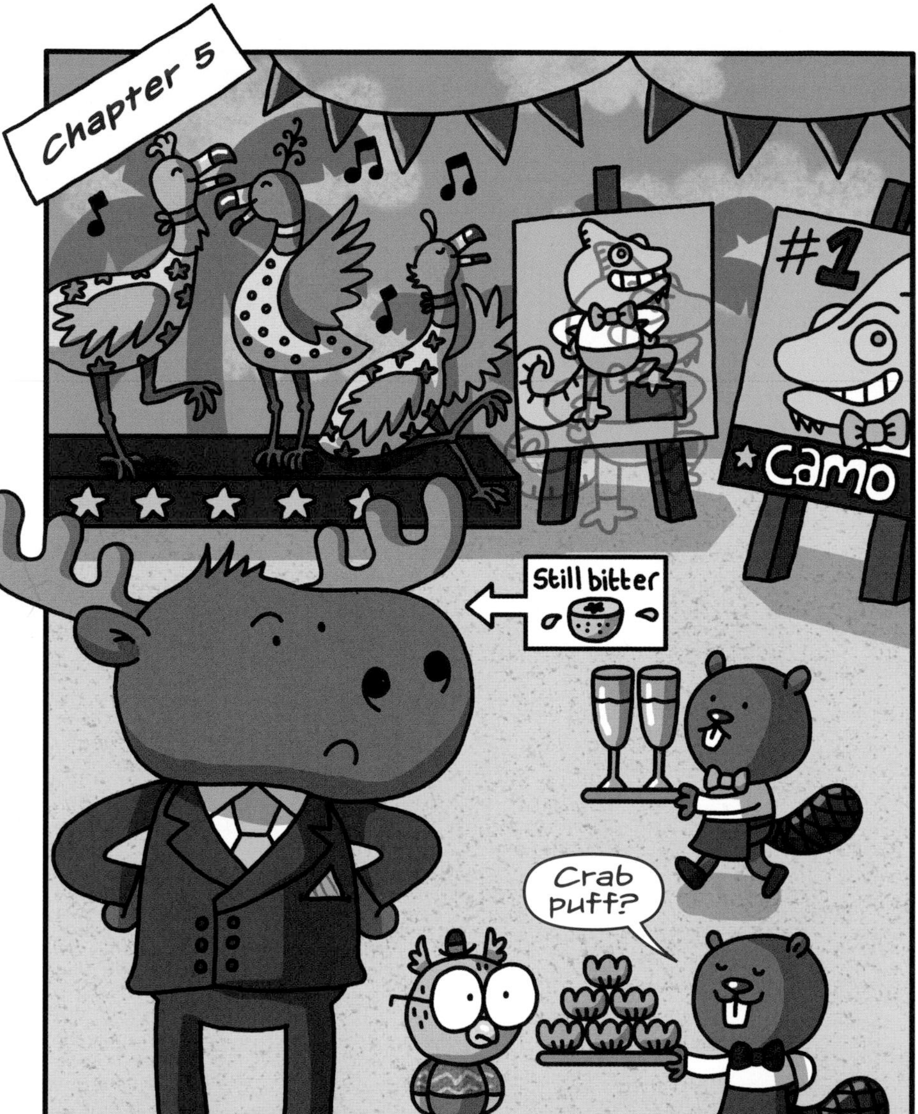
Chapter 5
#1
CAMO
Still bitter
Crab puff?

THIS IS A STRANGE DAY

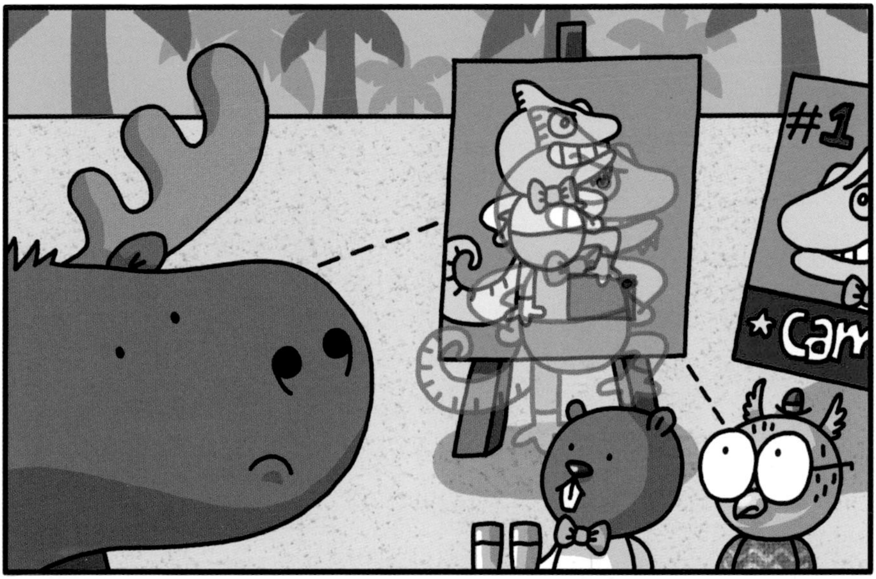
#1
Cam

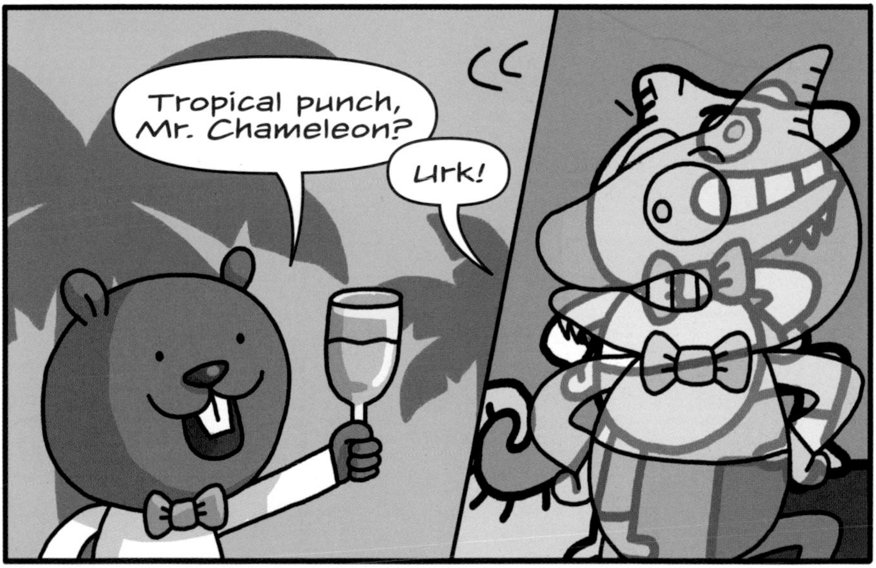
Tropical punch, Mr. Chameleon?
Urk!

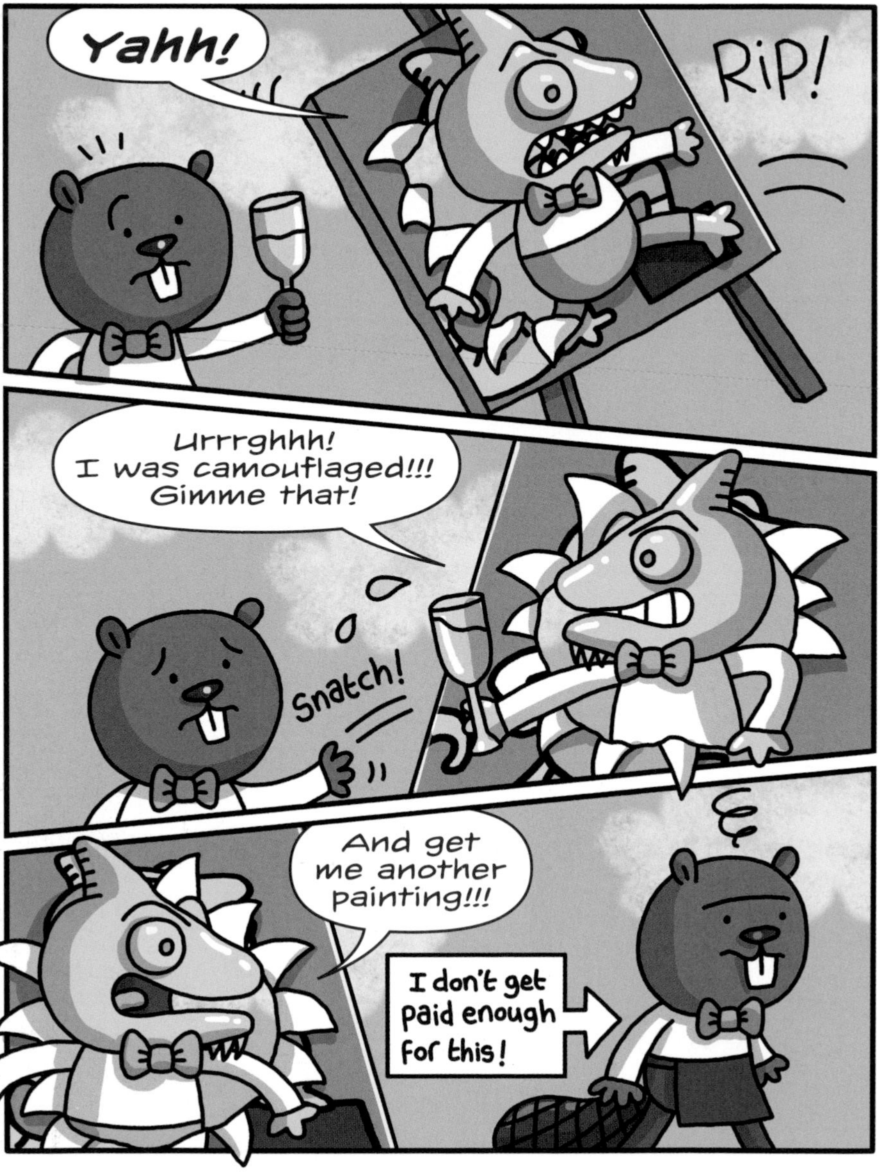
Yahh!
RIP!
Urrrghhh! I was camouflaged!!! Gimme that!
Snatch!
And get me another painting!!!
I don't get paid enough for this!

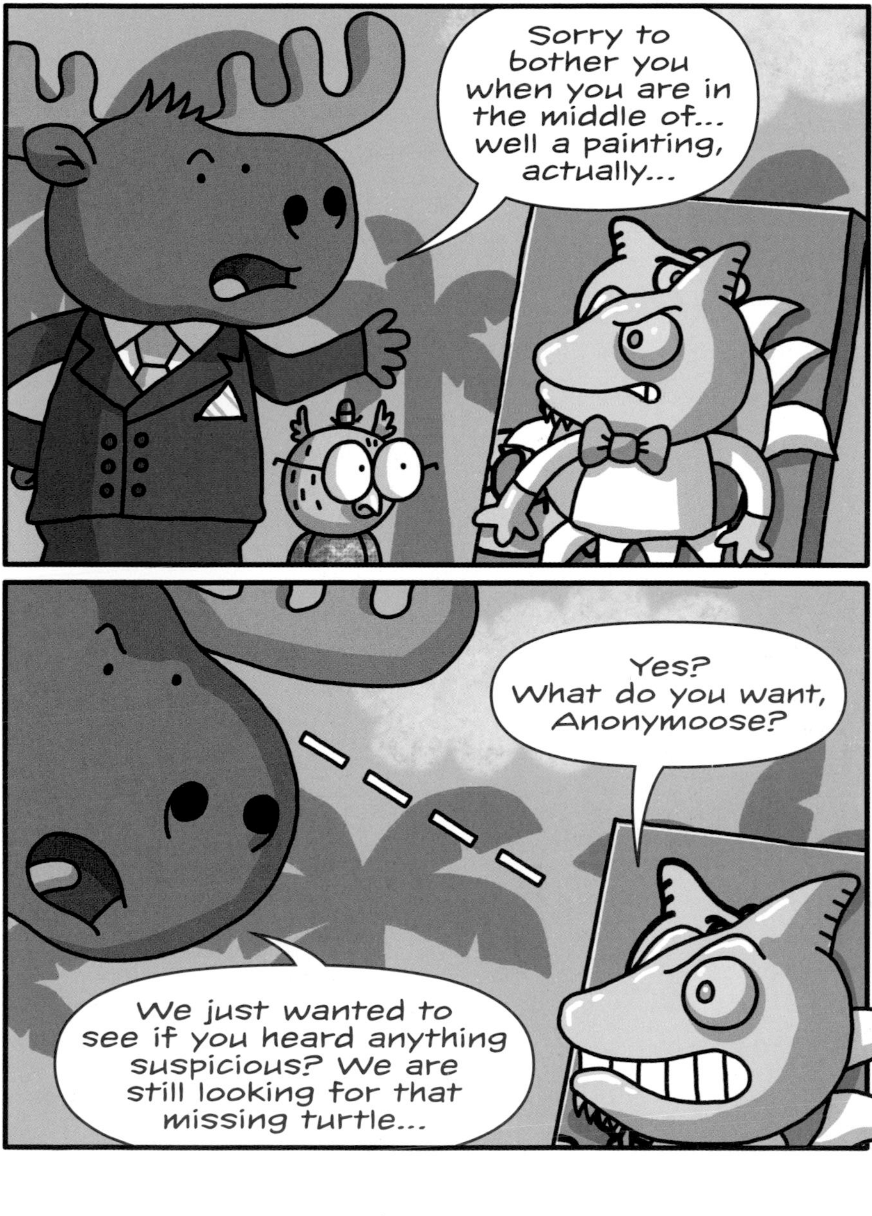
Sorry to bother you when you are in the middle of... well a painting, actually...
Yes? What do you want, Anonymoose?
We just wanted to see if you heard anything suspicious? We are still looking for that missing turtle...

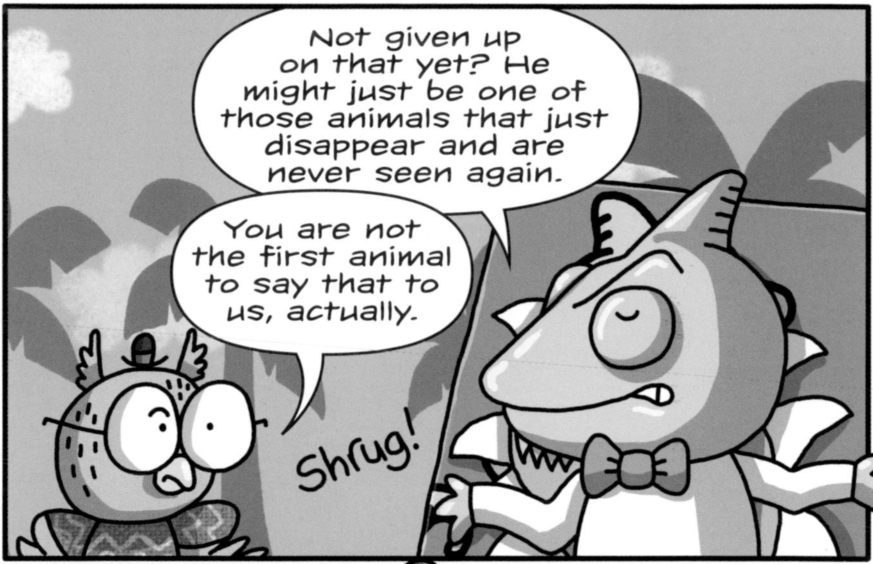
Not given up on that yet? He might just be one of those animals that just disappear and are never seen again.
You are not the first animal to say that to us, actually.
Shrug!

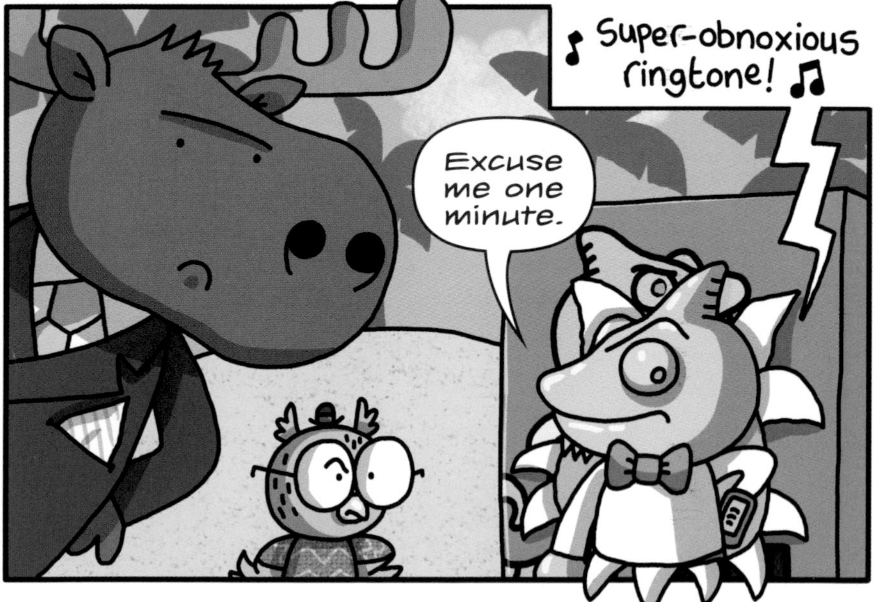
Super-obnoxious ringtone!
Excuse me one minute.

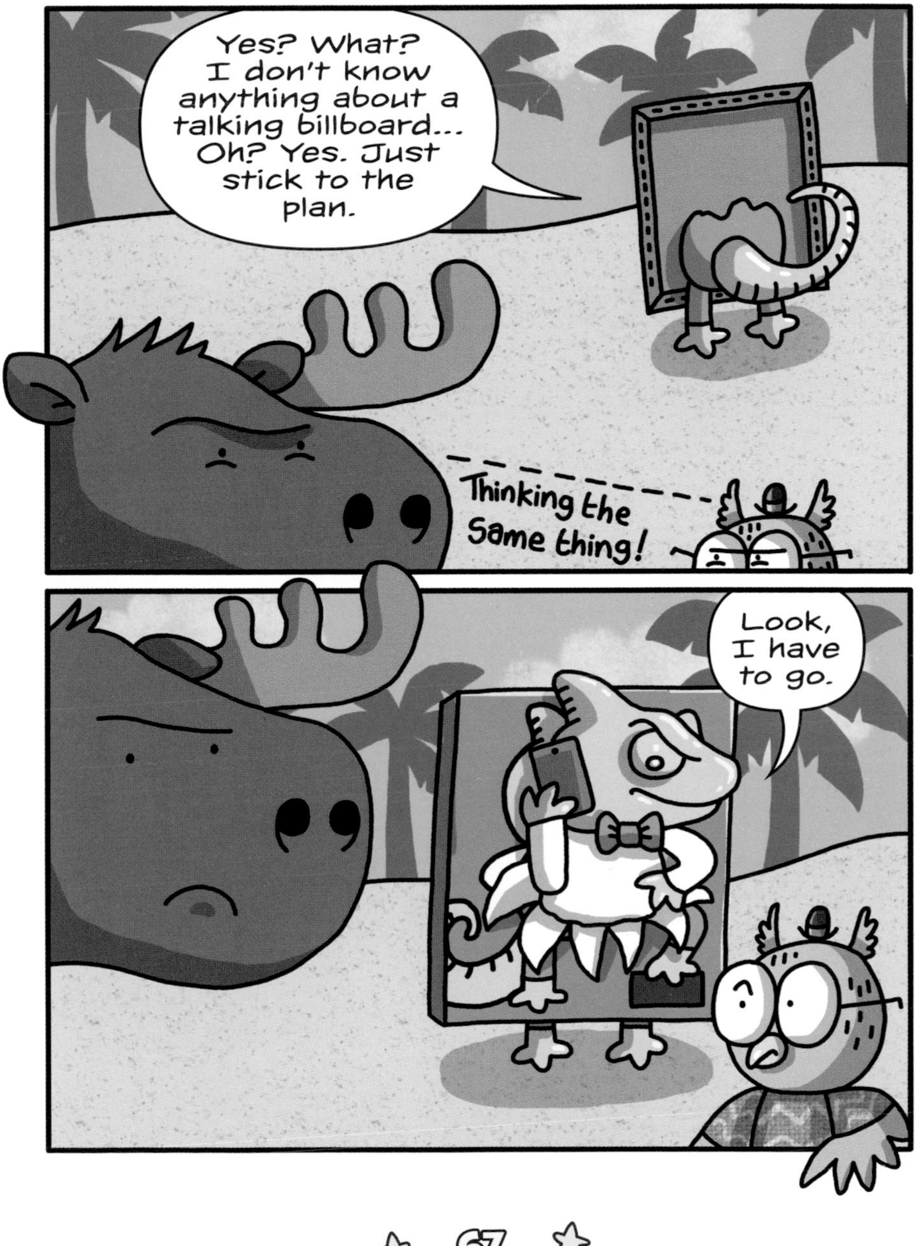
Yes? What? I don't know anything about a talking billboard... Oh? Yes. Just stick to the plan.
Thinking the Same thing!
Look, I have to go.

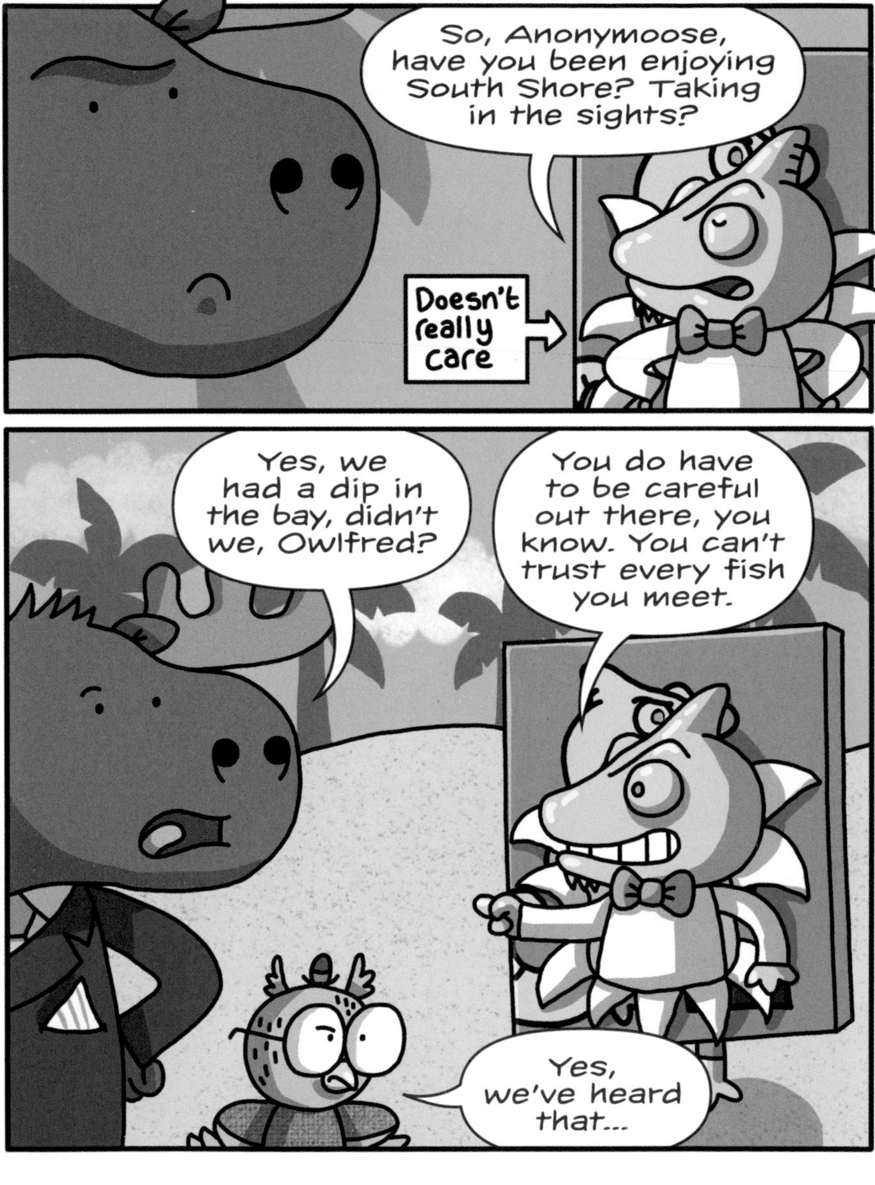
So, Anonymoose, have you been enjoying South Shore? Taking in the sights?
Doesn't really care
Yes, we had a dip in the bay, didn't we, Owlfred?
You do have to be careful out there, you know. You can't trust every fish you meet.
Yes, we've heard that...

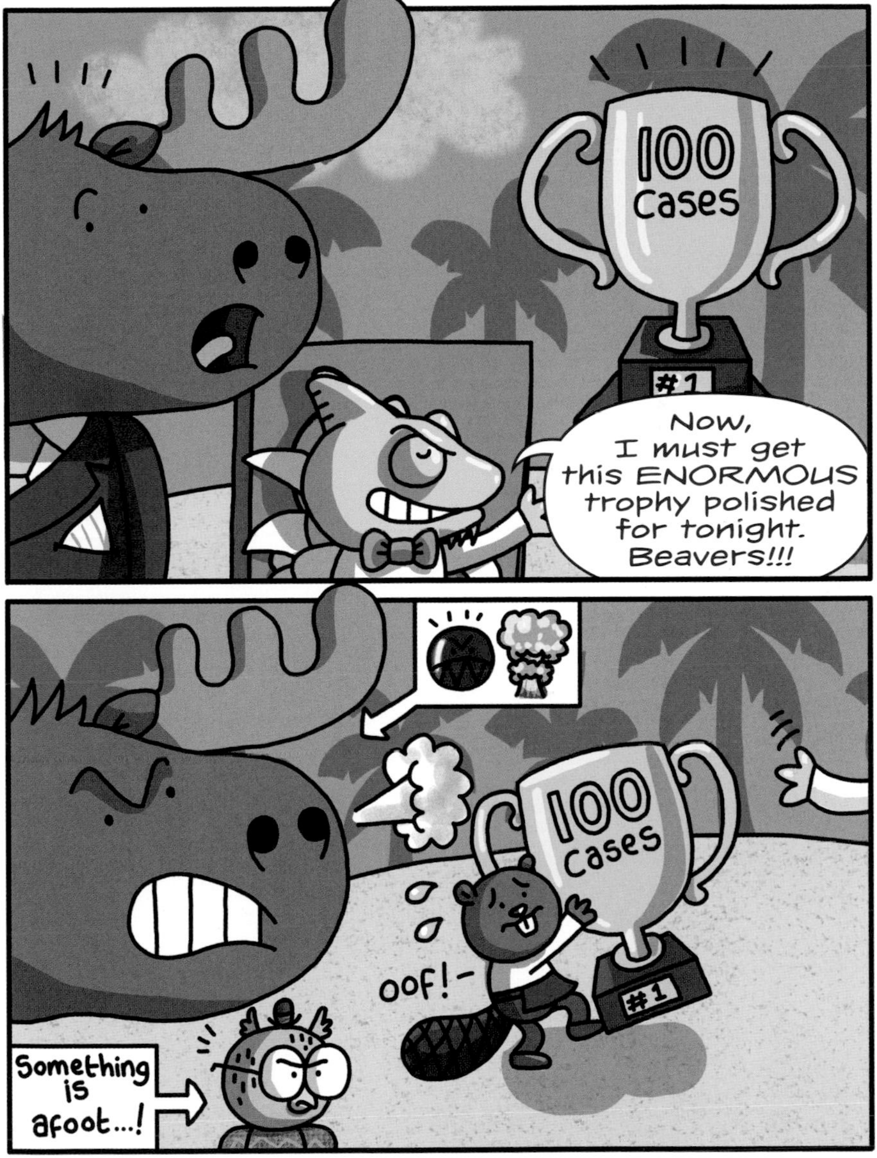
100 cases
#1
Now, I must get this ENORMOUS trophy polished for tonight. Beavers!!!
100 cases
#1
OOF!-
Something is afoot...!

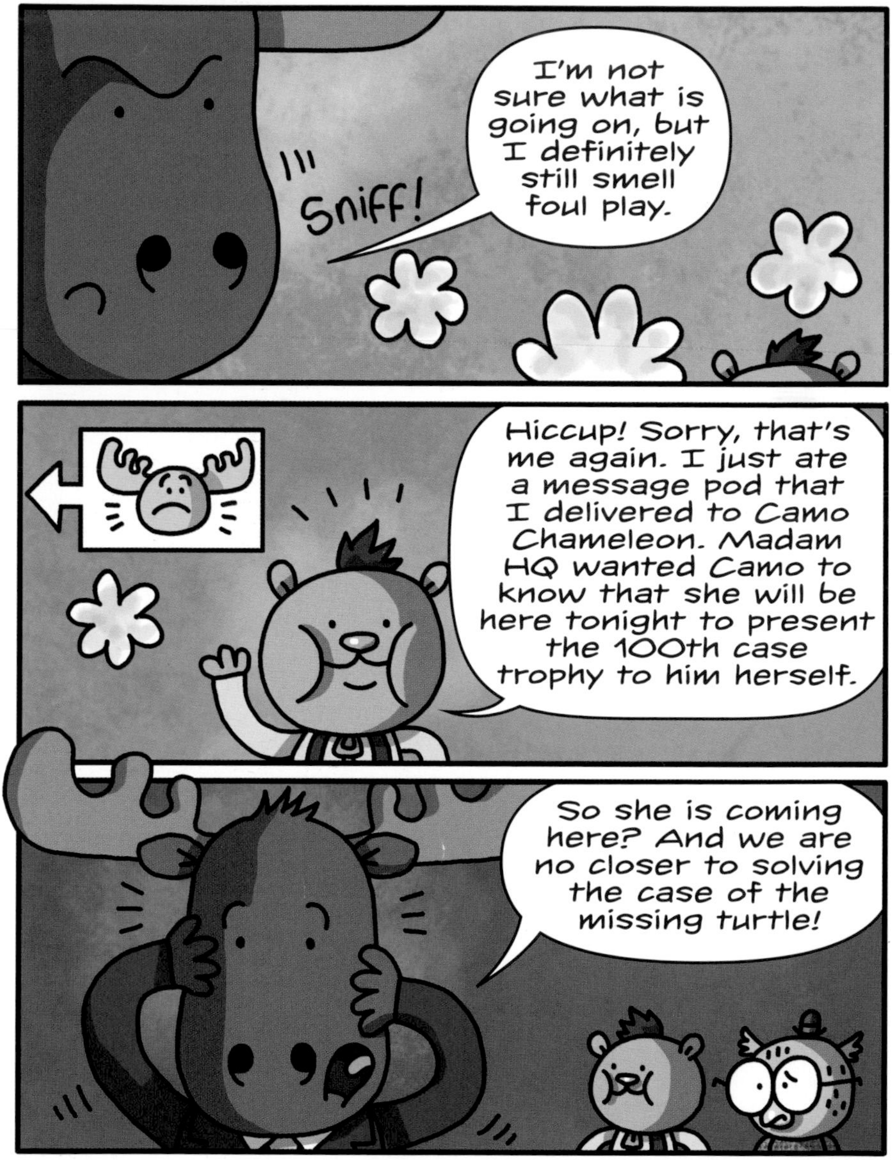
Sniff!
I'm not sure what is going on, but I definitely still smell foul play.
Hiccup! Sorry, that's me again. I just ate a message pod that I delivered to Camo Chameleon. Madam HQ wanted Camo to know that she will be here tonight to present the 100th case trophy to him herself.
So she is coming here? And we are no closer to solving the case of the missing turtle!

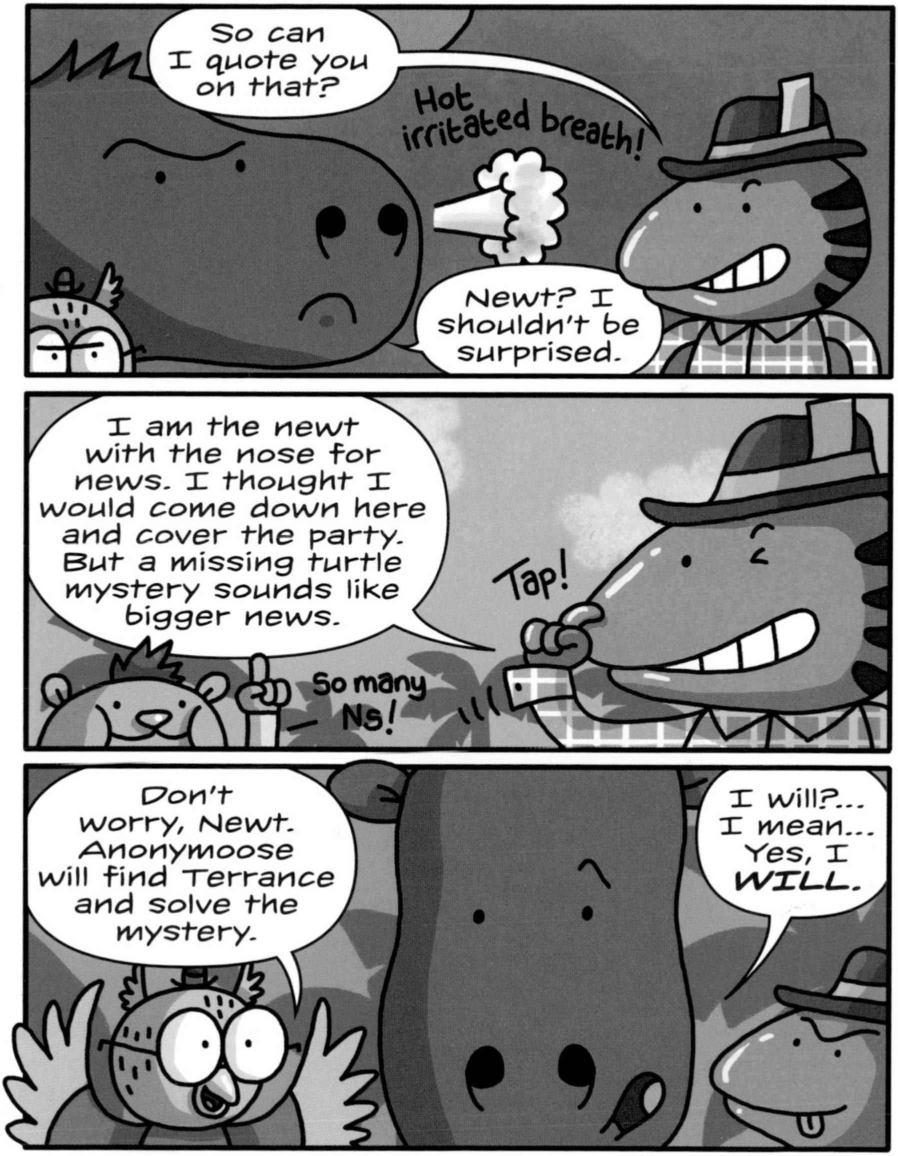
So can I quote you on that?
Hot irritated breath!
Newt? I shouldn't be surprised.
I am the newt with the nose for news. I thought I would come down here and cover the party. But a missing turtle mystery sounds like bigger news.
Tap!
So many Ns!
Don't worry, Newt. Anonymoose will find Terrance and solve the mystery.
I will?... I mean... Yes, I WILL.

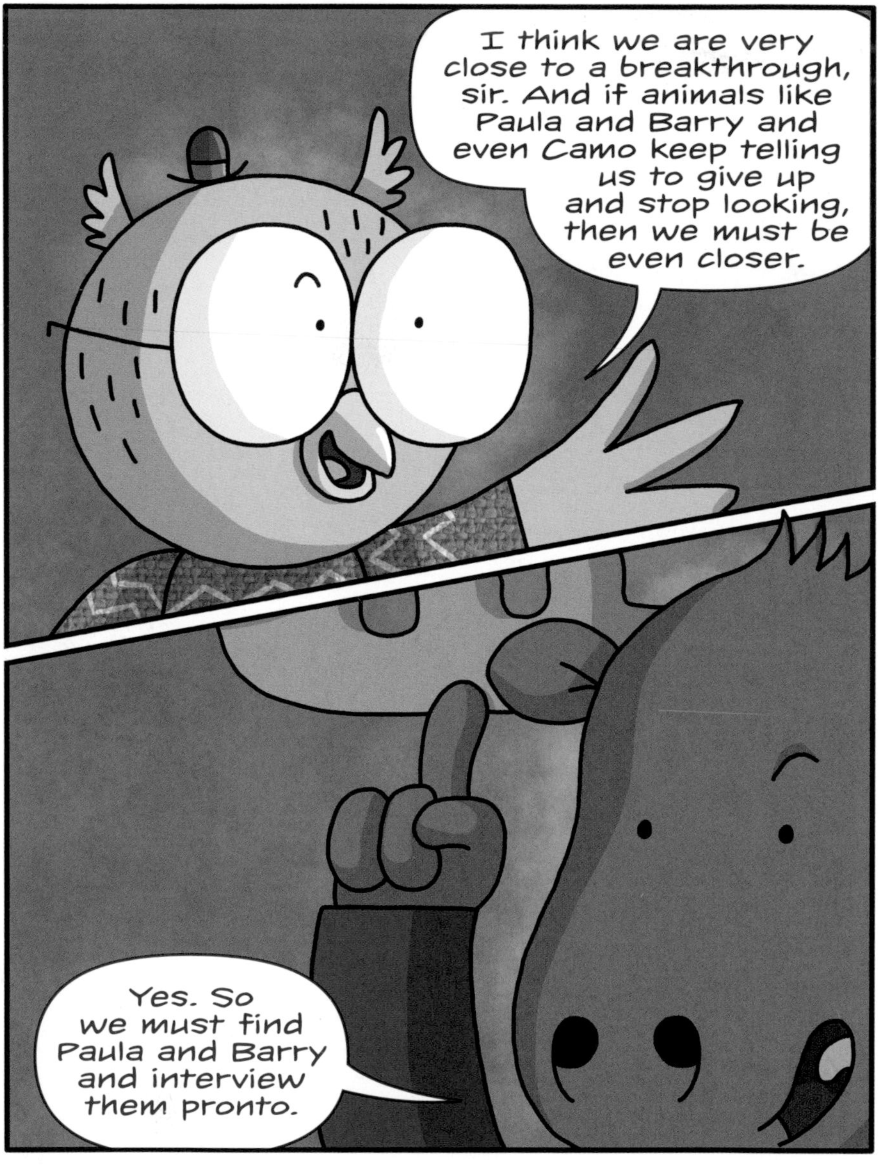
I think we are very close to a breakthrough, sir. And if animals like Paula and Barry and even Camo keep telling us to give up and stop looking, then we must be even closer.
Yes. So we must find Paula and Barry and interview them pronto.

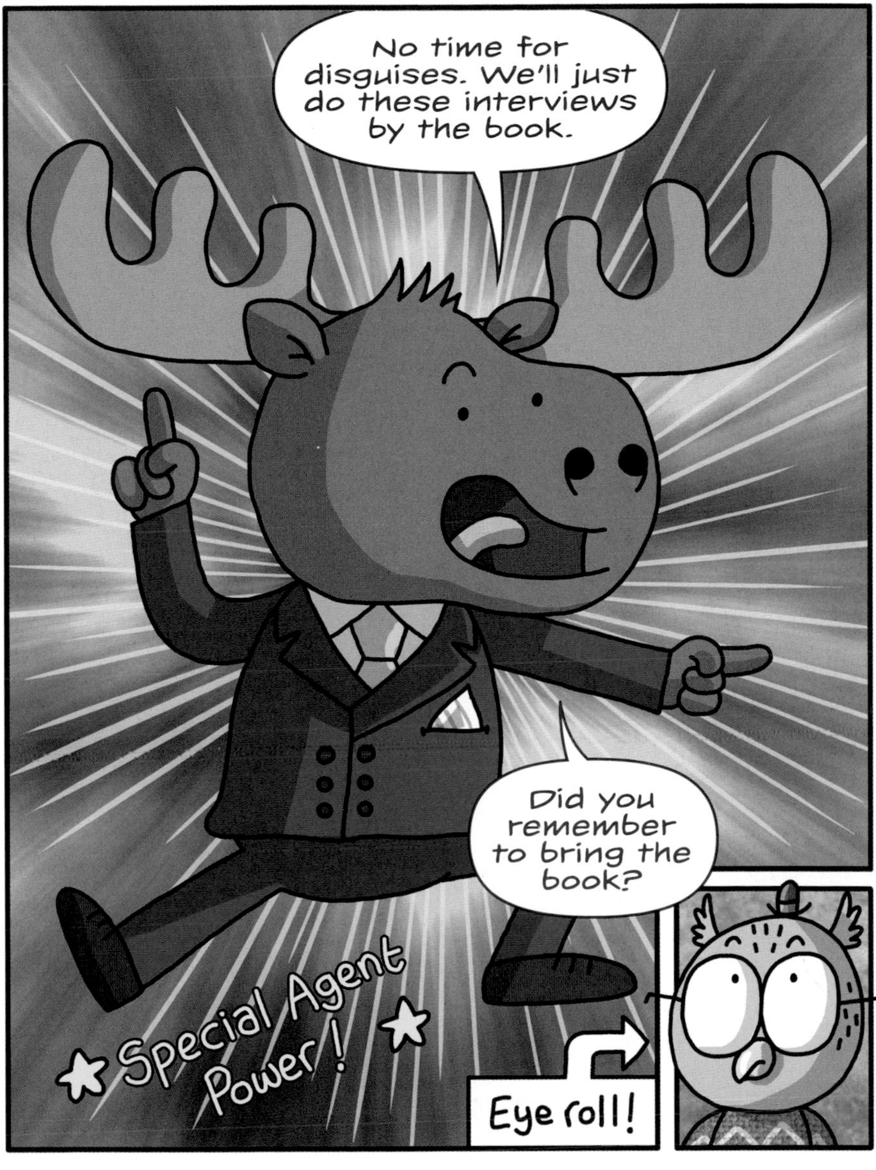
No time for disguises. We'll just do these interviews by the book.
Did you remember to bring the book?
Special Agent Power!
Eye roll!

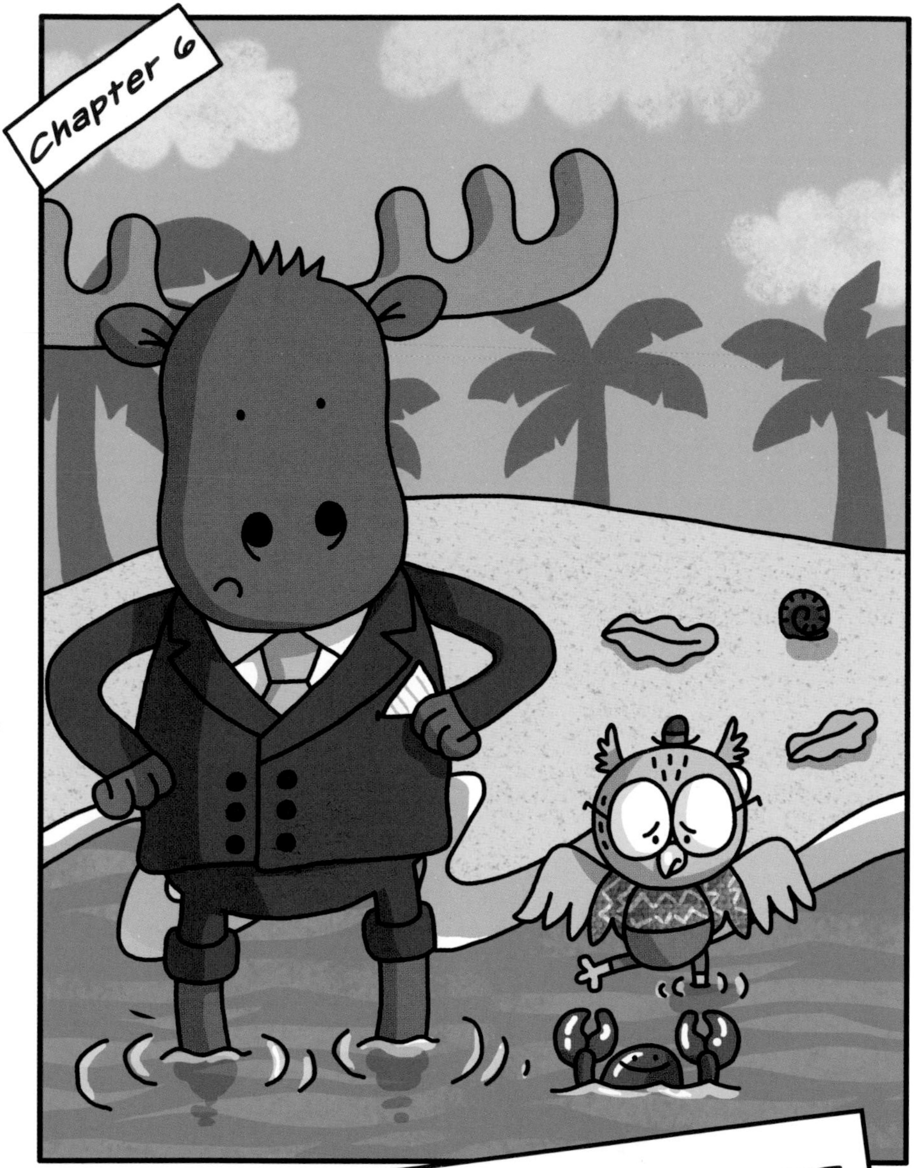
Chapter 6

GOOD OWL/BAD MOOSE

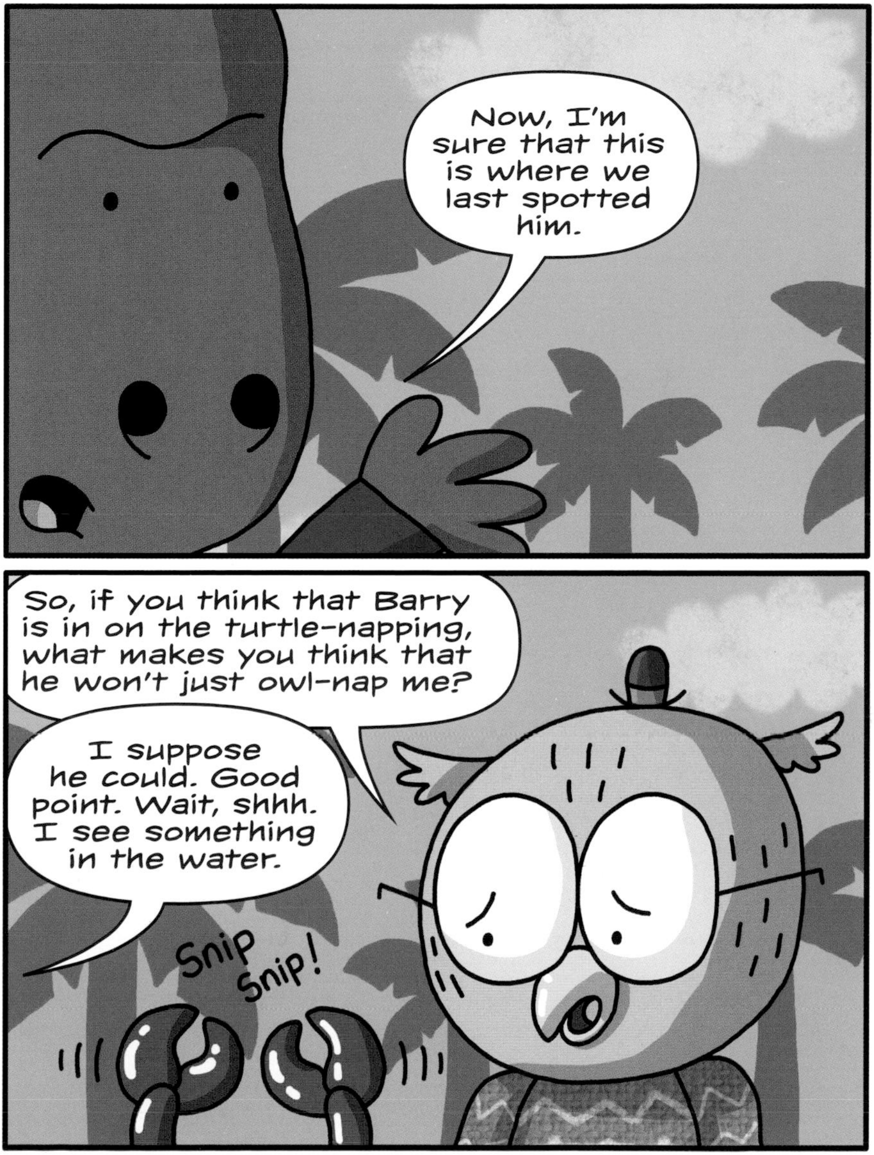
Now, I'm sure that this is where we last spotted him.
So, if you think that Barry is in on the turtle-napping, what makes you think that he won't just owl-nap me?
I suppose he could. Good point. Wait, shhh. I see something in the water.
Snip Snip!

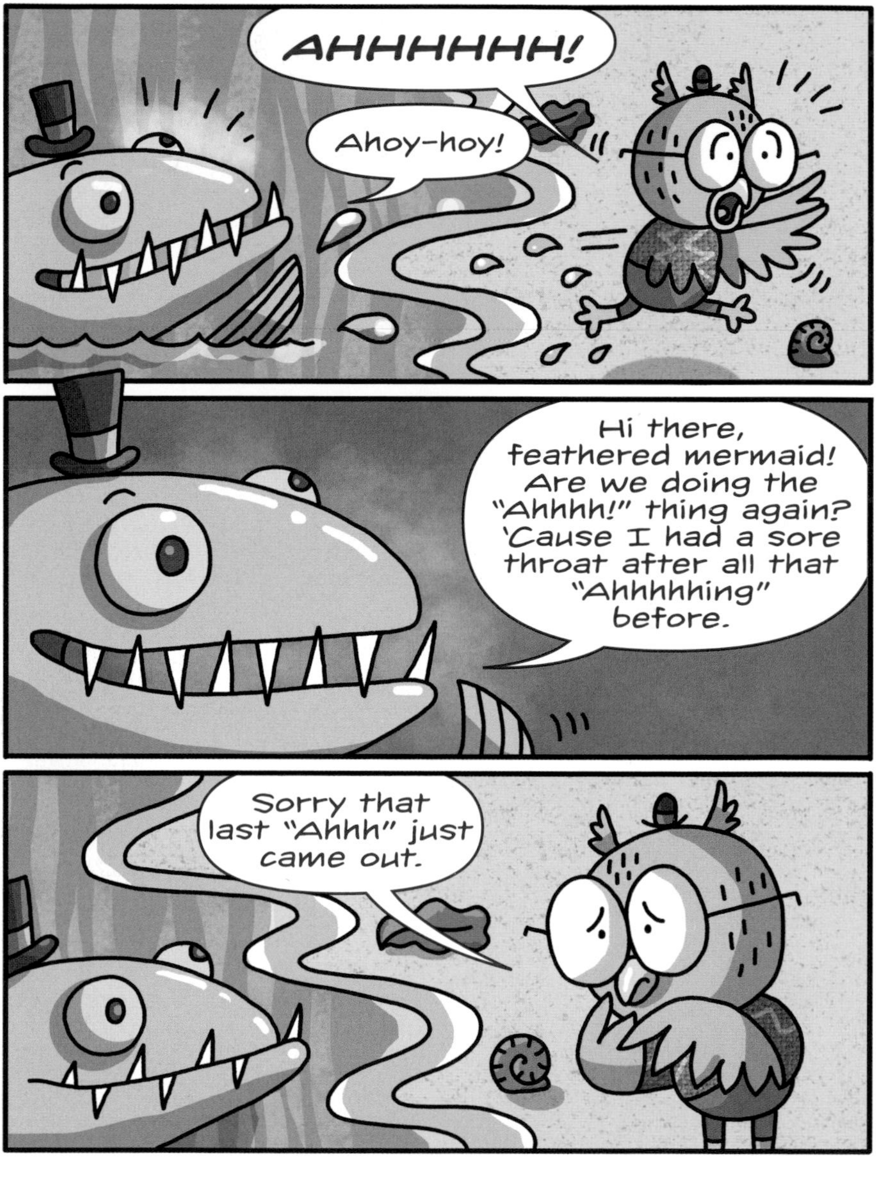
AHHHHHH!
Ahoy-hoy!
Hi there, feathered mermaid! Are we doing the "Ahhhh!" thing again? 'Cause I had a sore throat after all that "Ahhhhhing" before.
Sorry that last "Ahhh" just came out.

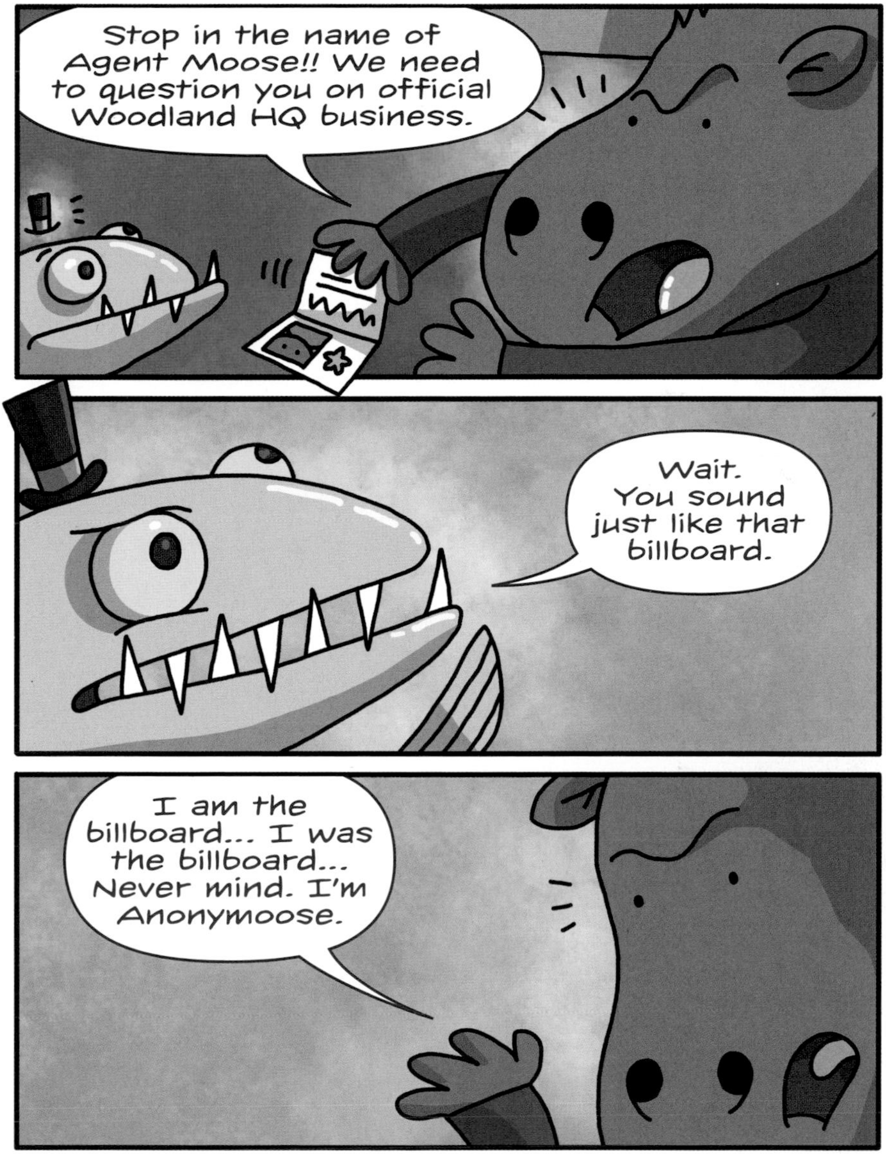
Stop in the name of Agent Moose!! We need to question you on official Woodland HQ business.
Wait. You sound just like that billboard.
I am the billboard... I was the billboard... Never mind. I'm Anonymoose.

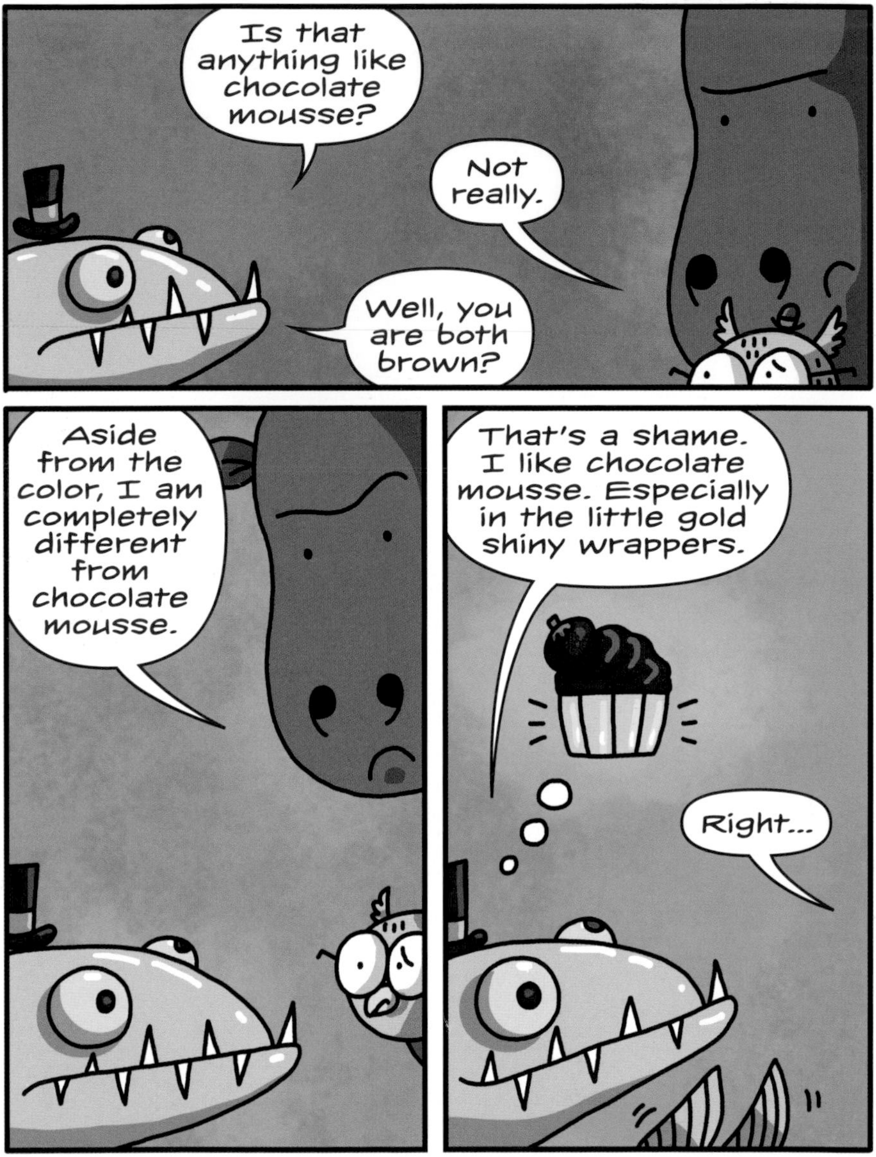
Is that anything like chocolate mousse?
Not really.
Well, you are both brown?
Aside from the color, I am completely different from chocolate mousse.
That's a shame. I like chocolate mousse. Especially in the little gold shiny wrappers.
Right...

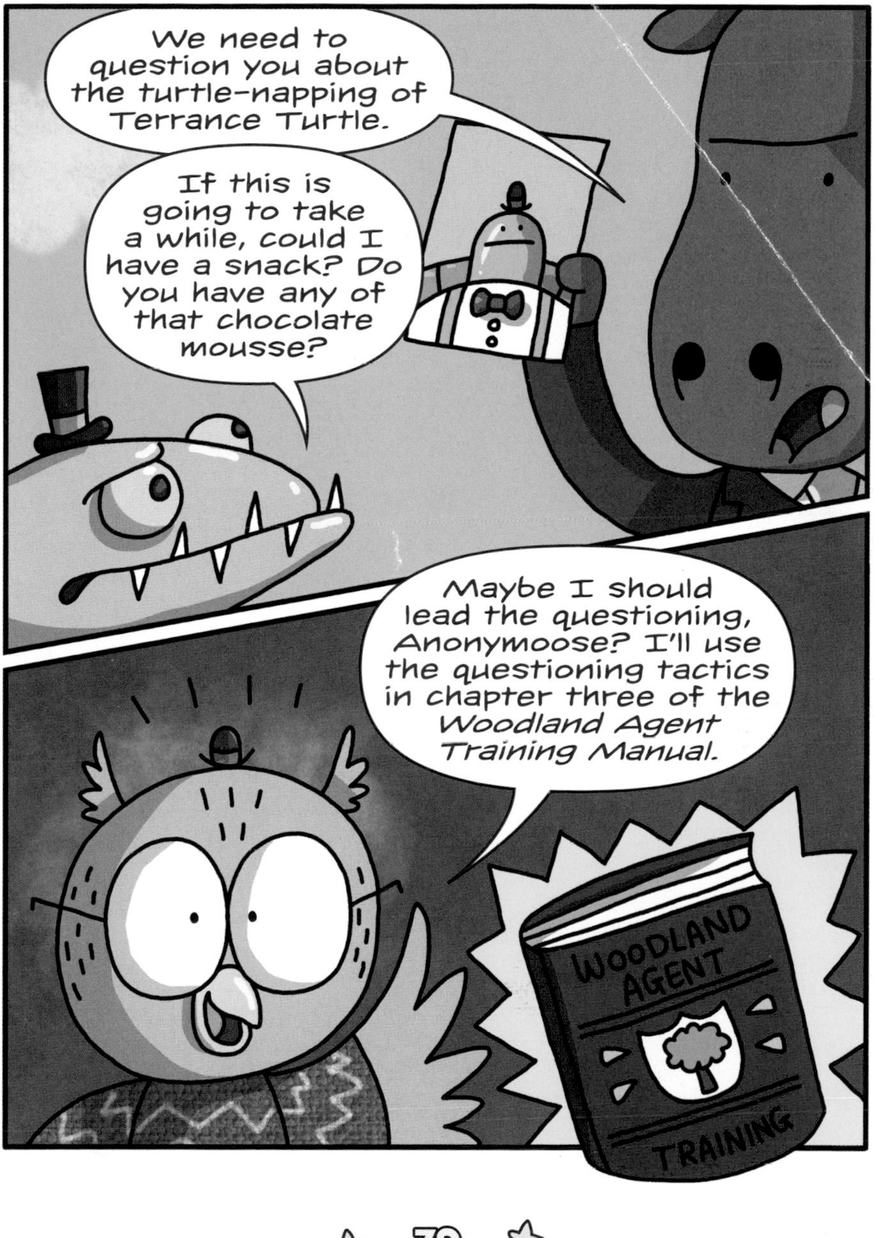
We need to question you about the turtle-napping of Terrance Turtle.
If this is going to take a while, could I have a snack? Do you have any of that chocolate mousse?
Maybe I should lead the questioning, Anonymoose? I'll use the questioning tactics in chapter three of the *Woodland Agent Training Manual.*
WOODLAND AGENT
TRAINING

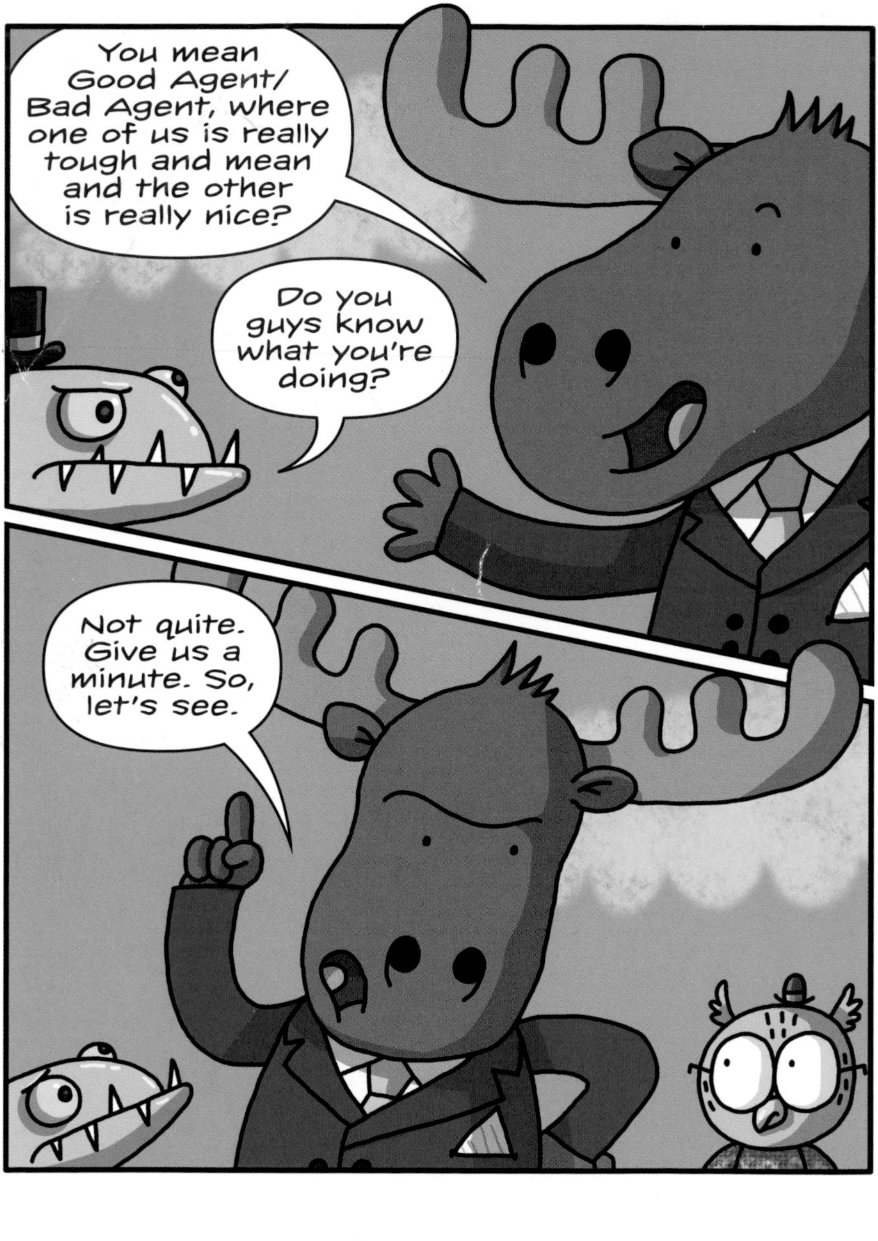
You mean Good Agent/ Bad Agent, where one of us is really tough and mean and the other is really nice?
Do you guys know what you're doing?
Not quite. Give us a minute. So, let's see.

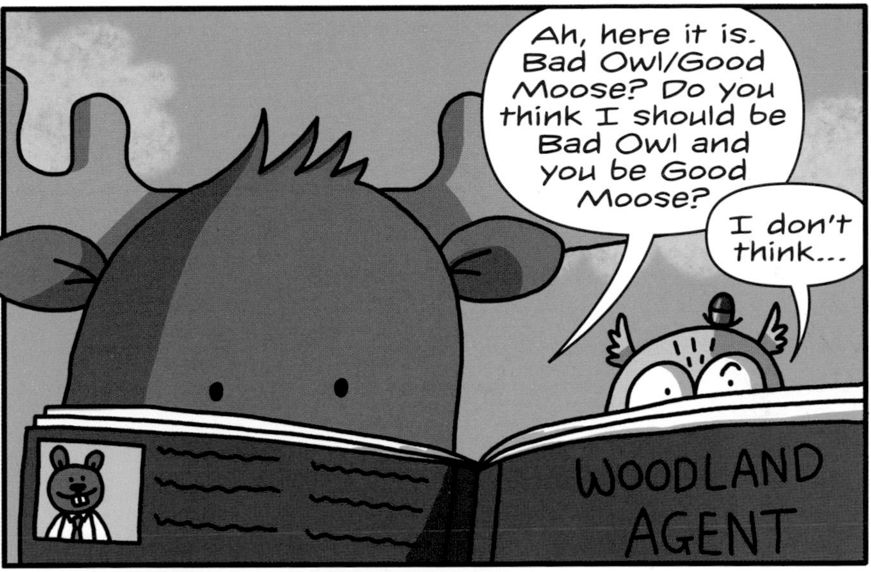
Ah, here it is. Bad Owl/Good Moose? Do you think I should be Bad Owl and you be Good Moose?
I don't think...
WOODLAND AGENT

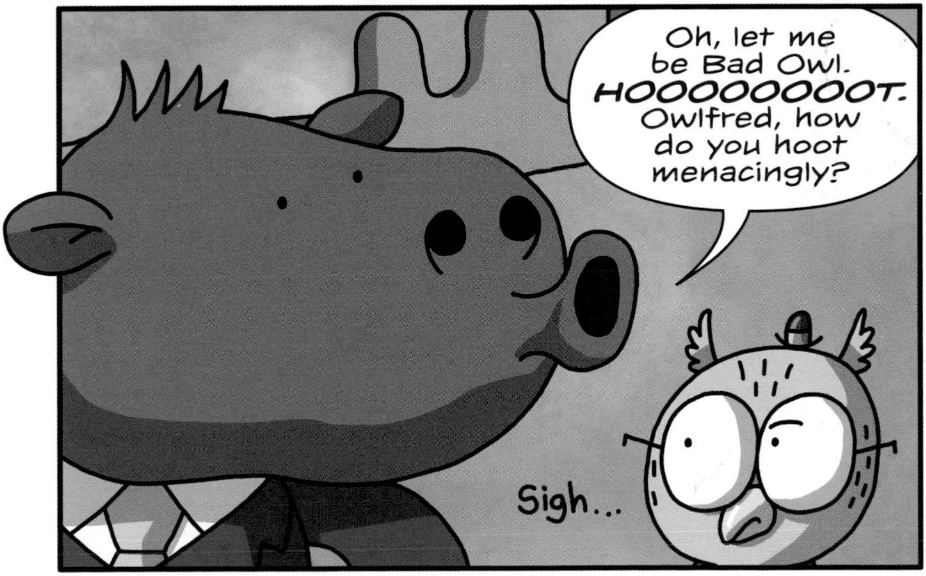
Oh, let me be Bad Owl. HOOOOOOOOT. Owlfred, how do you hoot menacingly?
Sigh...

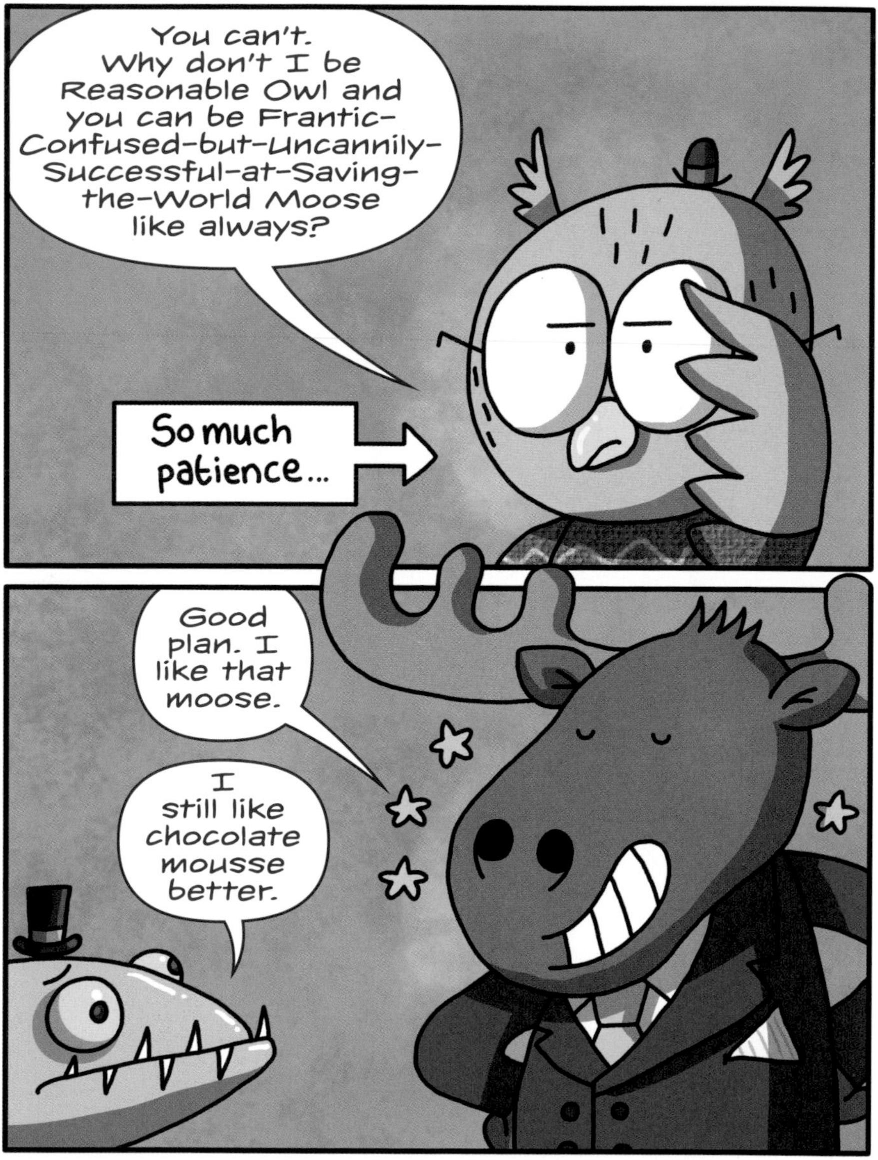
You can't.
Why don't I be Reasonable Owl and you can be Frantic-Confused-but-Uncannily-Successful-at-Saving-the-World Moose like always?
So much patience...
Good plan. I like that moose.
I still like chocolate mousse better.

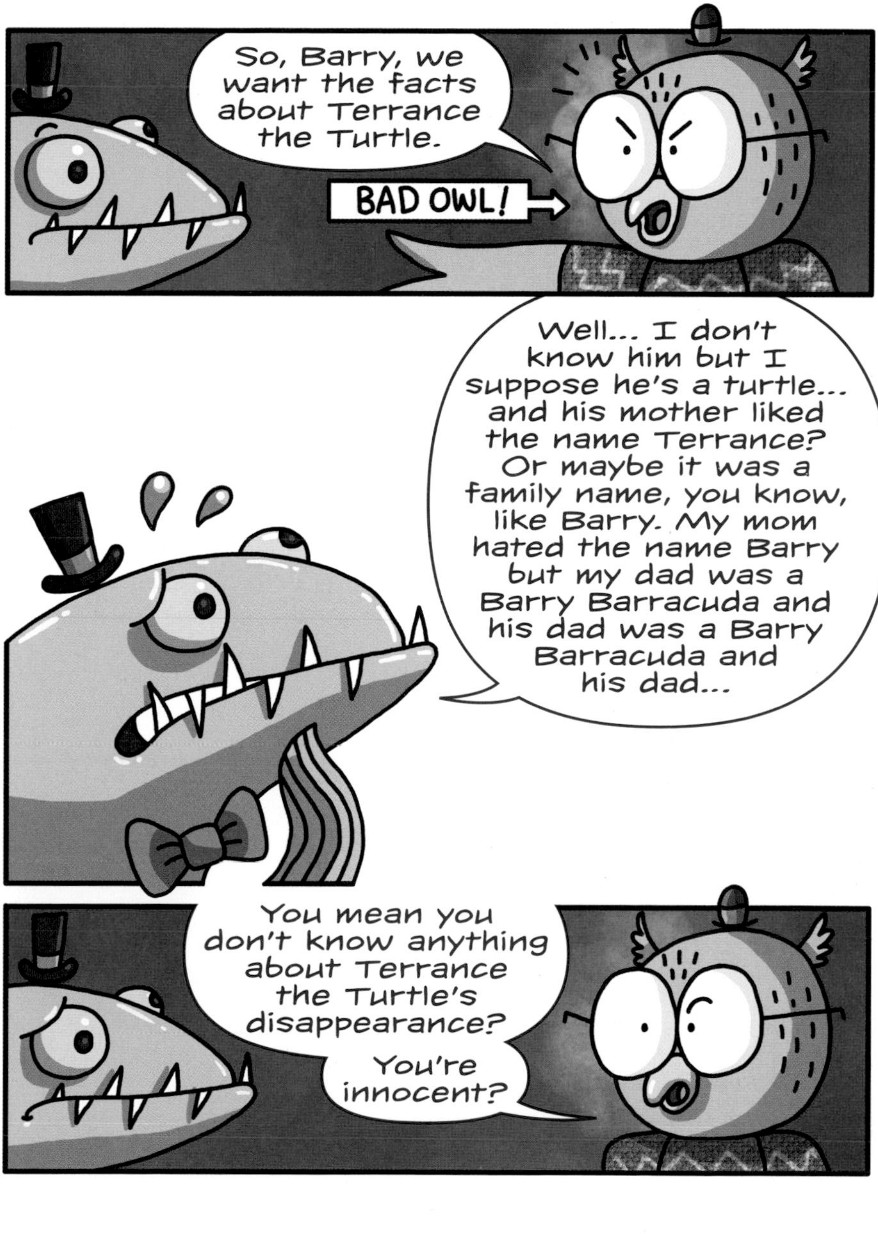
So, Barry, we want the facts about Terrance the Turtle.
BAD OWL!
Well... I don't know him but I suppose he's a turtle... and his mother liked the name Terrance? Or maybe it was a family name, you know, like Barry. My mom hated the name Barry but my dad was a Barry Barracuda and his dad was a Barry Barracuda and his dad...
You mean you don't know anything about Terrance the Turtle's disappearance?
You're innocent?

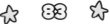

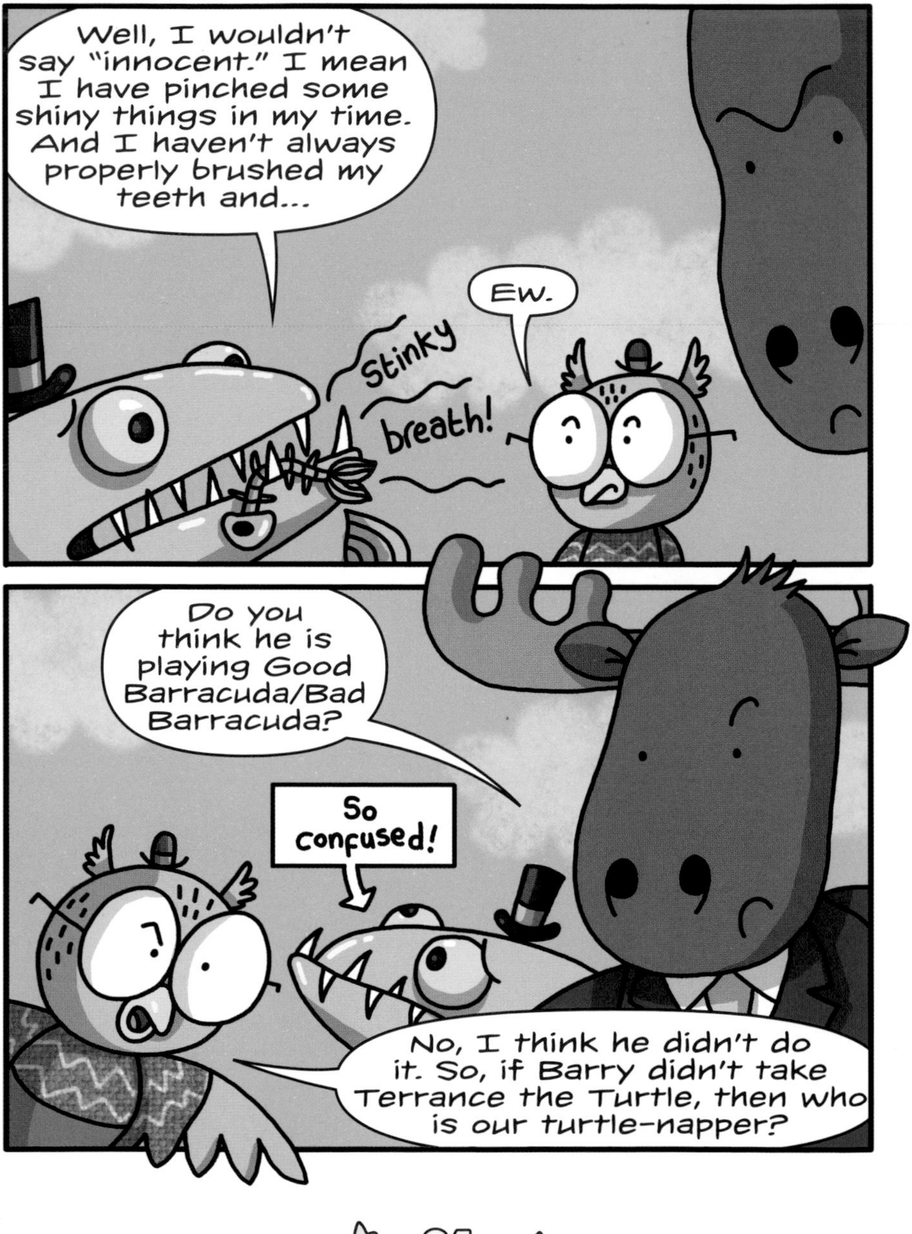
Well, I wouldn't say "innocent." I mean I have pinched some shiny things in my time. And I haven't always properly brushed my teeth and...
Ew.
Stinky breath!
Do you think he is playing Good Barracuda/Bad Barracuda?
So confused!
No, I think he didn't do it. So, if Barry didn't take Terrance the Turtle, then who is our turtle-napper?

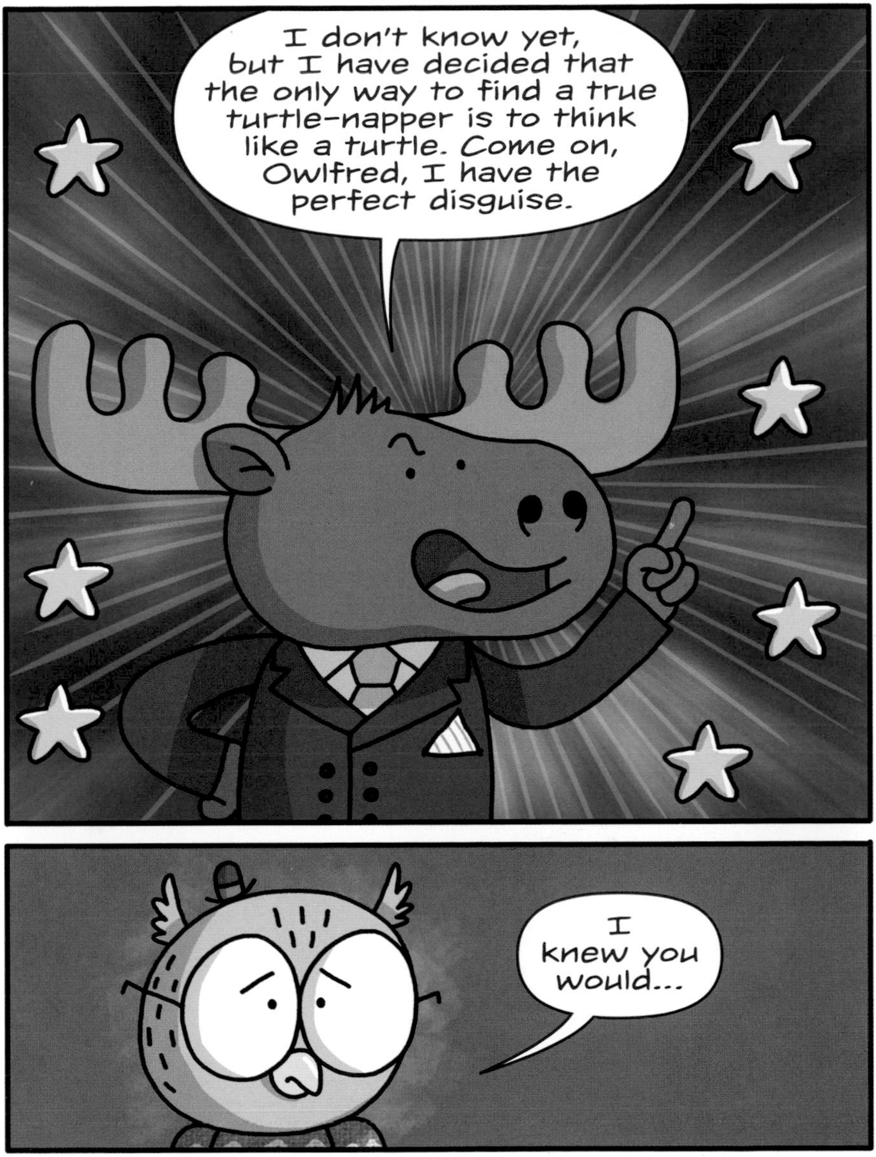
I don't know yet, but I have decided that the only way to find a true turtle-napper is to think like a turtle. Come on, Owlfred, I have the perfect disguise.
I knew you would...

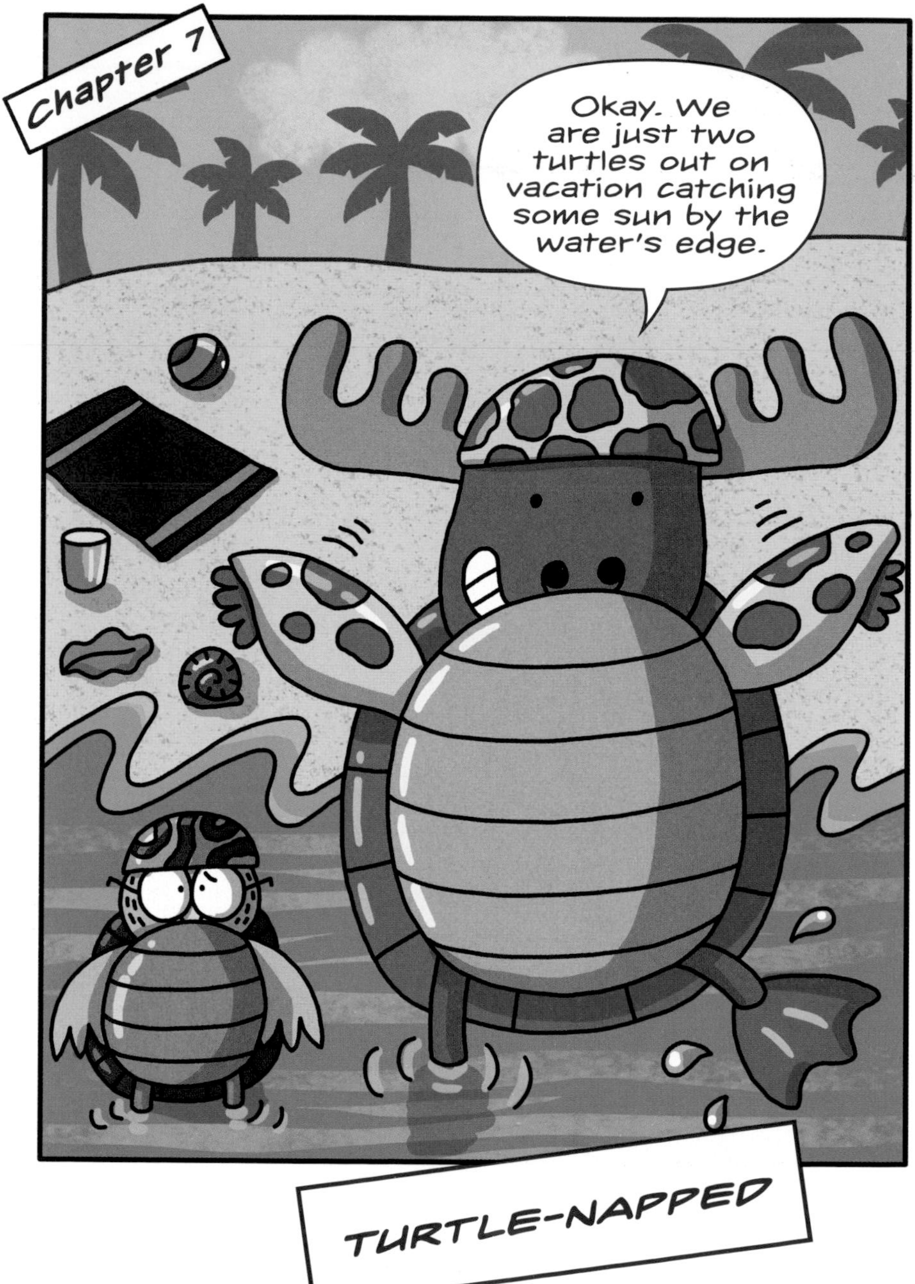
Chapter 7
Okay. We are just two turtles out on vacation catching some sun by the water's edge.
TURTLE-NAPPED

Turtle-napped

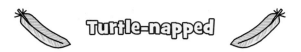

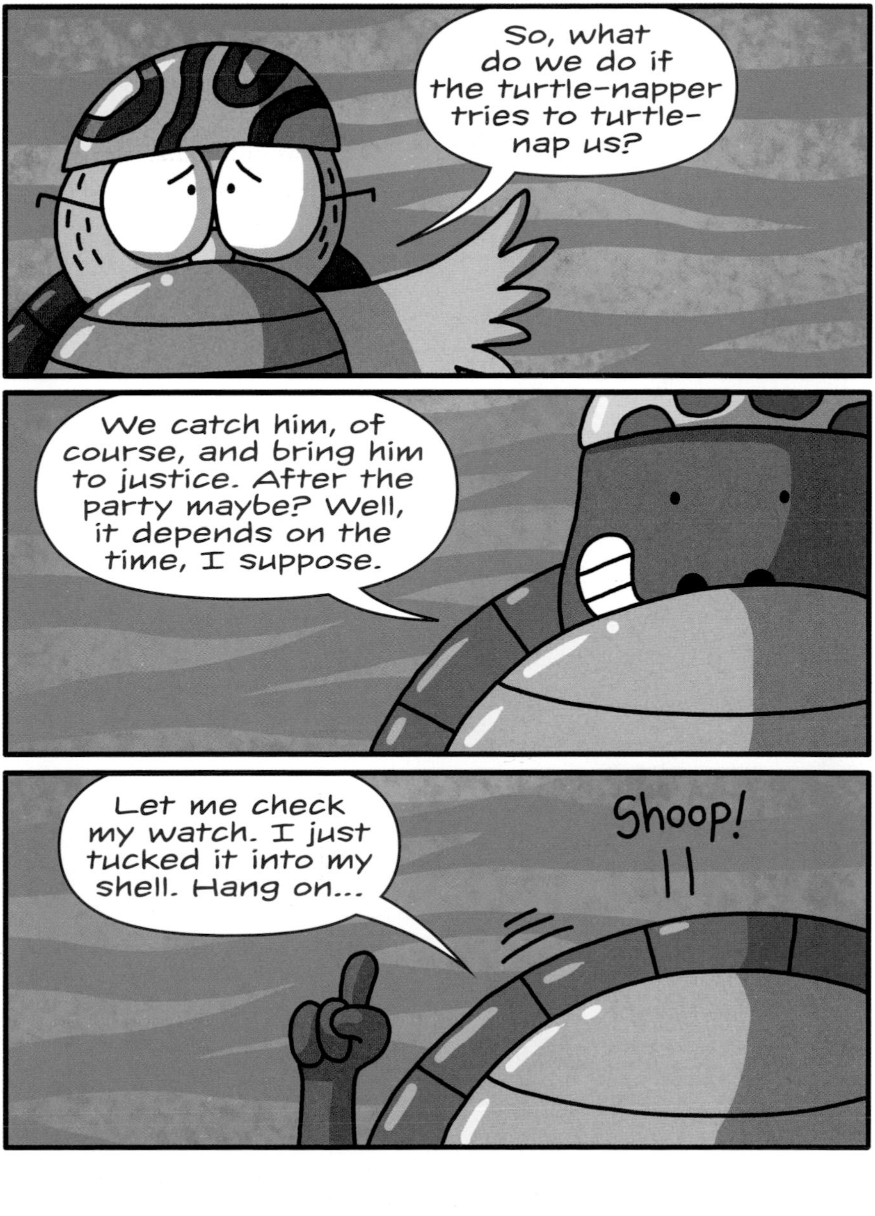
So, what do we do if the turtle-napper tries to turtle-nap us?
We catch him, of course, and bring him to justice. After the party maybe? Well, it depends on the time, I suppose.
Let me check my watch. I just tucked it into my shell. Hang on...
Shoop!

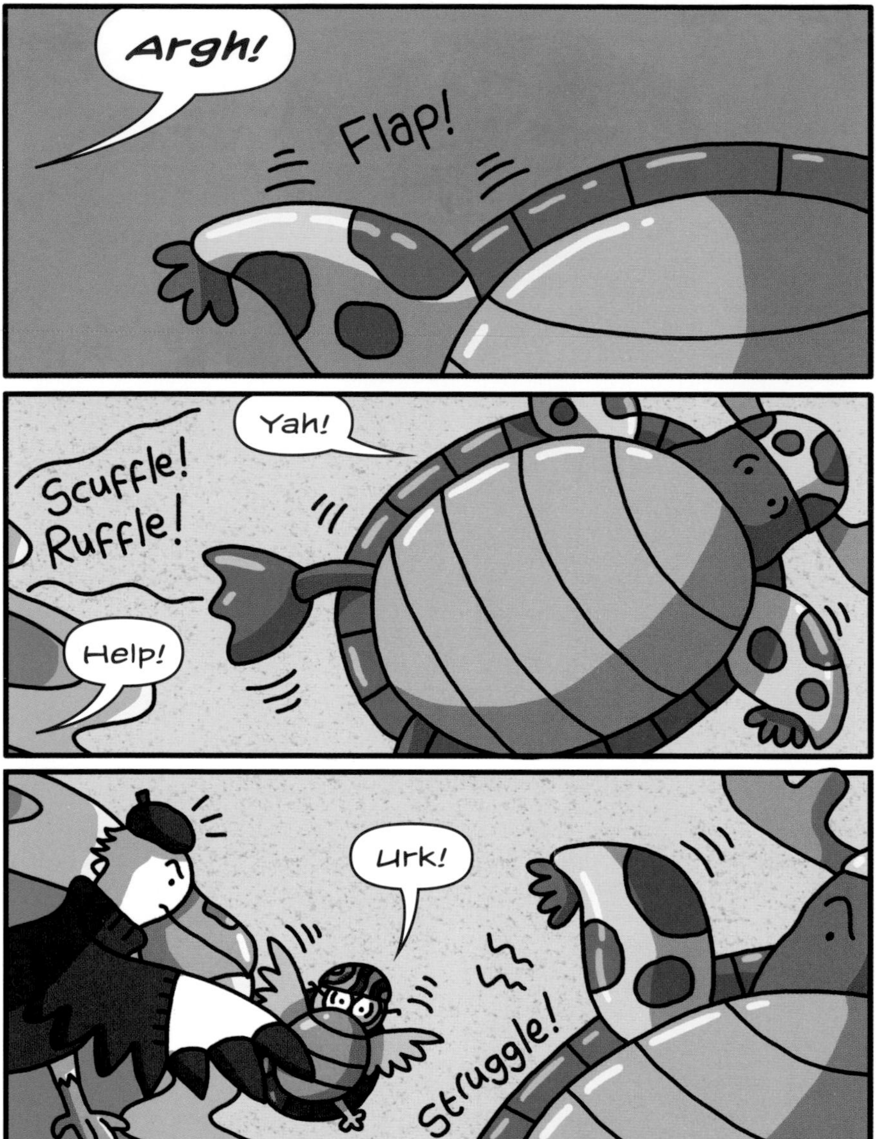
Argh!
Flap!
Yah!
Scuffle!
Ruffle!
Help!
Urk!
Struggle!

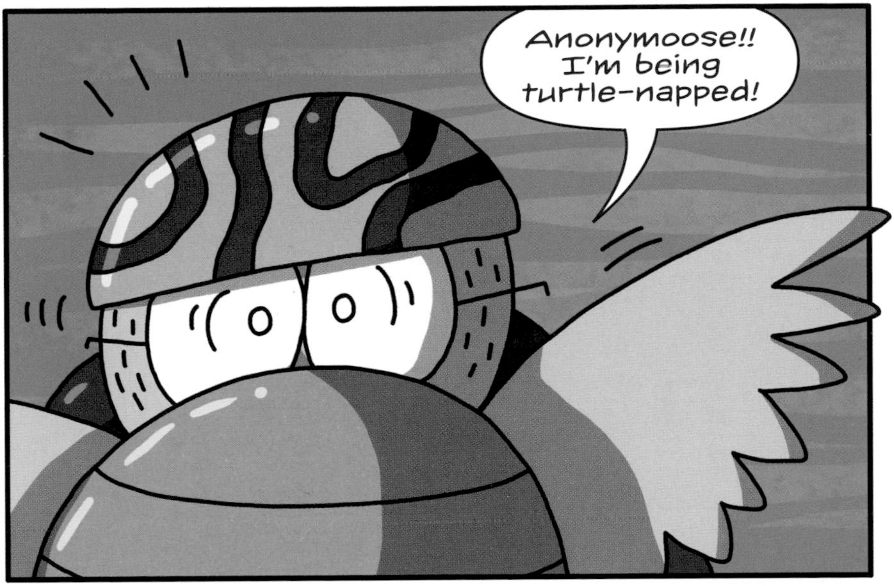
Anonymoose!! I'm being turtle-napped!

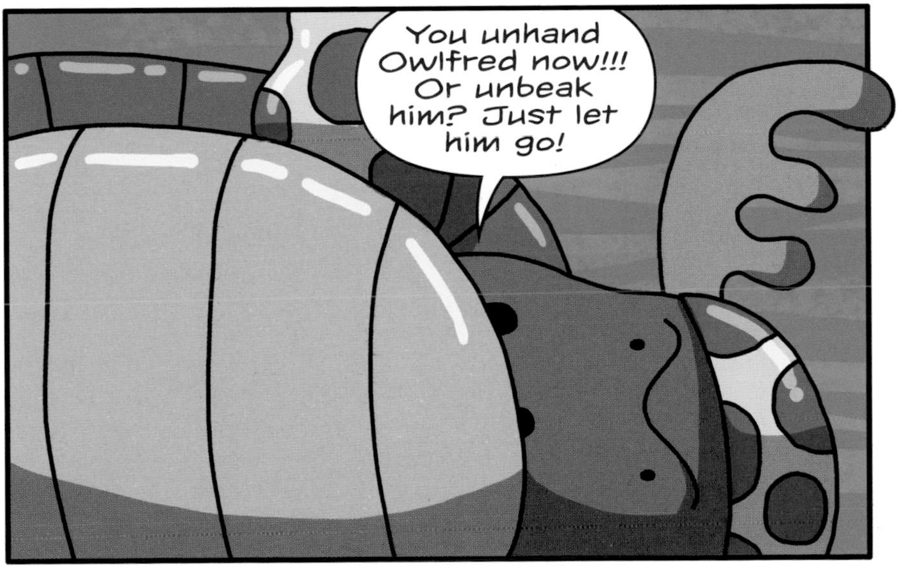
You unhand Owlfred now!!! Or unbeak him? Just let him go!

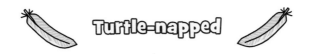

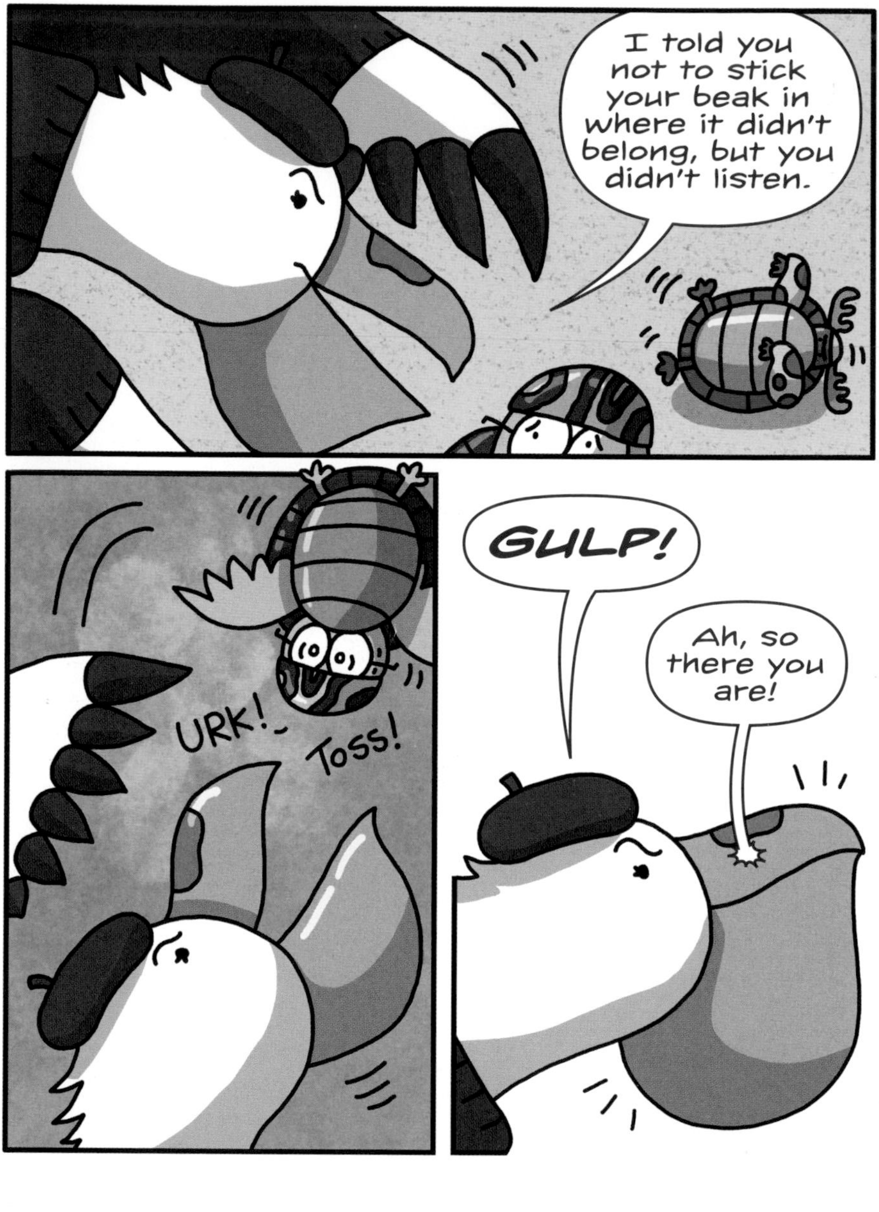
I told you not to stick your beak in where it didn't belong, but you didn't listen.
URK!
TOSS!
GULP!
Ah, so there you are!

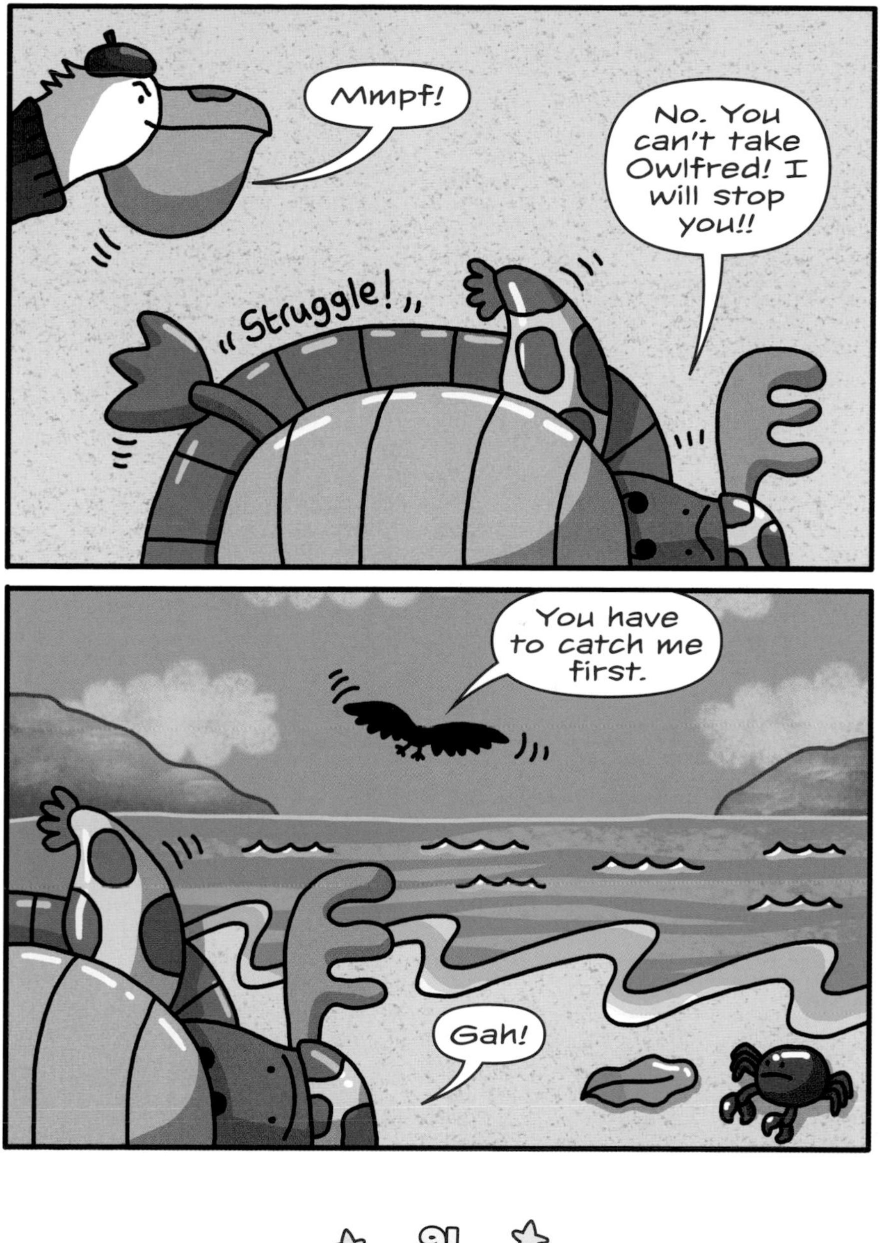
Mmpf!
No. You can't take Owlfred! I will stop you!!
"Struggle!"
You have to catch me first.
Gah!

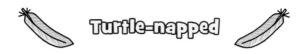

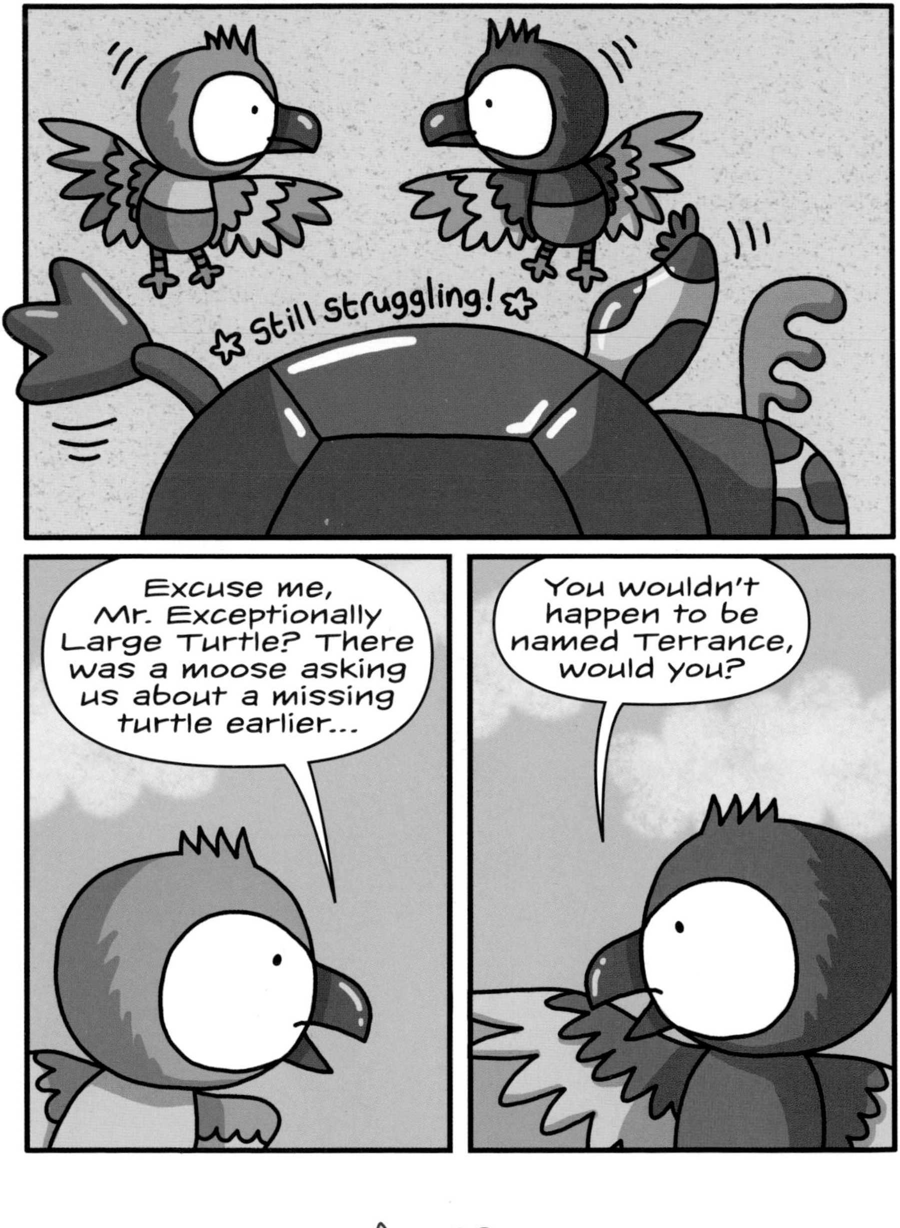
Still struggling!
Excuse me, Mr. Exceptionally Large Turtle? There was a moose asking us about a missing turtle earlier...
You wouldn't happen to be named Terrance, would you?

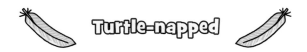

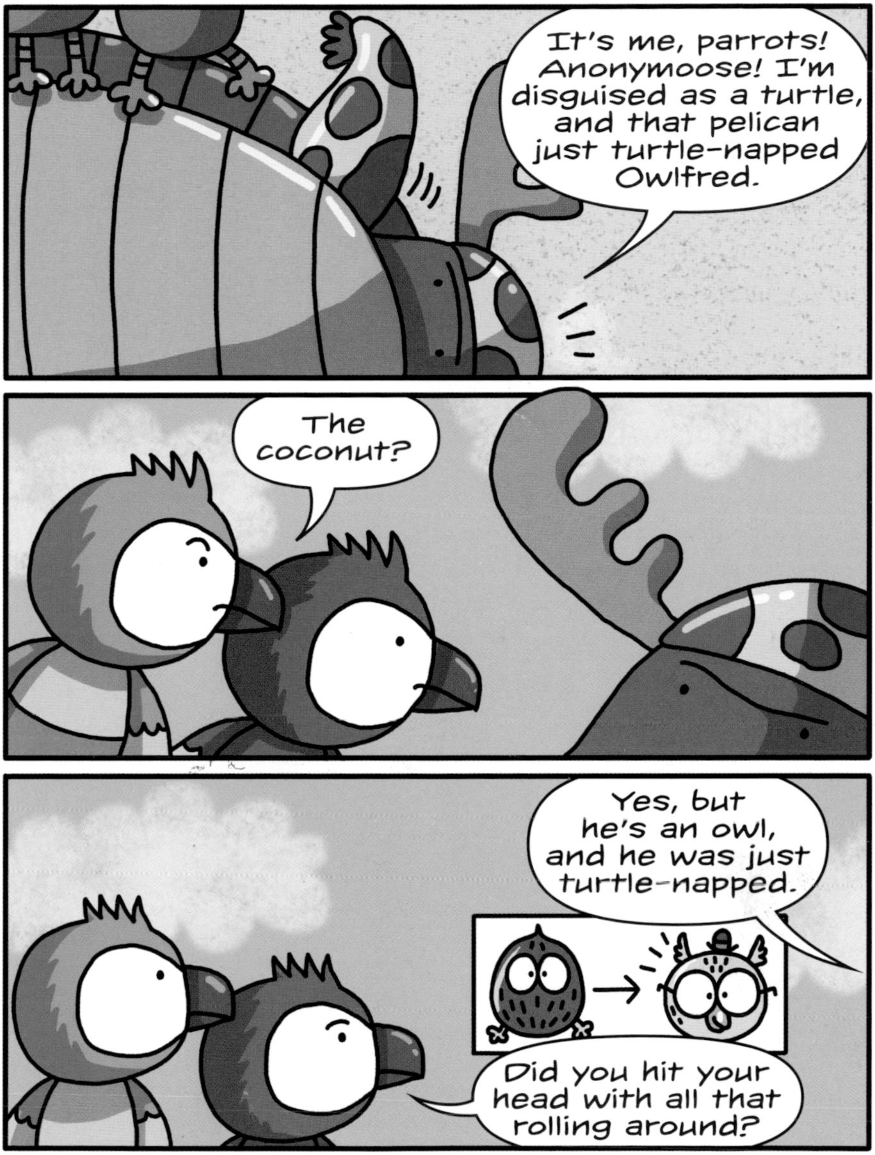
It's me, parrots! Anonymoose! I'm disguised as a turtle, and that pelican just turtle-napped Owlfred.
The coconut?
Yes, but he's an owl, and he was just turtle-napped.
Did you hit your head with all that rolling around?

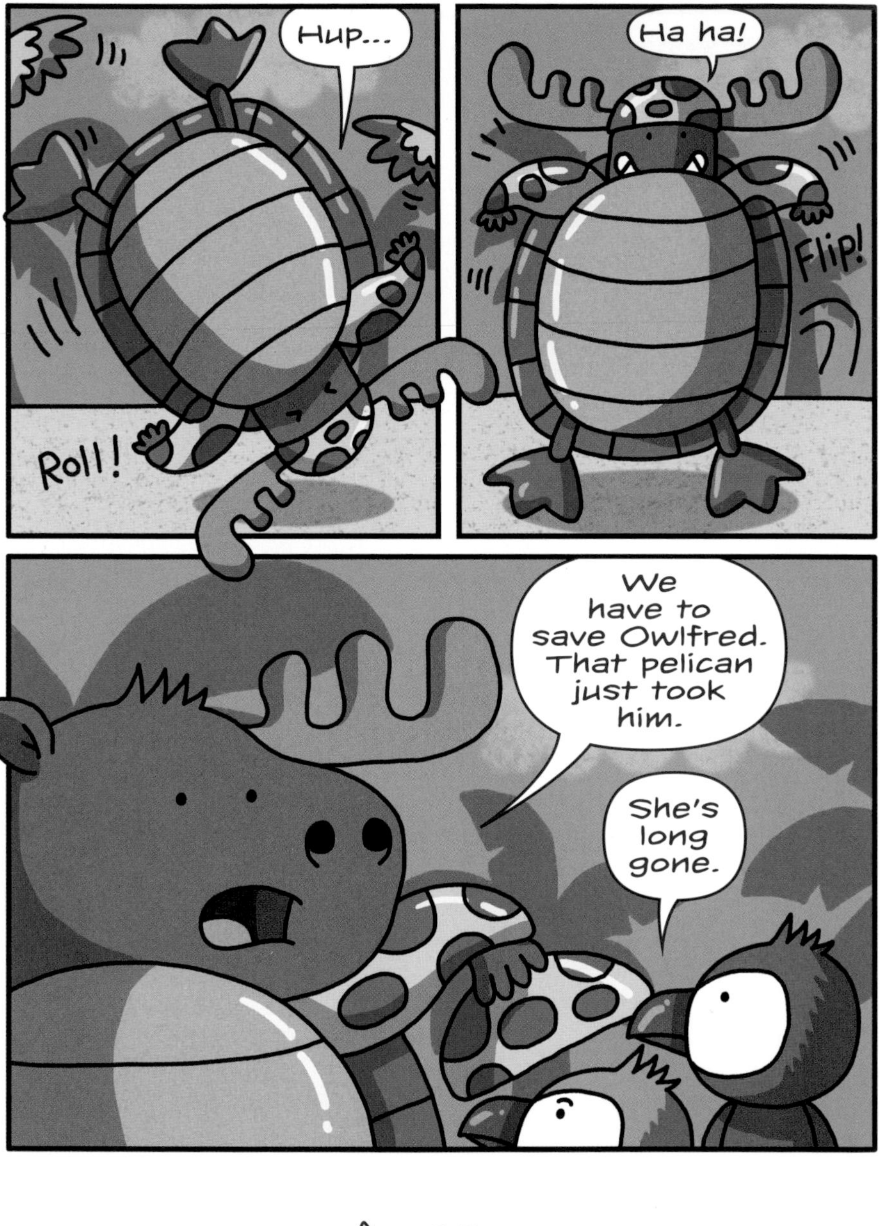
Hup...
Roll!
Ha ha!
Flip!
We have to save Owlfred. That pelican just took him.
She's long gone.

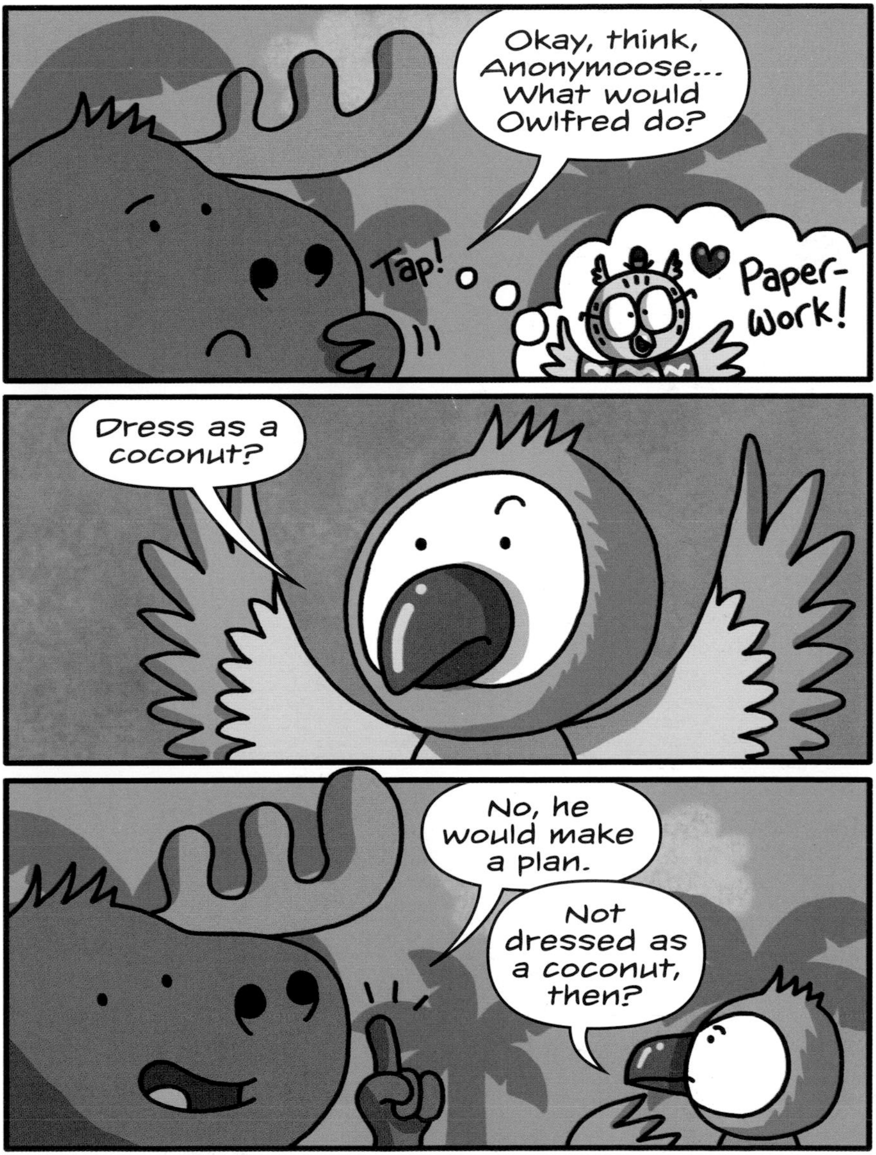
Okay, think, Anonymoose... What would Owlfred do?
Tap!
Paper-work!
Dress as a coconut?
No, he would make a plan.
Not dressed as a coconut, then?

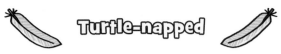

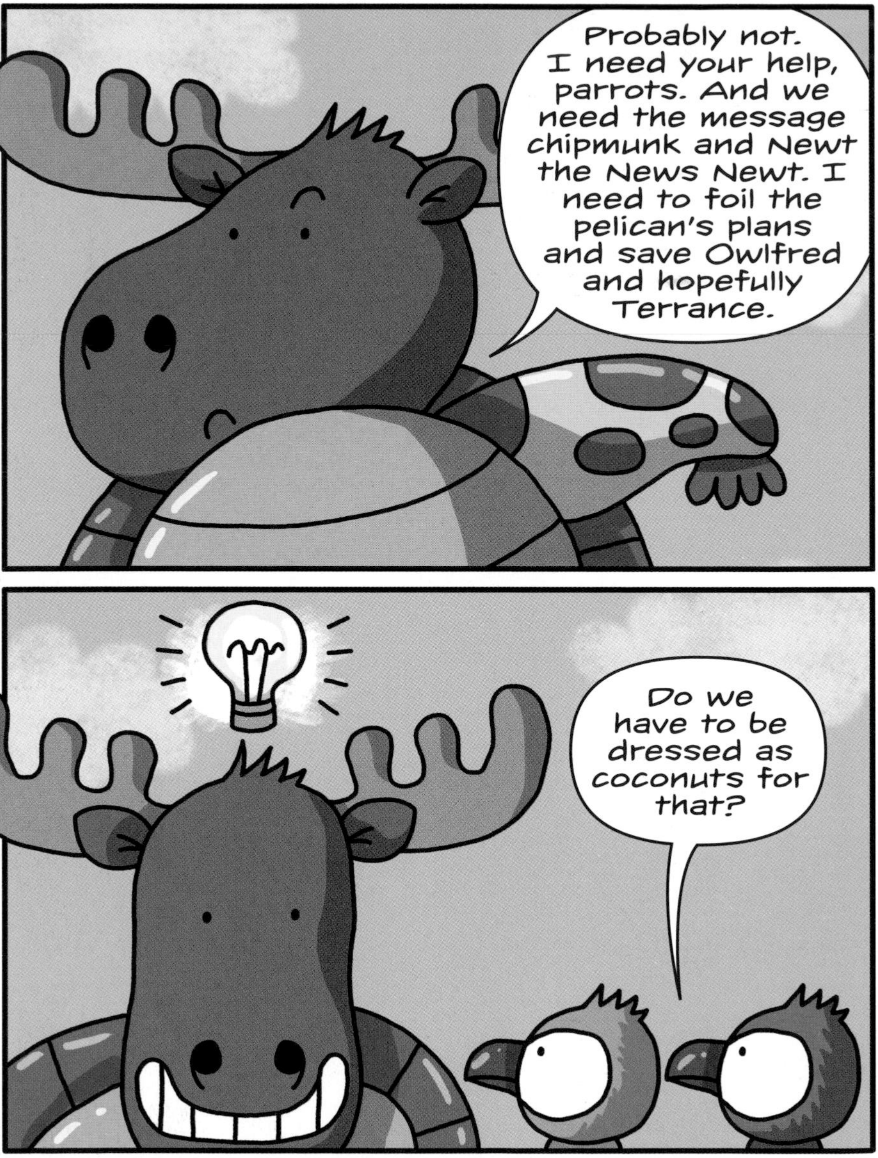
Probably not. I need your help, parrots. And we need the message chipmunk and Newt the News Newt. I need to foil the pelican's plans and save Owlfred and hopefully Terrance.
Do we have to be dressed as coconuts for that?

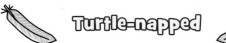

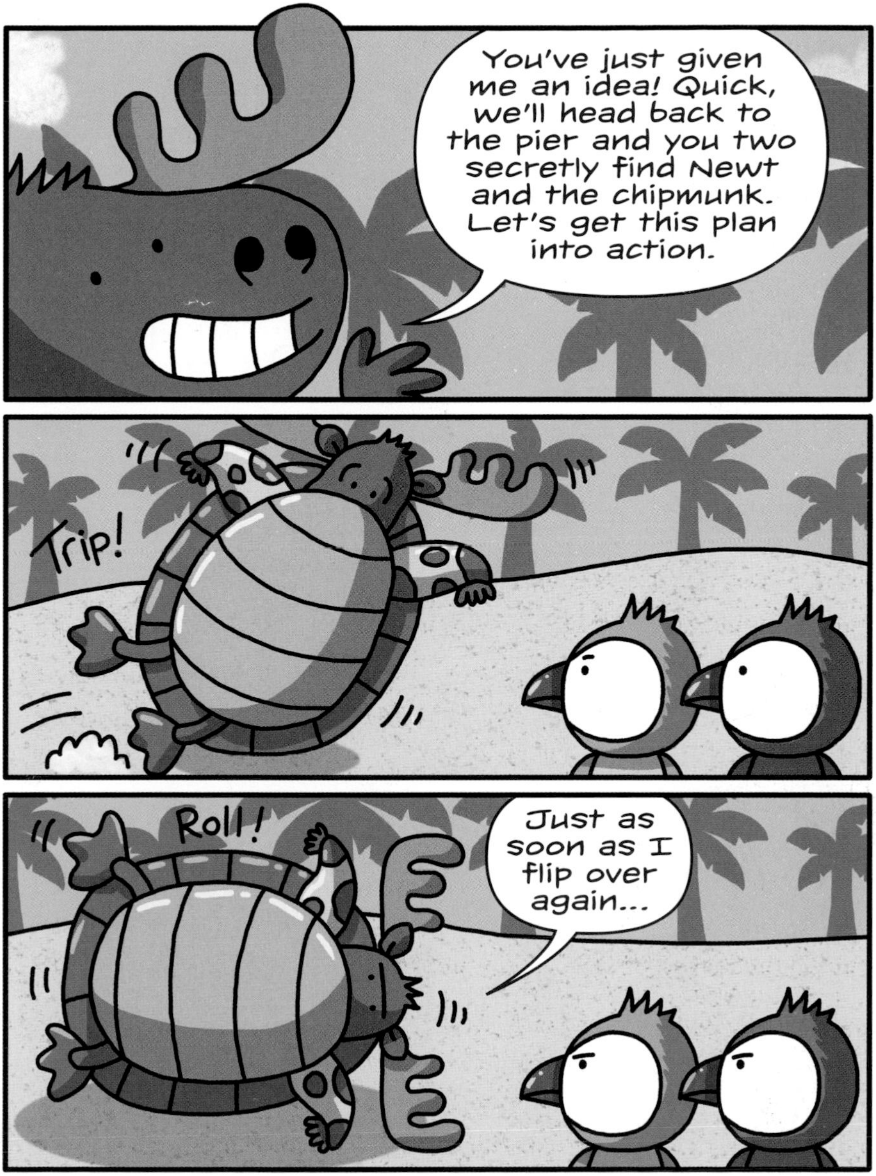
You've just given me an idea! Quick, we'll head back to the pier and you two secretly find Newt and the chipmunk. Let's get this plan into action.
Trip!
Roll!
Just as soon as I flip over again...

Chapter 8

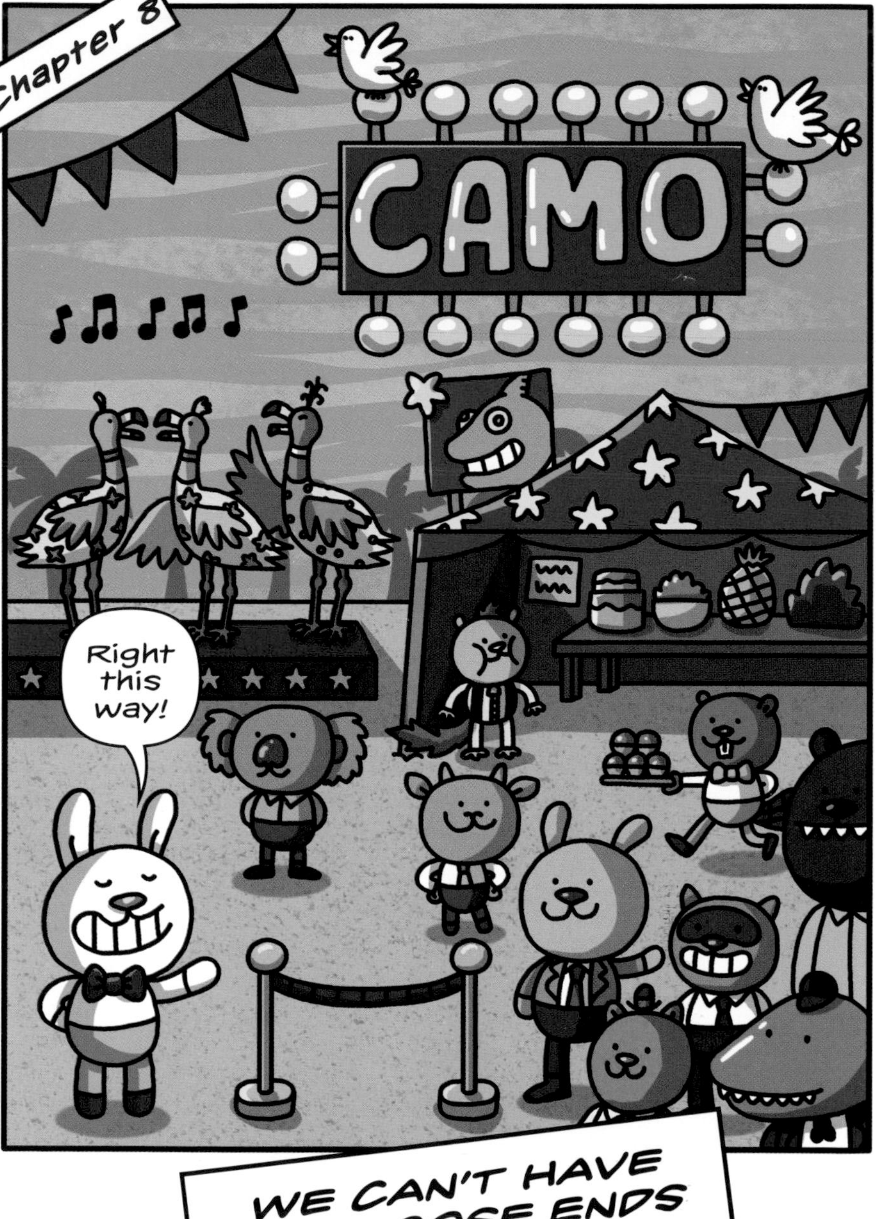
CAMO
Right this way!

WE CAN'T HAVE ANY LOOSE ENDS

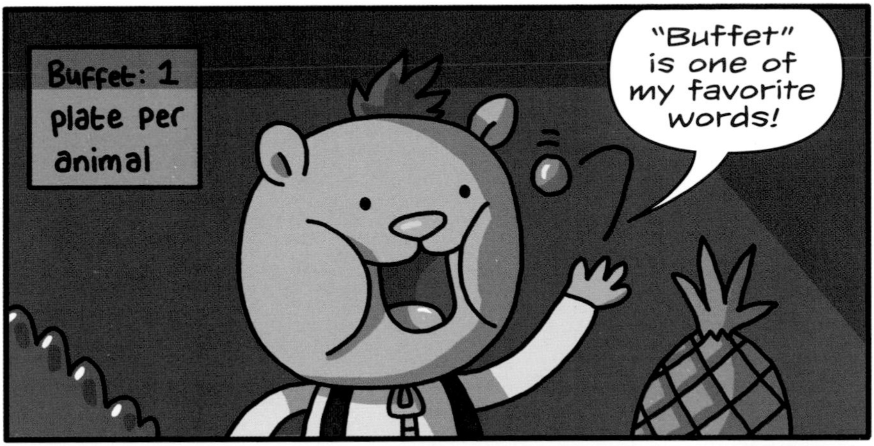
Buffet: 1 plate per animal
"Buffet" is one of my favorite words!

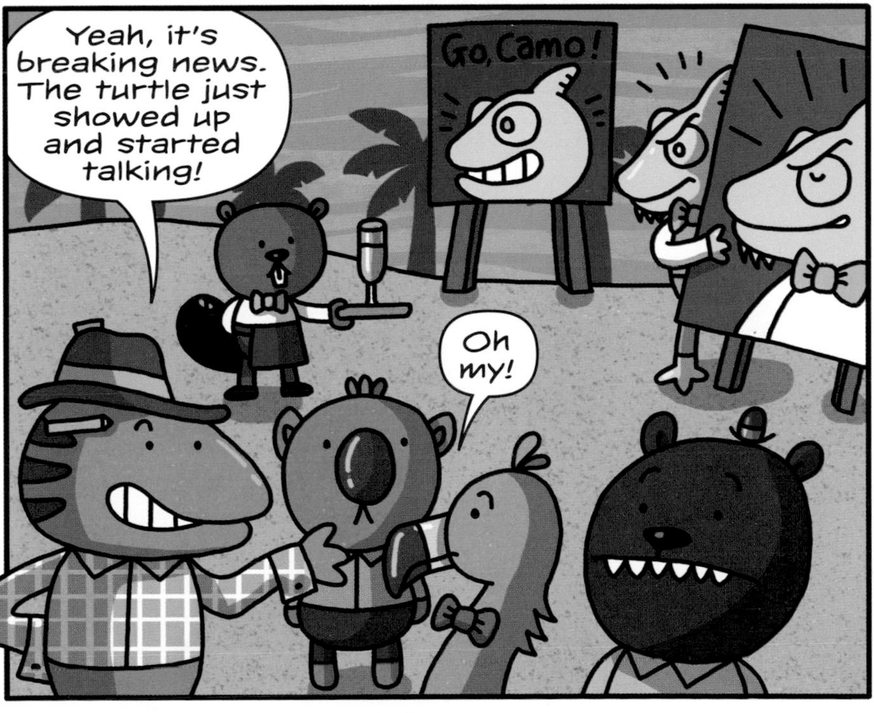
Yeah, it's breaking news. The turtle just showed up and started talking!
Go, Camo!
Oh my!

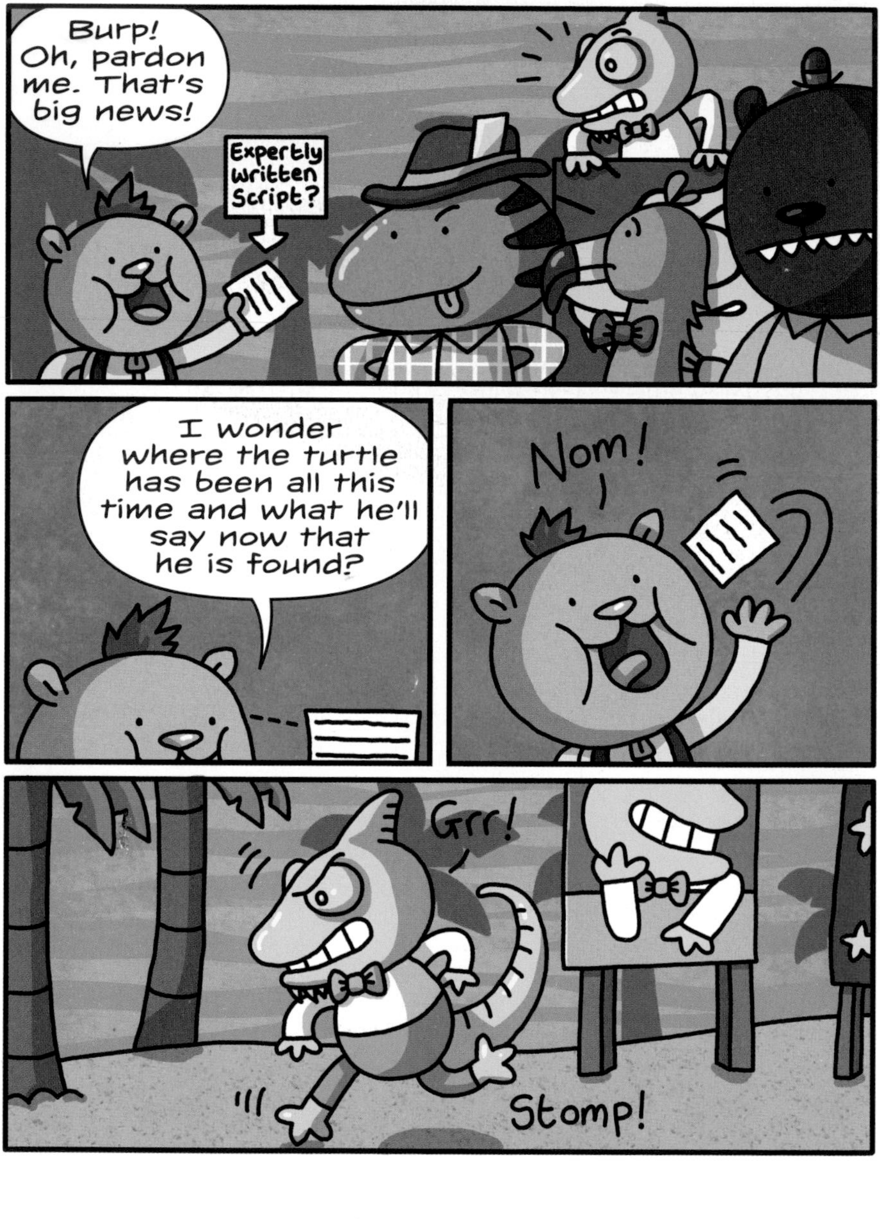
Burp! Oh, pardon me. That's big news!
Expertly written Script?
I wonder where the turtle has been all this time and what he'll say now that he is found?
Nom!
Grr!
Stomp!

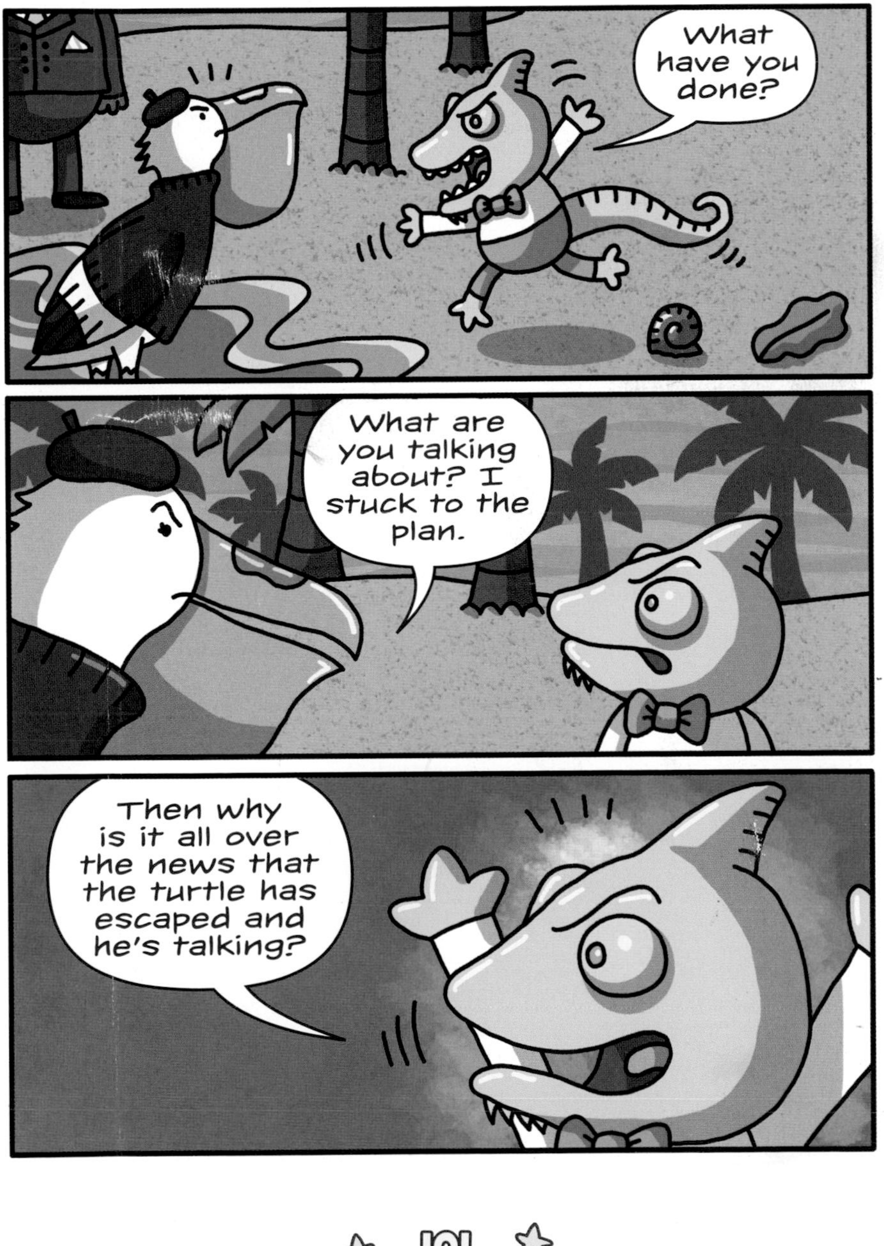
What have you done?
What are you talking about? I stuck to the plan.
Then why is it all over the news that the turtle has escaped and he's talking?

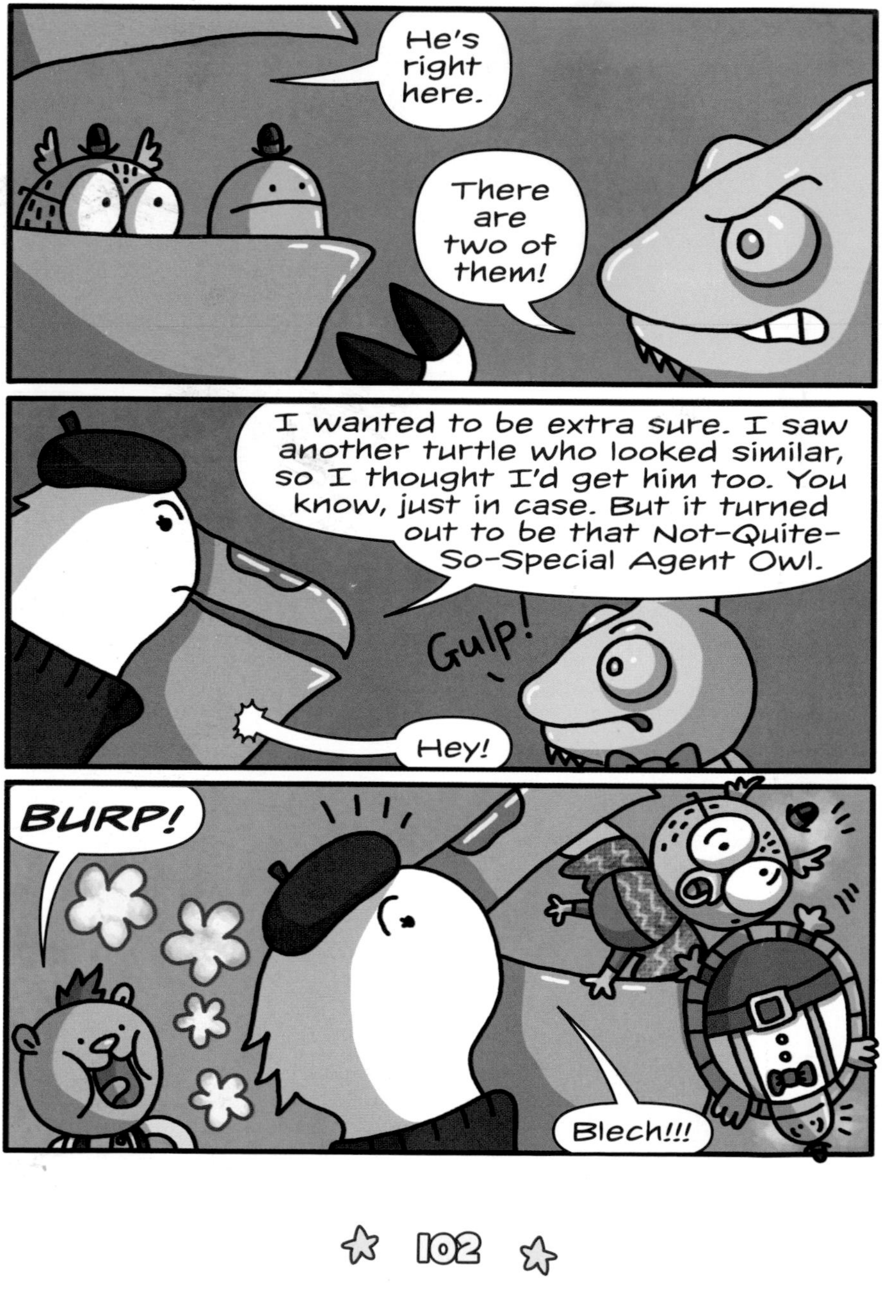
He's right here.
There are two of them!
I wanted to be extra sure. I saw another turtle who looked similar, so I thought I'd get him too. You know, just in case. But it turned out to be that Not-Quite-So-Special Agent Owl.
Gulp!
Hey!
BURP!
Blech!!!

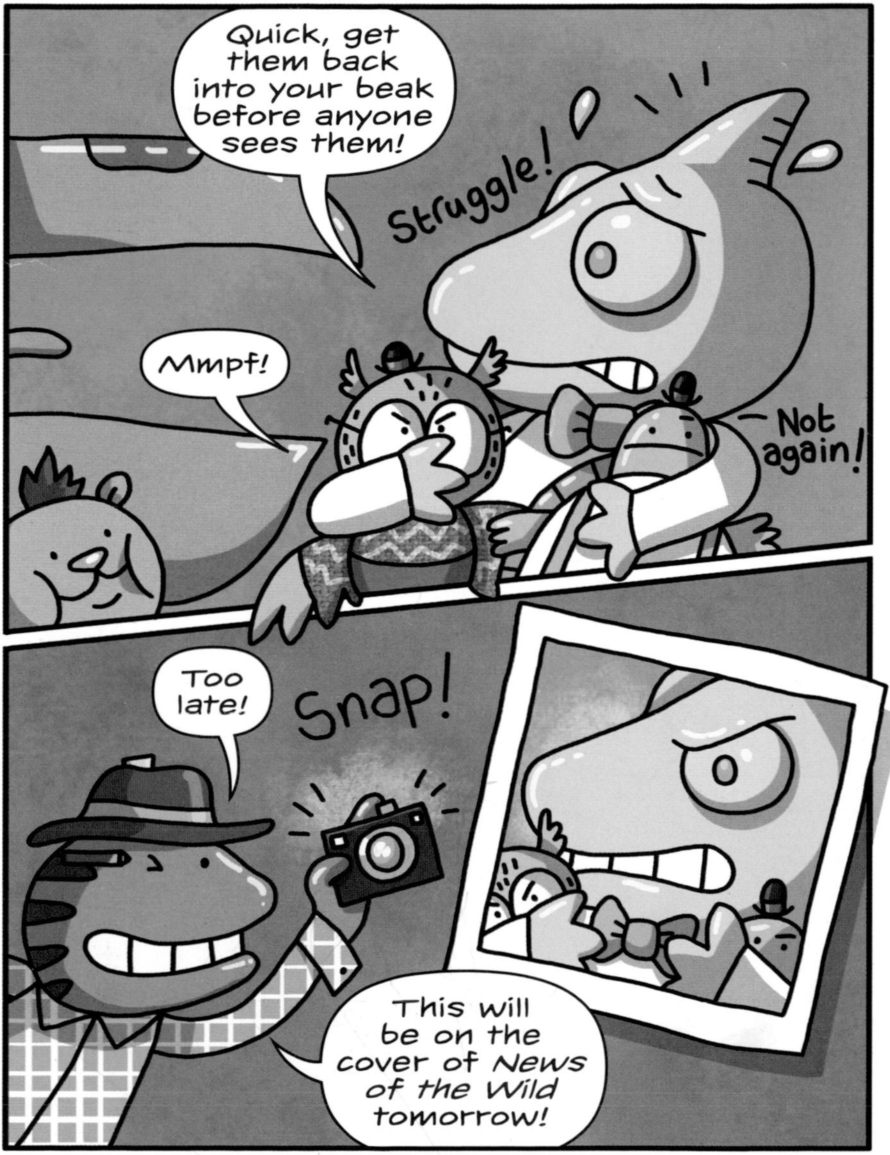
Quick, get them back into your beak before anyone sees them!
Struggle!
Mmpf!
Not again!
Too late!
Snap!
This will be on the cover of *News of the Wild* tomorrow!

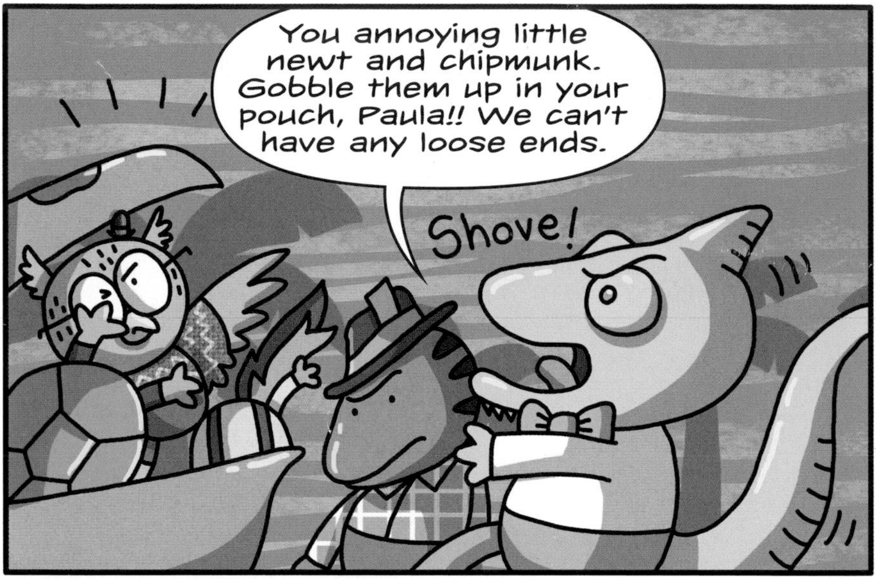
You annoying little newt and chipmunk. Gobble them up in your pouch, Paula!! We can't have any loose ends.
Shove!

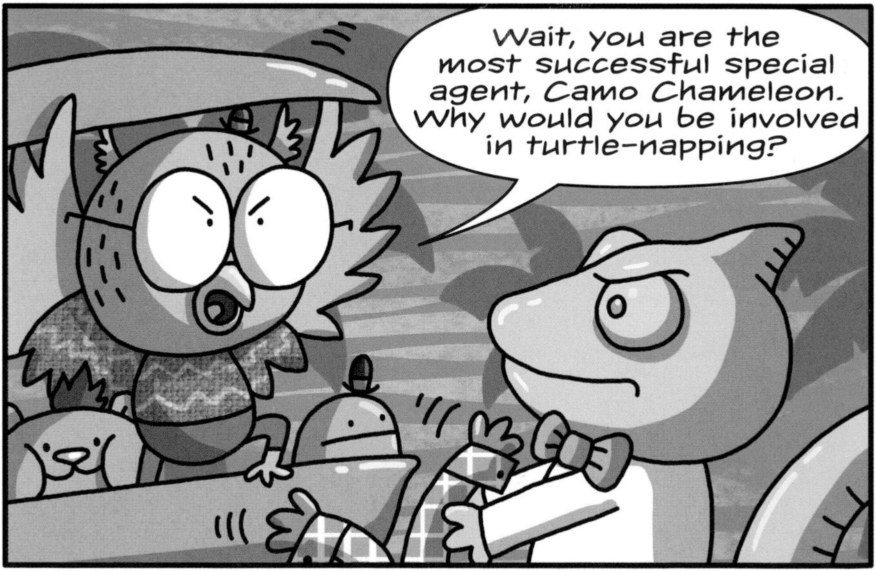
Wait, you are the most successful special agent, Camo Chameleon. Why would you be involved in turtle-napping?

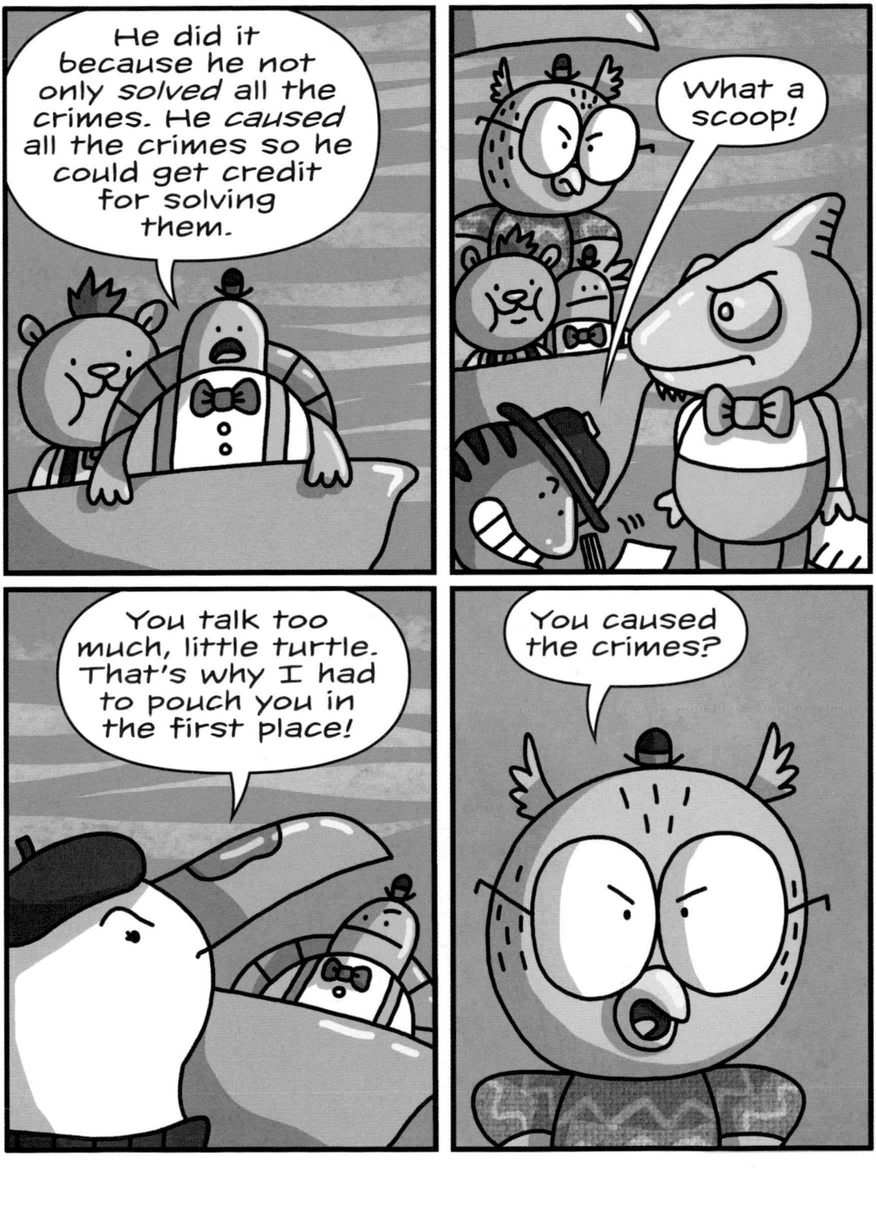
He did it because he not only *solved* all the crimes. He *caused* all the crimes so he could get credit for solving them.
What a scoop!
You talk too much, little turtle. That's why I had to pouch you in the first place!
You caused the crimes?

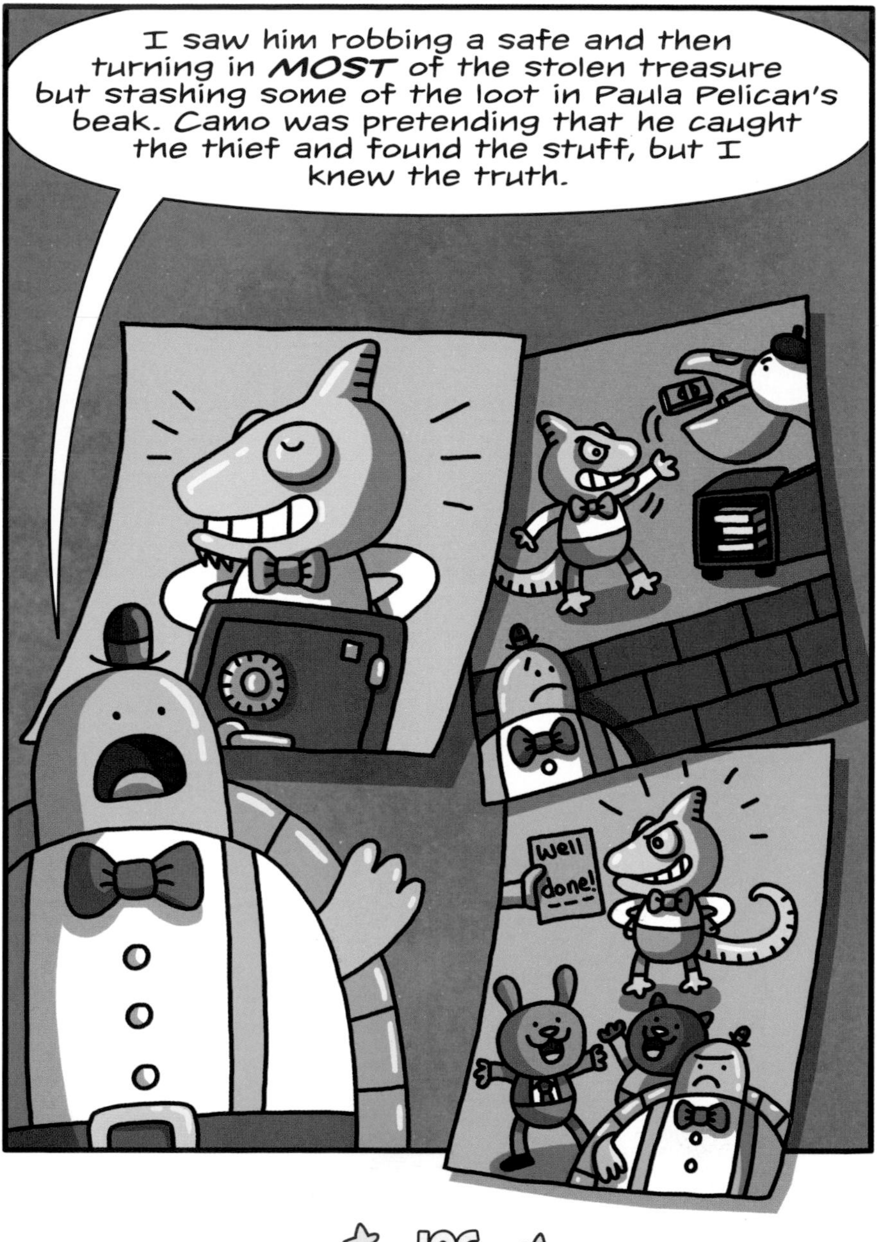
I saw him robbing a safe and then turning in MOST of the stolen treasure but stashing some of the loot in Paula Pelican's beak. Camo was pretending that he caught the thief and found the stuff, but I knew the truth.
Well done!

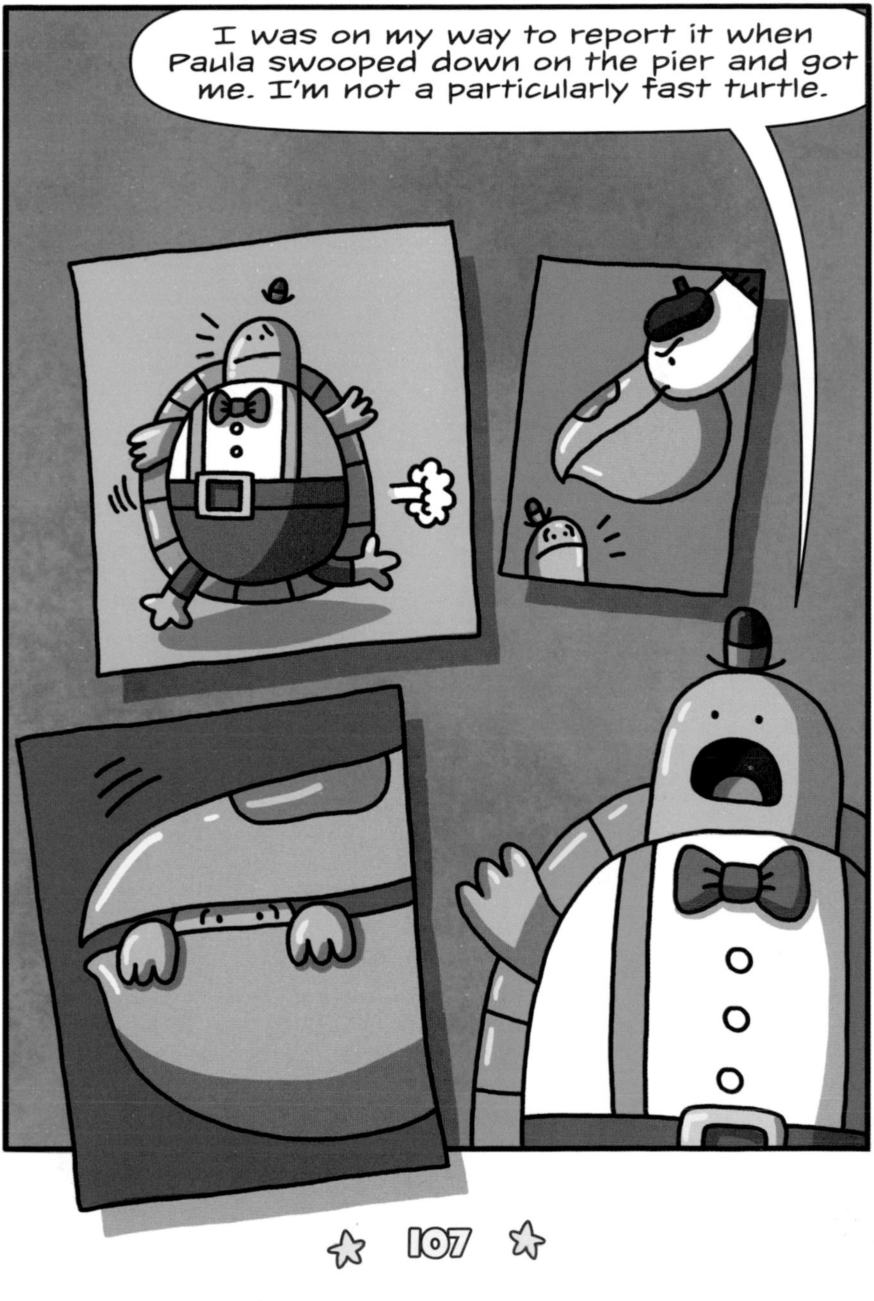
I was on my way to report it when Paula swooped down on the pier and got me. I'm not a particularly fast turtle.

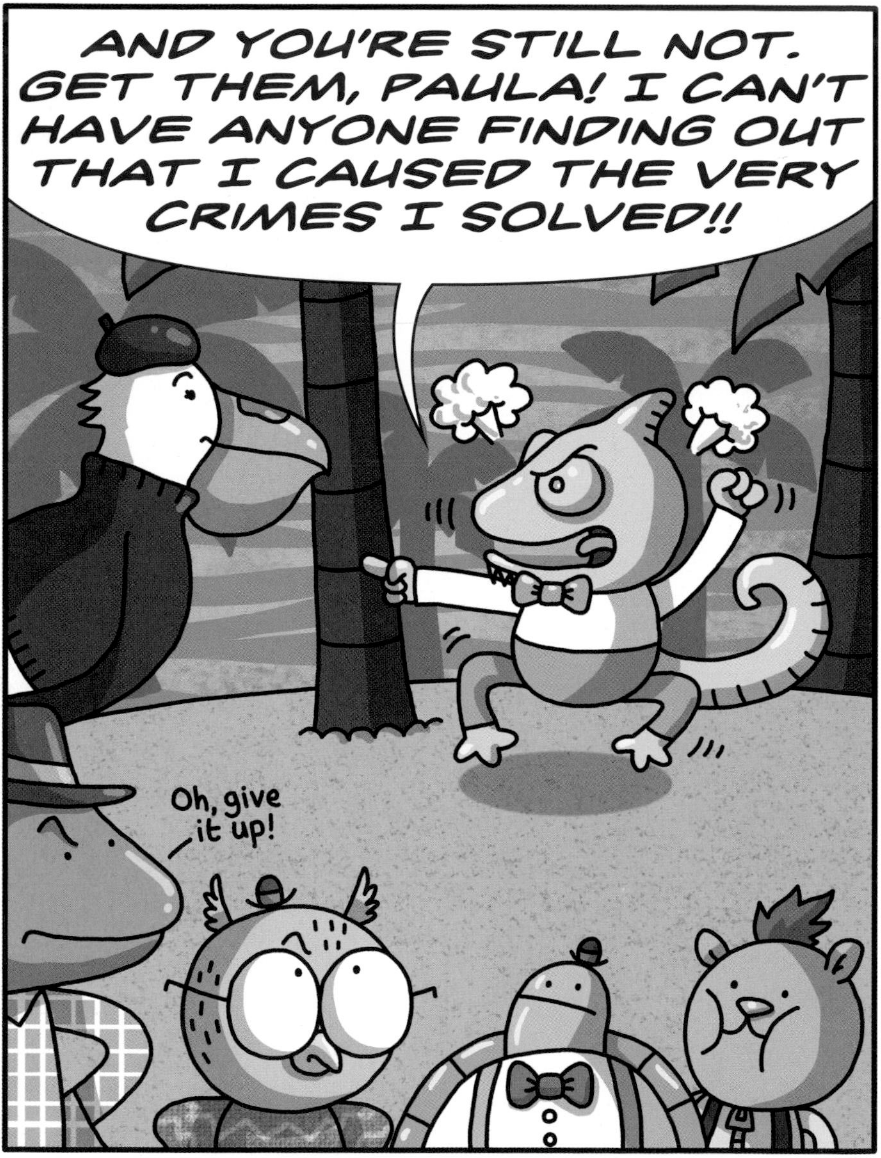
AND YOU'RE STILL NOT. GET THEM, PAULA! I CAN'T HAVE ANYONE FINDING OUT THAT I CAUSED THE VERY CRIMES I SOLVED!!
Oh, give it up!

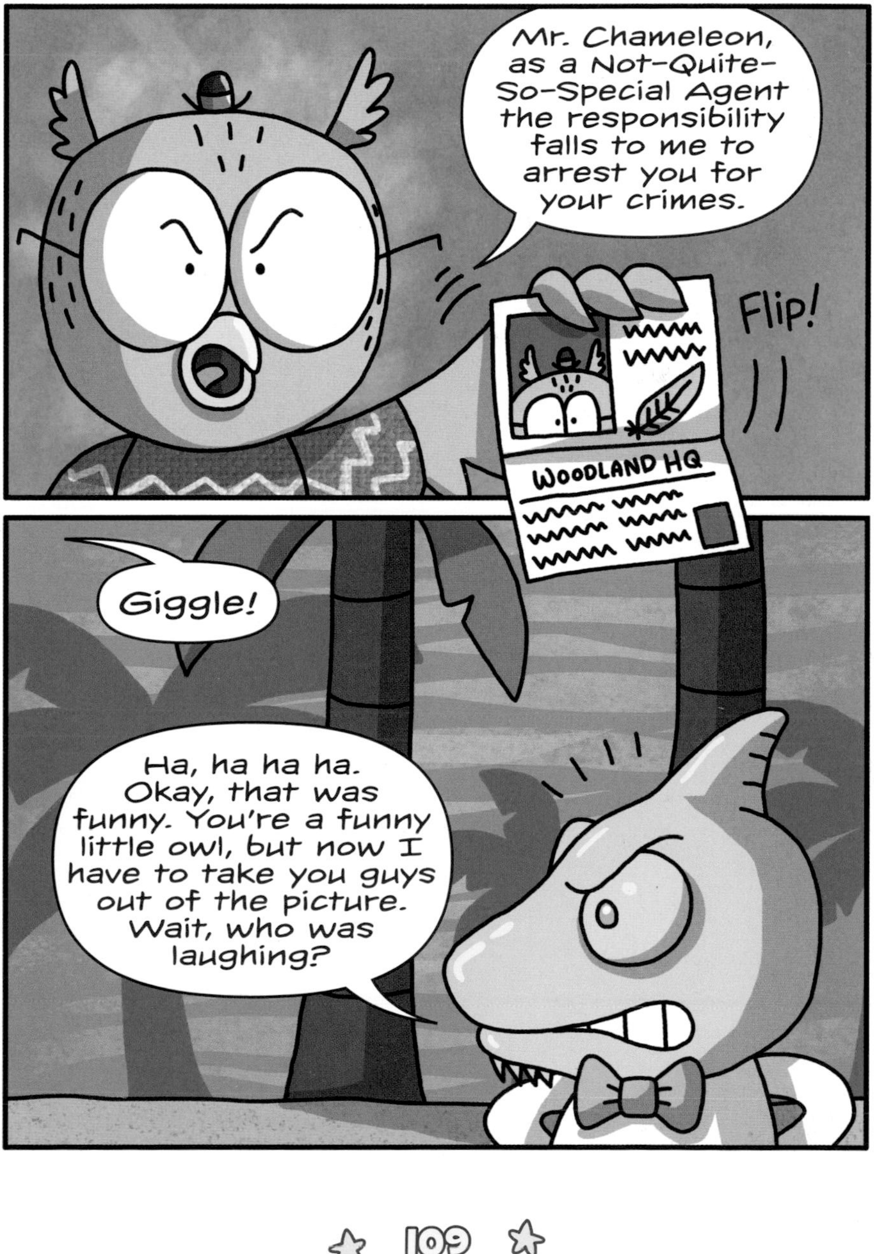
Mr. Chameleon, as a Not-Quite-So-Special Agent the responsibility falls to me to arrest you for your crimes.
Flip!
WOODLAND HQ
Giggle!
Ha, ha ha ha. Okay, that was funny. You're a funny little owl, but now I have to take you guys out of the picture. Wait, who was laughing?

Chapter 9

THE MOOSE WITH THE MOST

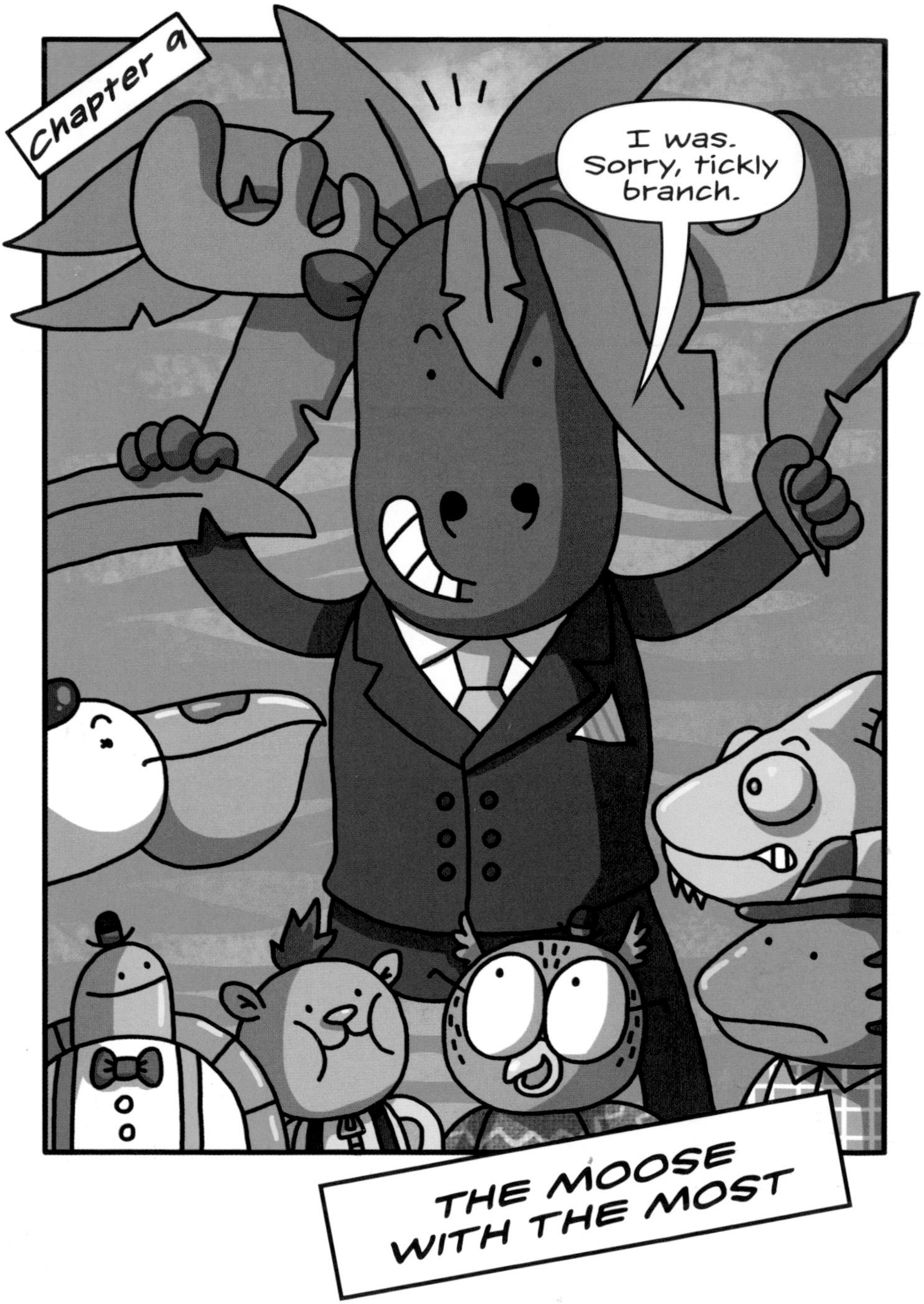
I was.
Sorry, tickly
branch.

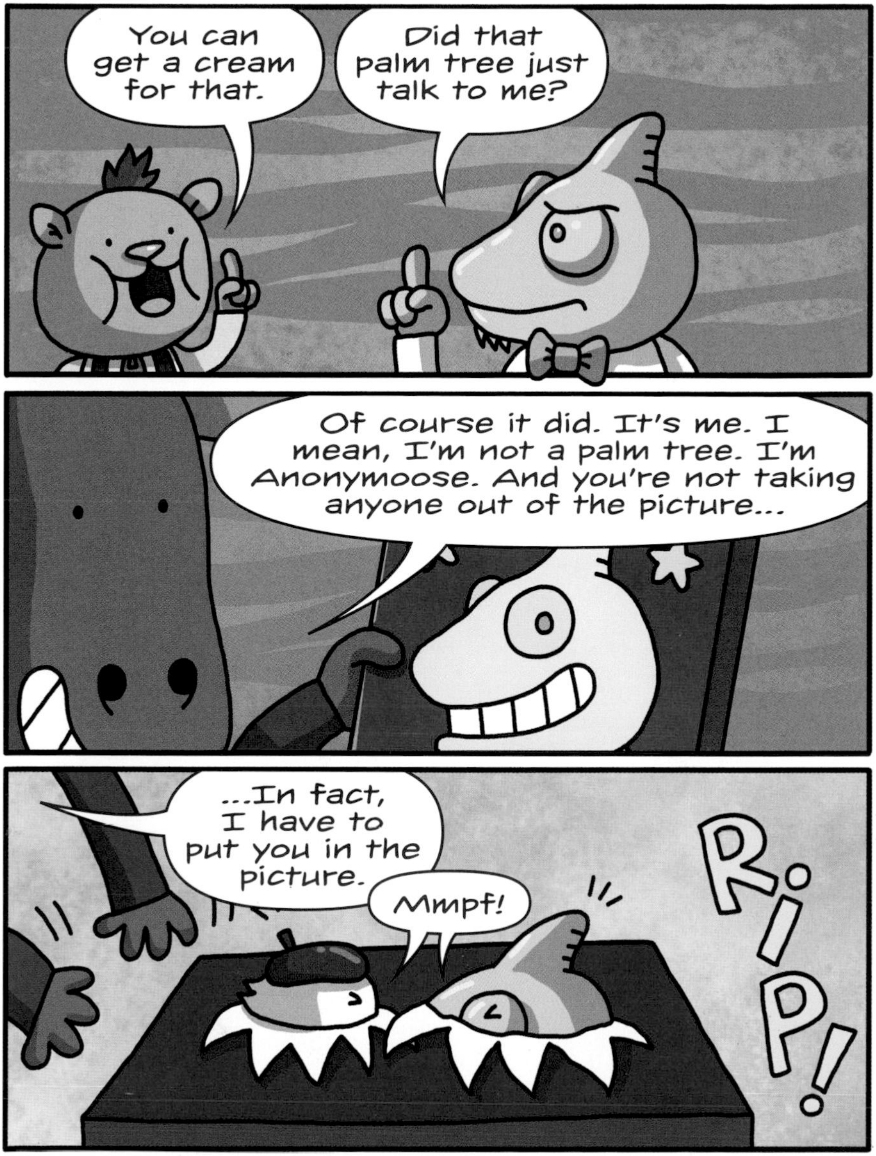
You can get a cream for that.
Did that palm tree just talk to me?
Of course it did. It's me. I mean, I'm not a palm tree. I'm Anonymoose. And you're not taking anyone out of the picture...
...In fact, I have to put you in the picture.
Mmpf!
RIP!

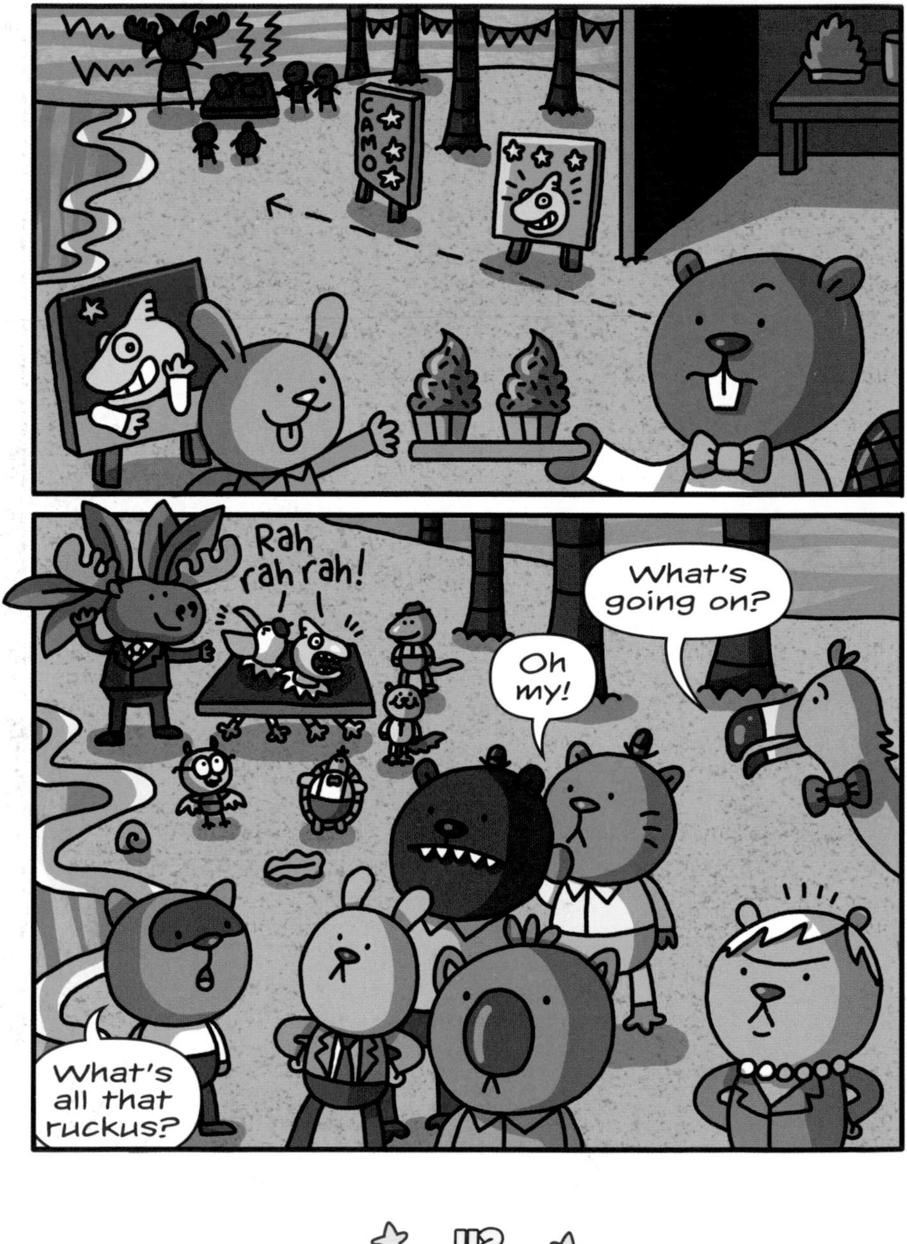
CAMO
Rah rah rah!
What's going on?
Oh my!
What's all that ruckus?

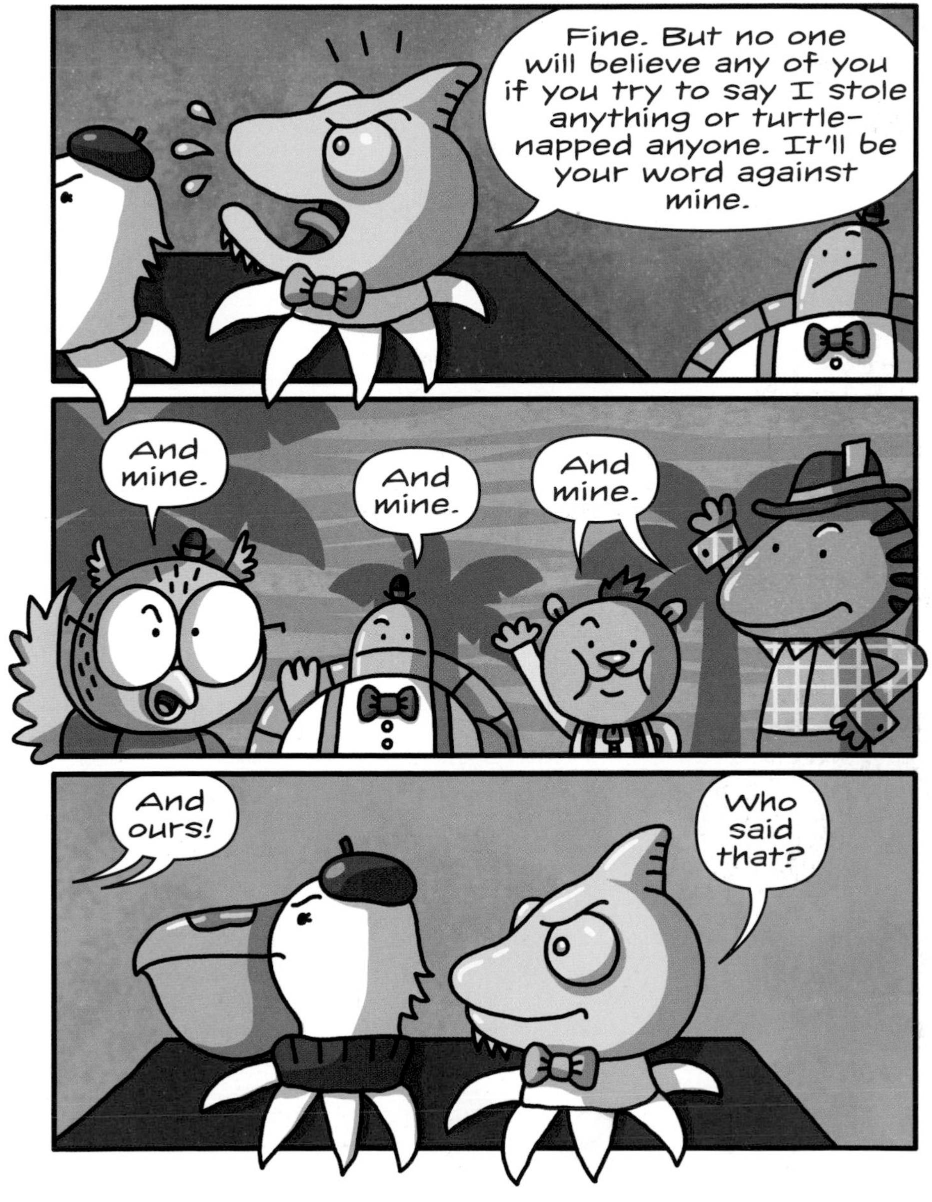
Fine. But no one will believe any of you if you try to say I stole anything or turtle-napped anyone. It'll be your word against mine.
And mine.
And mine.
And mine.
And ours!
Who said that?

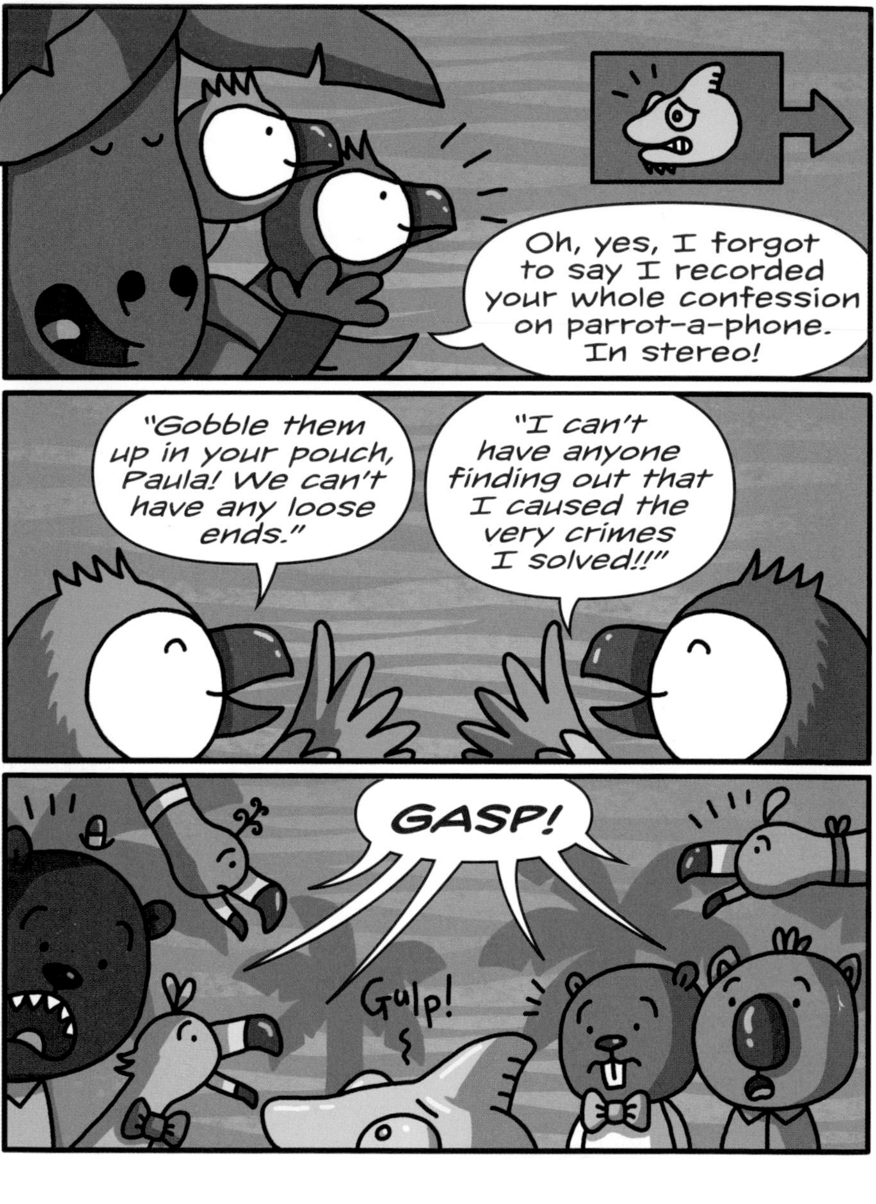
Oh, yes, I forgot to say I recorded your whole confession on parrot-a-phone. In stereo!
"Gobble them up in your pouch, Paula! We can't have any loose ends."
"I can't have anyone finding out that I caused the very crimes I solved!!"
GASP!
Gulp!

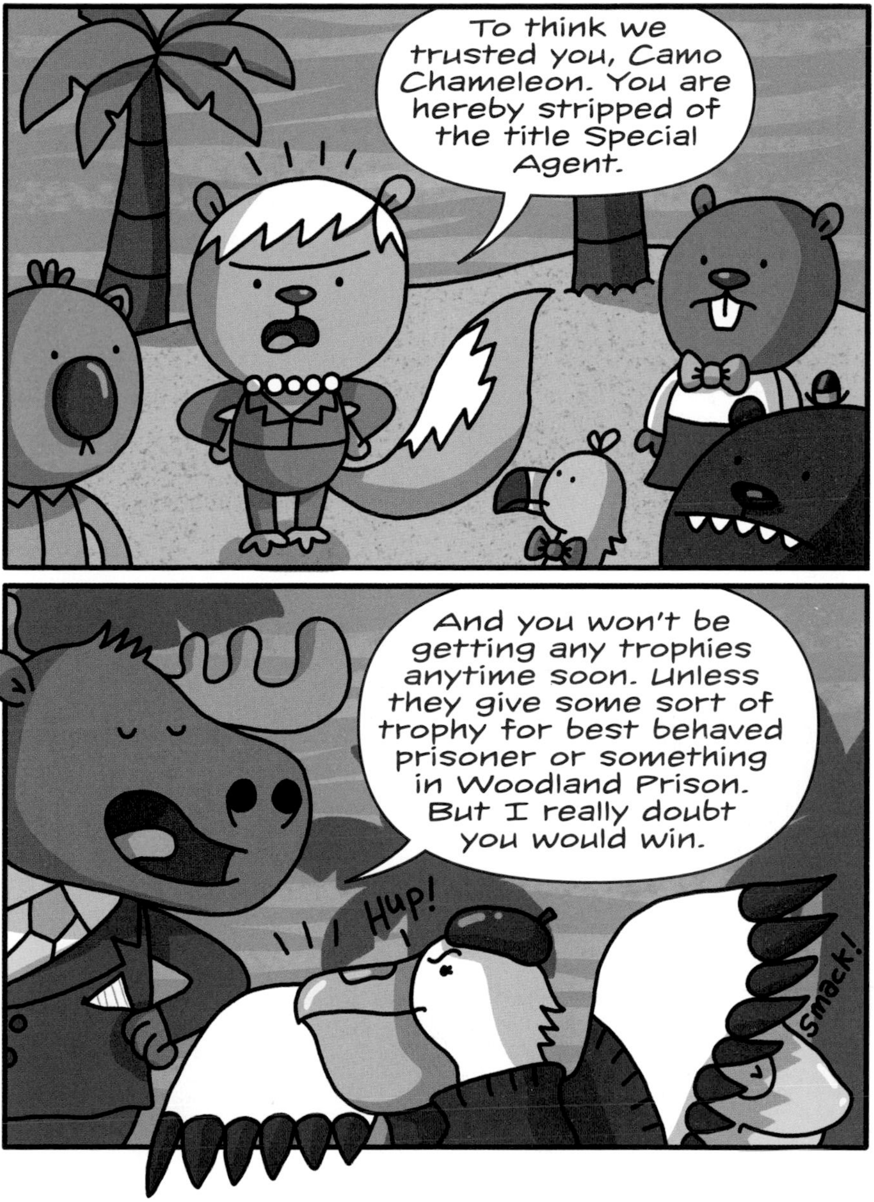
To think we trusted you, Camo Chameleon. You are hereby stripped of the title Special Agent.
And you won't be getting any trophies anytime soon. Unless they give some sort of trophy for best behaved prisoner or something in Woodland Prison. But I really doubt you would win.
Hup!
Smack!

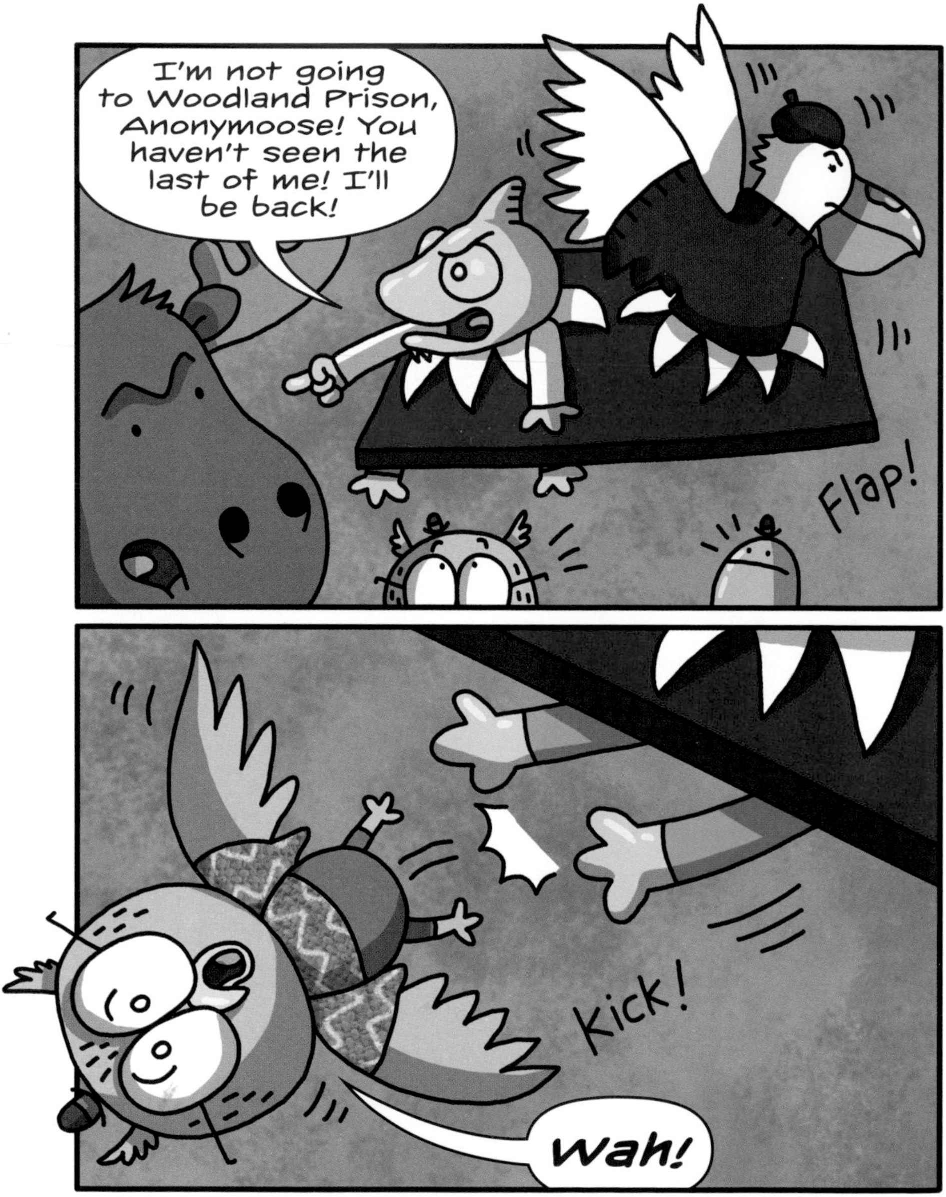
I'm not going to Woodland Prison, Anonymoose! You haven't seen the last of me! I'll be back!
Flap!
Kick!
Wah!

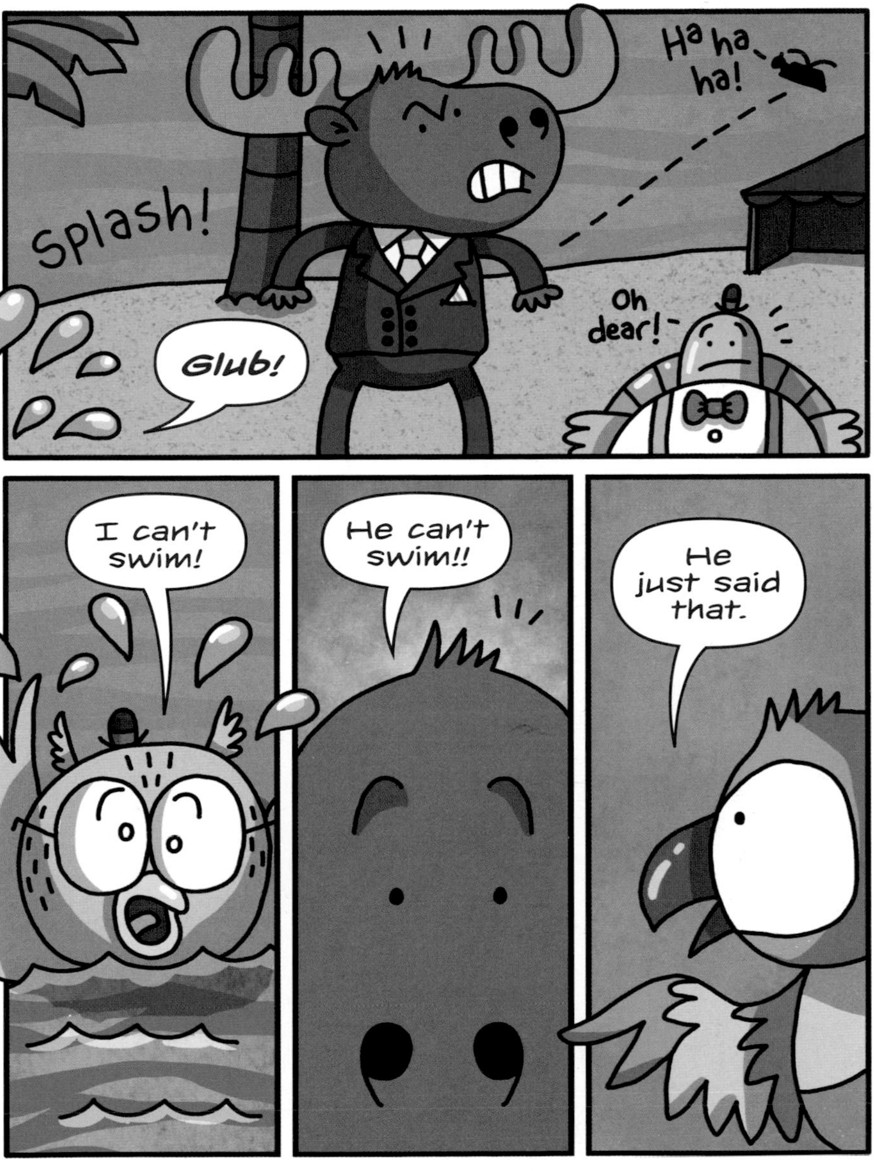
Ha ha ha!
Splash!
Oh dear!
Glub!
I can't swim!
He can't swim!!
He just said that.

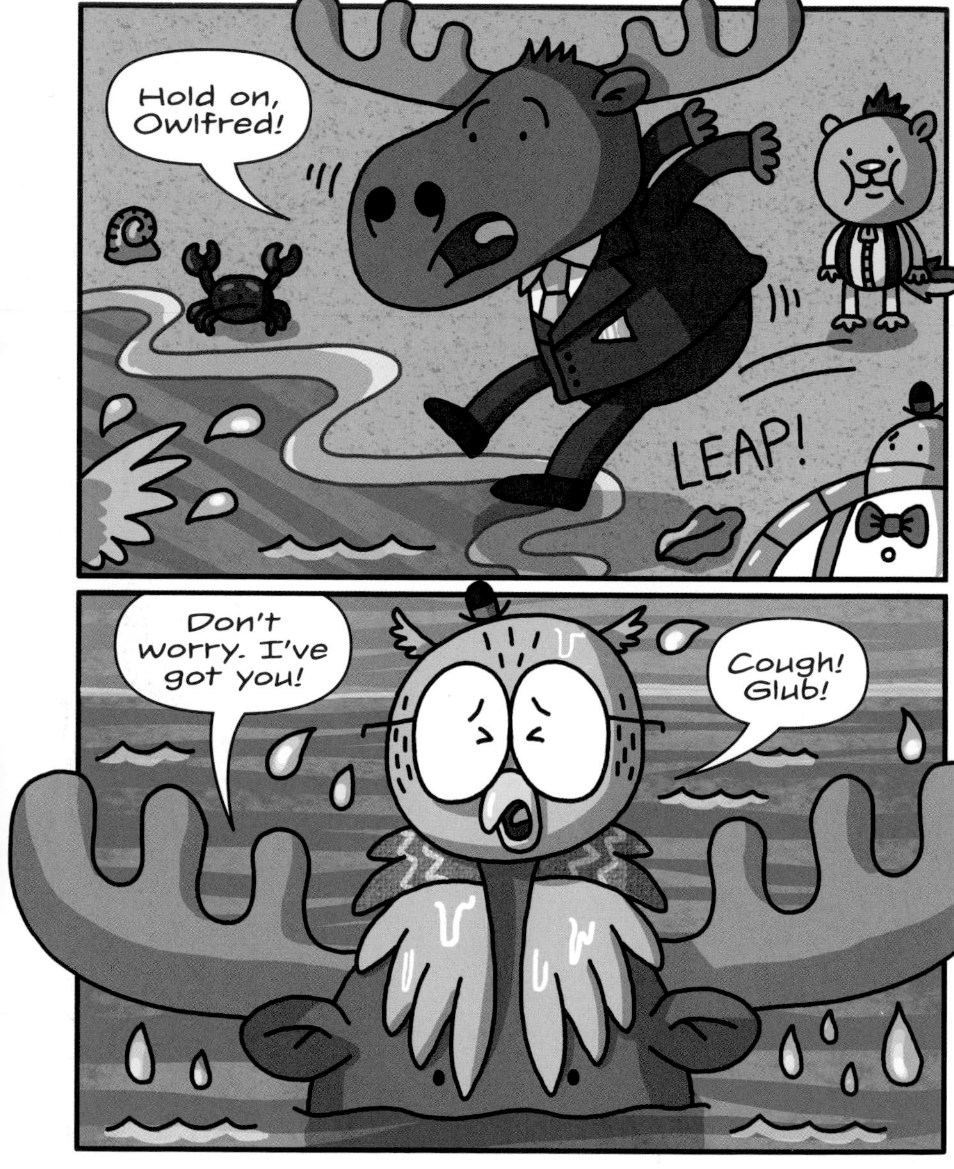
Hold on, Owlfred!
LEAP!
Don't worry. I've got you!
Cough! Glub!

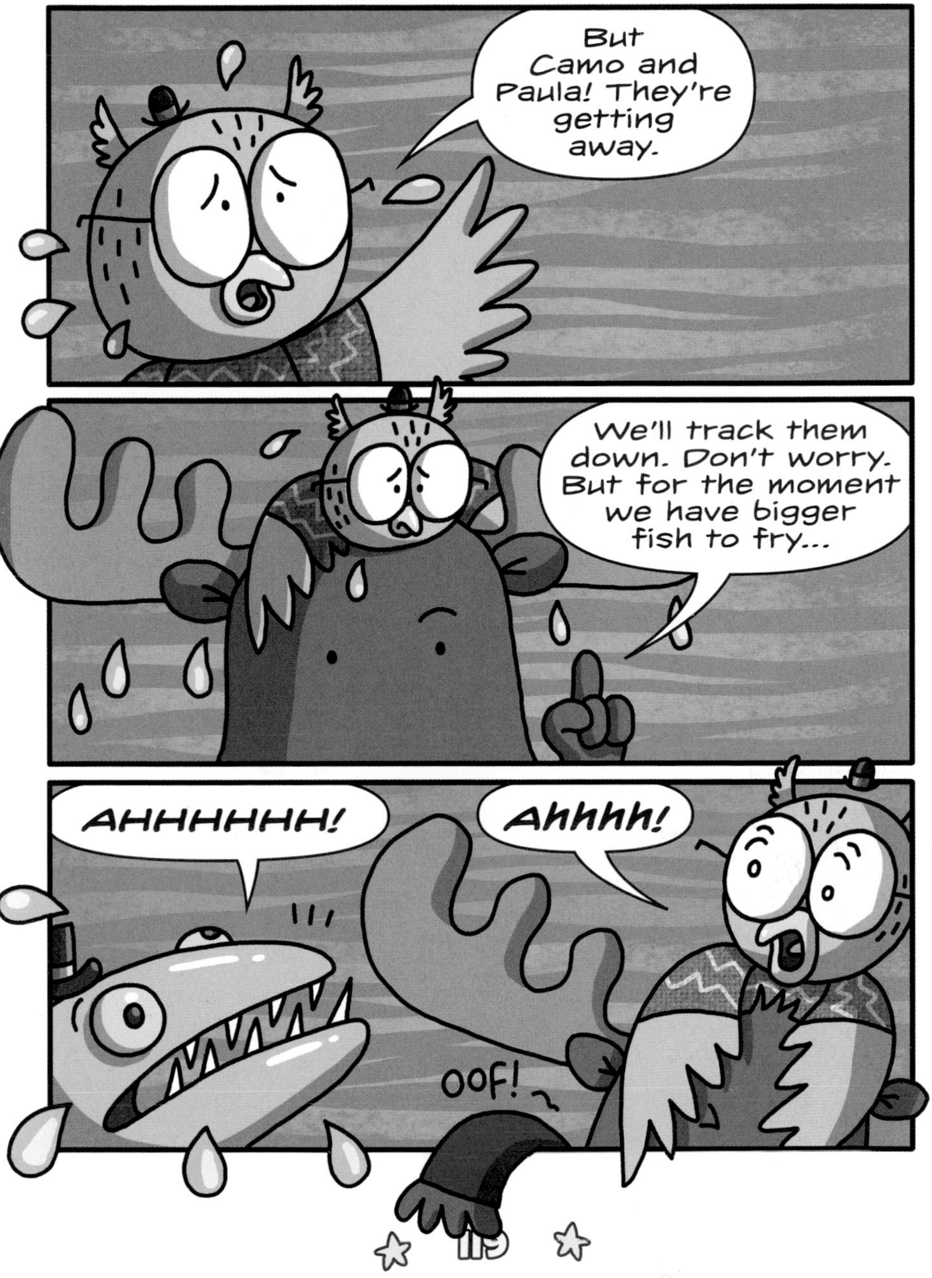
But Camo and Paula! They're getting away.
We'll track them down. Don't worry. But for the moment we have bigger fish to fry...
AHHHHHH!
Ahhhh!
OOF!

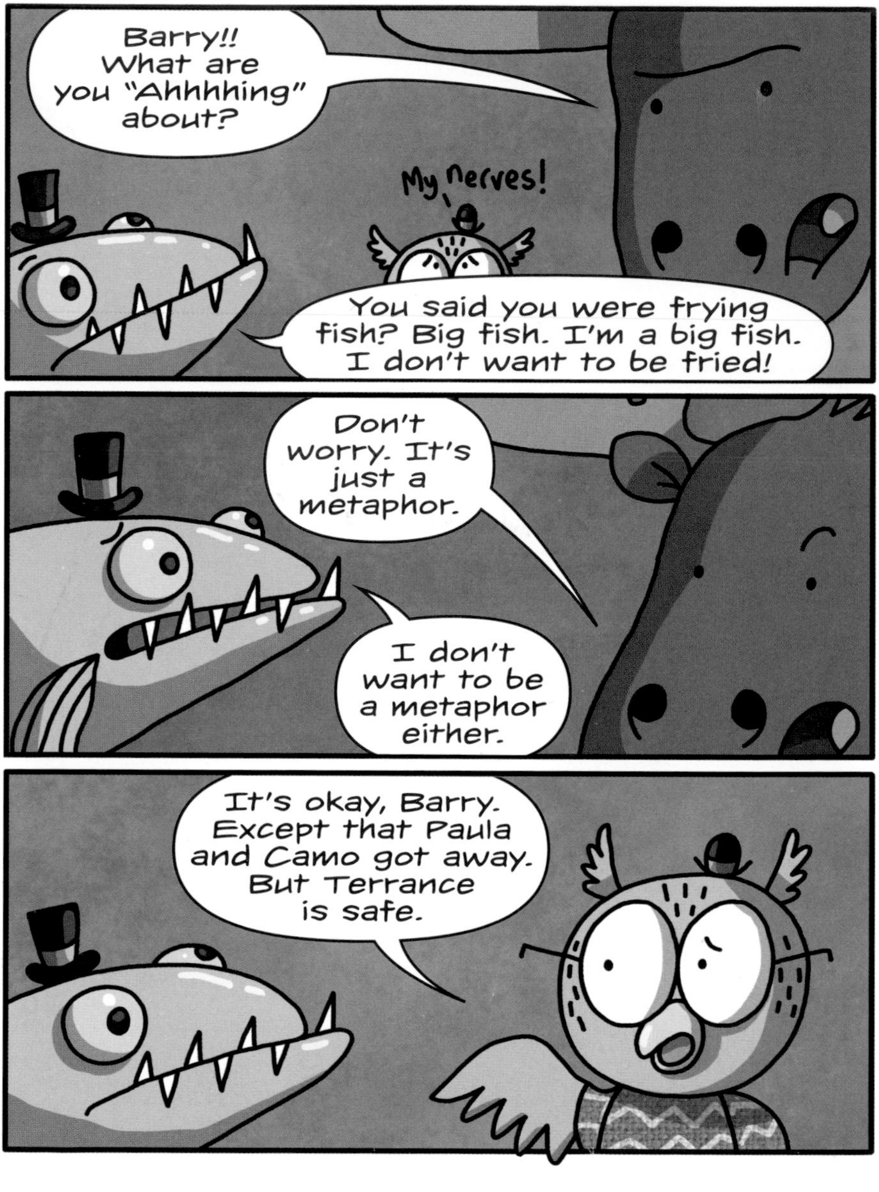
Barry!! What are you "Ahhhhing" about?
My nerves!
You said you were frying fish? Big fish. I'm a big fish. I don't want to be fried!
Don't worry. It's just a metaphor.
I don't want to be a metaphor either.
It's okay, Barry. Except that Paula and Camo got away. But Terrance is safe.

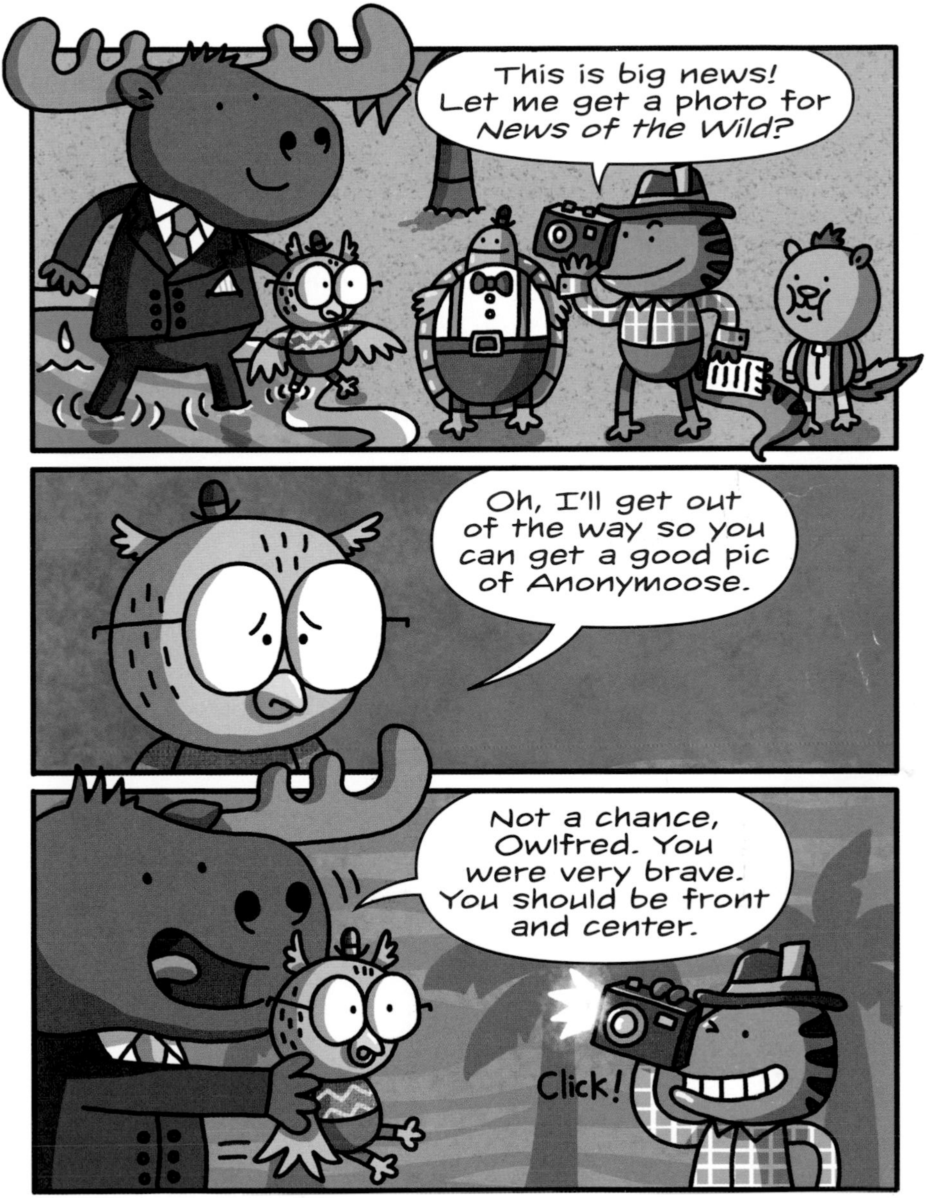
This is big news! Let me get a photo for *News of the Wild?*
Oh, I'll get out of the way so you can get a good pic of Anonymoose.
Not a chance, Owlfred. You were very brave. You should be front and center.
Click!

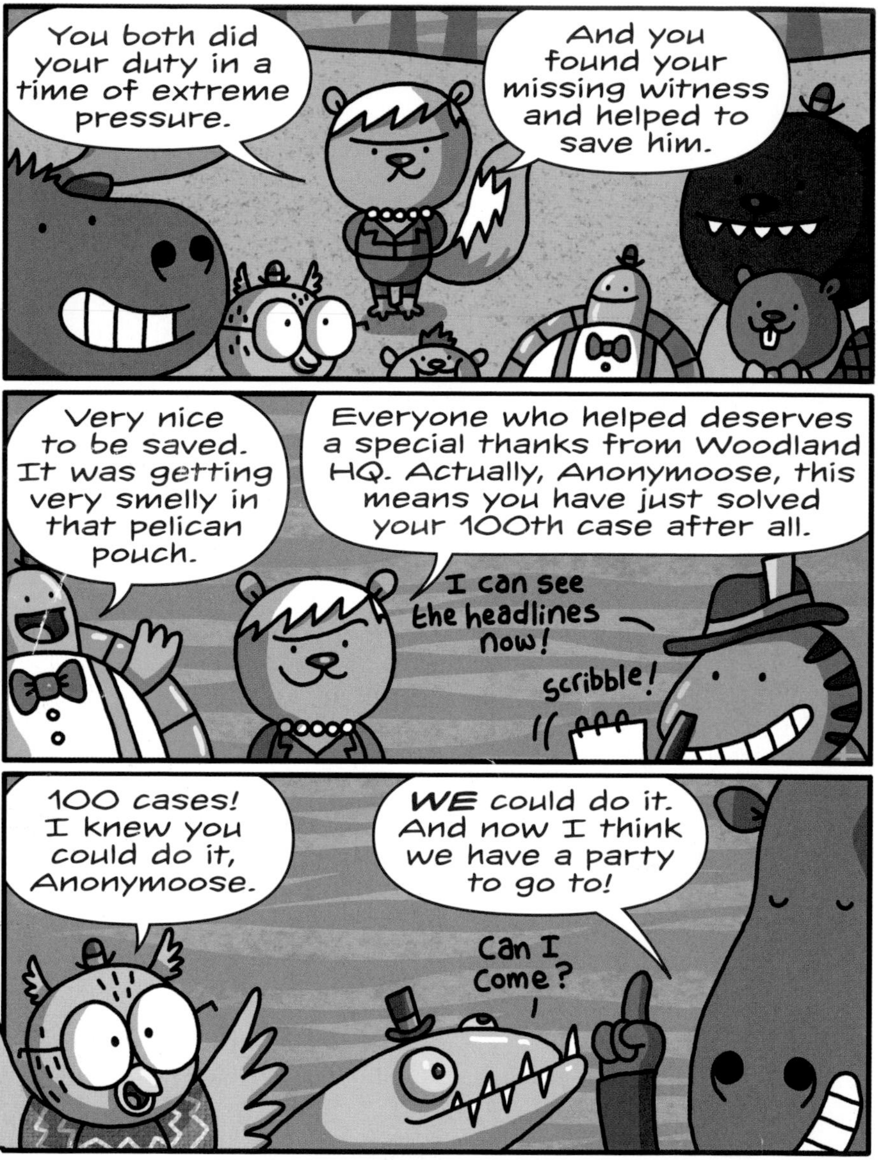
You both did your duty in a time of extreme pressure.
And you found your missing witness and helped to save him.
Very nice to be saved. It was getting very smelly in that pelican pouch.
Everyone who helped deserves a special thanks from Woodland HQ. Actually, Anonymoose, this means you have just solved your 100th case after all.
I can see the headlines now!
scribble!
100 cases! I knew you could do it, Anonymoose.
WE could do it. And now I think we have a party to go to!
Can I come?

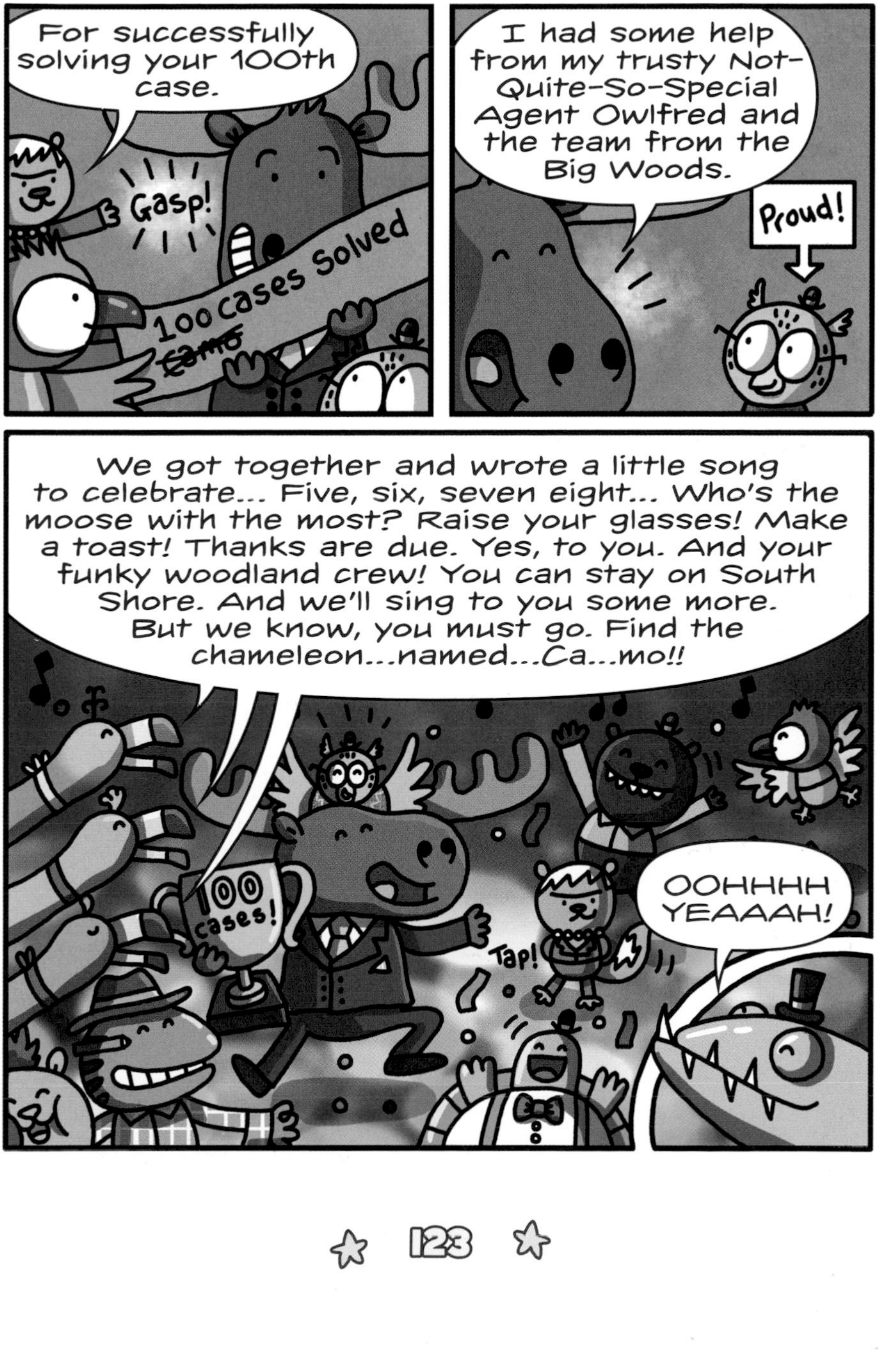
For successfully solving your 100th case.
Gasp!
100 cases Solved
~~Camo~~
I had some help from my trusty Not-Quite-So-Special Agent Owlfred and the team from the Big Woods.
Proud!
We got together and wrote a little song to celebrate... Five, six, seven eight... Who's the moose with the most? Raise your glasses! Make a toast! Thanks are due. Yes, to you. And your funky woodland crew! You can stay on South Shore. And we'll sing to you some more. But we know, you must go. Find the chameleon...named...Ca...mo!!
100 cases!
Tap!
OOHHHH YEAAAH!

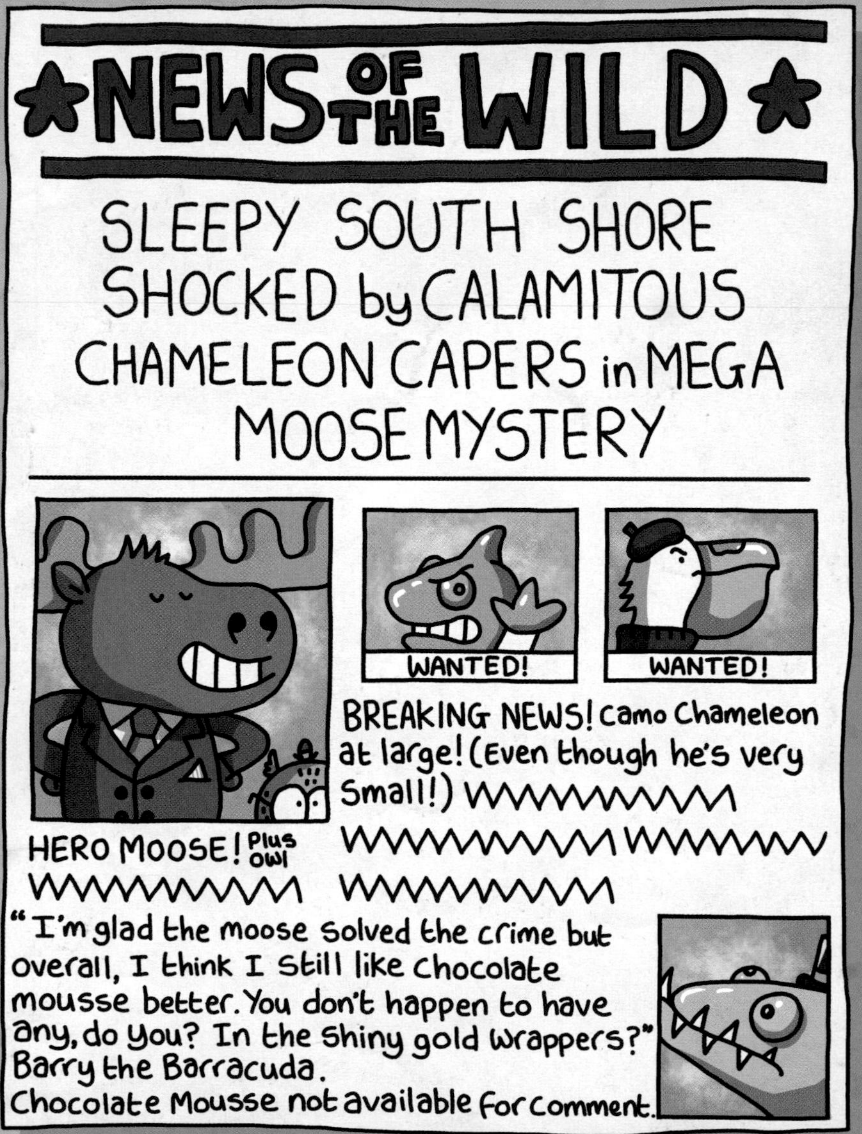
NEWS OF THE WILD
SLEEPY SOUTH SHORE SHOCKED by CALAMITOUS CHAMELEON CAPERS in MEGA MOOSE MYSTERY
WANTED!
WANTED!
BREAKING NEWS! camo Chameleon at large! (Even though he's very Small!)
HERO MOOSE! Plus Owl
"I'm glad the moose solved the crime but overall, I think I still like chocolate mousse better. You don't happen to have any, do you? In the shiny gold wrappers?" Barry the Barracuda.
Chocolate Mousse not available for comment.

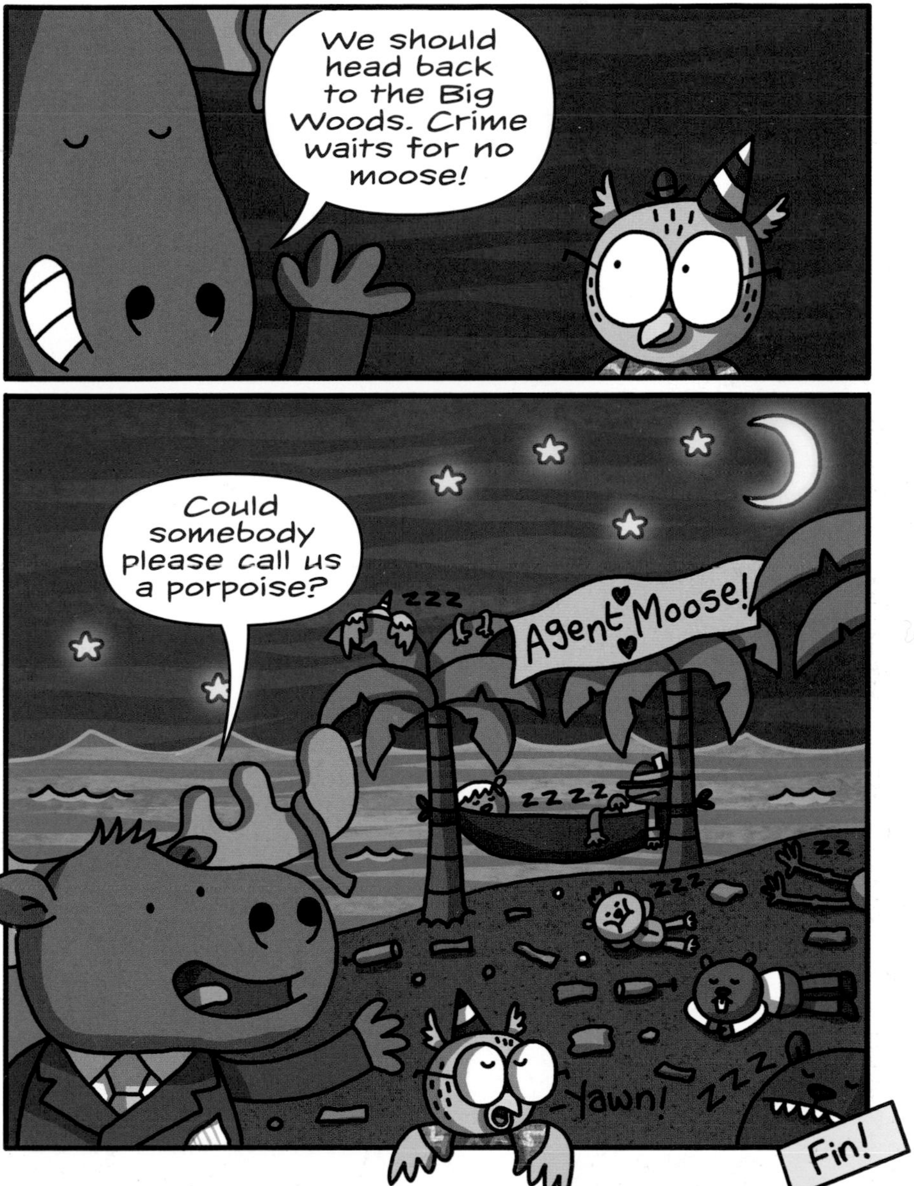
We should head back to the Big Woods. Crime waits for no moose!
Could somebody please call us a porpoise?
Agent Moose!
ZZZ
ZZZZ
ZZZ
ZZ
Yawn!
ZZZ
Fin!

THANK YOU FOR READING THIS FEIWEL AND FRIENDS BOOK.

The Friends who made

AGENT MOOSE

possible are:

Jean Feiwel, Publisher

Liz Szabla, Associate Publisher

Rich Deas, Senior Creative Director

Holly West, Senior Editor

Anna Roberto, Senior Editor

Kat Brzozowski, Senior Editor

Erin Siu, Associate Editor

Rachel Diebel, Assistant Editor

Emily Settle, Associate Editor

Foyinsi Adegbonmire, Editorial Assistant

Kim Waymer, Senior Production Manager

Liz Dresner, Associate Art Director

Mandy Veloso, Senior Production Editor

Follow us on Facebook or visit us online at mackids.com.

OUR BOOKS ARE FRIENDS FOR LIFE

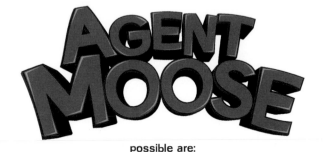